MISSING YOU

MISSING YOU

The Extraordinary Story of a WWII Airman's Girl

NANCY CARSON

First published in Great Britain in 2007 by
Severn House Publishers Ltd as *Linden Woods*

This version has been extensively re-written and differs from the
original.

Nancy Carson asserts the moral right to be identified as the author
of the work.

Except where actual historical events, places and characters are being described for the storyline of this novel, all situations and conversations in this publication are fictitious, and any resemblance to
persons, living or dead, is purely coincidental.

ISBN: 978-1-9163987-1-9 (eBook)
ISBN: 978-1-9163987-2-6 (Paperback)

Copyright © 2021 by Nancy Carson

| 1 |

Joseph Shakespeare had just returned indoors, after an obligatory spell in the back garden for the sake of his young daughter's modesty. She had been occupying the tin bath on the hearth in front of the fire in the parlour. Then it had been his task to empty the bath, one saucepanful at a time, into the drain in the backyard until it was light enough to drag outside without the remnants splashing about and soaking the podged rugs. Before long, the light of his life emerged. She stood on the bottom step of the narrow, winding staircase that was situated adjacent to the parlour's black-leaded fire-grate. Ready at last, she posed for him, fresh as a sunny spring morning, and raring to go.

'How do I look, Dad?'

Dad hesitated, but merely for effect, smiling his fatherly admiration as he looked her up and down.

'Passable,' he said, with a wink to Gladys, his wife.

'Only passable?' Disappointment was manifest on the young girl's lovely face. 'What's amiss then?'

'There's nothing amiss, my flower.' He answered sincerely, leaning towards her, and putting his hand on her arm reassuringly. 'You look smashing . . . smashing . . .'

The girl beamed back at him, her hazel eyes bright with an arresting vitality. 'Honest? You're not just saying that? He's not just saying that, is he, Mom?'

Joe laughed and turned to Gladys. 'Hark at her. You've got to reassure her all the time. She knows very well how nice she looks?'

'I feel nice, Dad, but a girl likes to hear it said. Even if it is a biased opinion.'

'Biased?' said Gladys. 'I should say he's biased.'

'But I like to think he's a good judge, Mom.'

'I should think I am,' Joe said. 'Years of experience doing the same for your mother has seen to that. What time's that young chap o' yours due to call for you?'

'He should be here any minute.'

Joe looked at the clock that lived on the mantelpiece, steadily measuring this close little family's existence, as it had done for the past twenty years, gaining about five minutes in the process every day, and having to be put right every couple of days. Beyond two days Joe lost track of when it was last put right, so could never be sure of the correct time thereafter.

'That clock'll be fast, by about four minutes,' he hazarded.

'Oh, it'll be near enough for Ron. It doesn't matter if he's five or even ten minutes late.'

'Well just mind your time getting back, our Libby,' Gladys cautioned. 'That matters.'

'Well, for goodness' sake don't wait up for me,' Libby pleaded. 'The dance won't finish till eleven. We'll be chatting outside for ages after I expect, saying our goodbyes and what-nots, then we've got to walk back.'

'Just keep your eye on your glass slippers,' Joe said. 'It'd be nice if you was back here by half past eleven.'

'That's not fair, Dad,' Libby countered with a girlish pout. 'Cinderella had till twelve. Her fairy godmother said she could. Why can't I have till twelve?' she looked at Gladys with an ir-resistible plea in her eyes.

'Because I'm not your fairy god-mother, I'm your mother,' was Gladys's stoic reply.

'Oh, Mom . . .' Libby implored. 'Don't expect me to rush back. Not tonight. The dance is specially for us school leavers. I might not see some of the girls ever again – nor the teachers come to that. And we've all been such good friends ever since the day we started at the school.'

Gladys looked at Joe for his assent, and got it with a nod. 'Very well, young madam. It's twelve and no later. And just you mind what you'm up to. Not that I shall sleep a wink till you get back.'

'I shan't get up to anything I shouldn't,' Libby assured them both. 'So you can sleep in peace.'

'Then you'd best take your key.'

She smiled impishly. 'I've already got it.' At that they heard footsteps in the entry. 'Hark. That'll be Ron. I'll be off then. See you in the morning.'

Libby swished around in a flounce of cotton dress, a string of glass beads tinkling around her neck. She gave her mother and father a kiss and breezed out with a delicious whiff of Chanel. As she opened the door, Ron called his greeting to Joe and Gladys.

'Bye!' they responded in unison.

'You look nice,' Ron said as she linked her arm through his. 'Cor! You smell nice as well.'

Libby beamed up at him as they began walking through the terraced streets of Kates Hill towards Dudley town. 'Thank you, Ron. You're looking very smart yourself.'

'Do I smell nice as well?'

She pretended to sniff him as they walked. 'Passable,' she teased, echoing her father's comment about her.

'Only passable, eh? Thanks. I should have expected nothing more from you. So how did it go yesterday, your last day?'

'A bit strange, really,' she answered. 'Happy and sad . . . I was happy to be leaving after all those years studying hard, but sad as well to be leaving all my old school mates behind. I shall miss them.'

'Life moves on,' Ron remarked, repeating a cliché he'd heard many times before.

'So they say. Now all I've got to do is get a job.'

'Well, you'll have no bother there, chick. You're eighteen, you're smart. Some girls would be off to university with the education you've had.'

Libby sighed. 'I know, and I'd love to go to university, but Mum and dad could never afford to send me.'

'It makes no odds,' Ron asserted with a reassuring smile. 'Girls going to university is a bit of a waste of time and money, if you ask me. They end up getting married and having kids, so hardly ever make use of what qualifications they get. Anyway, you've done all this shorthand and typing malarkey. Firms are always after good shorthand typists.'

'It's just as well. Dad's got me an interview at the Blower's Green Steelworks where he works. Did I tell you?'

'No, you didn't. But that's good news. You must be in with a chance, I should say.'

'Hope so. He had a word with the personnel manager. There's a vacancy, he says, so let's hope they like me.'

'Well, it's always good if somebody can put a word in for you, like your dad.'

'He is a bit biased, though, my dad – let's face it. Maybe they only agreed to interview me to humour him, 'cause he's worked there so long.'

'What, and waste everybody's time by going through the motions?' Ron said scornfully. 'No, big firms don't do that. Time's money to them. If they've said they want to employ a new shorthand typist, then you can bet your life that that's just what they intend to do.'

Libby squeezed his arm. 'D'you really think so?'

'I do . . .' He looked at her approvingly. 'So take my advice and wear your least showy skirt and blouse, in case it's a woman what interviews you. If it's a bloke smile pleasantly – as if you might be interested in him – but don't be too brazen o' course. Be nice, be yourself, talk sense and show some confidence, and the job'll be yours.'

'Lord! I'm getting nervous already at the thought of it.'

'We'll soon settle your nerves when we get to the Napper. It'll be a nice gin and lime for you, eh?'

The dance had been organised for the girls of the High School, and the boys of the Grammar School. These two schools existed symbiotically – their grounds shared a long boundary fence that effectively divided them – for fraternisation was never allowed, leastwise during term. Many older pupils, however, struck up romantic attachments outside school; once lessons were over they could hardly be prevented from meeting in the town centre outside Woolworth's in the Market Place.

Word had got round that many of those attending the dance would be meeting beforehand at The Saracen's Head, a respectable town pub known locally as The Napper; after all, no alcoholic drinks would be available at the school dance. The Napper overlooked the trolley bus terminus from Wolverhampton, about five hundred yards from the grammar school. Soon the place was buzzing with young folk, some just about old enough to be drinking legally. The stale odour of beer and tobacco smoke, absorbed over long years into the very fabric of the building, was familiar to Libby; not that she was a hardened drinker – she was not. However, as a small child and later as a young girl, she had accompanied her mother and father to the Shoulder of Mutton on Dixon's Green, Joe's favourite pub, and had mingled with other kids in the 'children's room'. The two pubs shared a distinctly similar smell, which reminded her poignantly of long gone summer evenings there.

Ron returned from the bar and handed Libby a gin and lime. She was new to the drink and, when she sipped it, she pursed her lips at both its sourness and sharpness. Ron put down his pint of Hanson's bitter on a table nearby and offered Libby a cigarette.

'You know I don't smoke, Ron.'

'Yes, but maybe you ought to try it.'

'What for?' She shook her head. 'I just don't fancy it.'

'Your dad smokes. Everybody smokes.'

'Not everybody smokes,' she riposted. 'And I don't want to.'

He shrugged and defiantly lit his cigarette. 'Can you see anybody you know?' he asked, puffing a blue cloud of smoke towards the ceiling. Ron was a stranger in both camps; never fortunate enough to have attended the Grammar School, although Libby privately reckoned he was sufficiently bright, if a bit lacking sometimes in the gumption department.

'Look, there's Irene and Doreen, from my class.' They spotted each other simultaneously, and Libby beckoned them.

After the introductions and small talk Ron gallantly squeezed his way to the bar to get drinks for Irene and Doreen. He brought another gin and lime for Libby, and she thanked him with a sparkle in her clear eyes, which were the colour of the sherry he'd bought for her friends. They laughed and joked about leaving school, and discussed which teachers they were happy to leave behind and those they wouldn't mind seeing again. Inevitably, talk veered towards what the future held for them, and hence their prospects now that they were being hurled into that exciting world where you were expected to find a job and earn your own living.

When they had each divulged their hopes and dreams Irene said, 'Did you listen to the wireless before you came out?' Her pretty face bore an ominous expression,

'No, why?' Libby replied, sensing angst in Irene's tone.

'Looks like there's more trouble brewing. This time between China and Japan.'

Ron shrugged. 'Well I heard about it, but I can't see as how that's going to affect us.' He took a nonchalant swig of his bitter.

'I think it's a sign of the times,' Libby remarked, her look delightfully intense as she tried to make herself heard over the hubbub of youthful laughter and the chinking of glasses. 'What with civil war in Spain, and Italy overrunning Abyssinia last year . . . and using that vile mustard gas to do it—'

'And what about Germany overrunning the Rhineland?' Irene added with a grave nod.

'Yes, I know,' Doreen exclaimed. 'And what about the king abdicating and marrying his beloved Wallis?'

'Don't forget, either, that they're mass-producing gas masks in this country,' Irene reminded them. 'We'll all get one. Why would we unless they think we're going to need 'em? Something's afoot.'

Libby rolled her eyes in apprehension at what all this mayhem might ultimately mean for them, whereas Ron shrugged again and took another slurp of beer. None of this was his concern.

'There's a war looming,' Libby said solemnly, and took another sip of her drink. 'My dad swears there's going to be another war. He says you can smell it a mile off. He reckons Hitler's got his heart set on making Germany bigger, by taking back land they reckon used to be theirs, like parts of Poland and the Rhineland. He says Hitler resents the terms of the German surrender in 1918, and wants revenge. You could never trust Hitler to be honourable anyway, my dad reckons.'

'I don't think there'll be a war,' Ron commented, trying to lighten the conversation. 'We've all got too much to lose – us, the Germans, the French – especially after the last war. And anyway, the Rhineland used to be part of Germany before. Hitler only wants back what's rightfully theirs anyway.'

'Yes, Ron, but it puts him a hundred miles closer to us,' Irene argued.

'So why is he predicting twenty-five years peace?'

Libby sipped her glass of gin and lime again. It was going to her head and she did not want to be made morose with uninformed speculation of war. She wanted to be happy, for tonight was supposed to be a time for letting your hair down, forgetting the unpredictable future for now, and celebrating the past few tremendous years at school. So she put the drink on the nearest table with no intention of returning to it.

'Hey, enough of this,' she exclaimed. 'Anybody else who talks of depressing things like war will be sent to Coventry . . . Agreed?'

They all agreed.

As the evening wore on Libby watched an ever-increasing number of her unescorted friends pair off with the available grammar school lads or their invited friends. Eventually, outside in the warm July night, everybody said their goodbyes with fervent and voluble best wishes for the future, all promising ardently to keep in touch, no matter what.

'We ought to hold reunions regularly,' one friend suggested.

'At least every four years,' another recommended with fitting exuberance, 'like the Olympic Games.'

They all agreed.

'That means we'll be due to meet again in 1941,' Libby remarked. 'I suppose it'd better be in Dudley.'

'Well, Dudley would be most convenient for everybody, I reckon.'

'And most central. We'll arrange it nearer the time.'

After Libby and Ron had left the dance and said goodbye to her friends, they walked arm-in-arm through Dudley's gas-lit streets, conversing little at first. She was beginning to realise how this night had been a turning point in her life. From now on, her daily routine would change inexorably. She had become comfortable in her school life, confident with all her many chums, ranking high in the pupils' hierarchy. From here on, she had no idea what the future might bring. Yet she did not fear it; rather she considered it a challenge, a time of new opportunities which she would embrace with eagerness . . . barring war, of course.

'You're quiet,' Ron remarked at last.

'So are you.'

He shrugged. 'I suppose I am.'

Libby looked at him and saw the streetlights reflected in his eyes. 'I was thinking about the friends I've just left.' She sighed profoundly. 'I'm sad, Ron. I spent twelve – maybe thirteen years with some of those girls, practically every day of the week except for holidays and weekends. I've been so close to them, got to know every mortal thing about them, even about their parents . . . Then suddenly, they're gone, like bubbles suddenly burst – to universities, jobs . . . I suppose some will find work in different towns and make new friends from other parts of the country. They'll marry, I expect, end up God knows where, have their own children . . . I know I'll never see some of them again. We'll lose touch, even though they're all so keen now to meet up again at some point in the future . . . Everybody's been such good pals over the years. I just think it's sad.'

He put his arm around her and pulled her towards him as they walked through the quiet streets.

'You're a sensitive soul, ain't yer?' he said sympathetically. 'You're a bit vulnerable, I reckon. You need to be protected.'

'Do I?' She looked up at him with eyes that seemed inordinately soft and wide in the half-light.

'You do. So I'm going to marry you.'

Libby stopped in her tracks and looked up at him again. 'Oh, Ron, did you say what I thought you said?'

He uttered a nervous little laugh and shrugged, unable to discern whether she was delighted or appalled at his suggestion. 'I said, I'm going to marry you.'

'Marry me? Well, fancy . . . Don't I have a say in the matter?'

'Course.'

'What if I don't want to get married?' she said, on the move again.

'Well what's wrong with it? I think it's a great idea. I mean, I'd ask your mom and dad first if it was okay.'

He saw in the half-light that she was rolling her eyes.

'Do I take it then that you don't want to?'

'I've just left school, Ron,' she protested, incredulous at his immaturity. 'I've only known you, what? Six weeks? That's no time. I hardly know you. Besides, I want to see a bit of life, not tie myself to the first person who asks me to marry him. I don't want to even think about marriage – to anybody – not for years and years.'

'I thought you'd be pleased,' he said, sounding hurt.

'I'm flattered,' she answered matter-of-factly. 'I'm flattered to think you might like me enough, but . . .'

'But what?'

'I just don't see the point. It's a joke. It's way too soon.'

'Why do I get the feeling, Libby, that I think a lot more of you than you think of me.'

'I like you a lot, Ron, but not enough to get married. Anyway, I'm just too young. My dad would have a fit.'

'The problem is, chick, I reckon I'm in love with you. But I'll wait . . . I'll wait till you change your mind.'

Libby did not want to say outright that she did not love him in return, even though it was true, because she had no wish to hurt him or belittle him. She liked him, he was her chum of six weeks, his attentions gave her confidence, pleased her, but it had never crossed her mind for a moment whether or not she was in love. Besides, she was often drawn to other chaps – the world was full of appealing young men and she certainly did not feel ready to commit herself already, especially to *him*. Anyway, she did not fancy Ron in the way that marriage would warrant.

Somehow, she felt she was on a different mental plane, brighter, more rational. The depressing discussion earlier about the likelihood of war typified what she meant; he'd never really thought about the world and its woes. He never seriously considered things like that – important things – he'd never considered the implications, and that was evident in his attitude earlier that evening, and in his comments. All he seemed interested in was whether his belly was full, football, what films were showing that week, and how much money he'd pick up on payday. She expected more than that from a man, and not unreasonably. A little bit of ambition wouldn't come amiss. She would only ever marry somebody who offered her some mental as well as physical stimulation.

'I'm just not ready even to get engaged and start courting seriously,' she answered simply.

'Well, here's another question for you then. D'you still want to go on seeing me?'

- - -

| 2 |

The Blowers Green Steelworks was situated in the most dismal part of Dudley, grey and drab, smutty with industrial smoke propelled into the atmosphere in thick coils by hundreds of red-brick chimney stacks, then dispersed by the whimsical wind to render grimy everything it fell onto. A couple of centuries earlier the area was an idyll of green fields, bluebell woods, grazing cattle and sheep. But the rapid advance of the Industrial Revolution, of which the town was the cradle, ensured that it quickly degraded into a gloomy grey panorama with the spoil of coal-mining spilling onto its pristine meadows like mountainous mole hills.

Such was this area's desolation that if even a dandelion had the audacity to pierce the dark-grey crust with its bright yellow head it stood out like a beacon, and was worthy of remark. The landscape here was criss-crossed by railways, some belonging to the Blowers Green Steelworks, some to other, even vaster enterprises that melted and rolled and re-rolled steel. It was noisy; the ear-splitting roar of blast furnaces diluted only by distance, the incessant clanging of metal, the unremitting thud of huge forging hammers that made the ground beneath your feet tremble as they walloped steel bars into pre-conceived shapes. The hissing and huffing of mineral-hauling locomotives and the shouts of men at work all added to the cacophony.

As Libby walked along Peartree Lane, over canals and under railway bridges, she feared for the whiteness of her blouse and the shine on her shoes, for the black dust, like soot, swirled around her in the breeze, whipped up by the lorries that chugged past her. If she were successful in her interview for this job, she would be walking this route daily. She tried to imagine it in winter in the cold and rain, and shuddered at the thought. It was nowhere near as pleasant as the walk through the town centre to the High School set in the lea of the old castle, among trees and meadows on the rural side. But, as Ron had told her in one of his worldlier moments, life moves on.

She pondered Ron and his surprising suggestion of marriage a few days ago. He must surely understand that she was far too young yet. She was just about to step into the bigger, wider world beyond the restricting limits of school discipline, and she had every intention of seeing what it had to offer before she committed herself to anybody. Meanwhile, she had no wish to stop seeing him; there would be no point to that either. He worked for a living, could afford to take her out once in a while. She enjoyed his company, she liked those friends of his whom she'd met, and they seemed to like her too. No, Ron was kind and gentle, he could be entertaining. But commitment? No.

She arrived at the works and dusted herself off as she presented herself at the commissionaire's hut. The amiable, uniformed gent with a military air pointed to a blue door in the side of a building that was evidently the office block and, with a smile of thanks, she headed there. A musty, dusty smell greeted her in the grand entrance hall of Blowers Green Steelworks. In a tiny room behind a hatch, two telephone operators sat, pulling and inserting plugs on red leads into and out of holes in the vertical boards that faced them. Each woman seemed to be wired directly to this board by a contraption fastened to her head, comprising earphones and a microphone. One, white-headed, with the look of a spinster and about the same age as Libby's mother, asked if she could help. Libby explained that she was expected for a job interview, so white-headed spinster suggested she take a seat while she told Personnel that she was here. Libby thanked her and sat down.

She looked around her. The walls were clad in panelled oak, and the lino on the floor incongruously showed the marks of where it had been recently wiped with a less-than-clean mop. Gazing down at her from above in a gilt frame was the photograph of a middle-aged man formally posed, clean-shaven, with greying hair and kind eyes behind his wire-rimmed spectacles. This, she presumed, was Charles Burgayne the owner of this huge and obviously successful enterprise. She had heard so many good things about him from her father.

About five minutes passed before another spinsterly middle-aged lady appeared, prim and straight-backed, with permed hair. When she spotted her visitor she approached and introduced herself as Miss Hardy. Miss Hardy looked Libby up and down, shook her hand and said in a pleasant voice how happy she was to meet her. She ushered Libby into a spartan interview room, also wood-panelled, with a solitary desk and chairs for three people.

Miss Hardy switched on the light, and closed the door behind her. She pointed out which of the chairs the job applicant should occupy, and said, 'Do sit down, Miss Shakespeare.'

'Thank you.'

'Of course, I know your father.' She smiled, as if the revelation might put her in good standing with her young visitor, and took the chair behind the desk.

Libby, now sitting demurely, her knees together, her hands clasped together on her lap, rolled her eyes as if to apologize for her father's very existence.

'He's a fine man and a good worker, and very well thought of. Employed here many years, I understand.'

'Since just after I was born, I think, Miss Hardy,' Libby replied, relieved that her father was decently revered after all. 'Straight after the war, I believe.'

'He served in the Great War, did he?'

'Yes, Miss Hardy. He was one of the fortunate ones to come home.'

'Well, we're all glad he did . . . Right. Down to business. This appointment . . . We're seeking a smart and reliable girl to work in our typing pool. She must be proficient at shorthand and typing, and be an excellent timekeeper – lateness is not tolerated at the Blowers Green Steelworks, Miss Shakespeare.' Miss Hardy looked challengingly into Libby's eyes. 'The successful applicant will be responsible for secretarial work for our Wages office. You're straight from school, are you not?'

'Dudley Girls' High, Miss Hardy,' Libby answered, not without some pride in the fact.

'I presume you attained your Pitman's Diploma there?'

'Yes, Miss Hardy. Ninety words a minute.'

The lady seemed impressed. 'Do you have your diploma with you?'

'Yes, Miss Hardy.' She opened her handbag and withdrew the certificate which she handed over. Libby watched the lady's reaction interestedly as she scrutinised it.

'That seems very satisfactory.' Miss Hardy handed it back. 'And your typing speed?'

'Sixty words a minute.'

Miss Hardy handed Libby a shorthand notebook and a pencil which she took from a desk drawer, along with a sheet of typewritten foolscap paper. 'I am going to read from this sheet of paper at normal speed, Miss Shakespeare, and I would like you to take it down in shorthand. Then I want you to read it back to me. Do you understand?'

'Yes, Miss Hardy.' Nervously now, she took the notebook and pencil.

What Miss Hardy read was an example of a letter containing typical words and phrases used in steelmaking, some of which were strange to Libby. Libby felt relieved when Miss Hardy ceased to read, but was anxious about reading it back.

She took a deep breath. 'Dear Sirs,' she began. 'Thank you for your letter of the fifteenth inst . . .' Words like ductility, Bessemer and molecular had given her a little trouble, and she glanced up at Miss Hardy apprehensively as she read back those words.

Don't worry, I'm not concerned at this stage over your unfamiliarity with some of the more technical words. I doubt you will be familiar with a great many of them at present, but regular use would make them familiar, of course. Apart from that you are accurate, and I commend you. How old are you?'

'Eighteen, miss.'

'And do you have any plans to get married in the foreseeable future?'

Libby smiled, recalling again Ron's proposal. 'No, Miss Hardy. Most certainly not.'

Miss Hardy smiled back and nodded, as if in approval. 'Very good,' she said. 'Now . . . The appointment will carry a salary of twenty-two shillings and sixpence a week, and the successful applicant would qualify for two weeks annual holiday after ten months service. We operate subsidised canteen facilities here, so meals are available at very modest cost. Staff working hours are eight-thirty in a morning till 6 o' clock evenings, Monday to Friday, and Saturday mornings eight-thirty till one. Do you have any questions you'd like to ask me, Miss Shakespeare?'

'Yes, Miss Hardy . . . When can I start?'

- - -

Ron called round that evening, wearing grey flannels, a white open-necked shirt, the collar of which was rolled over that of his sports jacket.

'How did you get on today, chick?' he asked as he sat down in the tiny scullery.

She grinned contentedly. 'I start on Monday.'

'Smashing!' he said, obviously pleased.

'And with my first week's wages I'll treat you to a night out.'

'I should hold her to that,' Joe Shakespeare exclaimed from his armchair in front of the black-leaded fire grate. 'It ain't often you get an offer like that from a woman. Leastwise, not in my day.'

'No girl could afford to pay for her chap to go out in your day,' Gladys chimed in, in defence of her sex. 'Times was hard.'

'Times am still hard,' he responded. 'But we've done all right. At least we put our Libby through high school, even though it cost twelve guineas a term.'

'It's as well you had a good job, Joe, else we would never have been able to do it.'

'I'll pay you back,' Libby exclaimed sincerely. 'It's always been my intention to pay you back when I can afford it. I realise how much you've sacrificed over the years for my sake.'

'Aye, well I shouldn't worry about it too much, my flower,' Joe said. 'It was money well-spent. It's given you a good education and a flying start in this world. That was my intention, and I wouldn't have had it any other way. To see you like you are now, with the world at your feet, is repayment enough. I desire nothing more.'

'Oh, Dad.' Libby leaned over, kissed her father and ruffled his thinning hair affectionately. 'Don't think I don't appreciate it. I do.'

'So go out and enjoy yourself, and make the most of it.'

'I thought we could go to the pictures tonight, chick,' Ron said. 'It could be a celebration for you getting this job. That film *Top Hat* is on again at the Criterion.'

'The one with Fred Astaire and Ginger Rogers?'

'Yes.'

'I've seen it. I enjoyed it.'

'I ain't. So – if you enjoyed it maybe you wouldn't mind seeing it again, eh?'

Libby beamed. 'Okay, why not?' she replied. 'I'll go up and get changed.'

'Well, be quick then. It starts in half an hour.'

- - -

The Criterion Cinema was close to the now deserted Market Place, whose red and white awnings rippled in the summer breeze as Libby and Ron walked past arm-in-arm on their way back to Hill Street on Kates Hill. She had enjoyed *Top Hat*, the dancing, the music, the romance, the spectacle. It was all so glamorous, and far removed from the routine of everyday life.

'Those folk in America seem to have a grand old time of it, if that film is anything to go by,' she remarked as they turned into Hall Street, narrow and confining, where the pavement was not wide enough to accommodate them both. 'I mean, the lovely clothes they wear, the beautiful motorcars and new buildings. Everybody looks so smart . . . And aren't the girls' hairstyles lovely?'

'I wouldn't mind emigrating to America,' Ron mused. 'I've often thought about it.'

'There's nothing to stop you,' Libby remarked provocatively. 'Except there's no work there because of the Depression.'

'When the Depression's over, I mean. It can't go on forever, the Depression. And things are getting better, they say, under Roosevelt. They're bound to re-elect him as well. Just think, if you and me was to get married – in a year or two, I mean – we could emigrate to America.'

'You don't think I'd leave my mom and dad, do you?'

His sigh was heavy with frustration. Of course, he should have had the foresight to realise that her loyalty to her parents created a self-imposed restriction. 'The way I see it, chick, you have to live your life for yourself, not for others, not for your mom and dad,' he reasoned. 'My mom and dad would never stand in my way if I told 'em I wanted to emigrate.'

'But your mom and dad have other sons, Ron. Mine only have me. I could never live far away from them, whatever happens.'

He felt thwarted at every turn. Even if they did get wed eventually, she wouldn't assent to his ideal of emigrating to America. Maybe Libby was not the right girl for him after all. But she was so beautiful, so alive, so bright, so wonderful to be with . . . There was no way he could ever give her up. They would just have to work out their differences, even if it meant staying in England for the sake of Gladys and Joe.

- - -

On her first day at work, Libby decided to walk to the Blowers Green Steelworks in her sensible shoes. The blue sky was daubed with billowing white clouds. Rain looked unlikely, so it would be a pleasant walk that would take her the best part of half an hour. The route was not direct; there were plenty of left- and right-hand turns before she reached Peartree Lane and its industrial gruesomeness. No doubt she could get there by bus and tram, but decided not to rely on public transport on her first day. Her father never did. He always walked, and had left home earlier to begin his shift at six.

When she arrived she reported first to the Personnel Department. Miss Hardy led her to the typing pool, and introduced her first to Miss Mayhew, the typing pool's supervisor. She was given a brand-new spiral-bound notebook, pencil and eraser, and shown to her desk, situated between two other girls of similar age. They smiled their welcome as she sat down on the well-worn swivel chair and inspected the typewriter she must work with, a fine Olivetti. But before she could explore the desk's drawers, or speak more than half a dozen words to any of the other girls, Miss Mayhew took her aside.

'I am taking you to meet Mr Webb, who is in charge of the Wages Office, Miss Shakespeare. You will be working mostly for him. So bring your shorthand notebook and pencil with you.'

So she skipped along behind Miss Mayhew nervously, clutching her new notebook, pencil and eraser, avoiding the eyes of other unfamiliar employees, male and female. Thus far, they were just nameless faces, milling about the corridors, but she felt their eyes weighing her up as another newly arrived office girl. Libby had not envisaged that she would be working for one particular individual. However, she shook Mr Webb's hand as she assessed him, and remarked that she was looking forward to working with him.

Webb was in his fifties, staid, wearing a stiff collar that looked a mite uncomfortable, striped trousers and spats which were unfashionable. It did not seem in his nature to smile – his face was a forbidding and mysterious mask – and Libby wondered if she was going to be happy working with such a cheerless person.

'Thank you Miss Mayhew,' Mr Webb said politely. He turned to Libby. 'Very well, Miss Shakespeare . . . if you are ready for some dictation . . .'

The work that Mr Webb gave her consisted of internal memos to other departments, and Libby, back at her desk, rummaged through her desk drawers for the correct headed paper, but found none.

'What are you looking for?' asked the girl on her right.

Libby smiled back amiably. 'I've got some memos to do for Mr Webb, and I don't seem to be able to find any blank ones.'

'I got some you can have,' the girl said helpfully. She opened one of her drawers and pulled out a sheaf of quarto sized paper. 'Here, this lot should keep you going a while. I'll take you to Thelma in the stationery stores after, and you can get all you need. You'll need white, blue, pink and old gold – quarto and foolscap – as well as letterheads. I'm Vera Bythe-way, by the way.'

Libby wondered at first if that was a double-barrelled name, but the girl's easy smile told her she had made her name the butt of a little joke. 'How do you do, Vera,' she replied, relieved the ice had been broken with at least one girl. 'I'm Libby Shakespeare.'

'I always think it's a bit nerve-racking when you start a new job somewhere and you don't know anybody,' Vera said considerately. 'Awful, it is. I remember my first day here. Didn't know a soul, didn't know where anything was, what was what or who was who. Didn't even know where the privy was. Same as you, eh? You'll soon get used to it though. And I'll show you where the privy is.'

'Thank you,' said Libby, amused.

'What did you say your name is?' the girl on Libby's left asked, butting in.

'Libby Shakespeare.' She smiled her introduction. 'Hello.'

'Hello, Libby,' the girl said pleasantly. 'I'm Hilda Homer.'

'Nice to meet you Hilda. How long have you two been here?' Libby asked them both collectively.

'Two years, me,' Vera answered. 'Hilda's been here about a year, eh, Hilda?'

Hilda confirmed the fact with a nod.

'It seems a nice place to work,' Libby remarked. 'I've just met Mr Webb – he seems a bit of a stick-in-the-mud though.'

'Yes, I know what you mean. But Nora, the girl who used to do his work before, got on all right with him, didn't she, Hilda?'

'I reckon so. He's harmless enough is Mr Webb. He's just a bit poker-faced. Mind you, with a wife like he's got it's understand-able. Got a face like a gargoyle, she has, and an attitude to match.'

'So why did this Nora leave?'

'She got married. I reckon she had to, to tell you the truth, but she never admitted as much to anybody, did she, Hilda?'

'There was no need. It was flippin' obvious. She was starting to get a right podge on her.'

'Anyway,' Vera continued, 'they don't operate a married workers policy here for women. So she would've had to leave, whether or no.'

'Shame,' Libby commented as she separated three sheets of white quarto with two sheets of carbon paper. 'You're not married then, I take it?'

Vera laughed out loud. 'I ain't that daft. Sort of courting, though, but not serious. I ain't about to get married anyhow. Not for a long time. I'm only just twenty. There's plenty time for all that softness. Unless somebody with pots of money shows up in the meantime.'

'Have you had many boy-friends?' Libby asked, curious.

'Loads.'

Libby laughed as she offered the sheets of paper to the rollers of her Olivetti typewriter, and turned the knob on the right-hand side of the machine to feed them through. 'So who do you work for, Vera?'

'Mostly Mr Vickers in Sales, but we all have to swap about from time to time, to even the work out.'

'What are the other girls like?' she asked in a lowered voice.

'They're all right. Most of 'em anyway,' Vera replied. 'Mavis over there can get a bit funny at times.' She nodded discretely in the direction of a fair-haired girl with spectacles, sitting two desks in front of them. 'Depends what time of the month it is. Mind you, we can all be a bit funny that way sometimes.'

Libby smiled and nodded, inclined to agree. 'Do you see much of Mr Burgayne?'

'Which one?'

'Oh, is there more than one?' Libby queried, with some surprise.

'There's the old man, Mr Charles, then there's Mr Hugh, his eldest son, who's also a director. He's about twenty-seven I reckon, and a right one for the women, I can tell you – so you'd better watch out for him, a nice-looking girl like you.'

'Thanks for the warning, Vera.'

'There's another son besides, but we never see him.'

'So Mr Burgayne has two sons?'

'The other one is at Cambridge university. I've forgotten his name. There's a daughter as well – Bunty. She seems really nice. She comes in from time to time and helps out when the staff get busy. I suppose coming here keeps her away from her horses. They say she's mad about horses.'

'So how old is this Bunty?'

'Our age. Nineteen or twenty. How old are you, Libby?'

She told her, and the conversation turned.

'Have you brought sandwiches with you, or d'you intend to go to the canteen at dinnertime?'

'I thought I might go to the canteen,' Libby replied.

'Then come with us, eh? We'll show you the ropes. It's always good to have somebody who can show you the ropes when you're new, I always think.'

'Thanks, I'm really grateful,' Libby said as she began typing. 'You're really kind – both of you.'

'Think nothing of it. It'll give you the chance to get to know some of the other girls.'

Libby duly accompanied her new friends to the canteen for the first time, and made more. They seemed a friendly lot, and she felt at ease with them. It was clear, even this early in her career at the Blowers Green Steelworks, that maybe Vera would be her closest friend and confidante. In the meantime, Mr Webb showed no sign of proving himself the ogre that he first appeared to be; rather Libby found him mild-mannered, perhaps a little shy and self-conscious in the presence of a young and very pretty girl, whom he seemed unwilling to even look at, let alone make eye contact.

Their relationship seemed to get off to a reasonable start, especially when her first batch of memos came back to her all duly signed and ready for the post room.

It had not been a bad first day at work.

- - -

| 3 |

Before Libby knew it, the works' annual shutdown had arrived. Office work was subsequently slack since many, barring staff and those involved in maintenance, were on holiday. Libby enjoyed the easy relaxed atmosphere, but found the days passed more slowly, and she was glad one day during the second week when Betsy Mayhew asked her to take her notebook and pencil to the boardroom for dictation. Nervous as to whom she might be working for, fearing it could be Mr Charles Burgayne or, worse, his womanising son Hugh, she tapped on the door, and was surprised when a female voice asked her to enter.

'Oh, hello,' Libby said cautiously to a girl who was sitting behind a huge oval table. She was young, slim and attractive, with blonde hair, bright blue eyes, and about the same age as herself. 'I was told to come here for dictation.'

'Yes, I asked for somebody,' the girl said with an affable grin. 'Do come in and sit down . . . We've not met before. Are you new here?'

'Yes, this is my second week,' Libby replied. 'I'm Libby Shakespeare.'

'Then, how do you do, Libby Shakespeare. Do you mind if I just call you Libby? I'm Bunty Burgayne.' She offered her hand, and they shook.

'So you're Mr Charles Burgayne's daughter.'

'The one and only. And do call me Bunty.'

Libby's surprise was matched only by her smile. 'I'm so pleased to meet you, Bunty. The other girls said you dropped by from time to time.'

'I could drop by more often, I'm sure, but Daddy insists I'm infinitely skilled at getting in the way. Anyway, I do hope you don't mind, Libby, but I have rather a mountain of pressing correspondence to wade through, and it would be such a fantastic help if you could do some typing for me. You must be frightfully good at it, whereas I'm a nincompoop in front of a typewriter.'

''Course. I'd be glad to,' said Libby, at once at ease with this girl. 'There's not much to do at the moment with the work's holidays and everything. I'm itching for something to do.'

'Well, just to explain, Libby, we're hosting a garden party at Buttonbridge Hall – that's the family pile – on the twenty-first of August – a Saturday – and I'm in a frightful panic to write to the butcher, the baker, the candlestick maker and a whole battalion of other trades people to confirm the orders for food and so on. Otherwise our poor invited guests will have sweet Fanny Adams to munch on, and will be totally unimpressed. Oh, and I shall be in the doghouse, of course.'

'I'll be happy to help,' Libby asserted.

'Actually, I can type a little myself, you understand,' Bunty admitted, 'but by the time I've got letters done without a page full of typos, I could have driven here and got a professional like yourself on the case. Hence the reason I asked for help.'

Libby chuckled aloud. 'I don't mind a bit.' She quite liked this Bunty. There was a warmth about her and, despite her cultured tones, she was unaffected, which surprised her, for she would not have expected it in a girl from her elevated background.

When Bunty had finished dictating her letters, all in a similar vein, Libby left her to type them up on the Burgayne family's personal headed notepaper. Within half an hour she was knocking on the boardroom door again carrying the finished articles, complete with typed envelopes, all in a neat pile. Bunty was ending a telephone call, and put the receiver down as Libby approached.

'That was quick,' she commented pleasantly. 'I'm impressed.'

'I do hope they're all right,' Libby said. 'Shall I wait while you glance over them, in case I need to re-type any?'

'If you like, Libby. Have a seat.'

She sat down opposite Bunty and studied the girl while she read the letters through and signed them in turn. This girl seemed as though she hadn't a care in the world. Her skin was fashionably tanned as if she had spent a great deal of time in the open air, living the country life. Libby had imagined her as a solemn creature, sedate and demure, wearing a pale blue twinset with pearls at her throat, and sitting at her father's right hand in the doubtless vast dining room of this Button-bridge Hall.

That perception was wrong, however. Bunty was not the twin-set type. She was unlike the preconceived notion that Libby had harboured all her life of how the daughters of the wealthy would be. Bunty would be fun, rebellious even.

'They all pass muster,' Bunty confirmed at length, and flashed a glimpse of her beautifully even teeth as she beamed.

Libby returned the smile, thankful that all was as it should be. 'Good. I'll seal them up and take them to the post room for you.'

'Thank you, Libby, that's jolly kind of you. But wait. There's no rush. Let's have a chat if you're sure you haven't got much to do. It's rather a novelty for me to talk to a girl my own age, especially here.' She instinctively looked about her as if somebody else might be in the room listening, and lowered her voice when she spoke. 'Normally, I'm stuck with Miss Evans my father's devoted secretary – do you know Miss Evans?'

'Not really,' Libby replied apologetically.

'She's a profoundly nice lady, but several decades older than a conker tree. And on holiday too . . .' Returning to a normal speaking volume, she went on: 'Thank goodness I say. Anyway, you claim you haven't got much to do.'

'It's true, but what about my supervisor if she wonders why I'm not at my desk?'

'Oh, don't worry about old Betsy Mayhew. If she says any-thing refer her to me. You say you're new here?'

'Yes. I left school in July, to be thrust into the big, wide world.'

'Bit of a sooty world, too, in this neck of the woods, don't you think?'

'Oh, isn't it just? So where is Buttonbridge Hall, if you don't mind me asking?'

'Out in the sticks. Between Kinver and Alverley if you know where that is. Rather lovely it is, actually, especially at this time of year.'

'I've heard you're keen on horses. I expect you get the chance to ride loads out in the country.'

Bunty gurgled with laughter. 'Is that what they say here? That I'm keen on horses? Well, also cars, bikes – chaps too. Anything that moves, frankly.'

'D'you have a boyfriend then?'

'Been getting through about one a month on average. No-body at present though.' Bunty shrugged self-effacingly. 'Not too many tasty unused chaps readily available out in the sticks, especially this side of the hunting season – I'm talking foxes here.'

'So you hunt?' Libby queried.

'If you can call it that. Actually, I have some sympathy for the poor fox, so really I just tag along for the ride. As far as chaps go, we could do with some interesting fresh specimens. Except for one, I've rather exhausted the local supply unfortu-nately . . . And you, Libby?'

'Mmm,' Libby answered wistfully. 'There's this chap I see. I've only known him a couple of months or so . . . He's my first real boyfriend. His name's Ron and I like him really, but he's asked me to get married already, the idiot. It would be daft at my age, so I'm keeping him at arm's length.'

Bunty gurgled again. 'Yes, you're far too young for marriage, having babies and all that palaver. So, best place for him, arm's length, eh? Do you have any brothers? Oh, I'm not fishing for an introduction – unless he's absolutely gorgeous, of course, so please don't jump to that conclusion.'

Libby laughed, dismissing the notion. 'There's only me. You have brothers though, don't you?'

'Two. Chalk and cheese.'

'I've seen Mr Hugh, of course. He always seems to be here.'

'Hugh? Oh, Hugh . . .' There was some disdain in Bunty's voice. 'I wouldn't trust him as far as I could throw him where women are concerned, but keep that to yourself for goodness' sake. Actually, he's engaged to a jolly decent girl called Laura Birch – the daughter of James Birch who owns a carpet factory in Kidderminster.' Libby shook her head; she had never heard of James Birch or his carpet factory. 'I'm sure Hugh doesn't deserve her at all, yet *she* thinks the sun shines out of his bum, poor fool. Somebody really ought to tell her.'

'But not you,' Libby suggested.

'Oh, definitely not me.' She turned down the corners of her mouth. 'It's nothing to do with me.'

'And your other brother, Bunty. What about him?'

'Edward. Oh, he's great. A year older than me. It's quite fun having him home from university for a while. At least I have somebody to play tennis with.' All at once there appeared a brighter gleam in Bunty's eyes, as if a brilliant idea had suddenly struck her. 'I say, Libby, do you play tennis?'

'I played a lot at school,' Libby replied.

'So you must be rather good?'

'Not bad, even if I say so myself.'

'Then you really must come over. Would you? I'm desperate for a lady tennis partner . . . somebody to make up a four. D'you think you might be interested?'

Libby was suddenly wide-eyed with surprise at such an unexpected invitation. 'Oh, I'd love to . . . if you're sure.'

'You fit the bill exactly. You have all the necessary attributes, not least because you you're a girl. You're also the right age and good-looking . . . and what's more you play tennis. So why not?' Bunty looked at her watch. 'I say, it's nearly one o' clock. D'you fancy a spot of lunch? There's this super pub I know.'

Libby sighed. 'If only I could. But I'd have Betsy Mayhew after my hide if I were late back.'

'Don't worry about Betsy. I'll square it with her. I'll tell her your working for me in a personal capacity. She won't question it.'

'Then I'd love to,' Libby agreed, delighted, flattered and surprised at being thus invited by no less an entity than the boss's only daughter, whom she liked. 'But how will we get there?'

'In my car.'

'You have a car?' Libby queried, incredulous.

'Yea, verily. Come on. If you take these letters to the post room I'll go see old Betsy Mayhew and tell her you're working with me elsewhere.'

- - -

Bunty drove the Riley fast and never stopped talking, while Libby felt compelled to cling on tightly but discreetly to the squab of her seat, her eyes never leaving the road ahead. Riding in a car was not something she did regularly. In fact, she could only ever recall having ridden in one other – an undertaker's car on the day of her grandfather's funeral. But this was hardly funereal; this was exhilarating.

After about fifteen minutes, the sight of a cattle market, closed today, signified their arrival at the village of Hagley, green with grass, and quaint houses painted white and black. It seemed a million miles from the industrial conglomeration they had left behind. They quit the main road and ascended a narrow lane before coming to a standstill outside an old red-brick building.

'Here we are,' Bunty announced, and clambered out of the vehicle. 'The Lyttleton Arms. It'll be quiet here today.'

They ambled to the front door and entered. Again, the familiar aroma every public house seemed to possess enveloped her.

'What's your poison?' Bunty enquired.

'Oh . . . I don't know. What are you having?'

'I'm having a pint of bitter. It's excellent here.'

'A pint of bitter?' *Men drink pints,* she thought. *Girls don't.* 'I don't think I could manage a pint of anything,' Libby declared.

'A half then?'

'A half of shandy, please.'

'A pint of bitter and a half of bitter shandy,' Bunty told the barman, who was waiting for the order.

'Coming up, Miss.' He grabbed a pint glass and proceeded to fill it from a beer pump.

'Are there any sandwiches available?

'There's cheese or ham, miss.'

'Two cheese and ham sandwiches, then, please.'

Bunty placed a half a crown on the counter and the barman handed her the change. The two girls moved to a table in the window with their drinks.

'Fancy you drinking pints of bitter,' Libby remarked matily, and not without some admiration. 'I wouldn't have the nerve – or the capacity.'

'Why shouldn't women drink pints?'

'But who'd have thought it? There's nothing to you. I mean, it's not as if you're big.'

'Eight stone wringing wet. But that's got nothing to do with it.'

'So where d'you put it?'

Laughing, Bunty said, 'Well, I'll have to visit the WC more often than you.' She took a good swig of the beer and sighed. 'Damn good stuff, this. You should try and develop a taste for it.' Then, after a pause: 'I say, do you really fancy making up a four?'

'Oh, yes. Who plays?'

'Edward, my brother, and his pal, Adrian Farrance. Adrian's sweetheart used to play with us, but since she ditched him we've been short of a girl. Actually, I'm rather glad she did. He's as pretty as paint.'

'You like him, then?'

'Like him? Rather! What's more, I fancy him.' She grinned impishly, her blue eyes sparkling, and Libby thought she looked extremely attractive.

'Does he fancy you?'

'Well, if he doesn't already, I'll have a jolly good go at making him.'

Libby broke into a chuckle. 'So when is the next match?'

'We could fix something up for Saturday, if that suits.'

'Okay by me.'

'Then let's hope the weather holds. I'll pick you up Saturday morning if you let me have your address before I leave today. You will be able to stay the night, won't you?'

'Stay the night? Really?' This was another huge surprise. 'You really want me to stay the night?'

'You'll be more than welcome. It'd be better for all concerned, too. Then we could get the lads to take us out for the evening . . . providing they've got nothing else fixed up.'

'Crikey, that sounds lovely. Okay by me. Thank you.' At once Libby's mind was awhirl. She would have to put Ron off. He wouldn't be happy about it, but he didn't own her. Surely her mother and father couldn't object though. Anyway, how could she possibly refuse an invitation to the home of Charles Burgayne?

If only her friends from school could see her now . . .

- - -

Gladys Shakespeare flitted around the cramped living room in Hill Street with a duster in one hand, a tin of Mansion polish in the other, as nervous as a kitten about the impending visit of Charles Burgayne's only daughter. She polished the sideboard, the chairs, the coal scuttle and the fender, then buffed up the black-leaded grate with a damp cloth, and stood back to assess the effect of her efforts. She adjusted the position of the ornaments on the mantelpiece, then spread the best chenille cloth over the table, which normally only saw the light of day on a Sunday.

Libby stepped down the crooked stairs and opened the creaking door onto the room to see her mother cleaning the imperfect windowpanes that looked out onto the veranda.

'I just thought I'd spruce the place up a bit afore that young woman gets here.'

'I wouldn't have bothered, Mom,' Libby replied, glancing around appraisingly. She had no intention of inviting the girl in – not wishing to put her off before she really got to know her. 'Best if I just run down the entry as soon as I hear her car.'

She noticed Gladys's hurt expression that she was not going to be allowed near Bunty Burgayne, and felt for her; her mother was doing her level best to make what little they'd got presentable. But the fussing made Libby acutely aware of the smallness, the humbleness of their little terraced home, compared to what Bunty was used to.

'She probably won't have time to come in and say hello,' Libby suggested placatingly. 'Maybe when she brings me back tomorrow.'

'Well, I would like to meet this Bunty Burgayne . . . I would like to think you're not ashamed of us, our Libby.'

'Oh, Mum.' She flung her arms around Gladys's neck and gave her a hug. ''Course I'm not ashamed. What a daft thing to say. I'm proud of you.'

They heard the thrum of a motor-car engine, the toot of a horn.

'She's here,' Libby said, and collected her things together. 'See you tomorrow, Mom. I'll be back for Sunday dinner.'

'Well, don't show yourself up, and just mind your Ps and Qs, our Libby. But try and have a lovely time.'

Gladys watched her daughter proudly as she hurried onto the backyard and down the entry to the street and the waiting motor car.

'Just throw your racquet and your bag on the back seat,' Bunty urged.

Libby did so, and jumped into the vehicle as quickly as she could, thinking that if Bunty hurried and drove fast through the awful narrow streets she wouldn't have time to notice the grubbiness. She did not know Bunty Burgayne well enough yet to appreciate that the girl was sufficiently well educated to understand that modest means did not necessarily mean modest intellect, nor a lack of fascination. Indeed, from the moment Libby first set foot in the boardroom to take dictation Bunty had liked the look and demeanour of her, recognising her not so much as a kindred spirit but more of a complementary personality. They were different, and it was their difference that attracted Bunty. In her own way, despite her lowly background, Libby seemed actually more refined; she was certainly more reserved, and Bunty was intrigued by the incongruity of it all.

'You must think it's pretty awful around here,' Libby remarked, feeling she should excuse the uninspiring scenery.

'Actually, I don't think that at all.' Bunty smiled her reassurance.

'But it can't be anything like where you live.'

'It's not. But that makes it all the more interesting. Look at the view from here.' They beheld a panoramic view overlooking Oldbury and West Bromwich, which Libby had never before considered attractive. 'It's terrific. And that's a pretty little cottage there, all covered in ivy,' Bunty commented as they turned left by the Junction Inn, into Cromwell Street, a canyon of red-bricked terraced houses and leaning chimneys.

'It is pretty,' Libby had to agree, thankful it was there, for it really was pretty with its fresh-painted wrought-iron railings, its foxgloves and lupins. 'So different from the other drab buildings. An aeroplane crashed into it once, years ago.'

'Really?'

'One of those biplanes. It was piloted by some young chap who lived around here. They say he'd built it himself, and he was showing off to his wife when he ran out of fuel.'

'What a blithering idiot. Was anybody hurt?'

'Apparently not. The railings were demolished, though.'

They left Kates Hill's narrow streets and drove to the centre of Dudley town crowded with Saturday shoppers, then headed out towards Stourbridge and beyond, alongside fields ripening gold under the summer sun. The houses they passed were big and beautiful with immaculately manicured lawns; flower beds and borders offered splashes of sometimes brilliant, sometimes subtle colours, but always eliciting a smile of pleasure and admiration from Libby.

They arrived at a crossroads. According to the signpost, they were now heading in the direction of Bridgnorth.

'Won't be long now,' Bunty exclaimed. 'Actually it'll be almost time for lunch when we arrive. And I'm starving.'

Over an undulating, winding road they travelled. Bunty swung the wheel left into a narrow lane. On the skyline, a clump of trees stood hazy in the distance, an island in a heaving sea of golden barley. The ground to their left dipped away from the road, cradling a hazel copse that looked dark, and soft as velvet. A little further on they were soon passing through two tall, wrought-iron gates hung on stone pillars, then along the sweeping curve of tarmacadamed driveway lined with tall elms and oaks, and vast stretches of lawn flanking each side. It seemed to go on forever, but when it skewed sharply a grand Tudor style house stood before them.

It was Libby's first glimpse of Buttonbridge Hall.

Before she knew it, she was ascending the front steps carrying her tennis racquet and her overnight case, with Bunty's hand encouragingly in the small of her back. She caught her breath as her roving gaze took in the entrance hall with its oak panelling, its arched and timbered ceiling. The antlers of long-dead stags branched out from wooden shields and, in a vast stone fireplace, fir-cones lay unlit in a wrought-iron basket. The place had its own distinctive smell, too; a blend of pot-pourri and stone, ancient wood and beeswax.

Almost at once a maid appeared.

'Libby, this is Jenkins. She'll take your things to your room.'

Libby smiled amiably at the girl who was in her early twenties, presentable and not at all unattractive. She offered the maid the overnight case, which she now realised was embarrassingly shabby. She was not used to servants and felt uncomfortable, aware that servants were normally people from her own class.

'Thank you very much,' she said self-consciously as the maid took the case and bobbed a curtsey.

'I'll show you your room later,' Bunty said. 'Let me introduce you to my mother first.'

They found Mrs Burgayne in the morning room sitting at a table, writing. She was a pleasant-looking woman in her mid to late fifties, as near as Libby could judge, neither fat nor thin; a woman who was holding onto her figure well.

'Mother, this is Libby Shakespeare, my lovely new friend.'

Dorothy Burgayne stood up and offered her hand.

'I'm delighted to meet you, Miss Shakespeare. May I call you Libby?'

'Oh, please do.'

'Bunty tells me you are a secretary at the works?' It was a question rather than an outright statement of fact.

Libby glanced at Bunty for reassurance. 'Not quite,' she said, wishing to be truthful. 'Actually, I'm just a shorthand typist from the typing pool, and fairly new there, Mrs Burgayne.'

Mrs Burgayne had no wish to appear condescending to Bunty's new friend, by suggesting she was demeaning herself by admitting being a mere shorthand typist instead of a full-blown secretary. Instead, she said, 'And here for the tennis, I hear. Do you play much?'

'When I was at school I played regularly. We were all encouraged to.'

'An active body aids an active mind is the theory behind that ethic, I suspect.'

Libby nodded and smiled. 'Yes, I suspect as much.'

'Edward has escaped for now,' Mrs Burgayne informed Bunty. 'He's meeting Adrian. I expect he'll be back soon.'

'He'd better,' Bunty said. 'He knew very well that Libby was coming here to make up a four.'

'Well, why don't you show Libby her room, and then have lunch. By then they might be here.'

'Right-ho. Come on Libby.'

Libby smiled. 'See you later, Mrs Burgayne.'

In the hallway again, she followed Bunty across the stone flags to a broad flight of stairs. In the gallery above, the polished wooden floor was uneven and creaked as they made their way over it to the kind of room Libby never dreamed existed anymore. It housed a four-poster bed hung with a cream-coloured tapestry with a design of pink roses, and richly coloured rugs on the oak floor. The mullioned windows were curtained with a material that matched the bed hangings, and Libby went across to catch the view outside.

'There's your case, look, Libby on the ottoman.'

'This is a lovely room, Bunty.'

'Glad you like it. There's a bathroom here . . .' She went through the door, out to the gallery again, and Libby followed. 'There, look.' She pointed to a door. 'You should have everything you need. If not, just ring for Jenkins.'

Ring for Jenkins! She wouldn't have the nerve to ring for Jenkins; she would rather die than ring for Jenkins.

'Anyway, do let's have lunch now, shall we, Libby? I could eat a horse.'

The two of them took lunch outside at a table and chairs set out on a lawn that stretched like a carpet before them, and shaded by elms that rustled gently in the light breeze. The flower beds were a riot of scarlet, purple, pink and white.

'I think your Buttonbridge Hall is beautiful, Bunty,' Libby remarked sincerely. 'The gardens too.'

'It's our home, Libby, and we all love it.'

'I'm a bit overawed by it all, though,' Libby added. 'Especially the servants. I'm just not used to servants.'

'The trick with servants, Libby, is to be respectful. Then they don't get all hoity-toity. I mean to say, if you really upset them there's no knowing what unspeakable things they might descend to when your back's turned. For instance, I once heard of a chap who was always awfully hard on his servants and rude too, so they used to wipe their master's favourite mutton chops round his bull-mastiff's backside before serving it.'

Libby giggled infectiously. 'That's disgusting! I take it this chicken hasn't had the same treatment?'

'Lord, no. Not here. I like to think Daddy runs a happy ship.'

'So tell me about your family. Have you always lived here? How far back do your ancestors go in this house?'

'Well, not as far as you might imagine. We're hardly aristocracy. Certainly not old money at any rate. This house was bought for a song, apparently, by my great-grandfather in the first flush of his prosperity. It was him who began steel-making – rather it was iron-making in those days, before there was any steel. As an ironmaster he did rather well and the business has been handed down and, with careful management it's grown. Not everybody has wanted to be part of it, though. Edward is one such – all he's interested in at present is aeroplanes.'

'I'm looking forward to meeting Edward,' Libby remarked. 'You speak fondly of him. What's he like?'

'Amiable . . . Yes, that describes him perfectly. He's amiable. Bright, too. I think you'll like him. I get on well with him.'

Libby wanted to ask if he was also good-looking, but such a question might give Bunty the wrong idea, so she desisted. Instead, Libby switched the subject to Bunty's string of past male conquests, and howled at her host's irreverence where chaps were concerned.

'D'you think you'll ever get married?' Libby asked.

'If I have to,' Bunty replied, then shrieked, 'Oh, Lord! I didn't mean it like it came out. Crikey, you must think me awful. What I mean is, it'll be sort of expected of me if the right chap comes along. So I might be persuaded . . .'

- - -

| 4 |

After lunch, the girls changed into their tennis dresses. On their way to the tennis court they dallied at a paddock to pat a new foal and admire its chestnut mother. Once at the tennis court they played a couple of hard-fought games, each testing the other. Libby won both. As they were about to start a third, two young men appeared in whites, bearing tennis racquets, and all the nonchalance and jauntiness of youth.

'You're late,' Bunty reprimanded them collectively, irked at their casualness.

One of them smiled, an icon of bonhomie. 'Sorry, old fruit. Had to get my racquet restrung. On my way back I called for Adrian, but he wasn't even up yet of course.'

So this was Edward. He was wearing a sleeveless pullover over a white shirt and his hair was a riot of unruly curls with some evidence remaining of a conventional parting on the left. Libby did not consider him strikingly handsome – at least not immediately – but there was something about him that appealed. He was the understated manifestation of what she considered masculine and elegant. His smile was broad and frank, and she perceived an innate warmth in his blue eyes that creased so attractively when he smiled. He was nice, and yes, he did seem amiable, just as Bunty had described.

'This is Libby Shakespeare,' Bunty announced to them both. 'Libby, my brother Edward . . . and Adrian Farrance . . .'

Edward greeted Libby with the wide-eyed smiling interest any healthy young man displays when introduced to a pretty girl. 'Pleased to meet you Miss Shakespeare,' he said sincerely.

'Oh, do call her Libby, Edward. You *are* going to leap around the tennis court with her.'

With a broader smile he offered his hand, and they shook. 'Your lovely name suits you,' he said. 'I'm delighted to meet you.'

'Thank you.' Libby smiled demurely, and felt herself blush.

Adrian offered his hand too, and she understood exactly why Bunty was interested in him. He was tall, lively, with an impish look in his eyes, a mop of dark curls akin to Edward's, and head-turningly handsome. He was evidently a rebel too, like Bunty.

'How do you do, Libby,' he said.

'I'm well, thank you.' Her round cheeks felt as if they were still glowing.

'You don't look quite your usual unsullied self this morning, Adrian,' Bunty remarked familiarly.

'Do I not?' he answered as if any personal disarray was unthinkable.

'You do not. Did you have a hectic night?'

He grinned waggishly. 'Momentous. I got invited to some stuck-up sort of do last night in Kinver. There were rather too many snooty types for my liking, except for one rather delicious girl who I did my best to woo. It so happened that she was of the same mind as me so we left together, and I hauled her around one or two of the local hostelries. Last thing I can remember is gazing at a half bottle of brandy and feeling rather sorry for it.'

'You're the limit, Adrian. What happened to the poor girl?'

'I honestly can't recall. Pity, really. She was really rather nice. Somebody, though, must have taken me home and poured me into my little bed, 'cause that's where I woke up. And now I don't feel any worse than if I'd been shoved through one of your father's rolling mills.'

'Well I think it's time you got over Juliet and settled down with a charming steady girl who'd put a stop to your nonsense.'

'Well, I always seem to be drawn back to you, Bunty, old love.'

'Ooh! For heaven's sake go away,' Bunty responded with a grin, but also blushing. 'Why don't we get on with the tennis?'

'Have we interrupted a serious match?' Edward enquired.

'If not serious, certainly significant,' she replied. 'I've just lost two games. This Libby Shakespeare is some player.'

'Well done, Libby. Are you ready for a four now?'

'I think so.'

'Girls against the boys, eh?' Edward suggested.

'That's hardly fair,' Bunty complained. 'You'll skin us.'

'You're joking. The state Adrian is in?'

'He'll soon rally round. Anyway, let me partner him, and you can partner Libby.'

'If that's okay with you, Libby?' Edward asked.

She nodded, smiling. 'Yes, okay by me.'

'You can serve first, Adrian.'

'Must I really?'

They all laughed, and the two couples parted to take their places at opposite ends of the court. Disregarding his aching limbs and throbbing head, Adrian began the onslaught, which Libby parried effectively, taking the point.

'Love fifteen,' exclaimed Edward. 'Well done, Libby.'

'Liven up, Adrian,' Bunty called, 'else we're going to be a pushover.'

It was an earnestly fought match, which Libby and Edward won two sets to one. This was quite some feat on their part, despite Adrian's self-inflicted incapacity, since Libby's long and shapely limbs distracted Edward as she moved across the court with all the grace and suppleness of a young gazelle. The bright sun, frequently behind her, shone through the flimsy material of her tennis frock, enticingly defining her form beneath it. She was oblivious to it, but Edward lingered to appreciate the treat on more than a few occasions, at the expense of several backhands and many points. Just who was this unassuming, pleasant and well-mannered girl Bunty had latched onto? She glowed like a lily in the sunshine. Her dark hair, which was pinned up, allowed stray strands to sensuously caress her elegant neck, now moist with perspiration. Her very kissable lips were pursed with concentration as she awaited Adrian's serves, usually returning them successfully as she danced around the court on tiptoes. Yet she seemed so innocent, so chaste, entirely unaware of her sexuality; and that made her all the more appealing.

- - -

None of them saw Edward's elder brother, Hugh Burgayne, watching, hidden behind the trees that encompassed the tennis court. His mother had mentioned that a new friend of Bunty's from the typing pool was playing tennis, and he wanted to catch a glimpse of her. Bunty wouldn't normally associate with employees, but their mother had remarked that she seemed a rather nice girl, and quite pretty too. This had aroused his curiosity. He had already spotted an extremely attractive new girl in the corridors at the office whom he very much fancied. He had wondered if this was the same girl . . .

- - -

At the end of the tennis all four were perspiring madly as they stood facing each other on the grass in the shade of an ancient oak, thankful that Jenkins had come along and planted a collapsible table, complete with two jugs of iced lemonade and four glasses beneath a tree.

'I must say, you played jolly well,' Edward said to Libby as he mopped sweat from his face with a handkerchief. 'Anytime you're in need of a partner at this game do let me know.'

'Well, this doesn't have to be a one-off,' Bunty interjected breathlessly, and radiant with exertion. She poured lemonade for each of them. 'Libby is welcome to play with us regularly, if that's okay with her.'

'I'd love to,' Libby replied, accepting a glass from Bunty.

'Except, Edward, that you'll be leaving for Cambridge soon.'

'I know it all too well,' he answered with what seemed like regret.

Libby sat down on the grass and Edward sat beside her, still studying her discreetly. To him she seemed the essence of femininity. Slim and perfectly proportioned, with all the grace and poise of a ballerina, her skin looked invitingly smooth, her eyes were crystal clear and long lashed, and her lovely mouth was so obviously made to give and receive delicious kisses.

'Are you staying the night, Libby?' he enquired.

'I think so,' she replied, looking at Bunty for reassurance, who sat on the grass, facing Adrian.

'Libby's having dinner with us,' Bunty confirmed.

'Excellent,' Edward exclaimed. 'So how d'you fancy joining Adrian and me for a day out tomorrow? We're playing cricket at Enville Hall.'

Libby looked from one to the other. 'Sorry,' she answered with sincere regret, 'But I shall have to get back home. My folks will be expecting me before one o' clock. Sunday dinner's a bit of a ritual at our house.'

As she took another drink, Libby realised she must sound ineffably plebeian, and her eyes latched onto Bunty seeking her reaction and perhaps encouragement to stay. But she was shocked to see that as Bunty sat with her arms around her knees, the hem of her short skirt had receded, revealing tracts of smooth, tanned thighs . . . and her white knickers. As Libby tried to warn her with eye signals, Bunty merely responded with an enigmatic smile. Libby twigged. *She's doing it deliberately while Adrian is sitting facing her. She means to lure him. She said she would.*

A little disconcerted, Libby tried to divert all attention away from glimpses of Bunty's underwear, and said to Edward, 'I'm told you're keen on aeroplanes.'

'Yes,' Edward replied enthusiastically, hoping to talk about his favourite subject.

'He flies one,' Bunty remarked.

'Oh, you fly one?' Libby couldn't help sounding surprised as well as impressed.

'His own plane,' Bunty added, now effecting modesty by wrapping her skirt around her thighs and thus hiding her knickers. Libby understood that her resumption of propriety was calculated.

'It's a Gypsy Moth, if that means anything,' Edward said. 'Would you like to see it?'

'Why? Is it here?'

'About a hundred yards away.'

'Then I'd love to. I've never seen a plane close to.'

'Come on then, I'll show you.'

All four scrambled to their feet, put their glasses on the table, and made their way in a group across the grass and through a line of trees to a long clearing.

'This is the strip where I take off and land,' Edward explained. 'The Moth only needs about a hundred and fifty yards for either.'

Libby turned her head from left to right scanning the swathe of short-cropped turf. 'So where is the aeroplane?'

'Over here.'

She walked beside him, while Bunty and Adrian fell further behind, absorbed in their own conversation.

'How long have you had the plane?'

'Nearly a year. My father got it me for my birthday. I'm hoping to fly to Cambridge next week, providing I can get permission to keep it at Duxford. That's the airfield we use. I belong to the University Air Squadron, you see.'

'I didn't know universities had air squadrons.'

He turned and smiled. 'Cambridge was the first, actually. Set up about twelve years ago. It's seen as a way of getting chaps with degrees to go on to a career in the RAF.'

'Is that what you want to do, then? Join the Royal Air Force?'

'That's my intention.'

'Doesn't the prospect of war with Germany scare you, though?'

'From the point of view of being involved? Not at all.' He turned to her and smiled. 'I understand the dangers an RAF pilot would face in war, but we would all have to play our parts.' He smiled again, with a rather sad look in his eyes, Libby thought.

'So what got you interested in aeroplanes?'

'Oh, ever since I was a small boy and somebody gave me a book on the aircraft of the Great War . . . Look, there it is . . .'

The aircraft, painted silver and blue with large letters marked on the side, lay under a canvas awning, akin to a large tent. Libby ran her fingers lightly along the leading edge of the lower wing as she inspected it. The covering was a material that looked like some sort of tough canvas, and the wings were secured by what she perceived as wire rigging, like sails on a yacht. Controlling rods and wires were attached to the outside of the fuselage.

'It's beautiful,' she said, almost breathlessly. 'And smaller than I thought it would be.'

'It carries two people. Would you like to go up in it with me for a whizz round?'

'Now, you mean?'

'Yes. It doesn't take long to get it ready. It's already fuelled up.'

'But it all looks a bit flimsy to me,' she said, uncertain now as to what she might be letting herself in for.

He was enchanted by her look of reticence. 'Actually, it's as safe as houses. Even if the engine packed up we would glide safely back to the ground.'

Libby turned to Bunty, hoping to obtain her advice. She must surely have flown in the contraption. Bunty was giving Adrian her full attention as they approached, and laughing at something he had just said.

'Bunty, Edward has asked me to go up in the aeroplane with him,' she said, almost as if he'd made an improper suggestion.

'Then you must wear something warm,' Bunty replied showing no sign of disapproval. 'It's freezing up there even on a day like today, and it'll blow you to bits. Forget it in your tennis frock. You'd better change into something warm.'

'Have you ever flown in it?'

'Yes. Once. It's great fun, actually.'

She looked at Edward, still with uncertainty in her eyes.

'You'll love it, Libby,' Edward assured her. 'Bunty has a warm jacket you can borrow, and I have a spare helmet.'

'You'll need some goggles too,' Bunty added.

'Don't worry, I have a spare pair of goggles,' Edward said. 'Look, why don't we go to the house, get togged up, then come back here when we're ready.'

'It all seems a lot of bother,' Libby reasoned, trying to wriggle out of the situation but not wishing to appear afraid.

'No bother at all, Libby. Come on, you simply must. We'll soon have you ready.'

So they returned with Libby to the house so that she could be suitably attired for what she imagined would be a hairraising flight in the open cockpit of an aeroplane. When they were walking back to the field, with Libby duly wrapped in a sheepskin jacket, a pair of Bunty's slacks, leather helmet, goggles and gloves and a headset with a microphone that hung beneath her chin, she could hear the throb and cackle of its engine, already warming up.

'Okay, Libby,' Edward called, trying to make himself heard over the din. 'Step up here and hold the wing struts for support, then lower yourself into the seat.'

'This front seat?' Libby yelled back, her voice almost drowned by the din.

Edward nodded.

As she clambered in, not without some difficulty, she wondered why she was placed in the driving seat and not Edward. Surely he didn't expect her to fly the plane. After all, how could he see where he was going and pilot it if he were sitting behind her? It made no sense. She flinched at the strength of the powerful airstream already being created by the propeller, as yet only idling. There was little room to move. Edward stood beside her on the wing and reached for the safety straps behind her, which he pulled around her in a sort of webbing. Then he asked her to reach down for another strip of webbing, that she had to pull up between her legs so that it could be fastened to the other. He clasped them all together in a central metal buckle.

'Don't touch the clasp until we're back on the ground,' he instructed in a shout. 'Are your goggles secure?'

She tightened them and nodded. He smiled reassuringly.

'The wire from the headset,' he said, and handed her the lead that had been dangling from the headset. 'Plug it in there and we'll be able to talk to each other.'

She did as he bid as he clambered into the cockpit behind her. When he had fastened himself in, he tapped her on the shoulder and, as she turned to glance behind her, he gave her the thumbs-up. Then the headset suddenly crackled into life.

'Can you hear me?' he asked.

'Yes,' she answered. 'Can you hear me?'

'Loud and clear. I'm about to get ready for take-off. You might notice an increase in the draught from the propeller.'

The first thing she noticed though was an increase in the speed and sound of the engine as Edward nosed the Moth into the wind and taxied forward. He opened the throttle fully and waited for the surge of power that would haul them into the blue. The blast of wind from the propeller intensified astonishingly, so much so that it ruffled the peak of the leather helmet she was wearing, and almost began lifting her goggles from her face until she tightened them further.

'Are you okay?' the voice asked through her headset.

'I think so.'

The little biplane did not disappoint; it rumbled along the clearing, gathering speed, the whole assembly vibrating alarmingly. Then the vibration suddenly ceased, and she was surprised at how quickly the ground beneath her was slipping away. She peered over the side as the aircraft banked. Bunty and Adrian, getting smaller and smaller, waved frantically. She waved back, scanning the landscape that was sliding away underneath her, for recognisable landmarks. A canal came into view, glinting like a length of shiny wire as it disappeared into the hazy distance.

It was strange and exhilarating to be up there, remote, flying with the birds, although birds seemed to scatter in all directions at the raucous sound of the engine.

'How high are we flying?' she yelled into her microphone.

'We're just coming up to two thousand feet,' came the reply.

Up here you could watch the world and all its troubles go by and somehow be untouched by it. They flew over countryside patched with gold and yellow and green, lush with trees while Edward gave a running commentary of what lay below them. To their right stood a stately home in magnificent grounds, with two shimmering lakes; it was amazing how many lakes and ponds there were down there. Through the summer haze, the spire of Top Church in Dudley became visible. Then Libby recognised the grey hulk that was the keep of Dudley's Norman castle, and the new modern buildings in its grounds that were a part of the new zoo. She recognised other landmarks too, including St John's church on Kates Hill, and her old school playing fields; she looked for the street in which she lived, but before she could find it she felt the flimsy machine roll to the left. The wings dipped alarmingly, the horizon became seriously skewwhiffed and Libby believed that but for the webbing that was securing her to her seat, she would surely tumble out.

'Time to turn back,' Edward announced.

'So soon?' she replied.

''Fraid so. Are you enjoying it?'

'Gosh, I love it, Edward. It's exhilarating.'

'Glad you like it,' he said.

It was intoxicating up here. Shame it must be so short a trip. Libby lost all sense of direction and orientation as they flew over the patchwork of golden fields and woods. All too soon she sensed that they were descending, the ground was getting closer . . . closer, ever closer. They skimmed a copse of trees, then she recognised the Tudor building that was Buttonbridge Hall. They were about to land. Ahead of her and below her she could just make out the clearing which served as the landing strip. She braced herself for the inevitable bump as the wheels hit the ground. But it was so smooth. The only clue that they were on the ground was when they rumbled across it and she felt the unevenness of the grassy surface that made the wings and bracing shudder.

Then the engine stopped . . . Silence . . . Silence like she had never known before.

She felt a bump behind her that suggested Edward was clambering out. She turned her head and caught sight of him hovering over her ready to release her from the harness.

He grinned laddishly as he took off his goggles and muffler, and motioned her to unplug the headset. 'How was that?'

'Brilliant!' She called, beaming back at him. 'Oh, I loved it, I loved it. I can't believe I've actually flown.'

'We'd better unharness you.' He reached into the open cockpit to unfasten the webbings. 'Okay, you're done. Careful as you climb out. I'll help you.' He jumped down onto the grass.

She raised herself up, aided by the wing bracing and lifted her leg to step out onto the lower wing. His hand was at once firmly on her ankle guiding her foot onto the built-in pad that would support her weight. Back on solid ground she removed the goggles to fully reveal her flushed cheeks and astonishingly bright eyes that told perfectly how much she had enjoyed herself.

'How long were we up there?' she enquired, taking of the fur-lined gloves Bunty had lent her.

He looked at his watch. 'About half an hour.'

'That long? It seemed like five minutes. It's so cold up there, isn't it?'

'Told you so,' Edward answered with a grin.

'I can't see Bunty and Adrian.' She looked about her, peering through the trees.

'Probably playing tennis again.'

'I expect so,' she said.

'Shall we go and find them, and let them know you're back in one piece?'

She smiled at him in unconcealed admiration. 'I suppose we'd better.'

- - -

There were six for dinner, which was a very informal occasion. Bunty had invited Adrian to stay, and he was still wearing his tennis whites. Libby had brought with her a printed cotton dress all fresh and summery, which turned out to be an ideal choice, while Bunty changed into black slacks and a blouse with a bold floral pattern. Mr and Mrs Burgayne were also at home, but Hugh had gone to meet his fiancée Laura Birch, Libby was told, and would doubtless be dining with her family, unless they had arranged to have dinner out.

Just before they sat down to dinner she met Charles Burgayne for the first time, when Bunty introduced them.

'I'm pleased to meet you, Miss Shakespeare,' he said as he shook her hand.

'You *can* call her Libby, you know, Daddy,' Bunty declared, rolling her eyes. Then, in an aside to Libby that was deliberately audible to everybody, added, 'Daddy is so old-fashioned sometimes.'

'It's an old-fashioned courtesy that I extend to anybody I've not had the pleasure of meeting before,' Charles responded, but with good humour. 'One just cannot take for granted that people are happy with such familiarities as being called by their Christian name.'

'But Libby is my generation, Daddy, not yours. We don't stand on ceremony. It's just too boring.'

'So, Libby,' he went on, choosing to ignore his daughter's denunciation but taking her advice anyway, 'I understand you've been up in the Gypsy Moth?'

'I have and it was a sensation,' she enthused. 'I loved every minute. It was good of Edward to go to all the trouble.'

Charles smiled. 'And I expect you're more than welcome to go up again next time you're here.'

'Goes without saying,' Edward asserted.

Charles made no comment about her being an employee of his company, and Libby was relieved that his attitude towards her was kind and considerate, a million miles from the reputation he had among his workers that he could be tough and uncompromising. But that was his business face. Now, though, he was in his own home, with members of his own family and their chosen friends, wearing his family face, which she liked.

They sat at the table in the large dining-room, where a maid who Libby had not seen before, served beef consommé.

'Are you going to the seaside for a holiday while the works are shut, Libby?' Dorothy Burgayne asked.

'I'm afraid not, Mrs Burgayne. Not this year at any rate. How about you? Shall you be going away?'

'Yes, I'm taking Bunty to Bournemouth. We leave on Monday. We're very fond of Bournemouth, aren't we, dear?'

'We are, Mother.' She turned to Libby. 'We have relatives living there,' she explained. 'Damn, I'd forgotten about Bournemouth. It means I shan't see you again, Libby, till I get back.'

'But perhaps Libby would still like to come and play tennis,' Edward suggested hopefully. 'She is rather good. I could always pick you up, Libby.'

'Her mother and father might strongly disapprove if they thought there'd be nobody here to chaperone her, Edward,' Dorothy suggested.

'Nor do I think her boyfriend would take very kindly to it,' Bunty added.

'Boyfriend? Oh . . . Sorry, Libby. I didn't realise you have a boyfriend . . .' He looked embarrassed and disappointed, and Libby felt herself redden as she met his eyes apologetically.

'It's nothing serious,' she replied, self-consciously.

'But he's asked you to marry him, hasn't he, Libby?'

Resolved not to blush, she put all her might into resisting the flow of blood to her cheeks, but the flow ignored her efforts as disobediently as a river in full spate would have similarly ignored her, and she blushed more vividly than she'd ever blushed before.

'He has, but I haven't accepted him,' she was anxious to let it be known. 'Nor do I intend to. I'm too young yet. I want to see something of life before ever I start thinking about marriage.' She glanced at Edward and smiled unsurely as their eyes met.

'I think you're very sensible, if you don't believe you're ready for marriage,' Dorothy exclaimed.

'Yes, good for you,' said Edward. He sighed to himself; though her wanting to see something of life would doubtless exclude him as a romantic interest anyway.

'Anyway,' Dorothy said, 'remember we have to be back from Bournemouth in good time for the garden party.'

'Of course, the garden party,' Bunty chimed. 'I say, Libby, would you like to come to the garden party?'

'I'd love to, but—'

'It is all right if Libby comes, isn't it, Mother?'

'Of course. If she wants to she's more than welcome.'

'Maybe I could help somehow,' Libby suggested brightly.

Bunty turned to her. 'Oh, Mother would have you slicing and buttering bread if you let her, but no, you'll be my guest, so that's settled. That boyfriend of yours will curse me, though, for dragging you away from him another Saturday night. Perhaps you'd better bring him too.'

'No, not on your nelly,' Libby answered emphatically, which made the others laugh, including Edward.

- - -

| 5 |

'My mother is dying to meet you,' Libby told Bunty as the Burgaynes' black Riley pulled up outside the little terraced house in Hill Street. 'You must come in and say hello.' She had been giving the matter some thought as they drove back, and to invite Bunty in seemed the proper thing to do in view of the fact that she'd enjoyed the easy friendship and hospitality of her family. That her own home was so undeniably working class, was unalterable.

'I'd be delighted,' Bunty replied. 'Who knows, I might have seen your father around since he works for my father.'

'Don't mind the house, though,' Libby said apologetically. 'It's hardly what you'd call grand.'

'It's home, isn't it?'

Libby gave a little self-conscious laugh. 'Oh, it's home all right.'

'And you're comfortable in it?'

'I suppose so.'

'So why should I mind it?'

'Well . . . The comparison between it and your house, I suppose,' Libby explained.

'If you're apologising for it, because you think it's small compared to the ancient mausoleum I have to live in, then don't bother. I'd prefer something much cosier. I bet your house is cosy. I bet your mother and father are cosy.'

Libby smiled, grateful for her friend's reassurances. 'It's just the difference in our backgrounds, Bunty,' she said candidly. 'Some people in your position would look down on us.'

'Some might, I daresay, Libby, but I never would. To do so would be to assume that you are less intelligent or less worthy, or less important than me, and I flatly refuse to accept such nonsense. I take people as I find them, and what I find in you I like. From the moment we met it seemed to me that we could become friends. Not because we are similar – we're absolutely not – but because we are different. So please, don't think so little of yourself or your background.'

'Well, I never do normally,' Libby said. 'I believe I'm as good as the next person—'

'And so you are . . . infinitely better than most. Edward thought so too.' Bunty looked at Libby for her reaction. 'I can tell.'

Libby smiled radiantly. 'Do you really think so?'

'Yes, I do.'

'And yet you told him I'd got a boyfriend.'

'Well, so what? If he allows that to stop him making a move on you, then he's not half the chap I thought he was. Anyway, even if you were interested in him, you wouldn't want him to think you were too readily available – at his beck and call. Am I right?'

'I suppose so,' Libby replied, smiling conspiratorially.

'It'll maintain his interest if he thinks there's just a slight chance, so toss him a crumb of hope from time to time.'

Libby laughed. 'You!' she exclaimed. 'You're a right one for playing games with men. How are you getting on with Adrian? Have you stirred his interest yet? I saw how you flashed him a glimpse up your tennis dress . . . And I caught him having a peep.'

'Brilliant!' Bunty's chuckle was almost musical. 'So he's had a glimpse of the promised land. Let's hope it's aroused some interest. But I'll still play hard to get. I shall have to assure him that I'm not a girl like that. It works wonders.'

'I must tell you, though, Bunty – I was a bit shocked when I knew he could see your knickers. I was even more shocked when I realised you were showing them deliberately.'

'Oh, but Libby, you must understand that I've never had the brass neck to do it before, but a girl I know once told me that she used it as a ploy herself – and it worked. So I thought I'd give it a try.'

'Gosh! I'm learning all the time . . .' Libby sighed and reached for the door handle. 'Well, thank you for everything, Bunty,' she said sincerely. 'I've had a smashing time. I wouldn't have missed it for the world.'

'You're welcome any time, you know. We'll get together again when I get back from Bournemouth.'

'I'm looking forward to it.'

'I'll ring you up as soon as I get back.'

'Well, don't forget.' She smiled happily. 'Now, come and meet Darby and Joan.'

Gladys Shakespeare was in the brew house peeling potatoes at the stone sink that stood below the window, beside a cast-iron mangle with bleached and cracked wooden rollers. In one corner was the wash boiler, a brick-built, copper-lined affair with a fire hole beneath for heating water on washing day. On the wall hung two maiding dollies for pounding the laundry in the tub, and alongside them hung the tin bath. Against another wall next to the door stood the gas stove, from which emanated the most wonderful, mouth-watering aroma of lamb roasting.

'My, that smells good,' Bunty at once remarked.

'Mom, this is Bunty Burgayne.'

'I'm pleased to meet you, Miss Burgayne,' Gladys said deferentially, turning from the sink to reach a towel and dry her hands. 'And if you like the smell of me lamb cooking you'm welcome to stop and have a bit of dinner with us.'

'That's really kind of you, Mrs Shakespeare, and do call me Bunty. Any other day I'd take you up on your offer, but today I must unfortunately dash home *toute de suite*. My mother and I are going away tomorrow, you see, and we have heaps of packing to do.'

'Well, have a cup o' tea then, eh? Our Libby, why don't you put the kettle on?'

'Course I will, mom.' Libby grabbed the kettle from the hob and filled it with fresh water. 'Where's Dad?'

'Need you ask?' Gladys replied. 'He's up the yard.'

'I didn't see anybody in the yard when we came through the entry,' Bunty offered.

'No, Mom means he's in the privy – which is up the yard.' Libby was mortified, and attempted to hide her discomposure by lighting the gas ring under the kettle.

'He'll be back in a minute. He's been up there twenty minutes already.'

'We don't need to know that, Mom,' Libby admonished. 'Is that cosy enough?' she remarked quietly to Bunty and rolled her eyes with embarrassment.

Bunty saw the funny side and laughed amiably. She turned then to Gladys. 'Mrs Shakespeare, I've returned your lovely daughter safe and sound, and I really do believe she's enjoyed herself enormously.'

'I have,' Libby confirmed. 'Enormously.'

'I hope she ain't been no trouble, young Bunty.'

'Not a minute's trouble, Mrs Shakespeare. She's behaved impeccably.' Bunty winked at Libby. 'We've enjoyed having her. So much so she's invited back again when I get back from Bournemouth.'

'Well, that's very nice of you, Bunty. Just so long as she ain't putting you to any trouble.' Gladys returned to the sink and rinsed her peeled potatoes in a colander, then dried her hands again. 'Let's go into the scullery and sit down while the kettle boils.'

The scullery was linked to the brew house by a veranda. Joe had erected it five years earlier, so that Gladys wouldn't have to endure the vagaries of the winter weather when darting from one to the other. Potted plants adorned the rough shelves and the window ledge, and an aspidistra sat majestically in a brass pot on an ancient but very solid round table that occupied far too much space on the stone-flagged floor.

Libby led the way to where a fire was burning bright in the black-leaded grate. A home-made podged rug, made from scraps of Joe's and Gladys's old clothes lay on the hearth. A stair jutted out onto the edge of the hearth and the door above it hid the staircase. Next to that was the cellar door, and both were painted the same leaf green as the cupboard and skirting boards.

In that small room, under the window that looked onto the veranda, stood a table adorned with the cherished tasselled chenille cloth, which matched the pelmet around the mantelshelf. Three varnished wooden chairs were placed around it. On the mantelshelf itself stood the black marble clock with Roman numerals that with reassuring reliability gained five minutes a day. On either side of it were matching porcelain vases decorated in a Chinese pattern, a letter rack and a jar of spills. A pincushion, bearing an assortment of needles and dangling threads in various hues, hung forlornly from the pelmet. On a cabinet next to the table stood a wireless and, facing the hearth was Joe's armchair. Behind the armchair and against the wall stood a sideboard adorned with crocheted mats and another vase of cut glass, at the bottom of which lay a hotchpotch of buttons and hairgrips.

'This *is* cosy,' Bunty remarked.

'And small,' Libby added morosely.

'But I do like it.'

Joe entered, carrying a folded newspaper under his arm as he dried his hands on a towel, having just washed them in the brewhouse.

'Ah . . . You'm back then, our Libby.'

'Hello, Dad. Yes, I'm back, and this is Bunty Burgayne.'

'Well, well . . . Miss Burgayne, this is an honour.'

'Please do call me Bunty,' she said.

'If you'll call me Joe,' he bargained, with a broad affable grin.

'It's a deal, Joe.' They shook hands.

'Dad always takes the paper with him to the privy,' Libby remarked, her embarrassment making it necessary for her to mention it and so appear to excuse it.

'Oh, my father does too,' Bunty replied. 'He says it's the only time he gets the chance to read the paper in peace and quiet.'

'I like the News o' the World meself, you know, Bunty. The football page is what I like best. And the cricket in the summer o' course. How's your father, by the way? I hope he's keeping well. I seldom see him these days.'

'He's quite well, thank you, except that he works too hard. He suffers with his chest, you know.'

'He always did. Is he thinking of retiring yet?'

'My father? Not he. He'll work till he drops.'

'Give him my regards, young Bunty. If he don't remember who I am – 'cause there's hundreds work there and he can't be expected to remember everybody – tell him I'm the one who pulled him out o' that great big gearbox he fell into on the number one rolling mill, when they was refilling it with grease one shutdown.'

Bunty laughed. 'I heard about that – it's a famous tale. Quite a hoot. He was covered in the stuff, wasn't he?'

'From head to toe. I thought we'd never get him clean. He thought so an' all.'

'We laugh about that still, you know.'

'We laughed as well at the time, but I don't think he saw the funny side of it. Not then at any rate.'

Gladys entered carrying a teapot cocooned in a bright woollen tea cosy. 'Tea up,' she declared, and put the tray on the table. 'Libby, will you get the cups and saucers and sugar from the cupboard, while I get the milk from the slab at the top of the cellar steps?'

'Let me get the milk, Mrs Shakespeare,' Bunty said. 'I'm dying to see your cellar steps. Is it that door?'

'That's the one,' Gladys answered.

- - -

That afternoon Ron called round. He was disgruntled because Gladys and Joe were full of this Bunty Burgayne who'd called in to pay her respects, and she was the cause of his being thrown over the evening before. Thus, he felt it was not in his best interests to condone either what Libby had done, or approve of where she'd been, or who she'd been with. So he tried his best to remain aloof as she recounted her visit to Buttonbridge Hall.

'I flew in an aeroplane, you know,' she wilfully goaded.

'You what?' He sounded highly sceptical.

'The Burgaynes' younger son Edward has his own aeroplane. A Gypsy Moth . . .' That certainly gained Ron's interest.

'A Gypsy Moth? And you went up in it?'

'It was absolutely brilliant. We flew over Dudley, and I saw the castle, the new zoo – everything.'

'How old is this Edward?'

'Twenty-one-ish And he's *very* good-looking,' she taunted.

'I suppose he was trying to get round you, eh? You want to watch out for these posh folk with money, who live in big mansions and have aeroplanes. They take what they want and then scarper.'

'Actually, he was really nice, Ron. Respectful, chatty, friendly.'

'So are you interested in this Edward?'

She shrugged, teasing him. 'Wouldn't you be if you were a single girl? Wouldn't you be interested in somebody with wealth, health, fine manners, who was handsome with it?' She paused a moment, looking thoughtful. 'And had an aeroplane? But then again . . .' She sighed theatrically. 'I suppose a lot depends on whether he's interested in me . . .'

- - -

The annual works' holiday was over, and Libby joined the throngs of people walking to work once again on the following Monday morning. Both Vera and Hilda, her closest workmates, had been on holiday, Vera to Blackpool with a host of friends, and Hilda to the Isle of Man. As they assembled in the typing pool, they were bubbling with enthusiasm to tell Libby about their respective exploits, and she listened to both with amused interest.

'Didn't you go away, Libby?' Hilda enquired, the fact dawning on her that Libby had offered nothing about holiday experiences to the conversation, only listening to them and laughing with them.

'Don't you remember?' she responded. 'I'm not entitled to any holiday yet. I was here.'

'Lord, I completely forgot. You poor thing. So was it quiet?'

'Very. But I did meet Bunty Burgayne. She asked me to do some letters for her. I think she's really nice.' Libby did not feel inclined to tell them that Bunty had since become a good friend and that she'd been a guest at Kinlet House. Such information was best kept to herself.

'And how's that Ron?' Hilda queried. 'Is he still as keen?'

'He seems it . . .' Libby shrugged. 'Sometimes I wish he weren't.'

'Why don't you just give him up?'

'To tell you the truth, Vera, I haven't got the heart. Anyway, I actually like him. It's just that I'm not serious about him. I'm not in love with him, and I don't want to marry him.'

Their chat was interrupted by the appearance of Betsy Mayhew, the supervisor.

'Miss Shakespeare, if you're not too busy Mr Hugh Burgayne would appreciate you taking some dictation.'

'Mr Hugh?'

'Yes, Mr Hugh. Miss Roberts, his secretary is still away. He's asked for you.'

Libby glanced at her two friends and the corners of their mouths turned down and their eyebrows arched simultaneously.

'Okay, Miss Mayhew.' Libby picked up her notepad and pencil and, smoothing the creases of her cotton skirt, made her way to the office of Hugh Burgayne. She tapped on the door, and entered when she heard him call her in. He was standing beside a huge oak desk and seemed tall in his dark pin-striped suit – taller than Edward. His hair was starting to thin already and he had a thin face with large eyes and a pointed nose – not half as appealing as his younger brother. His desk was a model of neatness; nothing was out of place, and such papers as there were, were stacked in neat, separate piles.

'Good morning, Miss Shakespeare.' He greeted her with a magnanimous smile and gestured that she sit down opposite him. 'I've a few letters I'd like rattled off, if you could manage that.'

'Yes, gladly, sir,' Libby replied.

'Excellent. We've not met before.'

'I'm Libby Shakespeare, Mr Burgayne.'

'Yes, I know who you are,' he said. 'You were a guest at Buttonbridge Hall over the weekend. Unfortunately, I never had the chance to say hello.'

She nodded and smiled self-consciously. 'I was, and I had a lovely time, thanks to your sister.'

'I'm sorry I missed you. I understand you and Bunty have become friends.'

'I like to think so.'

'So you had a good time.'

'Oh, yes, I had a wonderful time, thank you. Everybody was so kind . . . and Edward took me up in his aeroplane. I think that was the highlight of my stay.'

'Tut-tut. Edward and his aeroplane,' Hugh said, and his tone conveyed disdain. 'He'll get himself killed in that contraption one of these days. When he does, let's hope you're not with him.'

'Oh, but he seems a very capable flyer, Mr Burgayne. Very capable.'

'And you are able to judge?'

Libby shrugged, feeling mildly chastised. 'I know so little about aeroplanes and flying, perhaps I'm not such a good judge. But he returned me to Buttonbridge Hall safely enough.'

'Well be jolly careful, young lady. You're a very pretty girl, and it would be a sin to mar those delightful good looks in an accident with Edward. Or even worse, get yourself maimed.'

'I'm grateful for your concern, Mr Burgayne, really I am, but I think it's unlikely that I shall ever fly with him again. He's going back to Cambridge soon after the garden party, isn't he?'

'You know about the garden party?'

'Actually, I've been invited – as Bunty's guest.' She smiled pleasantly.

'Excellent.' He shuffled some papers. 'Naturally, I shall be in attendance, but under sufferance. My mother fondly believes she's doing something positive for the church and for the community by hosting a garden party every year. All we get from it, however, is a whole barrow load of litter, and lawns that take months to recover afterwards. Anyway, it will be a plea-sure to see *you* there, Miss Shakespeare.'

'It's nice of you to say so, Mr Burgayne. Thank you.'

'So . . . to the letters . . .'

Libby opened her notepad, and her pencil was poised. 'Ready when you are, Mr Burgayne.'

He dictated his letters, disposing of them in a capable and business-like manner, then resumed their conversation.

'Have you ever had photographs taken, Miss Shakespeare?' he asked unexpectedly. 'I mean formal, serious portraits? I'd say you're awfully photogenic.'

'Only snaps,' she answered, closing her notepad. 'Nothing what you might call formal.'

'I'm amazed.'

'Really?' She smiled. 'Why?'

'I'm astonished, frankly, that a girl so lovely hasn't. Has no-body asked you to sit before?'

'No.' She smiled again, wide-eyed, flattered that he should say as much.

'Such a waste. I happen to be a very keen photographer, you know. I have a studio and darkroom at Buttonbridge Hall. I'd be delighted if you'd agree to sit for me.'

This was totally unforeseen, and also astonishing. 'Well . . . I suppose I—'

'If you could come this Saturday or Sunday?'

Libby remembered what Bunty had said about being un-chap-eroned while she and Mrs Burgayne were away, and how her folks would have disapproved had she accepted even Edward's invitation.

'Sorry, Mr Burgayne, but I can't this weekend. I'm busy.'

'Perhaps when you show up for the garden party then? If you would allow me to steal you away from Bunty for an hour to take some serious photos. Does that sound feasible?'

'Yes, I suppose so . . .' She confirmed her assent with another enchanting smile. It was hardly possible to refuse, for Hugh Burgayne was a director of the company, and she would be enjoying his family's warm hospitality once again. 'I'll go and type these letters for you now, Mr Burgayne. It shouldn't take long.'

- - -

With the holiday season continuing for some, Libby found herself standing in for other secretaries from time to time, including Edith Evans, Charles Burgayne's ageing but utterly reliable helpmeet. She felt comfortable in the presence of Charles Burgayne, as she'd dined with him at Buttonbridge Hall, but was nervous about whether her work would be up to the standard of Miss Evans's.

'Have you heard from Bunty and Mrs Burgayne?' Libby asked him conversationally when he'd finished dictating a batch of correspondence.

'Why, yes, Libby,' he replied cheerfully. 'They telephoned last evening. It seems they are enjoying the sunshine and the beach. And I know my wife always sleeps remarkably well when she's in Bournemouth. So do I for that matter. Something to do with the sea air and the abundant trees, I think.' He coughed noisily, putting his hand in front of his mouth. 'Sorry about that. Maybe I should seek some of the same sea air to see if it will alleviate my cough.'

'Yes, you ought,' Libby agreed. 'That's quite a chesty cough, Mr Burgayne. Can I get you something? A glass of water perhaps?'

'No, please don't fuss.' He smiled to let her know it was not a reprimand. 'I'll be all right, my dear. I've always been prone to bronchitis, you know. Maybe I'm due an attack.'

'Perhaps you ought to seriously think about joining Bunty and Mrs Burgayne in Bournemouth. I'm sure it would help.'

He chuckled. 'I imagine you'd be quite the mother hen given the chance.'

'But it makes sense, Mr Burgayne. I'm sure you could allow yourself time away from here.'

He shook his head from side to side, weighing up her sage words. Then he burst out laughing which made him cough once more. 'I say, this is a bit of a turn round. Who's the boss here, I wonder? You're giving *me* time off!'

'I – I didn't intend it to sound like that,' she responded, full of apology.

He laughed again, amused at her consternation. 'Don't give it a second thought, Libby. I was jesting. Actually, I think you're quite right. It would do me good to get away from here and have a few days enjoying Bournemouth's clean, unadulterated air. There's no earthly reason why I shouldn't. Perhaps you'd be good enough to check the times of the trains for me.

If there's one tomorrow morning from either Wolverhampton or Kidderminster book me a first-class return, would you?'

'Of course I will, Mr Burgayne. What day would you like to return?'

'The Thursday before the garden party, I suppose. Hang it all, Hugh is quite capable of making any decisions while I'm away.'

'Wouldn't it be possible for Edward to fly you there in his Moth?'

He roared again. 'Are you serious? My dear, the purpose of the trip is that I survive it, not get blown to Kingdom Come.'

- - -

'You're going up in the world,' Vera remarked as Libby put down her notebook and sat at her desk. 'First it's Miss Bunty's work, then Mr Hugh's, then the gaffer's. They've took a shine to you, ain't they, the Burgaynes?'

'Not especially, I would've thought, Vera,' Libby replied diffidently, placing a sheet of carbon paper between two sheets of foolscap. 'It's just the way things happen. There's not much work from the Wages Office right now, and Mr Burgayne's secretary is away. Somebody has to step in, and I hadn't got much to do..'

'But I just saw you come out of Miss Evans's office. Have you been given permission to work in there as well?'

'Oh, it was just to use the telephone to book rail tickets to Bournemouth tomorrow for Mr Charles. His wife's there, and he wants to join her. To tell you the truth, he's got quite a nasty cough, and I reckon the break will do him good.'

'A nasty cough, eh? Why should you be concerned?' There seemed to be some resentment and even sarcasm in Vera's tone, which irked Libby.

Libby looked her squarely in the eye. It was time to be forthright. 'I am concerned, Vera. Mr Charles seems a very decent man. At least he's been really nice and very polite to me, so why shouldn't I be concerned? Besides that, he owns the firm that pays my wages, not to mention my father's. It doesn't hurt to give him the respect he deserves. Don't you think so?'

'I suppose you're right,' Vera admitted, humbled.

They remained unspeaking for a few minutes while Libby consulted her notepad and Vera resumed typing. Each was pondering what the other had said, and both realised that harbouring resentment might endanger their comradeship. They had to work together, and it was sensible to maintain good relations.

'Are you going to the canteen at dinnertime, Vera?'

'I expect so.' Vera smiled affably, relieved at the change of tack. 'And it's cottage pie today. I'd almost forgot. My favourite.'

Libby returned the smile, pleased that her matiness had worked. But perhaps it was time to clear the air a little more and reveal some snippets about her relationship with the Burgaynes . . . in strict confidence, of course.

Libby leaned towards Vera and Vera, in turn, cocked her ear towards Libby.

'Can you keep a secret, Vera?'

'Yes, I can keep a secret.'

'Well, if what I'm going to tell you gets out, I'll know it's you that's spread it, because you're the only person I'm telling.'

'Go on then. What?'

'Well . . . When I did that work I told you about in the holidays for Bunty,' she whispered, 'we got talking about things, and I told her I used to play tennis regularly. Well, she invited me to play with her and her brother Edward at Buttonbridge Hall where they live, because she wanted to get a four going, including Edward's friend. She fancies his friend, see. While I was there, I met Mr Charles Burgayne and his wife.'

'So get *you!* No wonder you're going up in the world. See, I was right. So what's the younger son like?'

'He's really nice. They all seem really nice, Vera. They made me feel ever so welcome . . .'

For the time being it was enough information.

- - -

| 6 |

The Burgaynes returned from Bournemouth on the Thursday prior to the garden party, and on the Friday Bunty telephoned Libby at the office and arranged to collect her from home next day at about eleven o' clock. The weather was set perfect for the occasion. She arrived later than expected and gave her apologies.

'I expect you've all been so busy getting things ready.'

'Just one hectic rush since we got back,' Bunty chimed. 'The gardener has been up since the crack of dawn mowing the lawns, and just after eight o' clock this morning a troupe of men arrived to erect the marquee. Oh, but they were so comical. You should've seen them. If it had been a circus tent being erected by clowns it couldn't have been funnier.'

'What about the food?'

'Well, food's all under control, thank God. Mother was flapping like a headless chicken earlier because the salmon hadn't arrived from the fishmonger, but it showed up just before I left to collect you.'

'Well, I hope I can be of help,' Libby said. 'There must still be plenty to do.'

'So there is, but you're a guest, Libby.'

'Whether I am or not, I'd like to make myself useful. I'm quite a dab hand at making sandwiches, you know.'

Bunty turned her head and smiled. 'You know, that's you all over. But you're not expected to do anything. We do have servants, you know. Just enjoy yourself.'

'Anyway, how's Edward?'

'Oh, he's fine. He wanted to collect you himself, but as it happened his car broke down. In any case I didn't think it was such a good idea. We wouldn't want your mother and father getting the wrong idea, would we? Not to mention that boyfriend of yours.'

'Poor Ron. He's not exactly ecstatic that I shan't be seeing him tonight . . . But I don't care.'

'Attagirl!' Bunty exclaimed with a mischievous grin.

'Have you seen anything of Adrian yet?'

'No such luck. But he'll be there this afternoon, or so his best chum Edward informs me.'

'And he's still unattached?'

Bunty grimaced. 'Crikey, he'd better be.'

'Oh, I forgot to tell you when we spoke on the phone yesterday. Hugh wants to take some photos of me. He wants me to sit for him today.'

'Does he, indeed?'

'I did some work for him, and we got talking. I quite liked the idea, to be honest. I might get a decent portrait out of it that I could give my mother and father. Otherwise, I've only really got school photos and a few snaps of me on the promenade at Rhyl.'

They arrived at Buttonbridge Hall hot after the stuffiness of the car. The temperature had soared to eighty-five, the air was still, the sky cloudless and the views across Shropshire were suffused in the summer haze. Libby noticed that the flower beds seemed to hold bigger and brighter flowers, the edges were well-manicured, the lawns greener and shorter. Bunty and Libby tucked into the plentiful sandwiches meant for guests with Mrs Burgayne, then went upstairs together to change and freshen up. Throughout the summer Libby's smooth skin had taken on the glow of a healthy-looking tan.

As they parted at the door to her room, she said, 'Bunty, d'you think it would be all right not to wear stockings at this garden party? I mean, it's so hot and sticky.'

'I think that's the most sensible suggestion I've heard all day.' Bunty, still stocking-free, lifted her skirt and assessed the colour of her shins and calves, thrusting each leg forward in turn. 'You know, I think with this bit of a tan I might just get away with it. How are yours?'

Libby raised her hem and peered down at her bare legs. 'Not quite as tanned as yours, but I think I might get away with it.'

They both laughed, enjoying the youthful excuse to cock a snoot at modesty and convention.

'Then let's leave stockings off.'

- - -

After lunch, people began arriving in waves, shaking hands, kissing cheeks, laughing and wishing each other well. Women in their best Sunday attire, appeared visibly uncomfortable in the heat, in contrast to the sprightly young daughters who accompanied them, vivid and vivacious in their light, unfussy summer dresses. Men old and young seemed to swelter under their jackets, waistcoats and straw hats in the intensity of the afternoon sun.

Members of the Burgayne family greeted all their guests in turn, with grace, attentiveness and welcoming smiles. Libby stood alongside Bunty who introduced her to so many people, the names of whom she struggled to remember. Eventually, a jazz band struck up from inside the sweltering depths of the marquee, its wailing brass and plinking banjo drifting through the air.

Unseen by either of the two girls, Edward sidled up to them when the tide of new arrivals had slowed somewhat.

'Libby Shakespeare! How smashing to see you again.'

Recognising the voice at once, her heart started thumping and she turned. 'Hello, Edward,' she beamed, delighted at seeing him.

'Sorry I wasn't here for lunch.'

'Your racquet needed restringing again?'

He laughed. 'Worse . . . My blasted car needed urgent attention. Carburettor. I had to splutter over to a little garage in Kinver that does odd mechanical jobs for us. Anyway, they fixed it, thankfully. If all had been well it was my intention to collect you this morning instead of Bunty.'

'That would've been nice, Edward.' She smiled again, her head tilted appealingly.

'I'm glad you think so.' His eyes creased with masculine appeal as he returned the smile.

Bunty butted in, detecting that her company was superfluous right then. 'If you don't mind, I'll leave you two to it. Seen Mother, Edward?'

'Wherever there's a tea urn . . .'

'See you later, Bunty,' Libby said contentedly, then turned back to Edward. 'So when do you go back to Cambridge?'

'Oh, probably Thursday.'

'And are you going to fly there, as you'd hoped?'

'Fancy you remembering that,' he answered. 'Yes, actually. I got permission to keep the Moth at Duxford after all. The only problem is that I'll have to send all my stuff by rail. Can't stow a fat lot in the Moth, you see.'

'I do hope you'll be careful when you fly. It beats me how you know where you're going when you're up there.'

He laughed. 'By following special maps that indicate landmarks. All rather basic stuff really.'

'I'm sure I'd get completely lost. I'd be useless.'

'Of course you wouldn't,' he said kindly. 'While you're flying you have time to pick out these landmarks and adjust your course accordingly.'

'So when shall you come home again?' she enquired.

'Christmas, I expect. Christmas is rather jolly here. It would be wonderful if you could spend some time here with us.' He raised his eyebrows questioningly.

'It's rather a long way off' she replied. 'Lord knows what I'll be doing. Spending it at home with my mom and dad, I suppose.'

'And that boyfriend of yours, eh?'

She wished at that moment that she had the power either never to blush, or to hide her blushes convincingly, for she coloured up like a peony. 'If he's still around by then,' she answered.

'Might he not be?'

She shrugged, her colour subsiding a little. 'It's up to him.'

'You have no say in the matter?' he asked.

'Well, of course I would have, but I hate the thought of hurting him.' She looked down, inspecting her big toe as it peeped out of the sandal on her right foot.

'He thinks a lot of you, then, Libby.'

'I think he does,' she said, meeting his eyes again but with a shrug. 'But . . .'

'But?' he queried, perceiving her indifference.

She sighed, deciding to be candid. 'But it's not because I encourage him. I don't.'

'Your looks and demeanour are the only encouragement he needs, I suspect.'

She laughed self-consciously, throwing her head back, enjoying the compliment nevertheless. 'I wish I could believe I have decent enough looks and demeanour, as you put it.'

'You'd do well to believe it.'

'Well, it's nice of you to say so, Edward.' She felt herself blushing again and was thankful for an unexpected light breeze cooling her face. 'Is Adrian here yet?' she asked, changing the subject.

'Yes, he's here. Why? Don't tell me you're interested in Adrian.' He sounded disappointed.

'No, not me. But I know somebody who is.'

'Oh, I see. And I think I can guess who . . . I say, Libby, you haven't got a drink. Let's get you something.'

'Thank you. Cold orange juice would be nice. Or even a glass of Vimto.'

They moved towards the marquee and the sound of the jazz band playing 'Honeysuckle Rose'. Everywhere, people were strolling in twos and threes, clutching drinking glasses, chatting animatedly. Some were standing, pointing out and naming the flowers, admiring the giant redwood trees that were almost as old as the house.

Although it was shaded inside the marquee it seemed hotter, stuffier than outside, and full of people chattering, vying to be heard over each other and the music. Standing next to the makeshift bar were Bunty and Adrian who seemed only to have eyes for each other, and were laughing at a shared joke.

'Hello, you two,' Edward greeted; then to the hired help who was tending to drinks, 'Two glasses of orange juice, please. As cold as you can make them.'

Adrian took out a cigarette case and offered it round. Edward took a cigarette, tapped the end against his thumbnail and put it to his lips. Adrian flicked his lighter and lit them both.

'I say, do you two have any plans for tonight?' he enquired casually, exhaling smoke.

'Nothing that can't be changed,' Bunty said, looking into Libby's eyes as if daring her to gainsay it.

'So, Edward, old chum, why don't we take these two delightful creatures out tonight?'

'I'm game, if they are.'

'How about it, girls?'

The two girls looked at each other as if seeking consensus, and their eye contact confirmed the agreement. They smiled and nodded simultaneously, saying how lovely.

'So what hot-spots have you in mind for us?' Bunty asked.

'No idea at all,' replied Adrian flippantly. 'But we'll have fun finding somewhere.'

Edward took the drinks handed him by the hired help and passed one to Libby. 'One cold orange juice,' he said.

She thanked him and sipped it, feeling it cool on her lips, soothing to her throat. 'Perhaps we ought to stand outside in the shade,' she suggested. 'It's so hot in here.'

'Good idea,' Edward said.

'But the tucker is about to be unveiled,' Adrian suggested.

'And you've had no lunch, I suppose?' Bunty remarked. 'Well, we can always come back for sandwiches. Libby is right – it'll be cooler under the shade of a tree.'

As they stepped into the open air again Libby looked around for sight of Hugh Burgayne. She had not seen him at all yet, and even though she was enjoying the present company she was still eager to fulfil her promise of sitting for photographs.

'I've never met Laura Birch,' she remarked, turning the conversation. 'Is she here? I wouldn't have a clue what she looks like.'

'She's on holiday in France, apparently,' Edward informed her. 'Her family have a place over there. Provence, I think.'

'Doesn't Hugh go with them?'

'Sometimes, but not this time. Too much going on at the works I expect.'

'What's she like, this Laura Birch?'

'Cigarettes, alcohol,' said Adrian glibly. 'Expensive clothes. You name it . . .'

'Twit!' Bunty exclaimed.

'No, she seems a nice lady,' Adrian affirmed, ducking Bunty's playful insult as if it were meant for the absent Miss Birch. 'She's a little plain for my tastes . . . And a trifle too broad across the beam. But she seems very affable.'

'Oh, Adrian, how can you be so unkind,' Bunty complained. 'She's not broad across the beam at all.'

'She's broader across the beam than you are.'

'She's not plain either. She has a lovely face.'

'If you're partial to Roman noses. Funny, ain't it, Edward?' Adrian commented, 'how women see women differently to men.'

'Because men have different priorities,' Bunty riposted. 'I suppose men look at women as potential mates, so they have to fancy them. And if you don't fancy somebody because she's broad across the beam, as you put it, then that's it.'

'Nature's way, old fruit,' Adrian answered.

'Look, Hugh's heading this way,' Edward remarked.

'Minus the broad-beamed Laura Birch, of course,' Adrian added.

Libby felt her colour rise again at the prospect of meeting Hugh, for he was likely to remind her of their photo session, which she had not had the opportunity to mention to Edward.

Hugh greeted them all in a collective 'hello', and commented how well-attended the garden party was.

'Libby,' he said, singling her out. 'I do hope you haven't forgotten our date.'

She glanced at Edward uncomfortably, before replying with a smile. 'Of course I haven't.'

'Then shall we go now?'

'Actually, Hugh, we were just contemplating grabbing some food,' Edward said, irked at his brother's unexpected intrusion when he was hoping to monopolise Libby for the rest of the afternoon.

'Food won't be ready for half an hour yet, I understand,' Hugh declared.

'In that case, why don't I go now with Hugh?' Libby suggested. 'And perhaps you three can save me a sandwich or something for later.' It seemed a diplomatic solution as she was unaware whether Hugh had told Edward that he'd arranged to take photographs.'

Hugh looked at the others, impatient for their assent.

'Yes, why don't you do that, Libby,' Bunty agreed. 'Come to the marquee when you're done, and we'll have a plate of divine curly sandwiches and jam tarts saved for you.'

Libby smiled her thanks. 'See you later then.'

'Any chance you'll be back in time for the raffle?' Edward called as she left the group.

Libby turned and smiled. 'I don't know,' she replied, and walked back toward the house in the blazing sunshine with Hugh.

Edward said, 'I didn't know Hugh had arranged a date with Libby. He has no business. What's he up to?' He felt as if his nose was being pushed out, and was decidedly unhappy.

Bunty detected the resentment and frustration in his tone. 'It's nothing, Edward,' she reassured him. 'Don't worry. He wants to use her as a model and take some formal photos of her, for his club competitions I imagine. He asked her a while ago, apparently, and today is the first and only opportunity. She's been doing some work for him while his own secretary has been away.'

'Oh, I see. Photos, eh?' He breathed a sigh of relief. 'Is that all? Just photos?'

'Why? Do you mind?'

'How can I mind?' Edward responded with a shrug. 'I have no claim on her . . . unfortunately.'

'But you wish you had?'

'Yes, I wouldn't mind at all, actually.'

'Well, maybe you'll get your chance if you can woo her away from her current beau. Shouldn't be too difficult from what I gather. Anyway – as to Hugh – she rather liked the idea of being able to give her mother and father a decent photo of herself. Something she's never had. I think that's rather sweet.'

- - -

Hugh's 'studio' was a conservatory on the north side of the house. Because it was in shade it was cooler than Libby might have expected under glass. He explained that it was ideally situated for portrait photography; the diffused light was preferable because it cast no hard shadows.

'I thought we might do a few close-up portraits first,' he said affably. 'Then we'll try some full-length ones . . . Do make yourself comfortable while I set up.'

There were a couple of armchairs, a stool and a *chaise longue* she could choose to sit on, so she opted for one of the armchairs.

'Have you been keen on photography long?' she asked conversationally.

'Ten years, give or take.'

'So what kind of camera do you use?'

He smiled. 'Are you interested in cameras?'

'I don't know a thing about cameras,' she said.

'Well . . . For this I'll use my Voigtländer Bessa. It gives a decent-sized negative, and has a sharp lens, so I can blow it up to a biggish print without too much loss of quality.'

'I see,' she said. 'Why does photography always seem so complicated?'

As he screwed the camera to the tripod, he grinned with delighted that she was declaring some interest. 'Well, there is a lot to learn,' he admitted. 'What with f-stops, shutter speeds, film speeds, depth of field and all that. And that's before you even get to the developing and printing stage, which is an entirely different world altogether.'

'Sounds terrifying.'

He laughed. 'I could teach you,' he added eagerly.

'Oh, I think I'm too much of a dunderhead,' she replied, attempting to acquit herself.

'Goodness, I'm sure you're nothing of the sort, Libby . . . Right . . .' He moved the camera and tripod assembly. 'We're ready. The camera's loaded. If you'd like to perch on that stool.'

She got up from the armchair and went over to the stool, smoothing the creases out of her dress. She wore a sleeveless cotton dress with a scalloped neck and full skirt, ideal for summer. It was pale yellow and complemented her dark hair beautifully.

'How do you want me?'

Her comment could so easily be interpreted as sexual innuendo, he thought, but he was well aware that she was innocent of any such notion, and that added to her appeal. He was tempted to let her in on the joke to test her reaction, but he thought better of it.

'Head and shoulders, three quarter face I think. It will show us a little of the shape of your nose.' He picked up his light meter and pointed it towards her, then adjusted the exposure settings on the front of the camera. 'You have a delightful nose, if you don't mind my saying so. And not just your nose – you have beautiful eyes as well . . . and your mouth . . .'

'Well thank you.'

'You're not too hot in here, are you?'

'No, just right.'

'Jolly good.' He adjusted the focus. 'Just a hint of a smile, please, Libby . . . Oh, yes, hold that . . .' She heard a click from the shutter, he looked up and grinned as he wound on the film. 'Promises to be good. We'll try that again but at a different exposure . . .' That done, he moved closer with the camera and tripod. 'I'd like to try one in real close-up. You have a lovely complexion – lovely skin . . . Tilt your head down just slightly, so you have to look up at me from under your brows . . . and smile . . . Yes, that's it . . . Gives you a delightful cheeky look.'

'I hear your fiancée is on holiday at the moment,' she said, making conversation, trying to divert attention from herself.

'Yes, she's in France for a month. Doubt whether I'll have time to miss her, though.'

'When are you getting married?'

'Nothing fixed as yet. I'm beginning to wonder if it will ever happen.' He gave a little laugh at that comment. 'And you, Libby? Are you stepping out with somebody?'

'Yes, there's this chap I see . . . Nothing serious though.'

'Would I know him? What's his name?'

'Ron Downing.'

'Does he work at the steelworks too?'

'Oh, no, he works for the GPO.' She felt so ordinary, so mundane, so plebeian, having to admit a fact that sounded so banal.

'But it's nothing serious, you say?'

'No. I don't want to settle down with anybody yet.'

'Especially somebody who works for the GPO, eh? It's a certain fact you could do much better for yourself, eh?'

She flushed with embarrassment. He must think her so commonplace. 'He's a genuinely nice chap, actually,' she said in Ron's defence. 'It's just that I don't want to be tied down yet. There'll be time enough for that when I'm older.'

'I applaud your common sense, Libby.' He wound the film on to the next frame. 'Two more portraits,' he said. 'One full face, and then one in semi-profile.'

'To show my nose off.'

'You have a very cute nose, so why shouldn't we show it off? But I want to capture the clarity of your exquisite eyes too..'

'You're being very complimentary. Thank you.'

He took the next two photos, as he'd intended. 'That was good. Right, some full-length pictures now . . . Can you jump on that table and sit facing me?'

She slid off the stool and sat on the table, her shapely legs swinging above the floor. He loaded a new roll of film, repositioned the camera and lowered the tripod a little, then refocused the lens.

'A nice wide smile now . . . That's lovely. Hold that . . .'

He walked towards her.

'For the next one I'd like to see your skirt up a little higher, showing more leg. A glamour shot. Would you mind?'

Before she knew it, his hands were on her knees and he'd lifted the hem of her skirt by about six inches. In so doing he managed to skim his fingers over her bare lower thighs, slicked with moisture wrought by the summer heat. Then he briskly proceeded to smooth out the creases of her skirt, momentarily stroking her thighs over the material.

It was over in brief seconds.

It was over even before Libby realised what had happened. He'd stroked her thigh, but what could she do about it? She could hardly complain, she must tolerate it. There was probably nothing behind it anyway, no malice aforethought, no over-familiarity, no lewd intention. He was a photographer doing a photographer's work. Photographers surely rearranged subjects' clothing for the benefit of the photograph. Besides, he was a director of the company that employed her, employed her father too. Once again she was at his home, enjoying the hospitality of his family.

'If you lean back a little . . . Yes, rest on your arms behind you . . . Throw your head back just a little . . . That's it . . . Now another of your cheeky smiles . . .'

Click!

'Smashing. Now, would you like to lie on the *chaise longue*, Libby? I want you to look all languid and sensual, as if you're enjoying some scandalously erotic thoughts.'

Erotic thoughts? *That would be a turn-up for the books. And how am I supposed to appear all languid and sensual?* she wondered.

She ambled over to the *chaise longue* and reclined on it, wondering if he was likely to touch her legs again.

'Would you mind taking off your sandals? Bare feet would look much more effective in a shot like this. Don't you agree?'

She raised her knees and unfastened the shoes, letting them drop to the floor.

'Do you want me to raise the hem of my skirt this time?' she enquired, thinking it would relieve him of the responsibility.

'Yes, rather . . .'

'How far?' She pulled the hem over her thighs and looked at him questioningly.

'Oh, a bit further would be marvellous, if you're comfortable with that.'

She generously complied, but Hugh misinterpreted her motive.

'Would you raise your left knee now? . . .'

She knew very well that the way she was posing he could see directly up her skirt, but how much he would be able to see she did not know. The image flashed into her mind of Bunty surreptitiously allowing Adrian a glimpse of her knickers. She smiled to herself, understanding Hugh's game, content to go along with it to some degree. Little by little he was trying to gain her confidence and ease her into exposing more of herself. Soon he would be asking her to shed her clothes and pose in her underwear, or even naked. But never would she agree to that in a million years.

'How do I look?' she asked perkily.

'Utterly vivacious . . . An icon of feminine abandon.'

Click!

She smiled feigning affability, but she'd had enough of his sneaky voyeurism. 'Can we call it a day now, Hugh? I'm getting quite hot. Would you mind?'

'If you're getting hot, why don't you take your clothes off? We could do some superb pin-up type pictures of you in your underwear, or even—'

'Gosh, I wouldn't dream,' she countered emphatically, interrupting him. 'You've got the wrong girl for that kind of stuff.'

'No, that's fine, Libby, if you're not comfortable with that. It was just a thought. But if you ever change your mind . . .' He wound on the film, mildly embarrassed that he had gone too far with his suggestion. 'I'll have these developed and printed in a day or two.'

'I'm looking forward to seeing them.'

'Er . . . I, er, wondered, Libby . . .'

'Yes?' She looked at him curiously.

'It occurred to me . . . If you're leaving here after the garden party and at a loose end, I wondered if you'd like to join me for dinner this evening? There's this lovely little place I know.'

'Actually, Hugh, I'm . . . I'm staying here at Buttonbridge Hall tonight,' she replied as diplomatically as she could. 'Edward and Adrian are taking Bunty and me out this evening. It's already fixed.'

'Oh, you're partnering Edward?'

'That's the arrangement.'

- - -

| 7 |

Edward and Adrian both owned two-seater sports cars, so the four were obliged to go out that night in the Burgaynes' Riley. Edward drove, Libby sitting beside him, with Bunty and Adrian close together on the rear bench seat. While the other three bandied wit and repartee, Libby was preoccupied; the encounter earlier with Hugh Burgayne was bothering her. It was not so much that he had contrived to paw her – and yes, she was coming to the conclusion that he had done it deliberately – but he had also invited her out that night behind the back of the girl to whom he was already engaged. That told her he was the sort of man no woman could trust, and she felt sorry for Laura Birch even though she did not know the girl. But she remembered Vera's warning, and Bunty telling her at the outset that as a woman she would never trust him.

But what sort of girl did he think she was to suggest such a tryst, and even suggest she take all her clothes off? Did he imagine she would be easy? Did he think that just because she was an employee of the Blowers Green Steelworks she should fall at his feet and be thankful for the opportunity to be gawped at or groped? Did he really think his superiority gave him the right to manhandle her just because she was a girl from the typing pool? Of course, Hugh could make things uncomfortable for her if he chose to. If he wanted to be really vindictive he could also make things awkward for her father. She hoped things would never come to such a pass, but she would have to be careful; such was the power he possessed.

She pondered whether she ought to tell Bunty about the incident. When they were alone together she might. Then again,

she might not. Bunty was Hugh's sister and blood was thicker than water. She was beginning to feel, because of the incident, that she was out of her depth with these people, that she really ought to refuse any further invitations. But it would be such a pity.

The car pulled up in the vast car park of a newish hotel called the Foley Arms, but better known locally as the Stewponey. An old pub, little more than a cottage, had stood on the site before, but it had been recently redeveloped, was now manorially vast, and even boasted a lido where the world, his wife and his entire family could all descend on sunny summer weekends and holidays for swimming and sunbathing.

'Listen, I can hear a band playing,' Adrian remarked as they each clambered out of the car. 'Let's see what's going on.'

It was a dance, so they paid to go in. Cigarette smoke drifted around, its thick aroma blending incongruously with sweeter feminine perfumes. Over the hubbub of raised conversations and laughter, the endeavours of the band and the shuffling of feet to a quickstep, Adrian hailed the drinks order to a barman. The four stood around the bar surveying the spectacle, soaking up the noisy, musky ambience while Edward, Adrian and Bunty lit up cigarettes.

'I say, you're quiet, Libby,' Edward commented exhaling a cloud of blue smoke. 'We haven't heard a peep out of you for ages. Is there something amiss?'

She smiled apologetically and shook her head. 'No.'

'You have been rather deep in thought, though, haven't you? Missing that boyfriend of yours? Or Hugh?'

She rolled her eyes. 'Neither, if you want the truth. It's a nice change having a Saturday night away from Ron. And I'm certainly not interested in your brother.' She wanted to say that it was rather nice being there with Edward at her side, but had no wish to declare her intensifying infatuation for him.

'I'm happy to hear it, Libby . . . So . . . Would you like to dance?'

'I'd love to,' she beamed sassily, delighted to accept.

Edward stubbed out his cigarette, they put down their drinks, and made their way to the dance floor, leaving Bunty and Adrian to their own conversation. The band was playing Night and Day, a Cole Porter song.

They faced each other, linked hands, he put his hand to her waist, and they launched themselves, swaying, into the surging sea of dancers.

For Edward it was divine to feel her body so close to his, as she moved smoothly to the rhythm of a slow foxtrot. She was so youthfully slender, and felt so warm and yet so delicate in his arms. He could detect the gorgeous aroma of her perfume, so clean and fresh. Freshness was a quality she had in abundance, unmistakeably, and 'fresh' seemed the perfect word to describe her. She was about five feet three, he estimated, deliciously petite. Sight of her skin was beginning to torment him; it must be fabulous to the touch. Her dark hair, cut in a fashionable bob that curled inwards around her neck, framed perfectly her beautiful oval face. Such a pity that she was already seeing that other chap; he could not be sure of the strength of feeling she might have for him, despite her claims that she was indifferent, always seeming dismissive of the poor bloke whenever he was mentioned. Yet that could be shyness, an unwillingness to talk about him because she felt embarrassed to.

'You dance well,' he said struggling at that moment to summon an original sentence. When she smiled, the curve of her lips rendered them so seductively kissable.

'Thank you. But so do you. I bet you go to lots of dances in Cambridge.'

'There's this place called the Dorothy Ballroom. Sometimes I go there with friends.'

'And there are lots of girls, I suppose?'

'Usually.' He wanted to say, but none like you . . .

'I bet you're looking forward to getting back to Cambridge now,' she suggested.

'I have no choice,' he replied. 'I have to continue my studies. But the thought of hanging around here a while longer, with the possibility of getting to know you better, has much more appeal.'

She lowered her lids at this surprising revelation, and her heart suddenly beat faster.

'I don't even know what you're studying at university.'

'Law. It's a bit dry, but—'

'Law?' she queried. 'I thought you said you wanted to fly.'

'So I do. It was my father who suggested I study law. I think he has me marked down as a future company secretary.'

'I see . . . Anyway, I thought the . . . the semester? . . . Is that the right word?'

He nodded.

'I thought the semester didn't start till September or October.'

'It doesn't.'

'So why do you have to leave early?'

'To further my flying experience. Did I tell you I'm in the University Air Squadron?'

'You did, but what can you do there that you can't do at home?'

'Well, we have lessons flying military training aircraft. And I just love flying.'

'Well, I do hope you'll be careful, Edward. Talking to Hugh, he seemed concerned for your safety.'

'Oh, Hugh . . .' He laughed dismissively. 'Well, what would he know? Which reminds me . . . I hadn't a clue you'd arranged a photo session with him this afternoon. Did it go well?'

'Hard to say, really. I won't know until I see the pictures. They might not have come out very well for all I know.'

'He'll possibly have them done over the weekend. I'll try and get a peep at them before I go back to university.'

'Oh, I wouldn't bother. They're probably awful.'

'A girl as pretty as you? I doubt it.'

The band finished their number and Edward unhanded her as they looked towards the musicians for an inkling of what was coming next. It was to be 'I'm in the Mood for Love'.

'Another?' he asked raising his eyebrows expectantly.

'Delighted,' she said, with another enchanting smile.

They held each other again, a trifle closer this time as they gently swerved along to the music.

'Tell me about yourself,' Edward said. 'I know so little about you, and I'm enormously curious.'

'There's really not much to tell. I live in Dudley, and I come from very ordinary parents. My father works at your father's steelworks, and my mother is just a housewife. I don't have any brothers or sisters – but please don't ask me why because I don't know. I've been lucky enough to have had a decent education – for which I'm grateful – thanks to the sacrifices my father made.'

'You certainly play tennis well.'

She looked into his eyes and laughed as they whirled around. 'So you say. Thank you.'

'Do you play any musical instruments?'

'The piano – a little. We have a pianola in our front room.'

'Your front room?' He laughed a little.

'Oh, please don't mock,' she said earnestly, looking into his eyes.

'I wasn't mocking, Libby, honestly,' he protested, afraid he'd humiliated her.

'Our front room is my mother's pride and joy, and only ever used on Sunday afternoons, if the weather's fine or when we're expecting visitors.' She was smiling again.

'I respect enormously the sanctity of your front room.'

'Well, now you are mocking even if you weren't before,' she complained, her smile changing instantly to a frown, pouting delectably, but in fact merely feigning umbrage. 'You said the "sanctity" of it. That's taking the mickey.'

'Apologies! Maybe "sanctity" is the wrong word,' he conceded, afraid he'd really put his foot in it. 'Maybe "sanctuary" might be more fitting.'

'Somewhat,' she said, smiling again. 'But "shrine" is even better. I admit it's my mother's shrine to respectability and convention. In our street, if you don't have a spotless front room to entertain the vicar, you're doomed. It's the same as pegging the washing out on a Monday. Dazzling white is essential. Once I went home and the whites my mother was pegging out on our line were grey. I was mortified, and I wanted to give her a piece of my mind there and then, because I thought our washing was a disgrace. But because she was talking to our next-door neighbour I kept my mouth shut. It was just as well I did – it turned out that the same grey washing belonged to the neighbour, and my mother was only pegging it out for her on our line because her line had broken.'

'That's a form of snobbishness.'

'Maybe so.'

He laughed appealingly. 'I think I'd like to meet your mother.'

'She really isn't anything special. Oh, I love her to bits and all that – with all my heart – but she doesn't stand out in a crowd. That's what I mean.'

'I detect some . . . Libby, I'm struggling for the right word here, so if it comes out all wrong to your ears please don't take offence, because none is intended . . . But I detect some embarrassment in you – some awkwardness – because of how you see yourself, or because of where you come from.'

She sighed. 'I'm well aware of my background, Edward . . . especially compared to yours. But please don't imagine for a minute that I'm ashamed of it, because I'm not.'

'Good for you, Libby. You have absolutely nothing at all to be ashamed of anyway. And if you imagined for a second that I might harbour some disdain because of it I'd be mortally offended. I don't hold with outmoded concepts of class distinction. Not that I'm a Socialist either, because I'm not.'

She flashed her eyes at him attractively. 'I'm glad to hear it. And I know that Bunty feels the same – not just because she's said as much, but I feel her friendship and I sense no barriers.'

'I hope you feel there are no such barriers between us.'

'I certainly don't want to feel any.'

He smiled openly and she warmed to him the more. He had such a lovely candid smile, and his eyes twinkled and crinkled so alluringly. She wanted to give him a hug, but did not dare.

'I'd like to think we can be close friends, Libby, and that you can discuss all sorts of things with me.'

'That's nice, Edward. I think I can . . . But I'm not so sure that Hugh is of the same mind as you.'

'As regards what?'

'As regards the class difference between him and me.'

Edward shrugged. 'He's inclined to be a bit snobbish, a bit aloof, is Hugh, but you're not likely to have that much to do with him, are you?'

'At work, I might. Who knows?'

'But he's not unfriendly towards you. After all, he has taken some photos of you.'

'Actually he's been very friendly towards me,' she said ambiguously.

'Well, there you are,' Edward said, failing to grasp her meaning.

She wanted to tell him she believed Hugh had tried to take advantage of his pre-eminence over her, but could not bring herself to say so. It would be grossly unfair to be the cause of any rift or mistrust between brothers.

The band stopped and promised a jitterbug for the next dance, so Edward, knowing he could remain within touching distance of her at the bar, but not if they were swirling round to a jitterbug, suggested they rejoin Bunty and Adrian. By this time, though, they had found a table at the back of the room and were sitting close together.

'We're talking about embarrassing moments,' Bunty said.

'Oh, go on then,' Libby exclaimed as she sat down, at once taken with the idea. 'Tell us yours.'

'I'll tell you mine first,' Adrian interjected with a gleam in his eye. He took a swig of beer. 'I'd just bought a new pair of shoes, and Lord, they squeaked like hell. Whenever I put them on I felt as self-conscious as an unfledged schoolgirl. But I was either bold or stupid enough to wear them for my cousin's wedding and, as I stepped up the aisle towards our pew, they sang their own processional hymn. By the time I reached it all eyes were on me and my damned shoes, and I was transfixed with shame.'

'How embarrassing,' Libby declared. 'I would hate that. . . So what about you, Bunty?'

'Oh, mine's better than that. I was at a posh dinner one evening, and I was the first to help myself to strawberries that were stacked into a neat, symmetrical cone in a bowl. Well, the one at the very top must have felt suicidal because as I approached it with the serving spoon it seemed to hurl itself to its doom and rolled off, leaving a vivid crimson stain across the hostess's pristine tablecloth. Then, as if that weren't enough, at my next attempt, half a dozen more followed suit, rolling in all directions across the table. I was mortified.'

'Yes, that's worse than Adrian's,' Libby sympathised, while the lads guffawed at the thought of it.

'The only redeeming feature was that none of the offending fruit decided to head my way and stain the pretty new white gown I was wearing.'

'What about you, Edward?' Libby enquired, looking at him with increasing admiration.

'The only thing I can think of on the spur of the moment was when I was travelling from Cambridge to Wolverhampton by train. By the time I reached Snow Hill Station in Brum I'd fallen asleep, and remained fast as a rock as far as Stafford, which is a fair few miles beyond my station and was the end of the line for that service. Actually, a guard woke me up. Unfortunately, I was too late to get a train back to Wolverhampton, so Dad drove all the way to Stafford to get me. He was not exactly delighted.'

'Especially as he had already gone to bed by the time you rang,' Bunty added.

'Now it's your turn, Libby,' Edward encouraged. 'What embarrassing moments have you suffered?'

'It happened only the other day,' Libby said. 'I was taking dictation for Mr Webb in the Wages Office, when somebody knocked on his door. He said, "Who the devil is that I wonder?" and, without thinking I actually put it down in shorthand as part of the letter he was dictating. It wasn't until I read back what I'd written that I realised what I'd done. Mr Webb thought it was hilarious. It was the first time I'd seen him laugh. He's normally so sombre.'

Edward finished his drink and stood up. 'I'll get us all a top-up. Same again, folks?'

'Aren't you going to ask me to dance, Adrian?' Bunty remarked. 'If I were you, I wouldn't be able to keep your hands off me.'

'Nor can I,' responded Adrian dryly. 'But the same could be said of Dr Crippen and Cora Tuner. However, I won't allow such thoughts to deter me, Bunty.'

She bobbed her tongue out playfully and they got up to dance, leaving Libby alone at the table while Edward fetched drinks.

At that point, suddenly left alone, Libby realised she was hungry; she hadn't eaten properly since her breakfast at home. Bunty had saved her a plate of curly sandwiches and cakes at the garden party, as promised, but the incident with Hugh had taken the edge off her appetite and she'd hardly touched any of it. Nor had she eaten much of the dinner later with the Burgaynes. Now, after drinking some alcohol, she was ravenous.

Edward returned with the drinks on a tray, which he set down on the table. He handed Libby hers, sat beside her and took a gulp of his beer. They talked about this and that, till Bunty and Adrian returned, glowing from the heat and the exertion of several energetic quicksteps.

'Would you like to dance again, Libby?' Edward asked.

'I'd love to, Edward, if I didn't feel so hungry – I've gone all wobbly. Can we find something to eat somewhere when we've finished our drinks or I'm sure I'll faint?'

'Of course,' he replied, with obvious concern.

'I noticed you didn't eat much at the garden party,' Bunty remarked. 'Nor at dinner. You must be starving. Where can we find some food for the poor girl, Adrian?'

'How about the nearest fish and chip shop?' he suggested.

'Ooh, yes,' Libby drooled. 'I could murder fish and chips, with salt and vinegar.'

'Fish and chips it is, then,' Edward agreed. 'I'm feeling a bit peckish myself.'

So they finished their drinks quickly and left the dance.

'There's a fish and chip shop I know in Kingswinford,' Adrian said. 'We'll try there. It's not far.'

Unfortunately, it was closed – to Libby's dismay.

'Fancy shutting a fish and chip shop on a Saturday night,' Edward remarked as they got back in the car. 'It has to be the busiest night of the week. Are you getting hungrier and hungrier, Libby?'

Libby nodded. 'I could eat a horse.'

'So we look for a field with a horse in it, eh?'

'Twit!' reposted Bunty.

'Actually, there's a fish and chip shop in Wall Heath,' Adrian informed them. 'In Enville Street – only a couple of minutes away.'

They arrived and were pleased to see it was open and doing plenty of business. They all clambered out of the car and joined the queue, laughing and joking, and Libby felt even hungrier when the aroma of fish, chips and vinegar assailed her.

It was soon their turn to be served and they placed their order.

'We called at that fish and chip shop in Kingswinford,' Adrian commented to the man who was serving them, 'but it was closed. Funny night to close, a Saturday, I would've thought.'

'Oh, there's a reason,' the man said with a gleam in his eye. 'I heard that the chap who owns it got home after taking his dog for a walk and found his wife in bed with another bloke.'

'Crikey!' Libby gasped, horrified.

'Good God!' Adrian exclaimed with a mischievous gleam in his eye. 'Sounds a bit fishy, that. Did he batter her?'

The man looked at him askance, and Edward latched on at once.

'So now he's got the plaice to himself?'.

'So he's in sole charge,' Libby added instantly.

'Even though he is down at eel as a result,' Adrian added for good measure.

While the four felt pleased with their collective wit, the man smiled patiently. 'Oh, very droll,' he said. 'You should come here every Saturday night, you lot, and do a turn for the customers.'

– – –

It was late when they returned to Buttonbridge Hall, and everybody had gone to bed. Bunty, loath to trouble Jenkins, made coffee which they supped sitting around the table in the breakfast room. Edward and Adrian lit up cigarettes, and they talked disconnectedly about the evening and where they had been.

'It's been ages since I've had so much fun,' Libby remarked. 'It was lovely to go dancing.'

'I agree,' Bunty said. 'We must all get together again next time Edward comes back from Cambridge.'

'But it'll be the middle of winter,' Edward said. 'Overcoats and scarves and gloves.'

Libby rolled her eyes typically. 'Oh, please don't remind us. I hate winter and having to scrape the frost off the inside of my bedroom window when I get up.'

'Do you really?' Edward asked.

'If it's that cold, yes.'

'Don't you have a fire in your bedroom?'

'There's a fireplace, but my mother reckons lighting a fire in a bedroom is far too extravagant.'

'You poor thing,' Bunty said. 'Not so cosy after all, eh?'

'No, not so cosy. Not in winter.'

Bunty yawned, and stretched her arms out.

'Are we keeping you up?' asked Adrian.

'I'm going to turn in, actually. Are you coming up yet, Libby?'

'I ought to,' she said, rising reluctantly from the table and looking at Edward with longing, in the hope that he might ask her to stay a while.

'Adrian and I will have a drink first, eh, Adrian?' he said instead.

'Smashing idea, old chum. Got any brandy?'

'I'll go and find some.'

'I might see you in the morning, Edward,' Libby said.

'Oh, I doubt it,' Bunty claimed. 'It'll be a miracle if he's up before you leave.'

'I'll say goodbye now, then, Edward. And to you, Adrian.'

'Goodbye, Libby,' Adrian replied. 'It's been great fun tonight, hasn't it? . . . Goodnight, Bunty – see you soon, eh?'

Libby was a couple of steps behind Bunty as they left the breakfast room, when Edward called her.

'I say, Libby . . .'

She turned to face him, and he walked up to her, put his hand to her waist, which set her pulse racing.

'I just wanted to say goodnight properly,' he whispered intently, and kissed her on the lips.

It lasted only a second but, in that magic moment, Libby felt the blood surge through her veins. Edward looked her directly in the eye, challengingly to assess her reaction, then kissed her again, lingering for some time before he broke off.

'I do hope I'll see you again next time I'm home,' he said.

'I hope so too,' she replied, conscious that her voice would waver and possibly break up with emotion if she said more.

'But I'll make a point of getting up early in the morning, before you leave. Then we can say goodbye again. So till morning . . .' He took her hand and squeezed it, smiling sadly, and seemed loath to let go of it.

- - -

| 8 |

Hugh's darkroom was a part of Buttonbridge Hall's cellaring that he'd petitioned off. In that small area he'd had running water installed as well as electricity, a geyser to heat water, two large sinks and two work benches, one for wet work, one for dry. On the wet bench lay three large, enamelled trays, one containing developer; a second, vinegar in water for removing and neutralising the developer; and the third had hypo in it for stabilising the prints. On the dry bench stood a photographic enlarger with a masking frame on its baseboard, a timer for timing the exposure of the negative to the light-sensitive print paper, and an electric print glazer. The whole was suffused in a dim orange glow from two safelights.

Hugh pulled a half-plate enlargement from the sink where several were being washed in running water, and inspected it by the meagre illumination. In the gloom a pair of bright, smiling eyes looked back at him from a print. His eyes lingered, devouring the image of Libby. He finally put it down, removed the excess water, then placed it face down on the hot glazer, which would give the photo an attractive gloss. Then he pulled out another print and inspected that too, and his desire heightened.

What gorgeous legs.

- - -

As Hugh was ascending the steps from his darkroom carrying the finished photographs in an envelope, Edward was on his way to find him. They met in a corridor at the rear of the house.

'Ah, Hugh . . . I was hoping I'd catch you. Have you developed and printed your photos of Libby yet?'

Hugh waved the envelope in front of him. He had no logical reason to refuse the request. 'Here they are. I've just finished them. Take a look.' Hugh withdrew them from the envelope.

Edward took them and scrutinised the first one, then looked back towards the light coming in through the fanlight over the door. 'Let's take them into the daylight. It's a bit dim here . . .' He moved towards the door and opened it to let in more illumination. Hugh followed him. 'She takes a smashing photo,' he beamed. 'Don't you think so, Hugh?'

Hugh gave a cursory nod, as if he could never be moved by youthful loveliness.

'Oh, I say, look at this one . . . sporting a lovely bit of leg . . . Would you mind if I took this one, Hugh?' He looked at his brother expectantly. 'I expect you have another copy?'

'I can always print one. Take it.'

'Thanks, old bean.'

'I understand you were out with her last night, Edward?'

'Yes, we had a great time. She's a jolly good sport. Of course, she's Bunty's friend, but because Bunty and Adrian seem to be getting it together, I was obliged more or less to accompany Libby. Mind you, it was no imposition I must say. She's rather a nice girl.'

'Lord knows what Bunty thinks she's doing befriending people from the works, and inviting them here,' Hugh said ominously.

'Oh? What makes you say that?'

'Well, I mean . . . familiarity . . . It doesn't do to get too familiar with employees. She's likely to blab it around the place. It undermines the family's authority.'

'So why did you ask her to sit for you?'

'She asked me. I told her I was keen on photography and she asked if I'd take some of her. She said she'd never had a decent photo taken of herself.'

'I understood it was the other way round.' Edward shrugged, really not sure of his ground.

'Anyway, you seem quite taken with her, Edward. My advice to you is, mind what you're doing, a girl like that.'

'What do you mean exactly by "a girl like that"?'

'Well, look at her . . .' He tapped the photo with the back of his fingers. 'I didn't ask her to pose like that, flaunting herself. She even flashed a sight of her knickers a couple of times – deliberately, of course.'

'Lucky you,' Edward interposed. 'But how can you be sure it was deliberate?'

'Because you will only ever see a girl's knickers if she wants you to see them, old fruit.' He tapped his nose with his forefinger as a sign that he was worldly wise to the ploys of women. 'As I said, she's just a shorthand typist at the works . . . An employee,' he added with sham disdain. 'Don't you see? She's trying to lure one of us into her Venus honeypot. Either one of us would be a damned good catch.'

Edward looked at his brother with astonishment. 'I think you've misread the girl totally,' he protested. 'I don't think she's like that at all. She's a delightful, sweet girl. And in any case, Hugh, I really don't see what her background's got to do with anything. As a matter of fact, I've already discussed it with her and, frankly, who cares whether she's the daughter of rolling mill hand or a duke? It's not her fault she's who she is . . . But I actually find her refreshingly different. I rather enjoy her company, you know. She's quite cultured for the daughter of a steelworker. An unbelievably smashing girl.'

'Edward, just don't get too involved. It's odds-on that she's out to entrap one of us. It just wouldn't do. She might be all right to practise on, and doubtless you'd have fun practising, but Mother and Father expect you to do better. A lot better.'

'Oh, Hugh . . .' Edward laughed in an effort to disguise his exasperation. 'I rather think you're jumping the gun there. I'm hardly likely to elope with the girl. In a day or two I shall be off to Cambridge and the possibility of seeing her, or even hearing from her until I come back, really is rather remote – more's the pity. Actually, I could become very distracted by Libby

Shakespeare, you know, but while I'm at university studying law and flying I don't think it would be such a brilliant idea.'

'Well that's sensible, at least.'

'Don't be too reassured. It's not to say I wouldn't like to.'

'So I trust nothing untoward went on last night.'

'Nothing untoward?' Edward gasped with indignation. 'Unless you consider eating fish and chips out of newspaper in Wall Heath untoward.'

'Fish and chips?' Hugh leered. 'Well, I expect Miss Shakespeare felt very much at home tucking into fish and chips,' he remarked sarcastically. 'Especially from a newspaper.'

Edward was incensed at his brother's attitude. 'Look, Hugh . . . Thank you very much for the photo. At least now I won't forget what she looks like. But your comments about the girl are rather churlish. I'm actually quite surprised – especially as she thinks you are quite friendly towards her. And your insinuations that she's a brazen trollop just don't ring true.'

- - -

It was on the Tuesday at the office that Hugh Burgayne requested Miss Shakespeare to do some secretarial work for him. She left her desk with a mixture of trepidation and anticipation. His brushing her thighs was still on her mind and she was anxious as to what his attitude might be. Carrying her notepad and pencil she tapped on the door of his office.

'Ah, Miss Shakespeare. Please take a seat . . .'

So, he was formal today; because they were at work: master and minion.

She sat down primly and just as formally, looking at him with secretarial expectation. But his eyes avoided her. Instead of looking at her he sorted through a small sheaf of papers on his desk, while she looked around the room patiently. Nothing was out of place. The walls were oak panelled, like each of the offices where the more prestigious people worked. Framed photographs ornamented the walls; of white-hot molten metal being poured into ingots, of men operating a rolling mill, as well as an aerial photo of the entire works. A clock with Roman numerals faced a barometer on an opposing wall. A wooden filing cabinet stood beneath the said clock, a table bore a sheaf of blue engineering drawings, and on Hugh's desk sat two identical black telephones, two small piles of papers, and a photograph in a frame which, although she could not see it, Libby presumed was of Laura Birch, the absent fiancée.

'Very well, Miss Shakespeare, when you're ready. I have half a dozen letters and memos I need done urgently. When my secretary returns we can revert to normality, and there'll be no further need for you to trip along to this office.'

'I really don't mind, Mr Burgayne,' she responded pleasantly. 'It's all the same to me whose work I'm asked to do. It's all good experience.'

'Do you enjoy this work?' he asked bluntly, as if such an attitude were foreign.

'I love it.'

He glanced at her indifferently then began his dictation. One letter was a reply to the Ministry of Defence and concerned increasing the production of steel for building warships, another was an enquiry about the best material for the production of air raid shelters. They only served to reinforce her opinion that the world was going mad, that all the speculation of war she was hearing on the wireless and reading about in the newspapers, was not all hot air.

And Hugh Burgayne was being very business-like, she thought. So much so, that you wouldn't know she'd been at his home over the weekend, treated almost as one of the family. You wouldn't have known that he'd taken photos of her, just the two of them together, and that he'd contrived to feel her bare leg.

Libby finished taking dictation then returned to her desk to type the letters. When she went back to his office with the work completed she stood before him, feeling like a schoolgirl in front of the headmaster's desk, awaiting judgment on an exam paper.

'Would you like me to wait while you check and sign the work?'

'Yes, wait, please.'

He read through each letter and memo, and signed them before handing them back to her.

'No mistakes?' she queried brightly.

'None that I've spotted, Miss Shakespeare.' He looked up and this time managed a smile. His manner was softening. 'Incidentally – I've got the photographs I took of you.' He withdrew an envelope from a desk drawer and offered them to her. 'They've turned out rather well.'

'Oh, thank you, Mr Burgayne. May I look at them now?'

He nodded. 'You might as well sit down then.'

'Thank you.' She sat down, opened the envelope and slid out the photos, glancing only cursorily at them. 'Oh, crikey, that's a bit revealing, isn't it?' she commented, and looked at him with an expression of wide-eyed innocence.

'Nothing untoward.' He smiled, and his voice was smooth as cream. 'I should say it's quite attractive, actually. I daresay that young man of yours will like it anyway.'

'I'm not even sure that I'll show him. It'll only invite too many daft questions . . . And I had such a lovely time at Buttonbridge Hall with Bunty and Edward . . .'

'Which you'll want to keep quiet,' he suggested. 'About the photos, Miss Shakespeare . . . It would be most appreciated if you would not show them to anybody here – your work colleagues, I mean.'

'I have no intention.'

'People might jump to the wrong conclusions. Leastwise people might wonder why you were at Buttonbridge Hall in the first place . . . It could lead to speculation about favouritism, which some people might resent.'

'I do understand,' she affirmed. 'It's not something I intend to shout from the rooftops. I value my friendship with Bunty, but it's my business – nobody else's.'

He smiled again, making a steeple with his fingers and resting his chin on it as he leaned back in his leather chair. 'And your friendship with Edward?'

'I value that too,' she replied frankly. 'Although I haven't known him long, I must say he seems to have accepted me completely, and I'm grateful for that. I like him – very much.'

'Well, not too much, I hope . . . Edward needs no distractions while he's studying at university. I'm sure you understand.'

'Yes . . . I think I do . . .' Libby was taken aback and annoyed, but she had to keep her cool, remain diplomatic and polite. 'But if you don't mind me saying so, Mr Burgayne, I don't think you have much to worry about on that score.'

She felt deflated and humiliated at what he was suggesting. He was warning her off. But why? Whatever occurred between her and Edward was nothing to do with him.

'Anyway,' he added, 'I understand you had a good time on Saturday evening after the garden party.'

'Yes, we did, thank you,' she answered, endeavouring to conceal her irritation.

'Oh . . . and, Miss Shakespeare . . . When I invited you to dine with me, you mustn't read anything into it.'

'Of course not.' Didn't he mean anything either when he deliberately felt my leg and made it look like a casual incident? She smiled politely.

'With Laura away, I was at a loose end. It occurred to me that you might be too. I was merely trying to be sociable. Nothing more. I didn't know you had already arranged—'

'Really, Mr Burgayne, there's no need to explain.' She rose from the chair, aware that her justified indignation was by now peeping through her normal composure; it was time to return to the safety of the typing pool. 'Anyway, thank you very much for the photos. Please let me know how much I owe you.'

He waved his hand in a dismissive gesture. 'You don't owe me anything. All I ask is that you give me permission to use one as an entry into my photographic society's annual exhibition. I think they're all good enough.'

She shrugged. 'Of course, if that's what you want to do.'

'And I'd relish the opportunity to take some more.'

- - -

That interview with Hugh Burgayne prompted Libby to take another look at her relationship with Bunty. If Hugh resented the presence of a lowly employee at Buttonbridge Hall, maybe she should make her excuses if further invitations were forthcoming. She had no wish to jeopardise either her own job, or especially that of her father, by upsetting one of the directors. In a way, she understood Hugh's point of view, but she was also acutely aware that it conflicted directly with the attitude of both Bunty and Edward. And it was Bunty and Edward who were her friends, not Hugh. It struck her that it would be best discussed openly and frankly with Bunty.

As if by stealth, the situation also impelled her to a greater closeness with Ron. She had kept him at arms' length, poor chap, preferring the company of the younger Burgaynes, allowing him nowhere near them. Having spent time with Edward, dancing with him, flying with him, talking alone with him, she had perceived his interest in her, which in turn had heightened her own interest in him. But she was fooling herself if she thought that anything would or could come of it. Even if it were to bud, it would not be allowed to blossom.

So Ron enjoyed warmer responses from Libby. When they went to the cinema she allowed him to lead her to the back row. She allowed his arm around her in the darkness, allowed herself to indulge in some serious and prolonged kissing, especially in the slower parts of the films. He was a decent, reliable chap after all. Her mother and father approved of him because they regarded him as steady and hard-working, from a respectable family, though not well-off. Yes, she decided, she could do a lot worse than to marry Ron eventually. If only she *fancied* him more. If only she could fall in love with him . . .

She tried, in fact, to imagine them married. She tried to picture herself lying in bed with him, doing what all young and newly married couples do. Somehow, the prospect did not excite her. Rather she viewed intimate physical contact like that as unsavoury. More precisely, the notion of physical contact as intimate as that with Ron was unsavoury; not necessarily with anybody else; Edward Burgayne, for instance. In fact, the business of intimate contact with Edward had occupied her thoughts often recently, and it had much more appeal. She had allowed and tolerated Ron's ardent kissing, found pleasure in allowing him to get himself worked up into quite a lather sometimes, but going all the way with him? No, definitely not. Going all the way with Edward Burgayne, though? Well, that might be a different kettle of fish.

She'd only ever received kisses from Edward when they said their goodbyes before he left for Cambridge. Yet it was enough to stimulate her imagination, it set her pulse racing, even if its promise was doomed for eternity.

Ron, meanwhile, was beginning to believe she had overcome her infatuation with the Burgaynes when he had relished four consecutive Saturday nights out with Libby. He was unaware, however, that she had pleaded unavailability to Bunty on a several occasions, preferring not to incur the further awkwardness that her presence at Buttonbridge Hall might provoke in Hugh.

But amidst all Libby's doubts, Charles Burgayne, Bunty's father, was only ever the epitome of politeness and pleasantness. Occasionally he had called upon her secretarial proficiency when his own secretary had been otherwise occupied. Charles not only acknowledged openly that she was a friend of his daughter, but seemed to respect the fact too. He addressed her by her Christian name, preferring not to stand on the distancing formalities of calling her 'Miss Shakespeare'. Everything he asked her to do for him she did with pleasure, and with an efficiency that did not go unnoticed. In short, he felt that her whole attitude was exactly right.

- - -

September arrived and the world remained sorely afflicted by its growing international lunacy. A British warship was attacked by an unidentified submarine off the coast of Spain, and Germany held the biggest ever Nazi rally in Nuremberg, with Hitler confirming that his nation needed more territory, and that they would be demanding colonies in the east, even at the expense of Russia. The Japanese bombed Nanking in

China leaving 200 people dead. On the day the League of Nations condemned the Japanese invasion of China, the German and Italian dictators, Hitler and Mussolini, staged a massive demonstration in Berlin where almost a million souls assembled in the Field of May, the stage of the previous year's Olympic games. They denounced the League's outrageous sanctions aimed at curbing Italy's war efforts, which had not stopped them invading and conquering Abyssinia in a frenetic chase to acquire a new Roman Empire.

Despite this global chaos ordinary folk went about their usual daily routine, eating, drinking, sleeping, working and playing, hoping that none of this folly would touch them and theirs. The serious business of life had to continue. There were wages to be earned, children to be raised and educated, old folk to be cared for and fed. Everybody wanted things to get better, not worse. But the unsettling shenanigans of the Nazis would not go away, and the future looked more and more uncertain.

Nazism was actually infecting some Britons. Even the recently abdicated King Edward and his new wife who, between them, had created constitutional mayhem, visited Germany and paid homage to the *Fuehrer*. In early October Sir Oswald Moseley, the leader of Britain's Fascists, led some 2,700 supporters – collectively known as the Blackshirts – through parts of London. More than a hundred well-meaning British patriots who tried to bar their route were arrested. On the tenth of that month Moseley was hit on the head and knocked unconscious as he prepared to address a crowd of 8,000 in Liverpool.

The day following that particular fiasco – a Monday – Bunty Burgayne accompanied her father to the steelworks, wearing a smart two-piece suit in indigo, which complemented her flaxen, sun-bleached hair. She made a beeline for Libby, asking her by internal telephone to an unoccupied office. The two girls greeted each other warmly.

'Been meaning to have a word,' Bunty said. 'What's up? You've been avoiding me.'

'Nothing of the sort,' Libby replied awkwardly. 'I've been really busy. Things Ron had organised mostly.'

'How is Ron?'

'He's well. And how are things progressing with Adrian?'

'I'm being dreadfully aloof at the moment, playing hard to get. So much so that I can't make up my mind whether I'm proud of myself or being a complete idiot. I've shown him the Promised Land, and I'm waiting for him to show some inclination to migrate to it. Trouble is, I might wait for eternity unless I give him a push. So it's time you and I made our marks elsewhere till he comes to his senses, Libby. Pastures new and all that.'

'Pastures new?'

'Men-wise. How do you fancy coming over and staying the weekend? There's a party on at the house of one of my friends. A twenty-first. It should be a riot. There'll be loads of chaps.'

'I don't know, Bunty . . .'

'Look, here you go again, turning me down. What's up? Has Ron finally got to you or something?'

Libby smiled sadly and shook her head. 'No, he hasn't,' she said, avoiding Bunty's eyes. 'Not at all.'

But Bunty was not happy with her friend's reticence. 'Somebody else has then?'

Libby shook her head.

'So what's the problem? I take it there is a problem.'

Libby hesitated, reluctant to tell her friend.

'Well?' Bunty urged.

'Promise you won't be upset.'

'Of course I won't be upset if you tell me the truth. Just tell me what's on your mind?'

'I've been warned off . . . Sort of.'

Bunty looked at her in amazement. 'Warned off? Warned off what? Warned off who? Where? By whom?'

'I really wasn't going to say anything.'

'You *must*, Libby. What's going on?'

'It's Hugh – your brother.'

'Tell me.' She folded her arms and rested them on her desk like a schoolteacher waiting for a plausible explanation of bad behaviour from an erring pupil.

'It's a long story, Bunty . . . '

'So tell me.'

'For a start, he warned me off getting too attached to Edward. He made it clear that Edward didn't need me as a distraction while he's studying. I think he was being a bit of a hypocrite to—' She stopped in mid-sentence, thinking what best to tell Bunty, what best to leave out.

'Go on,' Bunty urged gently, realising this was a sensitive issue for her friend.

'Did you see the photos Hugh took of me?'

'Yes. I thought you looked rather alluring.'

'Well, when he was taking them, he asked me to sit on that table he has . . . When I did, he came to me, raised the hem of my skirt, without so much as a by-your-leave, and ran his fingers up my thighs. Not far, but he did – he felt my legs – and if you remember we were wearing no stockings. It happened so quick, and I didn't know whether it was accidental or intended. But the more I thought about it afterwards, the more I realised it must have been intentional. Then he asked if I'd take my clothes off and pose for some pin-up shots as he called them. Course I said no. Then he asked me to go out to dinner with him that night . . .'

Bunty rolled her eyes in exasperation. 'What an utter cad! What can I say, Libby? I can only apologise. He fancies you, evidently, but that's no excuse for behaving like a blithering idiot.' She pondered a moment. 'And if he fancies you, perhaps he's jealous that there might be something stirring between you and Edward.'

'Maybe . . . but he's got Laura. He should be satisfied.'

'Laura's no oil painting compared to you.'

'Whether or not . . .' She sighed heavily. 'Anyway, just to confuse matters even more, Hugh made it plain as well that an employee of the company oughtn't to be too friendly with members of your family. I suppose he meant that if you get too familiar with employees you lose your authority over them, and I can see what he means . . .'

'And that's why you've refused all my invitations,' Bunty divined.

Libby nodded. 'I honestly thought it best,' she admitted glumly.

'The cheek of the man,' Bunty exclaimed, and stood up, aroused by her displeasure. 'I choose my own friends, Libby, not whoever Hugh or anybody else thinks is suitable. I will not have him upsetting my friends or interfering in my life. Who the hell does he think he is?'

Libby shrugged in response.

'Well, let me make this plain, Libby Shakespeare – Hugh certainly does not speak for the rest of my family. We all adore you. My father thinks you are wonderful, and only on Saturday my mother was asking when you are going to pay us another visit.'

'I'm glad to hear it,' Libby said inadequately, and sighed with relief that it was out in the open. 'So what should I do? Should I visit Buttonbridge Hall again and incur Hugh's contempt, or should I keep my distance?'

'You most certainly will not keep your distance. You're invited this weekend as my guest, and we'll go to that party as planned. Hugh can jolly-well fizz up and burst.'

'How is Edward, by the way?' Libby enquired. 'I take it you've heard from him.'

'Oh, he's fine, apparently. He telephoned yesterday. He sends his best wishes, by the way.'

'To me, you mean?'

'Yes, to you, Libby.'

Libby's face brightened with a delighted smile.

- - -

| 9 |

Libby had no idea whether Bunty had taken issue with Hugh over their friendship, but that weekend she was made to feel very much at home by the rest of the Burgaynes. When she did run into Hugh he was perfectly polite, although he affected to be a little detached. Yet for all his aloofness, whether contrived or real, Libby felt his eyes on her just the same, as if he were mentally undressing her.

She and Bunty attended the twenty-first birthday party. Adrian, too, was there, but Bunty, although extremely pleasant to his face, made sure that she and Libby talked to, and for much of the evening danced with, two other young men who were handsome and witty enough to plausibly warrant the girls' attention, as well as Adrian's curiosity which he masked successfully. Libby went along with it all, enjoying the attention of one of the lads, realising that their girlish flirting was all contrived by Bunty to arouse jealousy in Adrian. He merely responded by spending most of the evening with a particularly attractive red-haired girl, however, to Bunty's increasing frustration and dismay.

Yet while in the company of these people, one person Libby missed was Edward. She thought about him often, but at work and at home he was not part of her life, nor had he ever been, so in those places she had no memories with which to connect him. In this environment, however – his world – his absence was poignantly noticeable.

As the weeks passed, Libby found herself thinking about Edward Burgayne increasingly, wondering what he was doing, who he was spending his time with. She desperately hoped he had not met another girl on those Saturday-night jaunts to the Dorothy Ballroom in Cambridge, for if he had, she – Libby – would be the last to know. While her fixation for Edward increased, her interest in poor, long-suffering Ron waned again in direct proportion.

Her spirits were raised, however, when just prior to Christmas she received an invitation to Buttonbridge Hall that Bunty, privately aware of her friend's hankerings, intimated she should not miss under any circumstances.

'I'm inviting you to the Boxing Day Hunt,' Bunty said as she and Libby, who was at work, spoke over the telephone.

'Hang on,' Libby answered, at once apprehensive. 'I've never ridden a horse in my life.'

'You won't be expected to, you nit. You'll be a spectator.'

'Thank God for that! But you'll ride, won't you, Bunty?'

'Oh, nothing will stop me riding. I adore the hunt. You'll come, won't you?'

'Love to. Edward will be home, won't he?'

'It's Christmas. Course he will.'

'Great.' She wriggled with eager anticipation. 'So who shall I be spectating with? I expect Edward will ride as well, won't he?'

'Sure to. And so will Hugh, so you'll not be stuck with *him*. But my father won't ride, and my mother doesn't anymore. You'll spectate with them.'

- - -

Libby and Ron were ambling along Dudley's High Street, skirting the Market Place. He had his arm around her shoulder proprietorially. They had just left the Criterion cinema where kissing in the dark had been minimal due to her eyes being glued to the silver screen that had been showing the musical *The Great Ziegfeld*.

'I wish I could dance like that,' Ron commented.

'I know,' Libby agreed. 'Wouldn't it be lovely? And all those beautiful sets . . . That one, that looked like they were all spiralling round a great big wedding cake . . . Wasn't it good?'

'And those girls,' he said. 'They were gorgeous.'

'They were.' She agreed. 'So was that chap who played the part of the great Ziegfeld – Nat Pendleton, his real name. He's a masher.'

'A bit old for you, though, eh? He must be in his forties.'

'Maybe, but older men are steadier than young chaps it seems to me. And know how to treat a girl nicely.'

'Even so, there's a limit,' Ron protested, not relishing what he was hearing. He was so uncertain of his standing in Libby's affections, even after months stepping out with her. Sometimes she would seem keen enough, at other times she was cold, stand-offish, and he was sure it had something to do with those damned Burgaynes – in particular the one son who had an aeroplane. Ron had already begun to regard him as a serious rival.

He stopped to look in the brightly lit window of a furniture shop, pulling Libby with him.

'I like that three-piece suite,' he said pointing to a settee and two chairs. 'Leather as well. We should have something like that in our house when we get wed.'

'It's hardly likely to be leather at that price,' Libby replied, disdainful of his judgment, but also ignoring his comment about their being wed.

'But it looks all right.'

'It's not what I would choose, Ron.'

'So what would you choose out of those you can see here?'

'Nothing,' she replied. 'What's the point?'

'What d'you mean?'

She sighed heavily. 'You know what I mean, Ron. Because I can't see you and me ever getting wed,' she answered, and was immediately aware that she'd said something hurtful.

'Oh, not that old tack again.'

She shrugged, turned to face him and looked into his doleful eyes. 'I can't help the way I feel, Ron. You know I like you a lot. I enjoy your company, I appreciate you taking me out a couple of nights a week, but I can't promise you anything more. It's not as if I've not told you before.'

He put his arm around her shoulders again and they moved away, continuing their walk back to Hill Street.

'What are you doing on Christmas Day?' he asked. 'Would you like to come and have your Christmas dinner at our house. The family will be there.'

'I couldn't leave my mom and dad on their own,' she replied assertively. 'Not on Christmas Day. It's good of you to ask me, but I just couldn't, Ron.'

His arm dropped away from her shoulder.

'So I shan't see you at all on Christmas Day?' he remarked sulkily.

'Unless you want to come round to us on the night. You could come round on the night and have a drink with my dad while we all listen to the wireless . . . If you want.'

'Yes, I could do that,' he said in eager acceptance. 'What about Boxing Day then? My mom wondered if you'd like to come to us Boxing Day if you can't come Christmas Day.'

'I'm going out Boxing Day,' she was forced to admit. But it was the perfect opportunity to tell him, and she'd been anxious about it.

'Where're you going?'

'I've been invited to a foxhunt.'

'A foxhunt?' he queried mockingly. 'You?'

'I've never seen a foxhunt, Ron, and I'm looking forward to it. It'll be something different.'

'Oh, I see,' he said, peeved and scornful. 'I suppose it's that Bunty Burgayne or her brother who invited you, eh? So what shall I tell my mom? That you'd rather be with your posh friends?'

'It's not that I'd *rather*,' she replied, trying to be diplomatic, 'but I'd actually like to see a hunt, and this one just happens to fall on Boxing Day. You surely can't begrudge me wanting to see it?'

'Can't I? Well I can and I do. I'm getting a bit fed up with your regular excursions to them Burgaynes. I'm never invited, am I? I suppose you never put in a word for me to go with you. It's almost as if you're ashamed of me.'

'Course I'm not ashamed of you, Ron. What a ridiculous thing to say.'

'Then it strikes me there's something going on. I reckon you've got your eye on him with the aeroplane – or he's got his eye on you. I suppose he's the real reason you want to go. I suppose he *will* be home for Christmas?'

'How should I know?' she answered, feigning both ignorance and indifference. 'Why should he let me know what his plans are?'

'All the same, I expect he *will* be there.'

'Whether he is or not, he's no nearer me, nor is he the reason I want to go.'

'Huh! Says you. And you expect me to believe that?'

'I told you, Ron, I want to see a hunt – and I intend to. If you don't like it, you know what you can do.'

'So shall you stay the night again?'

'Don't be daft. I've got work next day.'

- - -

That misty morning on Boxing Day Bunty collected Libby early to deliver her to Buttonbridge Hall ready for the big event. The prospect of seeing Edward again after so long thrilled Libby and she made a special effort to look appealing by buying something to wear that was both chic and also suitable for the occasion. Normally, she would not wear slacks to go out, but she was dressed in readiness for the cold, wearing a new black pair that fitted perfectly. So much so that her mother commented, 'Look at her lovely little bottom in them trousers, Joe,' to which Joe replied, 'Well, her can hardly complain if her gets it pinched or patted a time or two.' To complement the slacks, she wore a bright red silk scarf, black hat, gloves and a thick overcoat, also new. The combination of minimal red and maximum black with her dark hair rendered her very stylish, and she felt good.

Charles Burgayne drove her and the other non-participating members of the family to the meet that was held every year at the Cat Inn at Enville. Dorothy sat beside him in the front while Libby sat in the back seat alongside Laura Birch, Hugh's fiancée. She had not had any opportunity to speak with Laura beyond their initial introduction.

As they sped between hedgerows bereft of leaves, the mist began to lift, and Libby saw how majestically still the fields and distant woods were in their winter bleakness. Solitary trees stood leafless in the foreground, tinselled in rime which was promising to thaw as the weak winter sun rose over the hills imparting a feeble warmth to the land.

'It's a fine day for it,' Charles exclaimed, speaking over his shoulder for Libby's benefit. 'A perfect day.'

'You've not been to a meet before?' Dorothy enquired.

'Never,' Libby replied. 'Nor did I ever think I would.'

'It's quite a spectacle,' Charles affirmed. 'And a long-standing tradition here on Boxing Day.'

They arrived at the Cat Inn which, by dint of a special dispensation from the vast Enville Estate – of which it was part – had been allowed to open specially for the occasion. It was set on a narrow bend in the main road between Stourbridge and Bridgnorth, and the hunt was to start from there; the wide-open space at the side of the inn served perfectly as a gathering point for the riders, their horses and the hounds. To the rear and running perpendicular to it, stood an avenue of cottages belonging to the estate, forming a quaint terrace that lined the drive to Enville Hall and its thousands of rolling acres.

Already the place was teeming with scarlet and black coats, grooms and sightseers holding warming drinks. Horses, scenting the excitement of the chase, stamped and scraped at the gravel, snorting with anticipation. The riders duly checked them, holding them still while they talked about livestock, crops, made jokes and laughed as they quaffed their favourite tipple. Libby watched it all with intensifying awe.

She heard somebody cough behind her and recognised it at once as Charles Burgayne. Due to her focus on the intriguing spectacle before her she had not missed him. He had slipped unnoticed into the pub, and returned with a tray of tumblers containing an amber liquid.

'Whisky,' he informed Libby. 'To warm you.'

'Well thank you.'

'However, I took the precaution of adding a spot or two of water to yours and to Laura's so as to take the fire out of it. Just in case you're not used to it.'

'Thank you,' Libby said again with a grateful smile, and took the glass. She sipped it tentatively, and it trickled, bitter and sweet, down her throat as it delivered its pleasant burning sensation.

'Hugh should be here soon with the others,' Laura commented from beneath an unflattering woollen hat. 'They were riding here over the fields together.'

As she spoke, Libby heard the clip-clop of horses trotting in a group, and saw that it was Edward, Bunty, Hugh and Adrian. They appeared together, riding abreast of each other along the drive that lead to Enville Hall.

She was disappointed that she had not had a chance to speak to Edward when she arrived at Buttonbridge Hall earlier, but she felt her heart skip a beat at sight of him now, unsettlingly handsome in his pinks, sitting high astride a beautiful chestnut stallion.

While Bunty, Adrian and Edward made their way towards her and the others, Hugh stopped to talk to another member of the hunt. Meanwhile, a kennel man shepherded the hounds along the same lane some minutes after them, their insistent baying becoming louder the closer they got.

'Merry Christmas, Libby,' Edward hailed from atop his mount. 'Belated, I know, but it's lovely to see you again.'

'Merry Christmas,' she called back. 'It's lovely to see you too.' She felt her smiling face go hot and flushed despite the cold. 'So how's Cambridge?'

'Cold,' he replied with an appealing grin. 'But no colder than here.'

He reached down to accept the glass which his father was offering him, and nodded his thanks. He raised it to Libby and she reciprocated.

Meanwhile, the whipper-in was trying to assemble the hounds into an orderly group, and he flicked his whip at the dissenters that broke ranks in their excitement. As the atmosphere grew more high-spirited, their yapping took on a more frenzied edge.

Libby found she was being increasingly gripped by the same fervour. She was growing more aware of the sweet, musty smell of the tensed horses and the humid warmth emanating from them. She was alert to the eagerness of the hounds, conscious of the cold intensity of the frosty air that caused breath to come in steam and noses to drip. She was mindful of the high-pitched, excited voices, all mingling to create a highly charged atmosphere. And all over a poor fox.

'You should get a good view of the proceedings from the Alveley road over the hill beyond the church,' Edward shouted to her above the cacophony of eager animals and people.

She smiled up at him. 'Maybe your father will drive us up there,' she called back.

'Oh, you'll have a job getting him away from the pub,' Bunty remarked. 'Actually, it's not so far to walk, but certainly you should get a better view there.'

'For a while at any rate,' Adrian added.

'Then maybe Laura will go with me,' Libby suggested.

'Of course I will,' Laura agreed.

'And do be careful, you lot,' Dorothy Burgayne warned. 'No heroics on those horses, do you hear? I want each of you back for lunch in one piece.' She turned to Libby and said privately, 'I do worry about them when they're on a hunt.'

'I'm sure they'll be very sensible,' Libby replied.

'Well, you know, Libby, Edward *is* normally quite sensible, it's a fact, but Bunty can be a frightful daredevil. She's far more reckless than either of the boys.'

'Hey, don't you just love this?' Bunty yelled, relishing the atmosphere, unaware of her mother's concern.

'I must go and see Hugh before they go,' Laura said, breaking in. 'I'll be back presently.'

Within seconds a sharp cry resounded. Ears pricked and hoofs grated amid a haze of steamy equine snorts.

'We're off!' Edward proclaimed. 'See you all later.'

'And please be careful,' Libby called, realising as soon as she'd uttered it that she earnestly meant it, although she realised he probably had not heard her plea in the cacophony.

Edward raised his hand and waved as he turned his horse round and broke into a trot. To the massed crackle of hoofs chafing the gravel, and hounds yelping as if suddenly sprung from traps, he followed the rest of the field heading towards the chase.

Laura returned having watched the departure from elsewhere. 'I just had time to give Hugh some biscuits in case he got hungry. And, of course, I had to wish him good hunting. Shall we make our way towards the church?'

'I'll drive you there, else we'll miss it,' said Dorothy. 'We'll leave Charles here and come back for him later. It'll do his chest no good to be outside in this cold air. He's much better off in the pub where it's warm.'

From the lane beyond the church that led to Alveley the three women watched, along with other spectators eager to monitor proceedings in the bland winter sun. In the distant they could hear the sound of hoofs thrumming over the hard, frosty ground. Then the hunt came into view pounding through the shallow valley below them, and Laura pointed excitedly.

'The hounds have checked, look. They must've lost the scent. See how they are sniffing about.'

'Have you seen the fox yet, Laura?' Libby enquired.

'I doubt whether we'd see it from here, but the hounds have certainly had a sniff.'

Then one hound bayed as he picked up again the lost scent, and the pack surged on behind him. The horn blasted, and the mass of red and black jackets gushed forward again, rising and falling like waves over the hedges.

'Can you pick out any of the riders?'

'Not from here, Libby,' Dorothy assured her. 'Everybody looks the same from this distance, especially with my eyesight. We should have brought the binocs.'

They watched, glued, until the hunt was out of sight, then returned to the warmth of the Cat Inn.

'Let's snatch another warmer with Father before we go home,' Dorothy suggested. 'If we stay here it could be ages before we catch sight of the hunt again. It'll probably end up in Alveley anyway, or by the river at Hampton Lode.'

- - -

It had taken many months of feminine wile, but eventually Bunty Burgayne, twenty years old, got the man she wanted. Adrian, too, seemed content with his catch and with being caught. Libby was delighted, for they were so obviously happy together. Both were spirited, indomitable, but it seemed to her that they respected that quality in each other, and neither would seek to hold dominion over the other. She sensed they might make it to the altar.

That Boxing Day evening, after the excitement of the hunt and the informal lunch and the more civilised dinner which followed that, the four braved the cold and went out together. Christmas festivities were still rampant in the pubs, for it had been a holiday for most, but tomorrow work would be beckoning. They tarried in a series of hostelries, each one closer to Dudley than the last, as they fulfilled their plan to deliver Libby home afterwards.

Naturally, they had talked about the hunt, recounted it almost field by field, and Libby was not sorry to learn that the poor harassed and harried fox had managed to evade his pursuers. It was a fair outcome, she thought, but it was an opinion she shared only with Bunty.

After closing time, Edward drove towards Dudley and Hill Street in the Riley, with Libby beside him in the front passenger seat, telling him the way to go, while Bunty and Adrian canoodled in the rear, whispering nonsense to each other and giggling over it between playful kisses.

'When do you go back to Cambridge?'

'Later this week.'

'Shall you be back home for Easter?'

'Unfortunately not, Libby. Flying school,' he explained. 'I hope I shall see you in the summer, though.'

'I hope so too,' she replied, smiling with secret pleasure that he should say so, but sorry it was so far in the future.

'I have a photograph of you, you know. One of those that Hugh took.'

'You haven't!' Any disbelief in her tone was smothered by her delight at the revelation.

He laughed at her reaction. 'Yes, I have.'

'Turn left here, Edward . . . Which picture, for goodness' sake?'

'The glamorous one . . . I mean the racy one.'

'Oh, God,' she exclaimed, embarrassed now. 'I think I know which one you mean.'

'You're my pin-up.' He grinned cheerfully. 'Gracing the wall of my room for all my friends to see. Do you mind?'

'Mind? No, of course I don't mind. I'm flattered . . . Oh, go right there.' She pointed out a road junction.

'It's a smashing photo. And this way, I can't forget what you look like . . .' He drove on, looking straight ahead, but after a few silent seconds he said, 'Libby, I'd like very much to meet you at some time in the summer hols. Just you and me if you've no objection. And I don't mean just once. We could go to a cinema maybe. Maybe have the odd day out, possibly drive to the seaside. What d'you think?' He glanced at her in the darkness and caught the catch lights in her eyes, warm for him.

'Gosh, I'd love to, Edward.' She replied with a broad smile. But the spectre of Hugh Burgayne reared up, and his ominous warning of months ago. Things had moved on since then, though; she now enjoyed the loyal friendship and protection of Bunty and Edward.

'Would you really?'

'Yes, really.'

'Are you still seeing that chap, though?'

'Take the next left . . . Yes, here . . . D'you mean Ron?'

'If that's his name. I only ask because I'd rather not get in the way of things, if . . . you know . . . if it's serious, I mean.'

'Well, I am still seeing him, Edward,' she felt compelled to admit. 'But it's not serious. He just takes me out from time to time. I can't see him putting up with me for much longer anyhow,' she added self-effacingly. 'I'm not in love with him.'

'If you're sure, then.' He smiled and, by the meagre light of the streetlamps flitting by, she saw the familiar twinkle in his soft eyes that always heightened her longing for him.

'Course I'm sure. I'd love it. Now turn right here at the end by the pub.'

'Well, it's a long time to wait,' he remarked as the car ascended Hill Street, 'but we'll let Bunty be the go-between, if that's all right.'

'Here we are, Edward. This is where I live, just on the right.'

He peered out of the window at the terraced house in the darkness and saw the front room window was illuminated.

'Would you all like to come in and say hello to my folks?'

'Has your dad got any brandy?' Adrian enquired, full of bravado and sudden interest.

'Brandy? My dad? He might have some beer.'

'I think we're late enough already, Adrian,' Bunty cautioned. 'It's half past eleven, and these good people have to be up for work in the morning.'

'No, you're welcome to come in,' Libby insisted. 'There's still a light on, look. They haven't gone to bet yet.'

'It's truly kind of you, Libby, but we have a half hour drive back as well.'

'Sorry, yes, I was forgetting.'

'See you next summer then,' Edward said, looking at her intently, seeking eye contact in Hill Street's poorly lit dimness.

'Yes, next summer.' *Roll on.*

He leaned towards her and it was obvious he was going to kiss her, so she met him halfway and offered her lips. He put his arms around her and hugged her as their lips met then, significantly, their tongues. She closed her eyes, and relished the sensation, aware of her heart beating fast and furious. It was such a scrumptious kiss, it excited her, and she wished it could last all night.

But a harsh tap on the window on her side of the car caused them to break off prematurely. Libby's heart turned a somersault at the startling interruption. She turned and looked to try and discern who it was. The agitated silhouette thrown up against the glow of the gas streetlamp opposite told her who it was, even though she had already guessed.

'It's Ron.'

Ron was beckoning her to get out of the car, and seemed inordinately disturbed.

'I'd better go.'

'Shall you be all right? Shall I have a word with him?'

'No, Edward. Best not to. I'll be okay, I can handle him. Look, I'd better go.'

'Be careful, Libby,' Bunty urged. 'I'll ring you at work tomorrow.'

Libby opened the door and clambered out of the car as she bade them goodnight. She faced Ron, who was hovering with proprietorial exasperation.

The car drew away slowly.

'I'll kill the brute if he so much as lays a hand on her,' Edward said grimly, pulling up after only fifty yards. He turned round to look through the rear window of the car.

'He's not that sort of chap,' Bunty remarked. 'She's talked to me about him, and from what I've heard he doesn't seem the violent type.'

'Jealousy can turn a man upside-down,' Edward replied grimly. 'And he's jealous all right. There's no knowing . . .'

'It's nothing to do with you anyway, Edward,' Bunty advised. 'It's Libby's business.'

'But she *is* getting to be my business. I can't help it.'

The eyes of all three of them in the car were fastened on Libby and her predicament, and ready to intervene should she need it. The couple, dark shadows against the light of the streetlamp, were arguing animatedly in the middle of the road, but then seemed to calm down. Libby moved calmly away from Ron towards the house, and he caught up with her, and seemed to put his arm around her. Then she waved to them, apparently a signal that everything was all right.

Edward sighed gloomily. 'He's taken her into the entry. I suppose he's smooth-talked her round. Maybe she's already pressed against the wall giving him some of those divine kisses I just sampled . . . Blast! Ah, well . . . I suppose that's the end of that little dream. What will be will be . . .'

'Don't be such a pessimist, Edward,' Bunty scolded. 'I hope you're not giving in that easily.'

He took off the brake and the car crept forward.

But Edward was labouring under a misreading of what had actually occurred . . .

- - -

'So that's you game,' Ron rasped angrily. 'Just as I thought. You're having it off with your posh mate's posh brother. He was halfway down your throat by the looks of it.'

'Slight exaggeration,' she proclaimed.

'Well it was more than just a peck on the lips,' he retorted.

'Oh, I agree,' she taunted.

'And he's only a friend, you reckon.'

'To be honest, Ron, he's getting to be more than just a friend,' she admitted, not wishing to perjure herself or give him reason to believe it meant nothing. 'But he's going back to Cambridge in a day or two. So I shan't see him anyway. More's the pity.'

'So you've been two-timing me all this time.'

'If that's how you see it. Anyway, you don't own me,' she said over her shoulder as she walked away from him. 'I never made you any promises. If you don't like it, you know what to do.'

'Typical,' Ron replied, but caught up with her and put his arm around her, despite what she had told him.

As she shrugged him off, Libby saw the car was still lingering, Bunty's and Adrian's faces just discernible at the back window. Sensing that Ron was dispirited at this news and calming down, she waved to signal that all was under control and, as she walked into the entry with him the car moved on, over the crown of the hill.

'Yes, I know what to do,' Ron hissed defiantly. 'I ain't prepared to put up with it any longer, I know that much. If you'd rather be out with them lot, then that's up to you, and I ain't gonna lose anymore sleep over it. I'm sick of mithering over you. You blow hot one day and cold the next, depending on whether you've been with him or not. Well, there's plenty more fish in the sea. But I warn you, you'll come to a sticky end with the likes of them . . . Them pair in the back should be locked up for indecency. His hand was right up her leg.'

'So you could see that much in the darkness, could you?' she argued. 'Anyway, good luck to her, I say. But you needn't pretend to be such a prude. I daresay you'd be glad to get your hand up her leg given the chance – or mine for that matter.'

'Huh! If that's the sort of talk your used to with 'em . . . You're turning into a right tart, Libby Shakespeare, and no two ways.'

'Is that what you think of me, then?' Libby asked, indignant and disappointed at insinuations. 'A tart? You know I'm not a tart better than anybody on this planet.' Tears glistened in her eyes.

She looked heartbreakingly beautiful in the gloaming, and so vulnerable, that Ron wanted to take her in his arms there and then. But he'd overstepped the mark. He had insulted her, and he would get no response.

'I think you'd better go,' she said huffily, and pulled a handkerchief from her coat pocket. She dabbed her eyes as she turned away from him, and strutted up the entry.

'Libby!' he called.

She stopped and turned to look at him. He was a forlorn silhouette against the faintly lit street visible at the far end of the dark entry.

'I am *not* a tart, Ron. Goodbye.'

- - -

| 10 |

Instead of telephoning, Bunty made it her business to visit the works next day especially to see Libby. She wanted to ascertain for herself that her friend had survived unscathed the unfortunate encounter with Ron. So when she arrived at the Blowers Green Steelworks she at once sent for Libby, under the pretext of requiring her shorthand skills.

'Well, you look all right,' Bunty said as they sat in the privacy of a vacant office. 'Are you all right?'

'Course I am,' Libby answered with a smile, grateful for Bunty's concern.

'Then at dinner break we'll go out, you and me, and you can tell me everything that went on.'

Libby smiled. 'Okay, so long as you square it with Betsy Mayhew.'

So, come the break, Bunty duly drove her into Dudley at Libby's suggestion, where they entered the Midland Café overlooking the market with its red and white striped awnings, and ordered sandwiches and a pot of tea. The weather was cold and dull, for rain had set in, and the street glistened as it reflected the glow of the naphtha lamps from the market stalls. The traders were already packing their unsold goods away, to return next day; it was obvious that, so soon after Christmas and it being so wet, there would be few paying customers today.

'So you didn't make it up with Ron?' Bunty asked, keen to know as much as possible about what had transpired. She had saved her questions till they were settled in the warmth and comfort of the café.

'No, I didn't. That's it. It's over.'

'You must have seen us stop a little way up your street.'

'I did.'

'To keep an eye on you. Edward was beside himself that you might need some help.'

'Bless him.'

'But when we saw Ron put his arm around you as you walked into the entry, we assumed you'd patched things up straight away.'

A waitress delivered their tea and sandwiches. The girls thanked her, and Libby took the lid off the teapot to give the tea a good stir.

'It wasn't like that at all, Bunty, even if that's how it looked. Ron was jealous. I'd never seen him that jealous before, but he'd seen Edward and me kissing each other goodbye. I had to admit to him that Edward was becoming more than just a friend, because I didn't see the point of letting him think he had a chance with me any longer. He said I'd been two-timing him, which I suppose is partly true. Then he called me a tart and that really upset me. I told him he knew better than any-body that I'm definitely not a tart. So I went off in a huff.'

'But fancy him going to your house when you'd arranged to come to ours.'

'I know,' she said, revealing her indignation. 'He came to spy on me. He knew I'd have to come home sometime because of work next day. So he came and sat with my mom and dad, twiddling his thumbs waiting for me. As soon as he heard your car outside he shot out, my mom said, and was down our entry in a flash.'

'Just to catch you.'

'Just to catch me.' Libby shrugged. 'To see who had brought me back home.'

'So have you arranged to see him again?'

'Do I look daft? I don't want to see him ever again, but I daresay he'll be round our house quick enough to apologise once he's thought things over and calmed down a bit . . . Knowing him.'

'But if you don't want him, Libby, don't you think this is a golden opportunity to be rid of him?'

'Course I do,' Libby replied. 'And I intend to be rid of him now. I've had enough. It strikes me that I'm best off without men at the moment.'

'Edward was noticeably quiet all the way home. You do realise he's very much taken with you, don't you?'

Libby smiled with pleasure at hearing it confirmed, but behind her smile was sadness borne of the conviction that nothing could possibly come of it. 'Yes . . . I know . . .' She took a bite of her sandwich and looked intently at her friend. 'I'm taken with him too, Bunty,' she remarked forlornly. 'I could very easily be head over heels if I let myself. Not that it would do either of us any good, I suppose. With him away at university most of the time I wouldn't be content courting from a distance.' She gave a little laugh as if to dismiss any notions of such an arrangement. 'I don't think he would either. So the idea of promising undying devotion would be a bit premature, to say the least. Besides, we could both do without the distraction. If he lived permanently at home, it might be different . . . Anyway, it's likely he'll meet some bright, exquisitely beautiful and educated girl in Cambridge, and be swept off his feet.'

'Maybe he will, Libby, maybe he won't. But how different you and I are,' Bunty exclaimed. 'If it were me, I'd be jumping in with both feet after the man I wanted. That's the way I am, though – impulsive. Too impulsive, perhaps.'

'You've not been impulsive with Adrian, though.'

'Crikey, I've had Adrian in my sights far too long for that'

'I must say, though, Bunty, I think you're ideally suited.'

'Well, I think so too . . .' Bunty smiled dreamily then bit into her sandwich and put it back on her plate, looking intensely thoughtful as she divested her slender fingers of crumbs. After a moment or two she said, 'Can I ask you something, Libby? Something frightfully personal? I consider you my best friend, so I feel eligible to ask, and there's something I'm awfully curious about.'

'Ask away.' Libby sighed with exaggerated drama. 'For you, Bunty, my life is an open book. You should know that by now.'

Bunty leaned towards her and, so as not to be overheard, said in a low voice, 'Have you and Ron ever done it together? The sex thing, I mean. You know, gone all the way? Penetration, and all that?'

'Lord, no,' Libby giggled infectiously at the notion. 'Not with him. I couldn't. I've never fancied him enough.'

'So you're still intact?'

'For better or worse. But I am only nineteen . . .' She rolled her eyes as if it were an appalling oversight to have remained a virgin at such an advanced age. 'I quite envy girls who aren't, though. So what about you, Bunty? Now you've asked me it's only fair that I ask you. Are you still . . . intact, as you so quaintly put it?'

'Me? No . . .' She shook her head and took another bite. 'Adrian was the first, mind you. I'm well aware that in certain quarters I earned a bit of a reputation as something of a fast cat, but I lost my virginity to Adrian, and not before. Well, I love him terribly after all, Libby, and he loves me, and it just all seemed so damned natural . . . It's brought us much closer. It's absolutely magical.'

'But that's ever so romantic, Bunty. I really do envy you.' She sighed dreamily. 'Did it hurt, though? First time, I mean? I'd love to know what to expect when my turn comes.'

'Stings a bit at first.' Bunty chuckled as she recalled it. 'But not for long, thankfully – infinitely more absorbing sensations soon take your mind off it, I can assure you. There was a spot or two of blood in my snowy white knickers afterwards, however,' Bunty added for good measure. 'It was the first time I ever washed my own knickers.' She put her hand to her mouth to smother her chuckle. 'Well, it wouldn't do to have the laundry maids speculating. Some things are sacred after all. But it just goes to show how romantic and practical the back seat of a car can be. It was so nice . . . and, I confess, it continues to be.'

Libby giggled again in this girlish conspiracy. It felt good to be so close to another woman – a friend with whom she could share such personal secrets. Meanwhile, some of the other patrons in the café looked on and smiled, no doubt wondering what it was that amused her and her friend so much.

- - -

Nineteen thirty-eight stormed in, bringing more anxiety and uncertainty to the world. Everybody was issued with a gas mask for fear that gas warfare was likely to be waged on Britain, and children were given drill at school on how and when to use them, made compulsory by a new law. Germany, meanwhile, annexed Austria and, as the Nazi troops marched into Vienna, the Austrians welcomed them enthusiastically. The Japanese bombed Canton in China and the number of innocent victims subsequently killed ran into five figures; nobody knew exactly how many.

Libby continued to apply herself conscientiously to her work. Her shorthand and typing speeds were increasing satisfactorily, and every task, every letter and memorandum that she handled brought her more confidence. Occasionally she was obliged to do work for Hugh Burgayne, and she began to feel more at ease in his company. She never enquired of him how Edward was, for to do so would reignite the flame of disapproval. But she talked amiably to him about other things, including his photography, and in turn he seemed to become much more amenable. She even agreed to sit for more photographs as a favour to him.

So Hugh drove her one pre-arranged dinnertime in spring to the ruins of the old Priory in Dudley. He wanted photos of her to enter into his camera club's annual exhibition. The wind was gusting, but the sun was shining, and he got her to pose, framed by those ancient limestone arches that remained standing, and on the crumbling grey walls, with the newly fledged trees and the Norman castle keep, high on its hill behind her, as a backdrop. This time though, she was careful to avoid letting him get too close. She did not risk allowing him near enough to touch the hem of her light summer dress and so afford him the opportunity to feel her leg again, but he did suggest that she should hoist the skirt herself for some 'pin-up' poses. Much of the time she had no need however; the capricious wind seemed more than willing to take on the onus, one minute pressing it sensually around her body and outlining her lovely figure, the next blowing her skirt sky-high, to reveal her shapely legs and more. Libby made the obligatory motions to modestly hold down her wayward skirt, but was invariably too late; Hugh seemed to have the knack of pressing the camera's shutter button at precisely the most revealing moments.

She excused herself and him, privately pleased that she must be sufficiently attractive to be asked to pose for such photos, and it was harmless enough done this way. The whole exercise was contrived to titillate him, poor pathetic soul, but she was content to go along with it. These days, apart from this one immature quirk, Hugh was behaving reasonably well.

Yet the weeks rolled on, and Libby thought it strange that Hugh never offered her any copies of the photos he took on that gusty occasion, nor even showed her any.

- - -

In August, the Burgaynes hosted another garden party. Libby was aware that Edward had returned home a day or two earlier, but was disappointed that she had not heard from him. So she resigned herself to what seemed the increasing likelihood of his having met and fallen in love with some incredibly lucky girl at Cambridge. This depressing possibility left her feeling rejected when she poignantly recalled that he had said how much he wanted to meet up with her during her annual summer holidays for days out. The bitter irony was that she herself was free. In any case, she hoped to see him at the garden party and establish whether or not he was still interested in her. At least it would release her from the thrall of her infatuation if he wasn't.

As usual, Bunty collected her from Hill Street, and as they drove they engaged first in random girl talk. But Libby was keen to learn about Edward.

'When did Edward get back from university?' she asked, unable to resist the inevitable question any longer. 'You haven't said.'

'I haven't said because I haven't spoken to you since he got back, which was only the day before yesterday.'

'Oh, I see. But I thought he broke up from university ages ago.'

'So he did, but more flying school held him up, I believe.'

'Not a girl, then?'

'A girl? I wouldn't have thought so. Leastwise, he hasn't mention anybody. Why? I got the distinct impression he was saving himself for you.'

'Well, I won't hold my breath anyway,' Libby said.

They arrived at Buttonbridge Hall around noon and the garden party was not due to open until two o' clock that afternoon. As Libby walked and talked in the deserted grounds with Bunty, admiring first the flower beds and then the horses in the stables, the weather was cooler than it had been the previous year. Grey clouds rolled across the sky, causing prolonged overcast periods.

Before long a familiar voice called her name some distance behind her.

Wide-eyed and her heart suddenly pounding, Libby managed to look decorously surprised, and hoped the shock might explain her blushes.

'Gosh, it's good to see you again, Libby,' Edward beamed as he hurried towards her. 'And you look gorgeous. Come and have a chat, will you? . . . if Bunty can spare you.'

Bunty, with a knowing look, said of course she could.

To Libby's mixed emotions of delight and apprehension Edward seemed eager to drag her away. He led her to the un-inhabited marquee and hauled two fold-up chairs to a small round table at which they sat opposite each other. Libby was becoming privately encouraged because he seemed genuinely delighted to see her after so long. Although she was suddenly feeling a little nervous as to the outcome of this impromptu tête-à-tête.

'How've you been?' he enquired. 'I've missed you.'

'Have you really?'

'Yes, really I have.' His smile was devastating.

She grinned self-consciously and cast her eyes down. 'I've missed you, too, Edward,' she said quietly, her eyes now meeting his. 'It's lovely to see you.'

'And you're even lovelier than ever.'

'Well, I try to make the best of myself, so it's nice of you to say so.'

'You changed your hairstyle. I love it.'

She flicked her hair self-consciously. 'I just let it grow a bit,' she answered.

'Well, it suits you. Really, it does. So how is the job at the Blowers Green Steelworks?'

'Busy. Actually, I've been doing quite a bit for your father lately – and Hugh. But how about you, Edward? Are you well? How's university?'

'I begin my final year when I return. Lots of studying, lots of exams to contend with.' He sighed ruefully.

'And lots of flying?'

He smiled at that. 'Yes, lots of flying, too.'

'And you still want to join the RAF?'

'Of course.'

'Aren't you worried, though, Edward, that there's going to be a war? That you'll be expected to fight?'

He shrugged. 'It's a racing certainty there's going to be a war. But that's what the RAF is there for – to help fight wars. Why? Dare I hope you might be worried about me?'

'Shouldn't I worry about you?'

His eyes devoured her. 'I'm awfully flattered if you do. I worry about you too.'

'Me? Honestly? Why?'

He lit a cigarette and puffed a cloud of smoke into the apex of the marquee. 'I worry about you and that chap Ron.'

'Well, you needn't worry about him anymore, Edward. He's history. We finished. Ages ago. Last Boxing Day evening in fact. You remember what happened?'

'Of course, I remember. I gathered as much from Bunty, but I wanted to hear it from you. All the same, I bet he can't leave you alone.'

'He still calls round to see my mom and dad . . . occasionally.'

'To see you, you mean.'

It was Libby's turn to shrug. 'That might be his intention, for all I care.'

'Of course he calls to see you. You must see that, surely?'

'But I've got nothing to offer him anyway. He knows that now. He finally accepted it. I haven't been out with him since last Christmas. Last Boxing night was the crunch. Maybe he's just having trouble breaking the habit of visiting Hill Street.'

Edward drew on his cigarette again, his eyes still feasting on her. She looked so achingly desirable with her longer hair style that added to her loveliness, the simple yellow cotton dress that accentuated her slender waist and pert young bosom. The dress was sleeveless, and her arms looked slender and smooth and beautifully contoured. He longed to hold her. 'I hope you're still free of him when I finish university.'

She blushed at what his words implied. 'As I said, he's history,' she replied softly. 'He's in the past.'

His eyes creased into another of his delectable smiles. 'I want you to know, Libby, that I'm terribly fond of you.' His voice was taut with pent-up emotion. 'And Bunty suggested a while ago that you . . . well, that you might be fond of me, too . . .' He drew on his cigarette and flicked ash nervously into the ashtray on the table, his eyes never leaving hers.

Libby smiled, aware of his nervousness as well as her own, and decorously averted her eyes.

Then he stubbed out his cigarette and reached across the table with the intention of taking her hand. Hers met his halfway, her heart beating faster. 'I understand any reluctance on your part, if you don't want to take this mutual regard we seem to have for each other any further while I'm at university. That's something else Bunty mentioned.'

'She's a good go-between.' Excitement was increasing within her because of where this might be leading at last. She did not want to lose any impetus, so decided to be perfectly frank and make her feelings clear. 'But I think what you call "mutual regard" is a bit of an understatement, Edward,' she whispered, meeting his eyes directly. 'For my part at any rate . . . I'd be more than happy to be your girl if that's what you want, but I don't know how I would cope with a long-distance courtship. Besides you have lots of studying and exams to sit in your final year. You wouldn't need me as a distraction.'

'Libby, I have great respect for your common sense, although it grieves me sorely . . . But look . . . I dearly want you to be my girl . . . So when I've finished university . . . do you think you might still be here for me? So I'm asking you . . . will you wait for me?'

She felt her heart suddenly pounding hard within the bodice of her yellow cotton dress, and looked earnestly into his eyes. She was still plagued by doubt that she was not good enough for him, that she might be rejected as a prospective daughter-in-law by the eminent Burgaynes, that in Cambridge he might still be swayed by a girl deemed more suitable.

'D'you think it's wise to be making such pledges, Edward?' she said, her tremendously respected common sense again getting the better of her emotions. 'I'm sure there must be lots of worthier girls in Cambridge.'

'There are lots of girls in Cambridge, it's true, Libby, but none more worthy than you. And certainly none that interest me.'

'So you say now.'

'Libby, my darling, it's true. I know how I feel – what I feel – and I trust my emotions. I would dearly love to hear you say that you are prepared to wait for me. It's you I'm interested in. I'm interested in nobody else.'

She smiled radiantly, more than happy to say what he wanted to hear. 'If you promise you'll wait for me, Edward, I promise I'll wait for you.'

- - -

That afternoon, she and Edward ambled round the grounds hand in hand, stopping to talk occasionally to people attending the garden party. That night they went out with Bunty and Adrian. Their intention was to relive the experience of the previous year's night; dancing at The Stewponey and maybe eating fish and chips later. They did it all, and had tremendous fun. The important things they wanted to say to each other had already been said and were not referred to again, but they held hands as often as possible, and exchanged ample kisses. Everything was understood between them. At this stage it would not do to become too intense about one another, but they were patently in love, and both sensed the promise of the future.

It had been arranged that Libby would stay that night at Buttonbridge Hall. She and Edward bid each other goodnight with delicious kisses, and they agreed they would play tennis next day, Sunday, if the weather held. Obligingly, it did. Evening came, a quiet evening spent with the Burgaynes, when Libby and Edward sat apart, concealing from their elders the affection they had declared for each other. When it was time for Libby to return home, Bunty feigned tiredness and asked Edward – for the sake of her friend – if he would be so kind as to deliver her back home.

As they sat in his MG outside the Shakespeare' home in Hill Street, Edward's arm went around her shoulders.

'I'm going to find it so hard to live without your kisses once I've left on Tuesday,' he whispered, prompting Libby to snuggle up to him as he drew her to him. 'I don't want to get too carried away before I leave, though. If I do, it'll be even more painful once I've gone. But it's so hard trying to be rational.'

'It's the same for me, Edward,' she breathed.

'I want to be with you every available moment, but I know that's impossible. So you'll write, won't you?'

She looked into his eyes, which reflected back the catch-lights from the streetlamp almost opposite. 'Of course I'll write, but it will only heighten my longing to be with you, and so hurt the more,' she answered philosophically. 'Maybe it's best if we don't write. I don't think I have the self-control to handle our love affair from afar. I just know I'll want to get on the first train to Cambridge to be with you and, as I said, you won't need the distraction. Anyway, I have a job to go to here.'

They fell silent for a few seconds, until Libby sighed profoundly, and said, 'I think my common sense, as you call it, suggesting we deprive ourselves of each other, will be my undoing. Or am I just being a complete idiot?'

'You're no idiot,' he replied tenderly and with a smile, his eyes reflecting the glow of the streetlamp close by. 'I love the idea of you coming to Cambridge to be with me. But I know exactly what you mean about being a distraction.'

'Oh, I think I'm too sensible for words, but remember we have agreed to keep it secret from your folks about us, except for Bunty. So why don't we agree not even to write, and let Bunty be our go-between. She can pass any messages, because you'll keep in touch with your family while you're away.'

'Lord above, Libby, how can you be so hard on a man? That'll be really painful.'

'It'll also be so romantic. I'll be thinking about you constantly and waiting, badgering Bunty for any messages.' She looked into his eyes appealingly.

'I'm doomed, yet I can see some logic in it,' he sighed. 'Okay, no letters. Just as long as you promise to wait for me.'

'I promise, Edward, with all my heart.'

He gave her a hug and they kissed again. 'I promise that too,' he whispered. 'I'm so much in love with you.'

They said their goodbyes that night. One aspect of their affair had remained unspoken, but deep in her heart Libby began to realise that the future was too uncertain to expect all their promises to be fulfilled. She read the newspapers avidly, listened to the wireless, and was filled with apprehension for the future. The RAF had launched a new recruitment campaign that was proving successful, and the government was spending millions establishing new airfields. The Spanish Civil War was rumbling on, with General Franco and his rebels gaining the upper hand. She was appalled and afraid for the Jewish families of Vienna when she read that their bread-winners were given a mere two weeks' notice by their employers to quit their jobs, just because they were Jewish. Clearly, some colossal, unstoppable evil was afoot.

Summer shifted surreptitiously into autumn, and her fears were bolstered when she heard that Mussolini had expelled all Jews arriving in Italy after 1918, while others were rounded up on the strength of trumped-up charges that they were plotting against his government. What awful, unspeakable deeds had the Jews perpetrated on the world to deserve such fiendish treatment everywhere? Surely not because their ancestors were believed to have betrayed Jesus Christ nearly two thousand years ago, for that would be vindictive in the extreme.

There was trouble in Czechoslovakia too; in carefully orchestrated rallies and riots the Sudeten Germans were calling for union with Germany, but the Czech government's response was to impose martial law, and appeal for calm amongst their countrymen who were hostile to Germany. Then, bewilderingly, the Czech government agreed to Anglo-French plans to cede the Sudetenland to Germany anyway, even though the rest of the nation protested vehemently. Hitler then called a conference of four powers, Germany, Britain, France and Italy, to discuss the crisis. On 30th September, Mr Chamberlain, the British Prime Minister, flew home from that conference and promised, as he waved a copy of the signed Anglo-German accord, that there would be 'peace in our time'. Libby viewed it with deep suspicion, and wished she were Prime Minister; it was so obviously a sell-out.

So she was not surprised to read that on 1st October the Nazis had marched into Czechoslovakia and occupied the Sudetenland, while Poland annexed other parts of the country. Hungary too was infected by the politics of greed, and annexed southern areas of Slovakia and Ruthenia. In December the German Navy announced plans to double the size of her fleet of U-boats.

But life went on. The Blowers Green Steelworks continued to produce and roll steel, and on Boxing Day, another hunt departed from the Cat Inn at Enville, to which Libby was once more invited. Edward, between delectable romantic interludes, informed her that the RAF was taking delivery of four hundred new aeroplanes a month. Once again she told him of her fears and clung to him fearfully while he was within embracing distance. Why were all these countries, Britain included, increasing the strength of their fighting forces if not to fight?

By March of 1939 it was clear that Poland itself was under threat from Nazi Germany and a military alliance was sealed between Britain, France and that country, pledging its defence of Poland under any circumstances. In April, the government announced conscription for military service, and compiled a national register of eligible men over twenty years of age. Conscripts would face six months of intensive training. For Libby, this was the clearest indication yet that war was just around the corner.

But, affording some light-heartedness into those anxious days, the month of May brought Libby's twentieth birthday. And something else . . .

- - -

Miss Hardy from the Personnel Department sent for Libby by way of a message from Miss Mayhew. At first she naively thought that out of the kindness of its heart the company was about to offer her a better salary, as a sort of birthday gift. She'd already received birthday cards from colleagues; both Vera and Hilda had handed theirs to her earlier.

'D'you think it will be to give me a rise?' asked Libby.

'You're kidding,' Vera replied tartly. 'They don't give rises here just for birthdays.'

So Libby made her way to the Personnel Department, tapped on the door of Miss Hardy's office and entered.

'Do sit down, Miss Shakespeare,' Miss Hardy invited.

Libby did as she was bid.

'How long have you been here now, Miss Shakespeare?'

'It'll be two years in August, Miss Hardy.'

'And you appear to have settled down very well.'

'I have,' Libby replied brightly. 'I really enjoy it.'

'You are very highly thought of, you know, in rather influential quarters, and I have been asked to "sound you out", so to speak.'

'Oh?' Libby's face was a delightful icon of bewilderment.

'You may or may not be aware that Mr Charles Burgayne's secretary Miss Evans is due to retire at the end of June . . .'

Libby was suddenly aware of her heart beating faster at the prospect of where this could be leading. 'Yes, I'm aware she's due to retire, but not the exact date.'

'Mr Burgayne himself has put your name forward as a possible successor, and I have been asked to get your reaction.'

Libby beamed with astonishment, manifest in her hazel eyes. 'Become Mr Burgayne's secretary? Crikey!' She laughed delightedly. 'I . . . I . . . I'm speechless.'

'Consider it an honour, Miss Shakespeare. I have never before known a woman of your tender years be considered for such an elevated position. But your work has been carefully monitored all the time you've been here, and Mr Burgayne obviously believes you are worthy of the post and capable of making a success of it.'

'Miss Hardy, I'm flabbergasted. Really I am.'

Miss Hardy put on her professional smile. 'So you must tell me, Miss Shakespeare – do you wish to be considered for the post?'

'Oh, yes,' she enthused emphatically. 'I enjoy working with Mr Burgayne. I enjoy working with him very much.'

'There would of course, be a significant increase in your salary to reflect the additional responsibilities and the extra work you will be expected to undertake.'

'What extra work, Miss Hardy?'

'Well, Miss Evans has been more than just a secretary here. She is more a personal assistant and, as such, she often works with Mr Charles and other members of the Burgayne family, sometimes even at their home, on things of a more personal nature. Her duties are not confined solely to the office.'

'I see,' Libby said thoughtfully. 'It sounds interesting.'

'You would, of course, from the day of your appointment, spend your time with Miss Evans getting to grips with the work, ready for the hand over at the end of June. You would be in contact with other family members as well from time to time.'

Libby was tempted to confess that she knew them already, but clearly, Miss Hardy had no idea that she did, so she decided it best to keep it to herself; she wanted no insinuations of favouritism.

'So what would my new salary be, Miss Hardy?'

'Thirty-nine shillings and sixpence per week.'

'Crikey!' Think of the new clothes and shoes I could buy, trips to a hairdresser . . .

'I will report your response to Mr Burgayne in a memo later today, and you can expect to hear further from him. Until you do, Miss Shakespeare, and until any appointment is decided, please do not to mention this conversation to anybody.'

'Yes, I understand, Miss Hardy. And thank you very much.' She got up from the chair, finding it hard to suppress her trembling. 'Oh, and please pass on my thanks to Mr Burgayne for considering me.'

- - -

'So what's it all about?' Vera asked when Libby returned to her desk looking preoccupied.

'What's what about?' she responded absently, her head still full of her conversation with Miss Hardy.

'What did Miss Hardy want you for? A rise, or the sack?'

'Neither.'

'What then? You look like the cat that got the cream.'

'I just found out something,' she said. 'But I daren't talk about it, Vera. So please don't ask. But I'll tell you at the right time. I promise you'll be the first to know.'

'Sounds blinkin' mysterious to me.'

After the dinner break Libby received another summons, this time to the office of Charles Burgayne. She tapped on his door deferentially and she heard him respond with a 'Come in,' and his customary cough.

'Ah, Libby . . .'

'Good afternoon, Mr Burgayne.'

'Please take a seat . . .' He shuffled some papers on his desk and leaned back in his big leather chair. 'I believe you know why you're here, young lady?'

'Yes, I think I do, Mr Burgayne, and I have to thank you.'

'Well, allow me to let you into a little secret, Libby . . . Ever since the very first time you did some work for me – and you'd only been here five minutes, as I recall – I was impressed with your work, with your demeanour – in fact, your whole atti-tude. I had you ear-marked even then for my future secretary, come the retirement of Edith Evans. I'm sure we shall con-tinue working satisfactorily together.'

'Oh, I am, too, Mr Burgayne.'

'You already have the advantage of knowing me and my family, as well as the understanding, I would imagine, that we all think very highly of you. The fact that you get on well with them all, and that you are not a stranger whom we should be wary of, was yet another factor in making you my choice. So congratulations, Libby . . .' He stood up, reached across the table for her hand, and they shook.

Libby beamed with joy. 'Thank you so much, Mr Burgayne, for considering me. I'll do my utmost never to let you down.'

'I'm sure of it,' he said kindly, and coughed. 'Now tell me, what have they offered you in the way of salary?'

'Thirty-nine and six a week,' she replied.

Charles winked. 'I'll see if we can't better that by at least another five bob, what?'

Her eyes widened with astonishment and joy. 'Thank you . . . I really don't know what else to say . . .'

When Libby arrived home that day, Gladys was emerging from the cellar heaving a bucket of coal. Her hands were as black as the coal she was lifting, and she placed a few lumps on the fire that was burning in the immaculately black-leaded grate.

'What's for tea, Mom?'

'I got a bit o' cod from the fishmonger. It'll be nice with some parsley sauce.'

'Shall I carry the bucket out for you?'

'No, I'll do it, or you'll get yourself all black and spoil your frock.'

'Well, if I spoil my frock I can always buy a new one.'

'Miss Moneybags, eh? Have you had a rise for your birth-day or summat?'

Libby grinned. 'In a way, yes.'

Gladys took the coal bucket out and Libby followed her through the veranda to the brew house. 'I thought you was looking pleased with yourself, our Libby. What's happened then?'

'You'll never believe it.'

'You'll have to tell me first.'

'I've been promoted, our Mom. I'm going to be Mr Bur-gayne's new secretary when Miss Evans retires at the end of June.'

'You mean the gaffer?'

'Yes. Mr Charles Burgayne.'

'Glory be!' Gladys looked at her daughter in a mixture of as-tonishment and admiration. 'I always knew you'd do well, our Libby, but I never thought you'd come to be the gaffer's secre-tary. Good for you, my flower. Wait till your dad knows.'

'I get a whopping rise as well. I can scarcely believe it.'

'Ooh, I think we'll have a celebration tonight then, eh, our Libby? I'll pop down to the outdoor after and fetch us a bottle of sherry.'

'No, I'll go,' said Libby. 'And I'll pay.'

They heard footsteps in the entry and turned to see Joe Shakespeare come through the veranda door. He was beaming as he greeted them.

'Blimey, here's somebody else grinning like a Cheshire cat,' Gladys ribbed. 'And what sort of a day have you had, dear husband?' she asked, in a mock-cultured tone.

'You'll never believe it,' Joe responded. 'They've made me up to foreman. Me – Joe Shakespeare. I can scarcely believe it.'

'Looks like a double celebration, our Libby, eh?'

'Does that mean two bottles of sherry, then?'

'Why what's happened?' Joe asked.

Libby told him.

'Well damn my hide. Looks like our ship's really come in at last.'

- - -

| 11 |

The telephone on Libby's desk rang, interrupting her work. She answered it, now installed in her own office as the recently appointed personal private secretary to Mr Charles Burgayne, for by this time Edith Evans had gone.

'Telephone call for you, Miss Shakespeare,' the firm's telephonist announced.

She waited, hearing a few clicks.

'Libby?'

'Speaking.'

'It's Edward.'

'Edward!' she replied, suddenly trembling at the sound of his voice and instantly sitting up straight. 'Gosh, what a lovely surprise. Are you home?'

'Got home last night. Late. Awful train journey. Hey, they tell me congrats are in order – they promoted you.' He sounded so cheery despite the crackles over the line that contrived to make his voice sound hard and distant.

'I know. Great, isn't it?'

'How's it going?'

'So far so good. Now I get to know some of the Burgayne family secrets.'

'You'll get to know more than me, no doubt.'

'Who knows!' she laughed. 'So how did your exams go?'

'Pretty well, I think.'

'So you've finished at university now?'

'Yes, thank God. That's it now. Finished. Which is why I called.'

'Is it to tell me you've waited for me, like you promised . . . or not?' The trembling began again. She needed to be reassured before she jumped in and made a complete fool of herself.

'In fact, it's to ask you whether you've kept your promise and waited for me.'

Her heart was thumping. 'Oh, Edward. Yes, I've waited,' she said in a whisper, her mouth close to the mouthpiece.

'Well, I've waited too, Libby, and I'm aching to see you. These last few weeks have dragged awfully. Have you changed since I last saw you?'

'Changed? Oh, maybe the hairstyle. That's all.'

'You're still as beautiful?'

She uttered a self-effacing laugh. 'Well that's always been a matter of opinion.'

'No, it's a matter of fact. So . . . When can we meet?'

'Tonight, if you want.'

'Excellent. I've waited long enough. Can you be ready by eight?'

'Okay.'

'I love the way you say "okay", just like they do in those Yankee films.' Now she heard the relief in his voice. 'So I'll pick you up at eight. We have a lot to talk about, Libby.'

- - -

She was ready and waiting when she heard the sound of Edward's motor car reverberating through the entry, followed by the beep of his horn. With her heart in her mouth she skipped down the entry to the street. When she saw him her eyes were bright with delight and anticipation, and her smile radiant. He was in his MG two-seater, the canvas roof was down, and his eyes followed her as she skipped round to the passenger seat to sit daintily beside him. He leant over and their lips met.

'It's so good to see you. And you look even lovelier than ever.'

She grinned appreciatively. 'You say the nicest things, Edward Burgayne.' As he sped away the wind blew her hair awry, and she laughed. 'I've spent ages doing my hair and as soon as I get in your car it's all over the place.'

He turned to look at her and grinned admiringly. 'I really don't know what you're worried about. You look absolutely ravishing, especially with your hair blowing everywhere. It's longer. It suits you. Makes you look very chic.'

'But it's not meant to blow all over my face.' She laughed at herself. It was as if they had never been apart. At once she felt sublimely at ease with him. 'Where are you taking me?'

'Kinver Edge. It's a lovely evening, don't you think? The sun's still shining gloriously, and we need to talk. And what more beautiful place to sit and watch the sun go down? We could go for a drink somewhere afterwards, if you like. Talking can be thirsty work.'

As he drove they brought each other up-to-date, spoke about his family, her new job, his experiences in Cambridge. They arrived in the peaceful village of Kinver, drove through the quiet main street, and turned left up a steep narrow lane. Eventually he pulled up at a quiet spot near the top of the hill, and they clambered out. Edward helped her over a style, and they walked hand in hand along a well-trodden path beneath a canopy of trees, content to be alone together. The path led them higher, winding one way then another, until they arrived at a vast clearing which was the top of the edge. The vista from that lofty elevation was magnificent in whichever direction they chose to look.

'I've never been here before,' she remarked, gazing about. 'Isn't it gorgeous?'

'I thought you'd enjoy it. Let's rest our legs and sit on the grass here and enjoy the view.'

He sat down first and reached for her hand as she knelt before him. The low sun lent a warm glow to her face and neck and to her smooth, slender arms as she smoothed the creases in her skirt, and looked at him expectantly.

'I've thought about you such a great deal, Libby,' he said, his voice low. 'I've missed you so much. I've thought about this moment a great deal too, trying to picture in my mind's eye what it might be like – our being together for the first time in so long. I had a little speech all worked out for you of what I wanted to say, you know . . . But it's all gone . . .' He laughed diffidently. 'I can't remember a word of it – I'm just too keyed up.'

'Do you think you needed a speech?'

'Not really,' he said. 'I realise that now, of course.' His expression changed, and he looked more serious. 'I just need to be sure that you still feel what I feel, my darling. My feelings for you are just the same as they were before I began my final year – stronger, if anything. Well, I'm free of university now, and I suppose I'm rather impatient for things to happen. I seem to have been waiting for ever for you . . . So . . .' He took her hand again and engaged her soft hazel eyes that were looking back at him so intently, drenched with the sun's gold. 'You admitted your feelings for me before—'

'And nothing's changed, Edward,' she breathed. Their eyes held and she looked so divinely intense. 'Nothing's changed since the last time I saw you. I've waited for you, and waited . . . and waited . . . just like we said . . .'

She paused, as if disinclined to bare her soul more just yet, and looked up into the sky momentarily where a buzzard was drifting on the breeze as he hunted for his supper.

'But?' he urged gently, sensing her reserve.

'Well . . .' She looked into his eyes again, intently. 'After all the promises we made each other, I only ever wanted you, Edward. Like you, I've been counting the days, the hours . . .'

He squeezed her hand, and leant forward to kiss her. 'That makes me so happy, Libby, my angel. I only ever dreamed of hearing you say such things. I only ever wanted you, you know. Come closer . . . Let me hug you.'

She swung round on her haunches and sat beside him and he wrapped her in his arms.

'Anyway,' she said, nestling up to him, 'I hoped you'd ring me at work some time to let me know you were home. But I could never be sure you would. Sometimes these things – like the promises we made – are said in the heat of the moment and can be forgotten just as quickly. And Bunty's been far too engrossed with Adrian to worry about my concerns for you.'

'So I gather.'

'It's been a long and lonely wait, Edward.'

'But you waited, my darling.'

'Because I knew you were worth waiting for, and I trusted you were waiting for me.'

'I was,' he whispered. 'Now kiss me.'

They kissed – rewarding, prolonged, lingering kisses that drew out once more all the mutual longing that had been pent-up through three long seasons and more. She melted at his touch and it was a vivid foretaste of how easy it would be to lose control of herself with this man whom she loved totally.

'Making up for lost time?' she asked teasingly when they paused.

'I've dreamt about your kisses,' he whispered. 'Every night before I went to sleep I kissed you in the photograph I have of you, and tried hard to remember your real kisses. If I tried hard enough, I really could imagine it all pretty well.'

'Well, we're together now . . .' She smiled as she fingered the shallow dimple in his chin, still barely able to believe she was here now, by his side on Kinver Edge. 'And there are no more barriers anymore to prevent us from being together.'

He was hers at last. So much had happened to her in the last few weeks – so much good, so much to be thankful for.

'But I think we should still keep quiet about it, don't you?' she suggested. 'I should hate your parents to think I'm getting too big for my boots, getting my claws into their younger son as soon as he's back from university.'

'Do you think so?' he queried.

'I've only just taken this job as your father's secretary. I think it would pay us to be discreet. I don't want to appear to be overstepping the mark. You do see, don't you, Edward? Although your father obviously thinks I'm suitable to be his private secretary, it doesn't mean he thinks I'm suitable as a potential daughter-in-law. I'm just a working-class girl, re-member – one generation away from a chamber maid, because that's what my mother was before she married my dad.'

'I hadn't really considered it, Libby. You know how I feel about such silly prejudices. Yet not everybody does, I realise.' He sighed disappointedly. 'I want to shout about us from the rooftops, but maybe you're right.'

'Well, it's a certain fact that Hugh won't approve.'

'Hugh . . . Cripes, yes. Ages ago he tried to warn me off you. I thought he was rather taking too much for granted at the time.'

'So it might not be all plain sailing, Edward, had it?'

'Bunty will be all right, though. You're her best friend.'

'Yes, Bunty will be fine.'

'Well, I'm prepared to outface the others if you are, if the situation ever crops up. I'll defy any outdated preconceptions some members of my family might have. I promise you that, my love. I take it your folks will be all right?'

'Oh, my mother will adore you, and my dad will hold you in fawning respect just because of who you are. Yes, my folks will be fine. I can just imagine my mother at her sewing circle gossiping and saying, 'Oh, our Libby's done well for herself'.' She chuckled at the thought. 'You must meet them soon, Edward. In the meantime, let's just enjoy what we have . . . Kiss me again . . .'

- - -

It was hard for Libby to gauge the impact that her promotion had had on the girls she worked with. Vera was aware that she had befriended Bunty Burgayne and doubtless believed that that friendship alone had triggered her meteoric rise. Nothing had been said about that, however, so Libby presumed that the girl had kept it to herself. At least Vera, Hilda and the other girls were still pleasant to her face, but what they might be saying behind her back she had no idea. Yet neither did she care. She tried hard to be the same with them as she had always been; friendly, approachable, and always willing to help out in whatever way she thought best.

These thoughts crossed her mind as she worked. But her daydream was disturbed by the ringing of the desk telephone.

'Miss Burgayne for you, Miss Shakespeare,' the telephonist announced.

The customary clicks and crackles ensued.

'Bunty!'

'Libby. You dark horse. Edward's been telling me everything. You never said, but it's official now, eh?'

'Except that we're keeping it from the rest of your family. Only you know – for now at any rate. You don't mind, do you, Bunty?'

'Mind? About you and Edward, you mean?'

'Yes.'

'Golly, no. Why should I mind? I'm delighted. I think you two are an ideal match.'

'Thank you, Bunty. I just hope the rest of your family think so.'

'Well, as you say, keep it under your hat for now. Listen, we want to make up a four for tennis before dinner. Edward says he hasn't arranged to see you tonight, so can you come? We'll be eating quite late, Mother says.'

'I could, but your father's not here to take me. He's out this afternoon . . . And I'd really rather not ask Hugh. If he thinks Edward and I . . .'

'Understandable. So book a taxi and charge it to the firm. Legitimate expenses. That's what Miss Evans used to do.'

'Why? Did she play tennis at Buttonbridge Hall too?'

'No, you goose!' Bunty chuckled. 'Lord, that would be a sight to behold, Edith Evans bouncing about in a short tennis frock.'

'Which reminds me, I'll have to fetch my tennis things from home first.'

'So use the taxi,' Bunty instructed. 'Edward will take you home afterwards. I daresay he'll want his kiss and cuddle.'

Libby laughed. 'I'll want mine, too.'

'I should hope you would.'

'So shall I be staying for dinner, Bunty?' Libby was almost afraid to ask for confirmation.

'Naturally.'

'Then I'll need something decent to change into.'

'Book the taxi for four o' clock, Libby, so you can leave work early. Try and get here before five. If Father's away he'll be none the wiser.'

- - -

At Buttonbridge Hall Edward greeted Libby with only affable politeness like he would any other house guest, but she knew it was to avoid arousing any suspicions. Yet out of sight of prying eyes he put his arm around her, hugged and kissed her affectionately.

The couple played tennis with Bunty and Adrian till about half past six, then they returned to the house, showered, and changed before going down to dinner. Showering was for Libby an exotic change from the tin bath on the hearth, or a thorough wash down at the stone sink in the brewhouse.

'Drinks outside on the lawn,' Dorothy Burgayne announced to Bunty and Libby as they reached the bottom stair together wearing light cotton dresses. 'It's such a beautiful evening.'

A table and seven folding wooden chairs had been set randomly on the lawn, which was dappled with wavering shafts of sunlight that pierced the foliage of the high trees. Charles had returned from his business trip meanwhile, and the men folk joined them.

This is very civilised, Libby thought, sipping sherry.

Taking Bunty's lead, she sat down and crossed her legs, dangling a sandal from her foot while Edward focused on the nail varnish neatly applied to her toenails, and Hugh admired her well-turned ankle and sensuous curve of her calf.

Talk was about the international crisis, while Dorothy tried vainly to steer it towards plans for the next garden party in August.

'If we're not already at war by then,' Hugh commented.

'Oh, nobody wants a war,' Libby said, glancing at Edward and thinking how traumatically it would affect their new relationship.

'Of course,' Charles agreed, 'but if and when it comes we must be prepared to fight.'

'I'll not fight, Father,' exclaimed Hugh. 'I'm a pacifist at heart. I shall register as a conscientious objector.'

'You mightn't need to,' his father replied sharply, obviously unimpressed by his older son's declared conviction. 'As a director of a steelworks you might find yourself in a reserved occupation anyway.' He coughed violently and went red in the face before he continued, everybody watching anxiously. 'Damn this cough . . . But I must say, Hugh,' he spluttered, 'I dislike and mistrust this creed of not being willing to fight for your country on grounds of pacifism. We could all adopt that silly attitude, then where would we be? It smacks of cowardice to me, my boy, especially when your younger brother is so obviously prepared to give his all, training for the RAF.'

'Edward's willingness to fight is Edward's business, father. It doesn't mean I have to be the same. Nor should you try to make me feel ashamed. I see nothing honourable or commendable in one human being slaughtering another in the name of patriotism.'

'I think you mean in the name of freedom and fairness, Hugh, because we do not want to be in the thrall, or under the control of Hitler and his National Socialist German Workers' Party. Besides, if we all felt the same as you, Hitler would invade us and marvel at our woeful lack of resistance, when after all, his obnoxious Nazi fascism is actually based on a fervent belief in belligerent patriotism.'

'I can't understand why all these countries who follow Hitler are so much against the poor Jews,' Libby remarked, changing tack. 'The way they treat them – even harming women and babies – is criminal by the standards of any civilised society. Can somebody explain it to me, please?'

'I believe it stems from a conviction that the Jews caused the death of, or in no way defended, Jesus Christ, who was himself a Jew, of course.'

'I wondered that,' Libby remarked. 'But that's madness. After all, those poor Jews in Germany and Austria and Italy are not responsible for what happened nearly two thousand years ago, are they? It's appalling. And I'm amazed that—' She was about to declare her amazement that Hugh would never offer himself to fight against such monstrous barbarism, but checked herself. Expressing such an opinion here would do her no good at all.

'I really do wish we could change the subject,' Dorothy interjected, trying once more to divert them. 'It's all too depressing. Let's talk about holidays instead. Do you intend to go to the seaside this summer, Libby?'

Libby glanced again at Edward. 'No, not this year, Mrs Burgayne. I'll just stay at home and maybe go out for daytrips, providing the weather holds.'

'And do you intend to go to France with the Birches this summer, Hugh?'

'I think not, Mother, even if they decide to go, and odds are they won't, because of the way things are shaping up on the Continent.'

'Look, I think dinner's ready,' Dorothy said, espying Jenkins. 'Shall we go in?'

- - -

Libby was thankful when dinner broke up. Hugh had been sitting opposite her, and she had sensed his eyes on her throughout, making her feel self-conscious.

Since the evening remained fine, Dorothy suggested they all take a stroll through the garden. It would do Charles's chest good too to get in the fresh, warm air. They could take coffee later. Nobody was inclined to refuse, and Bunty attached herself to Adrian, also a dinner guest, taking his arm devotedly as they strolled in a fragmented group.

Libby found herself behind them in a foursome that included Dorothy, Charles and Hugh, listening to Dorothy and Charles as they discussed this or that aspect of the garden.

Then Hugh, breaking free, lingered at a clutch of red-hot pokers, purporting to admire their vivid colours, but clearly intending to detain Libby. He said: 'Have you ever seen the fish pool?'

'No,' Libby replied. 'I didn't even know there was a fish pool.'

'Come with me. I'll show you.'

She looked for Edward, whose company she needed right then, but he was strolling way ahead, in conversation with Bunty and Adrian and oblivious to her plight. She wanted to call him, but how could she utter a cry for help without drawing attention to their relationship?

Hugh led her through a gap in an ancient grey stone wall where she imagined a gate must have existed long ago. On the other side of it, was a large ornamental pool surrounded by a well-tended lawn, and flower beds thick with blooms. Strange that she had never seen this part of the garden before.

To her great surprise and disappointment his hand reached for hers. She was shocked, but made no attempt to take it back and reproach him for it, not really sure what she should do.

'I need to talk to you, Libby. You see, I have a confession to make . . .' He stopped and looked at her, still holding her hand. 'I find I have feelings for you that simply won't go away.'

Oh, God. Of all the stupid idiots. How should I respond to this nonsense? What should I say? She averted her eyes, looking somewhat guiltily at the grass beneath her sandaled feet, biting her bottom lip in her angst.

'I understand how this might come as rather a shock to you, Libby, but I can't go on without letting you know how strong my feelings for you are. I hope you might give some thought to what I have to say and favour me with a positive response.' He regarded her steadily.

She heaved a deep sigh of anxiety. 'I don't see how I can,' she answered, picking her words carefully. 'You're engaged to Laura after all.'

'I'm not in love with Laura. So there seems little point in continuing the relationship. It only remains for me to make the break.'

She let go his hand and turned away from him. Somehow she had to stop this foolishness. *God, if he knew about Edward and me.*

'But I couldn't let myself be the cause of any unhappiness for Laura, Hugh. I like her too much for that. I've got to know her a little since I've been coming here as Bunty's friend.'

'Is Laura the only obstacle?'

'No . . . Not really.' She frowned, in two minds whether to confess there and then about Edward, and get it into the open. But to name him presented too many difficulties yet, and she struggled to find a plausible excuse. 'The thing is, Hugh . . . Something as serious as you're suggesting needs the assent of both people. It would be a bit one-sided, you see . . .'

'You mean because you don't feel the same for me?'

'Exactly . . . Oh, I'm very flattered, Hugh, don't misunderstand me. But I don't think I—In fact I'm sure I couldn't—'

'Return the affection?' he prompted.

'Yes, that's just what I was trying to say.' She frowned again as she looked candidly into his eyes.

'But I overheard Bunty say you're no longer involved with that chap you used to see.'

'That's true. But I'm involved with somebody else now . . . And I'm very fond of him . . . It's quite serious, actually . . .' She looked at her feet again, unable to give him the satisfaction of engaging his eyes. 'Actually, Hugh, I find this very embarrassing . . .'

'I see . . . Then I apologise.'

'I'm sure your feelings will change.'

'Oh, don't worry, Libby, I'll try and keep them under control . . . although I can't promise.'

For the first time she noticed the fish in the pool; large and golden and lethargically graceful as they slipped silent and untroubled between lily pads and reeds.

'I think we should get back to the others,' she suggested.

'In a moment.'

'If you'll allow me to be perfectly frank, Hugh,' she said, feeling herself becoming bolder, more able to handle this situation. Now was perhaps a good time to tell him what she really thought. 'I'm a bit taken aback. Especially after you'd given me cause to think I wasn't good enough even to visit Buttonbridge Hall, being only a servant of the company and coming from a working-class family.' There was nothing like the feeling of throwing something distasteful back in the face of the person who'd conceived it.

'Good God, if I gave you that impression, Libby, I can only apologise. It certainly is not the case.'

'Well, you did give me the distinct impression that it was, yet now you're confessing feelings for me.' Her voice was low, but her temperature was rising. Now was not the time to mince her words. She had the protection of his father these days, as his private secretary, as well as the potent friendship of Bunty and Edward. Besides, she disliked intensely his claim that he was a pacifist and would not fight in a war, when her beloved Edward, his own brother, was obviously prepared to die for his country.

'Maybe you misunderstood me, Libby.'

'Maybe I did, Hugh, maybe I didn't. But I really don't think I did. In any case I think it would be unworkable. In the office tomorrow you'll be Mr Burgayne, and I'll be Miss Shakespeare.'

'And ne'er the twain shall meet. Is that what you think?'

'Master and servant. I think that sums it up.'

She heard a voice call, 'Oh, there you are.' It was Edward.

She turned, smiled with relief and headed towards him, never before in her life so glad to see somebody. 'Hugh was just showing me the goldfish pond.'

'Lovely, isn't it? Have you seen Big George? He's a real whopper. You can't miss him.'

'I'm not sure.'

'Never mind. Some other time . . . Hugh, I'm going to steal Libby from you. We're off to the pub with Bunty and Adrian. Fancy coming along?'

'No, no,' Hugh responded, deflated. 'I'll have an early night.'

Hugh watched Edward and Libby walk away, and noticed how very much at ease this utterly desirable girl seemed with his younger brother. He was envious of how they smiled at each other and laughed with such obvious mutual affection, and found it difficult to subdue his jealousy. Was something going on there now that Edward had finished university? Was Edward the latest beau in her life, the man she'd referred to? Was Edward the lucky chap she claimed she was serious about?

- - -

| 12 |

The mood at the Burgaynes' garden party, held on 26th August in 1939, was noticeably more sombre than usual. The usual guests, as well as some new faces, trooped about in their summer finery with smiles on their faces. But conversations were generally confined to the imminence of war; Germany was banging on Poland's door demanding to be let in so that the Fatherland could reclaim its colonies there, yet audaciously requesting France and Britain to drop their pledge to defend the very neighbour it was bent on invading. But Britain was always honourable about upholding its treaties, and there would be no reneging. So serious was the threat of war by this time that all national treasures had been taken from museums and art galleries, and moved to safe storage. The Prime Minister had been granted wide-ranging war powers, in Poland and France army reservists were being called up. Life was about to be seriously disrupted, that much was clear, yet everybody accepted it with resignation.

That afternoon Libby and Edward had a deep desire to be alone.

'Why don't you take me to the fishpond to see if Big George is around,' she suggested.

Casual visitors were excluded from the fishpond. Because the family regarded it as somewhere to be kept private, Libby realised why she had never even known it existed until Hugh had whisked her behind the surrounding high wall to confess his feelings for her, out of sight and earshot of the others. Being there now reminded her of that unfortunate encounter. She had said nothing of the incident to Edward, not wishing to cause dissention between the two brothers. Yet in the quiet serenity of the place she thought with hindsight how churlish she must have seemed to Hugh. That night she loathed him for appearing to be a coward, adding to the resentment she still harboured over his previous implication that she was unworthy of being a visitor to Buttonbridge Hall – until it obviously suited him otherwise. Well, she had let him know how she felt – that she was not interested in him – as politely as she knew how. He had been decidedly cooler towards her since. For all his newly contrived reserve, however, she still felt his eyes upon her from time to time, looking her up and down.

'We haven't had two months together yet, and already I'm going to lose you,' Libby complained, as they sat on the low wall surrounding the pool, their arms about each other. 'I'm so scared of what might happen.'

'I'm scared too,' Edward whispered. 'Not of fighting the Germans particularly, but of being away from you.'

'It's the not-knowing, the uncertainty of it all. God, I shall miss you, not knowing how long it'll be before I see you again.'

He hugged her tighter. He had no other comfort for her.

'You'll be kept busy at the works, my love. With any luck you'll be too busy to dwell on thoughts of me.'

'You are joking, aren't you? I'm thinking of you every waking hour as it is, and you haven't gone away yet. I won't know where you are, what you're doing . . . What makes it worse is you'll be flying a plane. You'll be a prime target.'

'I might be a prime target, but I've got the biggest and best incentive in the world to get through it unscathed . . . You.'

She turned her face to him and he kissed her, a deliciously long kiss. When they broke off, she sighed, 'Oh, I do love you so much, Edward.'

– – –

During the morning of the following Friday, the first day of September, Libby was in her office. Ethel, the tea lady, had tarried to chat with her, as she did most mornings while she did her rounds with a tea urn atop a squeaking trolley.

'I'm gasping for this cup of tea,' Libby declared, and took a sip from her cup.

'How's his nibs today?'

'Mr Charles? Not too good, I think, Ethel. He's worried about what's going to happen. And when he's worried his cough always seems worse.'

'He's had that cough years. You'd think he'd get it seen to.'

'I don't think there's much they can do, to tell you the truth, Ethel. He's always been prone to bronchitis, from what I can gather.'

'He's a bit as'matical, I grant yer, is Mr Charles. I've always reckoned as much. But we all worry about what's happening with that swine Hitler. I wish I could get my hands on him, I'd murder the bugger.'

'Wouldn't we all? But I think Mr Charles is worrying about his son Edward. He's a trained pilot and he'll be in the forefront of any action with the RAF. He's bound to worry.' She sighed heavily. Charles Burgayne was not the only person worrying about Edward.

'There's a good many'll be worrying about their own. I remember the last lot, young Libby. You'd think they'd have more sense than start that softness all over again. Hundreds of thousands killed there was. No family escaped the grief of losing somebody. It'll be no different this time.'

That's all I needed to hear. Libby sighed again. Welling up inside her was the urge to weep, but she managed to quell it. Her eyes, however, glistened with the tears she was desperately pushing back.

'D'you know a lad, then, what'll be going?' Ethel asked, perceiving Libby's anxiety.

She nodded and, conceding defeat to the battle of the tears, took a small handkerchief from the handbag resting in an open drawer, and dabbed her eyes.

'Then may the Lord preserve him for you, my flower,' the tea lady said kindly.

'Thank you, Ethel. But it'll all be such a worry, such an upheaval.'

'Then make the most of him while you've got him, that's my advice. Make the most of him, you know what I mean?' She gave Libby a look that spoke volumes. 'Life's too short anyway, without the worry of war.'

Libby nodded and blew her nose. 'Yes, Ethel, I think you're right.'

'I know I'm right, young Libby. I lost the love of my life in the Great War. So cherish yourn while you've got him.'

As Ethel opened the door to return to the trolley she had left in the corridor outside, Libby's telephone rang. It was Edward.

'My sweetheart,' he greeted. He sounded down.

'Hello, love.'

'Just thought I'd better let you know – I got my call-up papers this morning.'

'Oh, no,' she sighed, and her heart sank, suddenly beating wildly at the prospect of losing him so soon.

'I have to travel to Cambridge tomorrow to join the RAF Volunteer Reserve. They even sent me a travel warrant.'

'So soon?' she groaned. 'War hasn't even been declared yet.'

'Not yet, my angel, but it's only a formality. Give it a couple more days at most. I just heard on the wireless that German troops invaded Poland at quarter to six this morning.'

'So it's begun,' she breathed. 'Oh, Edward, what are we going to do?'

'Well, if you're willing, I'm going to call for you tonight, and I'm going to lose myself in your arms while I still have the chance. Does that sound agreeable to you?'

'Most agreeable, but it won't last long enough. That's the trouble.'

'I'll pick you up about half past seven.'

'I'll be ready . . . By the way, do you want me to tell your father that you've received your call-up papers?'

'Better not, Sweetheart. It's best if I tell him myself when he gets home later.'

- - -

'How've your mother and father taken the news?' Libby asked as she sat beside him in the MG.

'Badly,' he replied sombrely. 'You could see father's colour drain away as I told him. Somehow, I think he blames himself – for encouraging me to fly, I mean – not least for buying me the Gypsy Moth in the first place.'

'He should be proud of you,' she said, sensing that the ambience between them needed brightening. 'I'm proud of you anyway.'

'I think he is quite proud of me really. He's just apprehensive.'

'Has Hugh said anything else about registering as a conshi?'

'Conshi' was a colloquialism creeping into everyday speech, an acronym for 'conscientious objector'. It carried overtones of scorn.

'He's said nothing to me at any rate.'

'He ought to be ashamed,' she said bluntly.

'I doubt whether he is. It's based on what he believes.'

'I think it's based on what it suits him to believe. He only ever thinks of himself, Edward. I don't think I ever met a more self-centred person.'

'You really don't like him, do you?'

'Not very much.'

'Why? What's he ever done to you?'

'Oh, nothing . . .'

They remained unspeaking for a while as they drove through country lanes towards Enville Common, the only place they knew where they could be really, truly alone. It was a vast expanse of common land clad in abundant bracken and fern, and dotted with silver birch trees. Devoid of people, it was an ideal spot for spooning under the stars if you had the means to get there.

'Are you all right?' Edward asked after too long a silence, on this night when no time should be lost on petty prejudices.

She smiled her reassurance. 'Yes, course I'm all right.'

Edward drove the car over some rough ground as they left the lane, towards a spot they'd visited once before. Some way in, surrounded by trees, he stopped the car and switched off the engine.

'I need a kiss, desperately.'

'No more than me.' She sighed, turned her face towards him, leant into him, and they kissed.

The unsettling events that day had heightened the emotions of both, and prompted heady thoughts of highly charged romance that night, the last night for heaven knew how long – possibly for ever.

'Tell me you love me, Libby,' he whispered. 'I need to hear you say it.'

'You know I love you, Edward. With all my heart and soul I do.'

He hugged her, nuzzling her hair. 'And I love you. More than I ever thought possible. Hell, I'm going to miss you.'

She began to feel a warm stirring within her and snuggled up to him. Again he kissed her softly on the lips. Eagerly, she responded, and her anxiety eased with every second of that embrace.

Then he broke off to reach for the blanket stashed behind his seat.

'Let's lie in the grass, eh?'

He clambered out of the car in the greyness of dusk, and spread the blanket on a patch of grass hidden by dense ferns.

She was shutting the car door when he scooped her up into his arms and laid her gently on the bed he had made, as if it were fit for a bride. She offered no resistance; there was no resistance left in her, there was no point in resistance; this was not Ron; this was Edward whom she adored, and they were deeply in love. As he lay beside her, she turned her face to him, smiled conspiratorially and held him close. She closed her eyes and felt his lips caressing her smooth eyelids with the lightness of a butterfly. His mouth found hers and she tasted him again with tantalising pleasure, running her fingers through his hair in an ecstasy of bliss at her absolute love for him.

In the twilight her love shone unmistakably through her clear, earnest eyes, and he kissed her again. Her lips felt so good. It would be forever impossible to have a surfeit of her kisses. He could happily kiss her till eternity.

After a while they broke off their kissing and his lips first brushed her throat and her neck, as light as the touch of a feather, then lingered at her ear. As she felt his warm breath she experienced sensations up and down her spine that she could not control. She could feel him pressing against her, urgently, and her heart was beating faster at the pleasure of it all. They kissed more, savouring each other's lips and his knee slid evocatively between her thighs. The feel of him pressing against her heightened her own desire.

Ethel's words came flooding into her mind.

It was time. There was no more time to waste. There might never be another occasion. He was going to war; he might never return.

As if reading her mind, and without further hesitation, Edward unfastened the buttons at the front of her dress.

'Wait, love,' she whispered. 'Let me take it off.'

She sat up and took off her dress, then her brassiere. He looked in awe at the tantalising curves of her breasts, the sensuous indentation of her navel and the contour of her belly as she undid and pushed down her underskirt. Soon, she was kneeling before him naked except for her white knickers, her slender body pale but exquisitely beautiful in the insipid, failing light.

He sat up to remove his jacket and his shirt. He pulled off his boots, then his trousers and his underpants. She watched him strip off till he was naked and saw that he was aroused.

Lust, simple and shameless – and entirely new to her – was increasing inexorably within her, as was the potent urge to flout straight-laced convention.

They lay beside each other. Her skin was chilled by the evening breeze soughing across the common, but she paid it no heed. He rolled onto her, kissing her on the mouth once more, one hand cupping a firm and incredibly smooth, virgin breast. He kissed her again. As she felt the pressure of his warm naked body, his chest against her compressed breasts, she sniffed his skin, breathing in her own ardent desire that seemed unquenchable.

'At university, when I was trying to get to sleep at night, I used to kiss your breasts . . . Naturally, such thoughts kept me wide awake.'

She hugged him, smiling to herself. His hands, so smooth, so caring, were gently fondling her, and it was such magical pleasure. As she felt his mouth on hers again she was all too aware just how desperately she needed this fast-flowing tide of passion.

His mouth skimmed her breasts delectably, his tongue teasing her nipples till she thought they would burst. He hooked his fingers behind the elastic of her knickers, and she raised her bottom to ease their removal. As he slid them down her slender legs he ran his lips tormentingly over the gentle curve of her belly, lingering where her delta of soft dark hair began.

There could be no turning back now.

'Oh, Sweetheart,' he breathed again, as if she had no other name. He was crouching on his knees as he looked at her longingly in the fast-fading light, and ran his fingers lightly between her thighs till they settled at the mystical triangle that had been the focus of so many of his erotic fantasies. She was so warm there, so soft, so deliciously moist and inviting, and she parted her legs a little to make herself more accessible.

She sighed, paralysed and astounded with pleasure and anticipation, lying sprawled, naked under the emerging stars of a clear evening sky. He lay down beside her, his fingers gently caressing her, his lips brushing over her body, exploring, lingering at her breasts. She was intoxicated, aching for him to enter her. Never could she have imagined anything like this even in her wildest, most sensual dreams. Never could she have envisaged such willing, enthusiastic submission as he shifted onto her and pushed against her wet softness for entry.

'Oh, Edward,' she sighed with longing. He entered her and she recoiled slightly. 'Oh, Edward,' she whispered again, trembling a little but trying to control it.

He drew back at once. 'Have I hurt you?'

'Hardly at all.'

He kissed her closed eyelids, her soft, round cheeks and her neck. He was so gentle, so afraid of hurting her, but each sharp twinge that accompanied each tender, tentative push was a delight, and she raised her legs to accommodate him the more as he probed deeper, deeper into her. The pangs were numbed in direct proportion to the pleasure, which increased with each gratifying, careful stroke, and they soon found themselves intertwined in a steady rhythm that was becoming more pronounced the longer they were joined. Her breathing came in short gasps as she gripped his buttocks, pulling him into her, rubbing herself more firmly against him. The pleasure intensified, until all knowledge, all sense of who or where she was, was of no importance.

In those precious, unforgettable moments she was conscious only of Edward and this strange, ethereal sensation rising in the pit of her stomach which she was consciously willing to a greater intensity. Her world was him. His quickening breath combined with hers, their hearts pounded together as one. She hugged him ardently in a fervour of passion. He groaned . . . and sighed . . . and eventually ceased to move . . . She was weeping as she cleaved to him, tears of relief that she finally had a reason to give herself entirely, because she was utterly, mesmerizingly in love.

Tomorrow he would go away and the waiting to be with him again would be intolerable, painful. He would come home on leave and they would make love like this again; but afterwards there would be only more anxious waiting. This was the way it would be from now on. This was the future. It was also the present and, for now, she wanted time to stand still, to exist only in this moment. She wanted this wonderful feeling of peace, which emanated from the very centre of her body and seemed to spread up into her head, to last till eternity.

He felt her tears wet against his cheek. 'Sweetheart, you're crying.'

She hugged him. 'Tears of happiness . . . But tears of sadness, as well . . . because soon we shall be apart again.'

'I know,' he said, with intense feeling.

He rolled off her and she felt moist with perspiration where he had lain on her, a little tender where he had been, but content. Oh, utterly content.

They lay silent. All she wanted was to sleep in his arms, to awaken with him at dawn and smile into his soft eyes . . . and perhaps make love again. Within her was a growing awareness of the enormity, the significance of what they had done, a growing awareness of the deeply satisfying heights of ecstasy they had scaled. There was no sense of shame, no guilt, no regret. It was done and there was no turning back. If only she could be sure there would be a next time.

- - -

| **13** |

4th September 1939

My own darling Libby,

I do so wish you had been able to see me off at the station on Saturday. It was all well and good my father and Bunty taking me, despatching me with their peculiar brand of bonhomie, when the one person I really wanted was you, and you couldn't be there. I am so looking forward to the day when we can be candid and open about our love, and I feel certain it will not be too long. People more privileged than me are going to face the common enemy cheek by jowl with others from what has hitherto been regarded as the "working class", so if nothing else, this war will drive home the message that we are all the same, all God's children, no matter what superficial stations in life we occupy.

Well, when I arrived at Cambridge a whole host of chaps like me were assembling at the station and we were marched en masse to where we were being billeted. We have since learnt that before we are allowed anywhere near an aero-plane we are to go through a period of parade ground drill, marching up and down till we can keep in perfect step. I can think of nothing more pointless or soul-destroying, but I sup-pose it's all about discipline. Lord knows how long it will go on, but now I'm here I'm itching to fly. At least marching al-lows me one luxury though – thinking about you relatively uninterrupted.

In truth, I cannot get you off my mind, my love, nor our wonderful evening last Friday. I relive it constantly, hardly able to believe that something so terrifyingly beautiful hap-pened to me. I long to be with you again. It was really quite the nicest goodbye imaginable! When I go to my bunk at night I allow myself to wallow in thoughts of what might be if the future is kind to us. Of course, it's all pie-in-the-sky at present, because nobody can reasonably make plans, but I have a dream, a vivid dream of the future with you, my dar-ling, and I intend to hold on to it. It will see me through all this madness.

Please write to me soon, my own sweet love, at the address above for now. When the square-bashing is over we'll be posted elsewhere.

I love you, and will always love you,
Edward.

- - -

Tuesday 5th Sept

My dearest darling Edward,

I was so relieved to get your letter. I am thinking about you constantly. I hope and pray this war will all be over by the time your training is finished so that you'll be able to come home to me unscathed.

I spoke to Bunty yesterday to ask if they'd heard from you, but she reckoned I was sure to be the first. It's just that I thought you might have telephoned them to say you'd arrived OK. Anyway, Adrian has decided he's going to join up and was due to go to a recruitment centre yesterday. So far I don't know whether he has. Bunty says the army is his preference.

Already a blackout has been imposed, and you daren't even smoke a cigarette outdoors lest the glow be seen by the Luftwaffe who might be overhead. Everywhere is as black as coal, and my dad said he could hardly find his way up the back yard to our privy last night, to which my mother's beautifully logical reply was that he'd best go before it gets dark in future. You have to laugh. They send their love, by the way.

You will notice that I have written this letter by hand, not on my typewriter. I always think a type-written letter is impersonal and I'm sure you would much rather get a handwritten one. I'm writing it in my dinner break, still at my desk.

I'm a little concerned about your father, Edward. He is terribly worried about you and it seems to be affecting him badly. He is normally quite jovial, but he is in a very sombre mood and looking quite pale. I don't wish to worry you with this, you have enough on your mind, but I think it's only fair you should know. To his credit, Hugh has taken over some of his work for a few days, and no doubt I shall be asked to do my share of the extra secretarial work he generates. I think it would be sensible if your father took a week or two off work before winter sets in. Perhaps you could suggest it in your next letter home.

I am ending this letter with a kiss. A real one, an imprint in lipstick of my lips at the foot of the page, so you can kiss me by proxy, knowing my lips have been there too. It's the nearest we shall get to the proper thing till you come home on leave.

Please write back at once, my darling. I need you and love you always.

Your very own Libby.

- - -

'Libby, I've decided to spend more time working from home,' Charles Burgayne said one day as she was poring over some files in his office. 'I'm rather aware that this chest of mine is not best served in the atmosphere that prevails around the works. I can benefit from the fresher, rural air of Buttonbridge Hall three or four days a week.'

'I think that's very sensible, Mr Burgayne.'

'Either Hugh or you yourself can bring me any correspondence, production reports, sales figures, et cetera, which need my attention. So, if you don't mind, you'll find it necessary to spend more time working with me at Buttonbridge Hall. Besides, there'll be a lot going on as regards the family now we're at war, and my wife will appreciate having somebody who can help her with her own correspondence and also help organising things. How do you feel about that?'

She turned to him and smiled. It was considerate of him to ask whether she minded, but that was typical of the man. 'I really don't mind at all, Mr Burgayne. Whatever is best for you. I agree with you about your chest and the atmosphere around here though.'

'Splendid. Arrange with the taxi firm to collect you from home those mornings you're needed at Buttonbridge Hall, and to deliver you back in the evenings. I'll have one of the unused bedrooms converted right away into an office for you, and we'll try and get a telephone extension installed as quick as the GPO can manage it. Order yourself a new typewriter and have it delivered there too – there's no point lugging the other one around with you – and arrange for a supply of stationery and postage stamps.'

So Libby became a working fixture at Buttonbridge Hall. Cups of tea were on tap, she was amply fed and from time to time enjoyed the welcome intrusions of Bunty and Dorothy for chats. The work was not entirely Blowers Green Steel-works business, although steelmaking was thriving owing to the war effort, so the amount of work she had to get through grew accordingly, and it all kept her busy. Charles was a hard taskmaster, but he was extraordinarily fair and considerate, and always impeccably polite and pleasant. She was perfectly happy doing what she was doing.

To Bunty's anguish, Adrian had joined The Staffordshires and had begun his training, so she decided that her own time could be usefully employed joining the Women's Royal Voluntary Service, ready for when things began to 'hot-up'.

- - -

Dorothy deemed it necessary that the family do their bit for the war effort. Between them all, they agreed to make parts of Buttonbridge Hall available as a sanatorium for the recuperation of injured servicemen, and Libby became involved in its organisation. The ancient house was duly inspected by the Red Cross and judged suitable. Together they repurposed and prepared downstairs rooms, and brought in and arranged beds, bedding and the other necessary paraphernalia in readiness for the influx of wounded servicemen. It was amazing how rapidly those domestic rooms began to resemble hospital wards.

- - -

One day in the middle of October when Libby was working at Buttonbridge Hall the telephone rang. She waited for a member of the family to answer it, since it would most likely be a private call, but it seemed to ring for ages. So, she answered it using the newly installed extension in her office.

'Buttonbridge Hall.'

'Hello. Is that you, Libby?' the voice at the other end enquired.

She recognised Edward's voice straight away and her heart leapt.

'Yes, Edward! It's me.'

'Sweetheart! Great Scott! I never expected to be speaking to you. How are you?'

'Missing you – a lot.'

'I'm missing you too, Sweetheart. Terribly. God, I'd give anything to be with you right now. Working for the old man at the house today, are you?'

'Yes. There's lots we can do from here. How's the square-bashing?'

'Absurdly tedious. Did you get my letter today?'

'Yes. You sounded really fed-up.'

'I am fed-up. Horribly. It seems such a waste of time marching up and down a parade ground when I could be doing something useful, like patrolling the skies.'

'I'm sure it won't be long now,' she remarked in consolation, even though she would prefer, for her own peace of mind, that he remain marching on the parade ground.

'We won't be allowed in combat anyway for some time, so you needn't worry,' he said reading her thoughts. 'We have to train in aerobatics, navigation, night flying and gunnery – all sorts of stuff – before we're let loose on an unsuspecting enemy.'

'By which time the war might be over.'

'That I doubt,' he replied darkly. 'The Germans will take some beating, believe me. From what we've heard here, it seems there will be little trench warfare in this war. You only have to look at the speed and efficiency with which they rolled into Poland. "Blitzkrieg", they're calling it – lightning war. Before their army moved in the Luftwaffe knocked out the railways and shot the Polish air force out of the sky. You have to hand it to them.'

'You're scaring me, Edward.'

'Oh, please don't worry, my love. Rest assured we'll be a different kettle of fish. They won't find us such a walk-over.'

The operator interrupted them to let him know he needed to put more money in the slot if he wanted to continue the conversation, and he replied politely that he only had six pennies. He fed them into the public telephone's coin mechanism, and she could hear the clatters as they fell.

'Who did you want to speak to, Darling?' she asked, remember-ing he had not expected to speak to her. 'Not that I want to let go of you yet of course.'

'Oh, anybody. Mother, Father, Bunty. But you'll do nicely,' he said warmly. 'Will you tell them I rang and that I'm all right?'

'Course I will. Shall you ring again?'

'Yes if I get the chance, but there's no guarantee I'll be able to speak to you, is there, my love?'

'Unfortunately not, but I'm sure your mother is going to be all right about things. We get on very well.'

'Great. I'm pleased. Anyway, I'll write again tomorrow and let you know the latest in parade ground politics. My last coppers are running out, Sweetheart. Look after yourself.'

The phone line went dead and, feeling both sad and uplifted, Libby rested the handset back in its cradle just as Dorothy Burgayne opened the door.

'Oh, Mrs Burgayne . . . That was Edward on the line. You just missed him.'

'Edward? Is he all right?'

'He sounds fine. He's just bored with all the drill they have to do, but he's in good health, I think.'

'You had a good long chat with him?'

'Not long enough really,' Libby answered truthfully. 'He was speaking from a public call box and his money ran out. But it was lovely to speak to him all the same.'

'I wish I could have spoken to him, Libby.' Libby felt her colour rise. 'You should have called me. I was only in the hallway.'

Then why didn't you answer the phone? 'Next time I'll be sure to, Mrs Burgayne.'

- - -

12th November 1939

My very own little darling,

Just a quick note to say I arrived at the RAF College Cran-
well about lunchtime, and I want to let you know my new ad-
dress. Please write to me here from now on.

It looks as though we'll be here about four months, but at
least we'll actually be flying. I might even be lucky and be al-
lowed a spot of leave soon. Even 48 hours would be brilliant,
so fingers crossed.

Will write again tomorrow.
My love always,
Edward.

Edward was indeed granted leave some weeks later, and on
Christmas Eve Bunty was about to collect him from Wolverhampton.

'I say, Libby, I bet you'd like to come with me.' Bunty suggested, knowing how much it would mean to her friend. 'Do
you have a huge amount of work to do for the old man?'

'Not much at all right now, but I can't just go without his
permission.'

'Leave it to me.'

Bunty left Libby and returned, beaming, a few minutes
later.

'You're coming.'

Libby grinned happily. 'How on earth did you manage
that?'

'Oh, I merely told Dad I wasn't sure where the station was,' she answered dismissively. 'I told him you knew, so was it all right if you went with me? He said yes, of course. Simple.'

'You're an angel, Bunty. Gosh, I'm so looking forward to seeing Edward again. But I'm so nervous.'

Christmas Eve was cold and damp, and the two girls were wrapped in their overcoats, hats, scarves and mittens as they climbed into the Riley. Libby was trembling more from anticipation than the chilly weather at the prospect of seeing Edward again, after nearly four months away.

'It's a frightful pity Adrian can't be home for Christmas too,' Bunty commented miserably as she drove through grey country lanes. 'God, I miss him.'

'I know,' Libby replied, aware of exactly how her friend was feeling. 'Have you heard from him today?'

'Yes, I got his usual letter this morning. He says there's not much happening in his part of France. I must say, Libby, it's a funny old sort of war when the only fighting is being done by the Navy at sea and the Finns on their border with Russia.'

'We should be grateful,' Libby said. 'At least it's keeping our boys safe.'

'But how long will it last? We all thought we would have been bombed out of existence by now, but there's been nothing.'

'Let's count our blessings.'

- - -

As soon as Libby saw Edward step down from the train in his RAF uniform her legs began to feel wobbly and her heart pounded. He was an icon of military fitness; leaner, fitter, taller, broader as he looked about him with a confidence that had not been apparent before. He was no longer the dewy-eyed, curly-topped university student she had fallen in love with, but a more masculine, more rugged-looking man and oh, so much more desirable. The locomotive that had hauled him home hissed and roared as she eagerly weaved her way towards him through the mass of folk spilling onto the platform. As soon as he saw her he dropped his suitcase.

'Edward . . .' She ran into his arms and pressed her head into his chest, tears of joy misting her eyes, then she looked up at him. 'Thank God you're home again.'

'If only for a little while.' He took her chin gently, lifted her face and kissed her on the lips. 'My, you don't know how good that feels.'

'Oh, yes I do,' she said with feeling. As she beamed up at him she saw the bright gleam in his eyes, a look of greater worldliness and authority. He picked up his bag, put his arm around her waist and ushered her towards the exit.

'Is Bunty with you?'

'Yes, she drove here. There she is.' Bunty was waving wildly, happily. 'You're much leaner, Edward,' Libby said as they approached her. 'I think I fancy you even more.'

He laughed. 'And look at you.' He gave a succession of hugs around her waist, assessing her trimness. 'You can't say that you've gained weight either, while I've been away.'

'It's the food shortages,' she said, smiling contentedly, for she was aware that her figure was sleeker now, a sleekness she was content with. 'Nobody will get fat in this war the way the Germans keep sinking our merchant ships.'

He greeted his sister affectionately. 'Thanks for bringing Libby with you, Bunty.'

'You don't think I'd leave her languishing any longer than necessary, do you?' she replied.

- - -

Later that afternoon, Libby presented herself at Charles Burgayne's study and tapped gently on the open door. He turned to look.

'Ah, Libby.'

'If there's nothing else this afternoon, Mr Burgayne, do you mind if I go home now?'

'That's fine, my dear,' he answered kindly. 'Is the taxi here?'

'No, but Edward very kindly offered to drive me home, so I cancelled the taxi.'

He smiled. 'Very well. I see you're taking the post with you.'

'Yes. I'll drop it in a post box on my way home.'

'Good girl. And don't forget to take all your Christmas boxes as well.'

She smiled appreciatively. 'Thank you all very much. Everybody's been so kind.'

'Merry Christmas, Libby.

'Merry Christmas, Mr Burgayne.'

When she had gone, Charles went to the breakfast room where he knew Dorothy would be, and requested a cup of tea of Margaret Jenkins, the maid. While he waited for it he sat down opposite Dorothy.

'I have a sneaking suspicion that there's romance blossoming in our midst,' he said quietly.

'Oh?' Dorothy looked up from the list of queries she had made regarding the convalescent rooms, still unoccupied.

'Edward and Libby, no less. She's cancelled her taxi in favour of Edward driving her home.'

'Now that you mention it, Charles . . . He rang a few weeks ago and she answered his call. Nobody else had a chance to talk to him, and she blushed like a rose when I said something. Do you think we should discourage it?'

He waved his hand dismissively. 'Discourage it? Why? There's a war on, and you can hardly blame the lad – she's such a pretty little thing. Let them have their fun. Frankly, I admire his choice. If I were in his shoes I daresay I'd be doing the same. I take it he hasn't said anything to you, my dear?'

'Nothing.'

'Then it'll probably amount to nothing.'

'Let's hope he doesn't do anything rash. You know the old saying about absence making the heart grow fonder.'

'Well, as I see it, we can hardly discourage it if we don't know for certain that there's something going on.'

'We can discourage his driving to Dudley and back willynilly, with petrol rationed the way it is,' Dorothy said. 'Especially in this blackout as well. It's just too dangerous.'

Charles gave a little laugh. 'Frankly, I doubt whether that argument will hold water when there's petrol aplenty available for the works.'

- - -

Edward stopped the car at a post box at Libby's request, and they took advantage of the break in the journey to indulge at the side of the road in a kiss or two, heightening their already intense hunger for each other.

'Where can we go where it's quiet?' Edward asked.

Libby wracked her brains trying to think of a suitable location. 'Let's try Oakham Road. There's bound to be somewhere by the golf course.'

There was hardly any light to guide them. The blackout was total, but for the sporadic lighting up of the sky as the various steelworks around randomly tipped their white-hot slag. The resultant flares reflected vividly off the low clouds. But, driving slowly, meeting little traffic, they found their way. Edward turned into a narrow, bumpy lane that led to a deserted, worked-out quarry some way off the road. He stopped the car and switched off the engine.

'I've missed you, Libby. God, I've been longing for you.' He took her in his arms. 'I haven't been able to get you off my mind. I simply can't forget that night we had before I left for Cambridge.'

'I'm glad,' she breathed, her heart thumping. 'I keep thinking about it as well. It was so beautiful.'

He felt her shiver in his arms. 'You're cold, my love.'

She nodded against his chest. 'But I'm warm inside now I'm with you.'

'Kiss me.'

She tilted her head, offering her lips, and they kissed . . . a long, lingering kiss that inflamed their mutual desire.

'Let's get in the back,' he suggested.

In the darkness she smiled to herself, remembering Bunty's comment months ago that the back seat of the Riley could be a wonderfully romantic place. Biddably, Libby clambered into the rear, and Edward followed.

Outside an owl hooted. Only the owl had eyes wide enough and round enough to witness this secret escapade in the darkness. In the concealing safety of the blackout, they fell into another embrace, more passionate. He unfastened the buttons of her overcoat and unwrapped the scarf that was around her neck. He undid the row of buttons on her winter cardigan, then the tiny buttons of her blouse. As he peeled back the layers of winter clothing he unfastened her brassiere. Only then did she feel the chill of that cold December evening on the smooth skin of her bared breasts, and she shivered. But the cold would not deter her. She was with the man she loved, and the warmth of desire was lighting her up as his hand softly kneaded one firm but exquisitely pliable breast. She found herself sliding down against the backrest until she was lying horizontally along the full width of the seat. Her skirt had ridden up in consequence, baring her legs. He thrust his knee between them, and she felt him hard against her.

When he pulled the hem of her skirt up to her waist and ran his hands hungrily over her thighs, lingering at the bare silky-smooth skin above the tops of her stockings, she sighed in anticipation. He felt between her legs, slid his fingers inside the leg of her knickers, and she was as aware as he was of her own readiness as he tantalisingly caressed her. When she raised her backside he slid her knickers down and she dislodged them from her feet with a small deft kick. Both were panting like hounds on a hunt when he unbuttoned his trousers and she reciprocated by sliding her hands into the waist of his trousers and easing them over his backside. She manoeuvred herself beneath him and shivered with pleasure at the sensation of his lean, manly body on top of her. Her hands gripped his buttocks, pulling him to her, and she uttered uncontrollable little sobs of pleasure as he guided himself in.

It had been so long, and the sensation was so exquisitely sweet. She had been so lonely without him, despite being surrounded by her own family and his. As they settled into an easy rhythm that belied their inexperience, tears of joy welled up in her eyes again at the relief and absolute bliss of being so physically and spiritually close to her Edward once again.

Soon though, the tears ebbed, supplanted by indescribable sensations emanating from the very centre of her being and radiating out; sensations that became mesmerising as they intensified, creating a crisis of ecstasy that had her gasping.

Afterwards, they lay in silence, stunned at the utter beauty and power of their love, and at the sheer pleasure they were able to give each other. Their hands still roamed affectionately over each other's cooling skin, for they were still gaining familiarity with each other's bodies.

But the cold was creeping in and it was time to go. Her folks would wonder where she was.

'That was the best Christmas present ever,' she quipped as she fumbled in the darkness trying to locate her knickers.

'For me as well.'

'Well, I've bought you something else,' she said. 'I left it under your Christmas tree. I hope you won't mind the inscription.'

'Inscription, eh? So what have you bought me?'

'I'm not telling . . .' She found her knickers and put them back on. 'Anyway, shall I see you tomorrow? I know you won't be able to come to us for your Christmas dinner – that wouldn't be fair on your family – but can you come for tea? Mom and Dad would love you to – as would I.'

He pulled her to him affectionately as she was fastening the buttons of her blouse. 'I don't see why not. About six?'

'Oh, earlier, if you can. Say five.'

He kissed her. 'I'll do my best, I promise . . . I love you, little Libby Shakespeare.'

She reminded herself that she only had him for two more days before his return to Cranwell, and she shivered at the impending loss. *Life before Edward has been nothing*, she thought. *Life without him now would be unbearable, a void. And if I'm pregnant after this, I shall be so pleased.*

The inside of the car was all steamed up and, as Libby deftly scrambled through to the front passenger seat, Edward grabbed a chamois leather from the parcel shelf and wiped the windows.

'We've certainly generated some moisture,' he quipped, and she tapped him playfully on the arm.

- - -

| 14 |

The Christmas tree that stood tall and broad in the hallway at Buttonbridge Hall had been grown on the estate, and Libby had helped to decorate it with Bunty and Dorothy a few days earlier. On Christmas Day it glittered and glowed as the family handed their gifts around in turn from beneath it, creating mounds of torn wrapping paper on the floor as they opened them.

'Here's another from Libby,' Dorothy remarked, picking up one of the remaining gifts, a small cube. She turned it over and read the label. 'For you, Bunty.'

Bunty took the cube and opened it carefully. 'Perfume.' Her blue eyes brightened along with her smile of appreciation as she took the top off the pretty bottle and sniffed its contents. 'Oh, it's simply beautiful. It must've cost a fortune. Do smell it, Mummy.'

'Mmm . . .' Dorothy gave a nod of approval before she stooped down to pick up another. 'And another from Libby . . . for Edward this time . . .'

Edward took the small package hesitantly, but made no attempt to open it, merely waiting for the next gift to be handed out.

'Aren't you going to see what it is?' Bunty asked.

'If you insist,' he answered reluctantly, and all eyes were on him as he unravelled the tasteful wrapping paper. After a second or two he withdrew a silver object. 'A cigarette lighter,' he beamed, and immediately placed it back in its box to avoid reading the inscription Libby had told him about in front of them.

'I asked her to come and see the hunt on Boxing Day,' Bunty said, aware of Edward's discomfiture. 'But she said she wasn't sure. She said she didn't think it was fair that we should have to travel to fetch her with petrol rationing the way it is.'

'I'll fetch her,' offered Edward. 'There's petrol enough in my car. If you think about it she could stay Boxing Night as well, then she'd be here ready for work the following morning. That would save fuel as well.'

'But might not her parents have something to say about us depriving them of their only daughter over the Christmas holiday?' Hugh suggested. 'Let's face it, she spends an awful lot of time here already working for Father. Why should she want to come here on her Christmas holiday?'

'Because she enjoys our company?' Edward suggested.

'If you don't mind my saying so, Edward, dear, you seem quite keen to enjoy Libby's company yourself,' Dorothy remarked astutely.

'I'm very fond of Libby, Mother.'

'And I suspect she's quite fond of you too,' Hugh said grudgingly. 'I always thought she was Bunty's friend, first and foremost, as well as being father's private secretary.'

'Yes, well I consider her my friend as well these days,' Edward retorted. 'You might as well know, Mother, that we've been writing to each other ever since I joined the RAF.'

'Ah.' Dorothy glanced at Charles for his reaction before she turned back to her son. 'Are you sure that's a good idea, Edward?'

'I don't see why not, frankly.'

'There's always the danger that it might develop into something more,' Hugh said.

'Danger?' Edward queried. 'You make it sound horribly undesirable.'

'It rather depends on the girl, I suspect, and her suitability.'

'Oh, I think Libby is eminently suitable – and if there's any likelihood of romance I certainly wouldn't shy away from it.' He turned to his father. 'What's your opinion of Libby, Dad. She is your private secretary.'

'She's my private secretary because she works hard, is jolly reliable and very capable. I also happen to think she's not only a rather sweet girl, but also quite delightful to behold. Therefore, I can understand Edward's interest perfectly. So, if she and Edward see fit to write to one another while he's away, I certainly won't begrudge them their pleasure.'

'Thank you, Dad,' Edward said.

Hugh turned away and went to his room.

- - -

Gladys and Joe Shakespeare were neither surprised nor resentful of the suggestion that their only daughter should be whisked away to the country home of Charles Burgayne for the remainder of the Christmas holiday. They had taken to Edward as if he were the son they'd never had, and were delighted for her in their typically unselfish way. Libby had done well for herself, and her proud parents wondered whether there might be marriage at the end of it, the war and survival permitting. What more could they possibly ask for? The sacrifices they had made, in order to pay for her education and raise her above the life they were used to, were paying off handsomely. Just think if the Burgaynes and the Shakespeare should become related by marriage . . .

So Libby left them with a kiss apiece, while Edward carried her small cardboard suitcase, bearing her clothes and toiletries, down the entry to his car.

At Buttonbridge Hall the Christmas festivities which the Burgaynes enjoyed were on a level which was completely new to her. Christmases at home in Hill Street were generally quiet affairs, with grandparents, uncles, aunts and cousins sometimes dropping by to pay their respects. When that happened, they would drink beer and whisky, normally bought just for the occasion, and the jokes and the gossip would grow louder the more they supped. As the evening progressed, Libby would generally be asked to make a pot of tea which the womenfolk would consume before departing into the frosty December night, bound for their respective homes. But even that didn't happen every Christmas. Sometimes they would sit, just the three of them, and listen to the wireless; in latter years Ron would have sat with them.

But Christmas among the Burgaynes was different.

Libby was staggered at the amount of musical talent that surfaced in the drawing room that night. Bunty and Hugh played piano duets together with such gusto and technical expertise that she felt compelled to applaud enthusiastically. Dorothy Burgayne also excelled on the grand piano with renditions of Chopin, only to be followed by Hugh who changed the mood completely with modern pieces by George Gershwin.

Then Bunty sang, accompanied by Hugh, a song that she said was for Adrian; it was 'I Get a Kick Out of You', and Libby thought it seemed rather poignant in the context of his absence. After that, she was surprised when Hugh beckoned his Laura, still his fiancée, to his side at the piano and suggested she sing her favourite song. She obediently sang 'They Can't Take That Away from Me' with a stunningly mellow, jazzy voice, and delivered the song with surprising panache.

The girl has hidden talents, Libby thought. She can't be stupid, so why can't she make more of herself and her talents? And if she's not stupid, why can't she see through Hugh?

'Do you know any songs, Libby?' Hugh enquired, raising his eyebrows in a manner that suggested long-standing friendship.

'I can't sing,' she protested, hoping she would not, nevertheless, be hauled up to make a spectacle of herself, for not even the sherry she had been sipping gave her the courage to do that.

'I don't believe it,' he replied. 'Try "Over the Rainbow".' He took a gulp of port, and began playing the accompaniment.

'Honestly, I can't sing, Hugh.' She glanced at Edward for help, but he was laughing, egging her on to sing. 'In any case, I don't know the words.'

After some discussion, they took her at her word, but when Edward produced a book of Shakespeare sonnets she agreed to a recitation of one as her contribution, and was rewarded with a stirring round of applause.

Eventually the mood became more sombre as the entertainment gave way to talk of the war. Depressed by it, Dorothy Burgayne decided she'd had enough and retired to bed. Charles followed shortly after. Hugh poured himself another drink and offered Laura a top-up, since she too was drinking port.

'No, thank you, Hugh, I'm off to my room. It's been a hectic day and I'm awfully tired,' she said. 'See you in the morning. Are you coming up, Libby?'

'Maybe it's time we all turned in,' Edward suggested. 'You'll want a clear head for the hunt tomorrow.'

'But you're not riding, are you?' Libby said, alarmed at the potential for him to get harmed.

'Gosh, no. I'm safer in a plane than on horseback, the way I ride,' he answered with a self-effacing laugh. 'And anyway, it wouldn't do at all to get myself maimed being thrown from a horse after the government has spent a fortune training me to fly fighter planes.'

She smiled. 'I'll see you in the morning then. Goodnight, all.'

Led by Laura, they went to their respective rooms, leaving Bunty, and Hugh downstairs finishing off their drinks.

Libby shut the bedroom door behind her and, lit by the glow of the fire burning in the grate, went across to the window. She parted the curtains and peered out. The silhouettes of trees were just visible against the lighter night sky. *Who would believe we are at war*, she thought to herself. *It's so peaceful.* She let the curtain fall, and walked back across the room to the light switch and flicked it on, hoping no light was escaping into the night to be seen by marauding German aeroplanes. Among the clothes she had brought with her she found her nightgown. As she undressed, carefully hanging her dress and folding her underwear and stockings, she wondered whether Edward would risk coming to her room later. Her heart pounded at the possibility. Maybe she would not put her hair in curlers that night, just in case . . .

- - -

Hugh Burgayne left his bedroom and closed the door shut as quietly as he could. Laura's room was along the landing in the west wing of the house, and his intention was to pay her a nocturnal visit. It was a practice he'd employed for some time on those occasions when she stayed the night, and hitherto had proved perfectly safe and satisfying, for nobody was ever any the wiser. But then he remembered that Libby's room was in the same direction and he was seized by a befuddled impulse, fuelled by too much alcohol, to visit her instead. After all, Libby Shakespeare was a sight prettier than Laura Birch, and so much more desirable. She might even welcome him into her bed; she'd been more socially amenable of late, and Edward's perpetual absence could hardly be satisfying for her.

To any onlooker, the exaggerated stealth of his movements to avoid creaking floorboards suggested that not only was he about forbidden commerce, but that the port he had drunk was taking its toll. He reached Libby's door in the darkness, the only scant illumination from the starry night sky entering through an oriel window on the landing. It was chilly and he shivered as he curled his fingers around the cold brass door-knob. She might have grown attached to his brave, heroic brother; they were writing regularly – or so Edward had asserted – but she was certainly not yet secured, or even claimed. With Edward away for so long maybe now was the right time to turn her head. Maybe he ought to groom her for the lengthy periods that Edward would be away; she was sure to feel the need for some love and affection from time to time. And how he ached to feel her warm, naked body pressed against him.

But he hesitated. Was this quite wise, this creeping about the house to the bedroom of the girl who was also his father's secretary? What if he were caught? What if she screamed in horror at his uninvited presence and woke the whole household? What a downright cad he would look; what a complete bounder, what an idiot. His sometimes warm, sometimes cool affair with Laura would be finally decided. His mother would be ashamed of him, as would his father. Libby would spread it around the works that he was a thoroughly lecherous beast.

He would be a laughing stock, unable to uphold his authority as a director of the Blowers Green Steelworks.

Maybe it was the cold that was bringing him to his senses. In any case, he loosed the doorknob.

Then, to his horror, he heard the creak of a floorboard and was sure the sound did not emanate from beneath his own feet. Instinctively, he darted away in the opposite direction to that from which the sound had come. His heart started pounding at his own rashness and the narrowness of his escape. He hid behind a corner, waited, and watched. The dim light was just enough for him to see the ghostly, pyjamaed figure of Edward, creeping almost as stealthily as he had done . . . to Libby's room.

Things seem to have progressed beyond merely writing letters,' he pondered, thankful that he had not done what he had so foolhardily set out to do.

- - -

In the new year two million British men between the ages of 19 and 27 were called up for military service. Among them was Hugh Burgayne, who suffered the indignity of having to visit Dudley Labour Exchange to justify his claim that he was in a reserved occupation. As an executive director of a steelworks employing nigh on five hundred men in the borough, and was intimately involved in government contracts. If this plea were turned down, only then would he resort to declaring himself a conscientious objector, since he was aware of how much his father disapproved of that stance in the face of Edward's bravery. After due investigations, Hugh learnt that his plea had been accepted and registered. He could remain at work, doing a vital job.

That out of the way, he decided it was time to appraise his relationship with Laura Birch, and coldly ended the affair. In consequence, he received a letter from her father's solicitor containing threats of litigation for breach of promise. Laura's father, it seemed, had taken it as a personal snub, rather than a snub to his daughter.

Libby's natural apprehension about the reliability of her monthly visitor was lifted, and she shared the news with Edward in her next letter that she was not pregnant. She understood how the heat and urgency of their passion had removed from their minds all regard for the possible consequences. Next time – providing there was a next time – they really must take more care.

In early March Libby received a letter from Edward. She read with eagerness of his love and longing for her, but one paragraph contained news she had been secretly dreading. It read:

After months of perfecting slow rolls, stall turns, bunts, spins, dives and all manner of aerobatics, after hours in the air practising map-reading, low flying, night flying and high-altitude flying, I have finally got my 'wings'. Pretty soon now I shall be transferred elsewhere for practice in the chivalrous art of gunnery. I'm told we shall be sitting on the tails of other aircraft trying to blast away a little red cone trailing behind it. Sounds like fun.

In April the slow, 'phoney' war, as it was being called, where nothing seemed to happen, was over when the Germans invaded Denmark and Norway, and British and French troops joined the battle, albeit somewhat ineffectually.

May ushered in Libby's twenty-first birthday. The Burgaynes held a small party for her at Buttonbridge Hall and Edward, by prior arrangement, rang up and reversed the charges so he needn't worry about having sufficient coins. Bunty related the latest news of Adrian before she handed Libby the receiver.

Libby smiled gratefully at her friend and a knowing look passed between them as she put the receiver to her ear.

'Hello, Edward . . .'

'Sweetheart, many happy returns of the day, and congratulations of course.'

'Thank you.'

'I just wish I could be there to share it with you.'

'I do too.'

'Did you realise you are old enough now to marry me without having to ask permission from your father?'

'I know.' She warmed inside, her smile broadening to a contented grin.

'Well, at least you don't sound displeased at the prospect.'

'Of course I'm not. Not at all.'

'Just sounding you out, Sweetheart. Who knows what the future might bring?'

'Yes. Who knows,' she repeated guardedly, because of her listening audience.

'What's the matter, Angel? Are you tongue-tied?'

'It's not that,' she said quietly into the mouthpiece, turning away from the rest of the family present.

'Oh, I see. Stupid of me. You're surrounded by large, flapping, Burgayne ears, aren't you? So when I tell you how much I love you, you can't say the same to me.'

'Not without some . . . you know . . .'

'Giving the game away.'

She laughed. 'Spot on . . .'

'Better change the subject then, eh? How's rationing?'

'Rationing? Well, we're getting quite used to four ounces of butter a week, twelve ounces of sugar, and three and a half ounces of bacon. We'll none of us get fat, that's for certain. Anyway, what's the latest with you?'

'We finish our gunnery training in a few days, then I'm being posted.'

'Where to?'

'No idea yet.'

'Are you likely to get some leave soon?' It was an uncontroversial question, of general interest.

'That I couldn't say, either. Do you miss me terribly?'

'Of course,' she answered deceptively for the family's digestion.

'Oh, darling, I miss you too.' The frustration in his tone was obvious. 'This dratted war . . .'

'I know.'

'But write tomorrow, eh? As soon as I know my new address I'll send it to you.'

'Okay.'

'I do love the way you say that.'

'So you say.'

'Does anybody else want to say hello while I'm on the line? You'd better ask.'

'Hold on . . . Does anybody else want to talk to Edward? . . . Yes, your father does.'

'Bye, then, darling. Write soon. I love you.'

'Bye, Edward.' With a self-effacing, half guilty smile she handed over the receiver to Charles.

- - -

A few days later, on 10th May, Holland and Belgium fell to Germany's 'blitzkrieg'. It was obvious that France would be the next country overrun, with Britain the victim thereafter. On the same day, Winston Churchill assumed the role of Prime Minister of an all-party coalition government, after Neville Chamberlain, utterly discredited, was forced to resign against a background of military and political catastrophes. By the 21st of May, German troops had reached the River Aisne in France and were only sixty miles from Paris. Their advance was so rapid that by the twenty-seventh they had taken Boulogne, cutting off British and French troops. The only escape for them was via Dunkirk, and British soldiers were bombed and machine-gunned as they waded out toward ships and small boats that had been despatched in their thousands to retrieve them.

The battle for Britain was on.

| 15 |

My Own Darling,

Blessed with a posting close to home would have been grand, and might have afforded the opportunity to see you more often, if only for a few hours, but it was not to be. A squadron based at Biggin Hill, south east of London, is where I am needed, so that's where they have sent me. However, I might as well be based on the moon as far as getting to see you is concerned, since we're on 30 minutes notice at most. There are some jolly decent chaps here and I think I've slotted in pretty well. On our first night off we're honour-bound to visit at least one of the local hostelries, which I look forward to immensely.

Already I've been involved in some action over Dunkirk, trying to protect our fleeing troops. Naturally, one gets rather nervous on these sorties, but everything happens so quickly, and I'm comforted by the fact that my Hurricane is the most manoeuvrable of all modern fighter planes. It's not as fast as a Messerschmitt, for example, but no Messerschmitt can out-turn me, and if he's fool enough to try I'll dive beneath him and come up behind him in a trice, and he'll be squarely in my sights. That hasn't happened. I can't yet claim a notch on my gun, but conversely I haven't provided a notch on the gun of any Luftwaffe pilot either . . .

- - -

It was on 6th June that a visitor called unexpectedly at Buttonbridge Hall, a day when Libby was working there. Jenkins let in a highly agitated and emotional woman who asked to see Bunty. Amelia Farrance was in her late forties but always looked as if she was in her thirties. But not today. Today, she looked older than her years and careworn. As soon as Bunty saw her she knew the news would be traumatic.

'Oh, Mrs Farrance,' she cried, a horrified look on her face. 'Oh, dear God, no . . . It's Adrian, isn't it?' She rushed to the older woman and threw her arms about her, for both support and to give consolation. Tears began to flow from both women.

'I just received a telegram to say he's been wounded in action, Bunty,' Mrs Farrance said quietly, endeavouring to remain calm. 'But we don't know to what extent. It happened at Dunkirk while he was trying to board a boat.'

'Where is he?'

'A hospital in Brighton. As I opened the telegram I feared the worst. Thankfully, he's only wounded. I hope and pray it's not too serious.'

'I'm going to see him, Mrs Farrance.'

'Oh, Bunty, I hoped you might, and I'm so glad. I would come with you, but I really couldn't face seeing him suffering, maybe even fighting for his life. It would crucify me.'

'Depending on how bad he is, maybe I could even arrange to get him here as a convalescent.' Bunty's face lit up at the prospect.

'Oh, Bunty, please try.'

'Thank you so much for coming to let me know, Mrs Farrance.'

'I had to come,' the older woman replied. 'I know how close you two have become. It hardly seemed appropriate to let you know by phone.'

'Do come into the breakfast room and I'll get Jenkins to make us a cup of tea. My mother's at a Red Cross meeting this morning, but I want to get the all-clear from Daddy for a trip to Brighton. Come on through, Mrs Farrance . . . Please . . .'

Bunty led Amelia Farrance into the breakfast room, sat her down and ordered a pot of tea. 'If you'll excuse me a moment.'

Bunty raced to the room that had been converted into Libby's office.

'Are you all right?' Libby enquired, looking up from her work. 'You look as if you've seen a ghost. What's the matter?'

'Adrian has been wounded. He's in a Brighton hospital. I'm going to see him. Would you mind very much going with me?'

'Of course I will, Bunty, if it's all right with your father.'

'Naturally. But he'll agree to it, have no fear.'

'When do you want to go?'

'As soon as possible. Today.'

'But I don't have a change of clothes or anything, Bunty.'

'You can borrow my things. You're the same size as me. Take whatever you need.'

'But I'd have to let my mom and dad know.'

'We'll phone the works and get a message to your father. Would you find out the times of trains meanwhile, Libby?'

'Course I will.'

\- - -

The journey to Brighton seemed to take an eternity. Bunty was on tenterhooks the whole time, preoccupied with thoughts of Adrian and how she might find him when they finally arrived at the hospital. Libby consoled her tearful friend and pacified her in the best way she could, and was utterly sympathetic. If the tables were turned it would be herself that was devastated, dashing across the country to see Edward and help support his recovery with all her affection. The thought horrified her.

When they arrived in Brighton, Libby suggested they find somewhere to stay for the night, for both thought it unlikely that they would return home that same evening. A taxi driver took them to a boarding house he knew of where they hurriedly inspected and took a room. From there, the taxi driver delivered them to the Brighton Municipal Hospital where they were taken to see Adrian.

Drained after the emotional anguish and the long train journey Bunty had fallen asleep. When she awoke, she looked about her totally disorientated. She was in a strange place . . . obviously a hospital ward, surrounded by screens – and a bed . . . But it was not a ward that had been created at Buttonbridge Hall. It took a second to assimilate where she really was and what had happened. She was sitting up in a chair, but her head had dropped forward and her neck ached as a result.

The bed contained Adrian.

So the nightmare was real after all . . .

Libby was there too, still asleep, sitting up in a chair on the other side of the bed, also drained with fatigue. Bunty heard footsteps outside in the corridor, the door swung open and a nurse approached.

'Good morning, nurse . . .'

Nurse Radcliffe stopped when she reached the bed. 'Miss Burgayne,' she answered gently, overflowing with sympathy. 'You're awake. How does he seem?'

'I don't know, Nurse Radcliffe,' Bunty answered apologetically. 'I dropped off to sleep.'

'You've had a long journey to get here, and you've been here all night with the poor lad, haven't you? Why don't you go for some breakfast, or a mug of tea or something?'

'What time is it?'

'Just after seven.'

The nurse inspected Adrian, whose upper body was swathed in bandages through which blood had oozed, and was probably still oozing. She took his pulse. He had not regained consciousness and the doctors had told Bunty that his chances of survival were slender, after losing part of his right shoulder and his arm. It was on learning this that Bunty decided she must stay with him until the end, appalled as she was at the extent of his wounds and the witnessing of his dear sweet life ebbing away.

'Have you got time to stay with Adrian for a few minutes?' Bunty enquired. 'I desperately need to have a wash, and clean my teeth.'

'I shall be on the ward all the time, Miss Burgayne, so I shall be able to keep my eye on him,' the nurse replied kindly. 'Why don't you wake your friend and the two of you go together?'

'Thanks awfully.'

Bunty roused Libby, who awoke equally disorientated. The groans of other soldiers and seamen, also suffering atrocious wounds, quickly reminded her of her whereabouts.

'How is he?' Libby whispered, rubbing her eyes.

'No change, it seems.' Bunty sighed heavily. 'Come on, we're going to freshen up and hunt down a mug of hot tea. Some breakfast too if you can stomach it. Nurse Radcliffe will keep an eye on Adrian.'

Libby got up from the chair and rubbed her neck where it ached from its unusual and uncomfortable angle of repose. She stood up, smoothed out the creases in her skirt and picked up her handbag. She looked again at poor Adrian, and was horrified. If this should be Edward . . .

'I'm so sorry to inflict all this on you, Libby,' Bunty said. 'You really are a true friend. It must be beastly hard on you, too – I know you must be thinking about Edward. I know you must be frightfully worried.'

'I try not to think about him ever getting hurt, Bunty. Otherwise it drives me mad.' She gave a profound sigh. 'Come on then, and we'll spruce ourselves up.'

Bunty took the opportunity to telephone Amelia Farrance as soon as she spotted a payphone. She told her in detail about Adrian's condition, preparing her as gently as she could for what was inevitable. Then the two girls went to the boarding house they had been taken to on their arrival in Brighton.

They washed and changed, requested tea and buttered toast to sustain them, before hurrying back to the hospital.

'I've been to see him a few times, Miss Burgayne,' Nurse Radcliffe reported on their return, 'but there's no sign of him coming round.'

'Think I should try to wake him?' Bunty asked.

'Why don't you just try talking to him?'

Bunty nodded and smiled sadly. She sat beside the bed and leaned across to Adrian. 'Adrian,' she whispered. 'Adrian, can you hear me? . . . There's so much I want to tell you, if only I thought you could hear me . . .' She took his hand, which was lying on top of the counterpane and she stroked it lovingly. 'Do you remember the very first time Edward introduced us, Adrian? I fell for you straight away, you know, but you'd always got that girl Juliet around you, hadn't you? Yet I knew instinctively that someday we'd be together . . . that I'd marry you. Well, hear this, my love – I'm going to marry you when you get out of here . . . So please get well . . . Please . . . I don't mind how long I have to wait. I'll wait for ever if need be, only please, please get better. And when you are feeling just a little better I'll get you sent to Buttonbridge Hall to convalesce, and I can look after you myself . . .'

Libby heard Bunty's poignant words and was touched. Her eyes misted and tears ran down her cheeks.

'Oh, Bunty, if only I could do something to help,' she said.

'Just being here helps, Libby.' Bunty's eyes filled with tears, due as much to Libby's genuine concern as to her own grief. 'Last night he came round for a second or two.' She sniffed and wiped her tears with her handkerchief. 'He looked at me and smiled. I'm sure he knew me. At least, that's what I shall keep telling myself. He hasn't come round since, though, as far as I know. But he seems feverish now . . .' She sighed again, resignedly. 'Feel his forehead, Libby. Tell me what you think.'

'But I'm no doctor, Bunty,' Libby answered quietly. Nevertheless, she felt Adrian's forehead. 'Yes, he does feel hot. Maybe we should open a window.'

'I need a cold damp cloth to put on his forehead to help cool him down.'

Just then, a doctor appeared. He ordered the screens to be put around Adrian's bed and asked the girls to leave them for a while.

- - -

Outside in the cool air of morning, Bunty laid her head on Libby's shoulder and wept bitterly, while Libby consoled her in her arms. Libby understood what her friend was going through, appreciated the mixture of emotions that were tormenting her, and she pitied her. The tighter Libby held her and the greater the manifestation of her sympathy, the more Bunty wept. But she was not the only woman weeping in Britain over the loss of a lover, a son, a husband, wrought by the evacuation of Dunkirk.

'Come on, Bunty,' Libby said kindly. 'Let's go and sit on one of those benches over there. Have a good cry and talk to me. I'm sure it'll help, just talking.'

'Oh, Libby, I want to die . . .' Bunty snivelled into her handkerchief, trying in vain to stem her weeping. 'I love him so much,' she cried. 'It's a travesty that he should suffer like that, such a young man who had everything to live for.'

Her crying came in plaintive wails during which Libby said nothing, merely holding her, allowing her friend to weep to her heart's content. Libby figured it was something Bunty must do to get Adrian Farrance out of her system, though it might take months and even years, for she had set her heart on this man as her lifelong partner.

When they returned to the ward, the same doctor saw Bunty and asked her to step into the office.

'You are not the wife of Captain Farrance, are you?'

'No, Doctor, he doesn't have a wife, but I am his fiancée,' she answered. 'Captain Farrance's mother was unable to come due to family commitments, and she asked me to come instead.'

The doctor nodded his understanding. 'So I may speak frankly and in confidence?'

'Of course.'

'Captain Farrance is in a desperate condition, I'm afraid. I am firmly of the opinion that gangrene has taken a hold – hardly surprising in view of the length of time between his getting wounded and receiving any proper medical treatment, and the extent of his wounds. I'm dreadfully sorry to have to say this, but you should prepare yourself and his family for the inevitable. I really am most terribly sorry.'

'How long has he got, Doctor?'

'Hours . . . At most.'

- - -

Captain Adrian Farrance passed away at ten minutes to one that same afternoon, and Bunty Burgayne wept again over his lifeless, blood-stained body.

At his funeral some days later, wracked with grief, she decided that she needed to do something for other men wounded and maimed in this war.

'Libby, I've got to make myself useful,' she announced afterwards. 'I'm going to train to become a nurse. Convalescents are already being sent to Buttonbridge Hall, and my help would be welcome there, as well as being useful experience.'

'I think that's a brilliant idea, Bunty,' Libby agreed. 'I think you should.'

- - -

Events moved on. With the courage of a jackal lurking in the shadows of a bolder beast of prey, Mussolini cynically declared war on the Allies, hoping to share as cheaply as possible in Hitler's spoils of war, for Germany would win this conflict easily. The Germans took Paris, and Hitler himself was present when the French signed their surrender, and gloated over their humiliation.

So Britain was left to fight a formidable foe alone. The Luftwaffe attacked shipping in the English Channel, and decided that Britain's air superiority must be destroyed before the kingdom could be invaded. Thus began the systematic bombing of airfields.

Libby received a letter from Edward dated 15th August 1940, part of which read:

My own darling Libby,

I am writing this letter late into the night. I was going to leave it until tomorrow, but I can't sleep because I am so hyped up after the day's events, that I feel I must write to you about them and get them out of my system, or I'll never sleep.

The day started insignificantly enough, but just after midday all hell broke loose and we heard the scream of a Spitfire squadron as it took off. My squadron was scrambled soon after and we took to the air under no illusions as to the significance of what this all meant. I should explain that two squadrons of fighters are not sent up unless something drastic is afoot.

You can imagine how extremely apprehensive I was, to say the least. Strangely enough, though, my fear was very soon replaced by sheer excitement, with the result that I have never in my life felt as alert as I was then. Having your wits about you on occasions like this is what saves your life. Once over the sea we maintained a height of about 12,000 feet and were about twelve miles out to sea when we first spotted a closely-packed formation moving across the sky towards us in a swarm. Of course they were too far away to be identified as yet, but as we closed in it became obvious it was bombers escorted by fighters. I wanted it to be all over and done with, as if some time-slip could take place and pitch me out at some point in the future beyond the inevitable action. Yet another part of me was eagerly anticipating the encounter, for this is exactly what I have been trained to do.

Anyway, the instruction came through my headphones that I, along with the rest of my section, was assigned to deal with the fighters while six of my colleagues were assigned to downing the bombers. So we split up and six of us headed towards the fighters; and I must tell you we were vastly outnumbered about four to one. No matter; one of my team, Harry Drummond it turned out, scored a hit first time and I saw a Messerschmitt 109E blow up into a ball of flame, showering scraps of metal through the clouds below. My first thought was 'there but for the grace of God go I'. At that, the rest of the German fighters forsook the bombers they were escorting, leaving them at the mercy of our two other sections. Their tactics then were to fly round in a defensive circle, everyone looking out for the other, so we dived after them, breaking it up. Then, suddenly, A Messerschmitt passed right in front of my very nose and I followed him, firing tracers after him. And guess what – I got him. He didn't burst into flames but down he went. I must explain that in the split seconds all this was going on, moral principles didn't matter, and the thought crossed my mind that this could feasibly have been the very pilot who had hit Adrian with machine gun fire while he was trying to scramble onto a ship. If so, justice had been done, and I was not in the least sorry.

That's what I felt then, but looking back now from the peace and comfort of my bed, I do hope that the pilot, whoever he was, made it safely to the relative tranquillity of the sea below and was picked up. You see, after all he is somebody's son, fiancé or husband and if he was killed, that somebody will be grieving over him, in much the same way that Bunty is still grieving over Adrian. Not only that; it could so easily have been me.

Anyway, next time I looked around I was alone. I imagine the Messerschmitts had taken refuge under the clouds below us, so I went chasing after them, but they had disappeared. We patrolled the skies for some time afterwards and heard or saw no more of them.

Of course, when we landed we were all so excited. In all, our squadron and the Spitfire Squadron combined, had twenty confirmed downs and a dozen unconfirmed, with many more damaged. We escaped with no losses. If nothing *else, the escapade confirmed our superiority in the air, both in expertise and machinery . . .*

- - -

The Luftwaffe continued the aerial bombardment of Britain and Edward was invariably involved. Then came the news that Biggin Hill airfield had been heavily bombed, and was unserviceable except as a base for one squadron only. Edward was thus posted to Exeter where his squadron was needed to protect the important Naval Bases at Portland and Plymouth, as well as to intercept bombers on their way to sorties over Wales, the Midlands, and even the North West of England.

Flying Officer Edward Burgayne, recently promoted, settled himself in his bunk before tea with a fountain pen and writing pad, and began writing his daily letter to his beloved Libby. He told her how that day he had already flown 3 sorties, due to having only eight operational pilots available, he was tired and needed some leave to recuperate. Besides which, he was longing to be with her again; for too long they had been kept apart.

No sooner had he finished the second paragraph than they were scrambled again. It was half past five in the afternoon. Edward checked on the men, some of whom were showering, some asleep, but within five minutes the depleted squadron of eight Hurricanes was airborne.

'Control reports thirty-plus bandits approaching west of Penzance,' Edward heard in his earphones. 'Currently headed northwest over the Celtic Sea from Brittany.'

The voice was calm, measured and reassuring and Edward's keen eyes searched the empty sky. Visibility was good. The air was frosty, the sky was cloudless, the moon and stars were clearly visible. The squadron flew north west across the Severn Estuary in tight formation at about fourteen thousand feet, scanning the void around them for sight of the invading formation. They were to intercept enemy planes over the Celtic Sea, that area of the eastern Atlantic bounded by the southern portion of Ireland, Wales and Cornwall. The extreme western coast of Pembroke was barely visible in the darkness.

A few minutes later, an excited voice seared into Edward's headphones.

'Bandits at ten o' clock. Bandits at ten o' clock. About two miles.'

With practised precision, the eight Hurricanes turned as one towards the enemy aircraft.

'Approach from the side,' yelled the squadron leader. 'I repeat, approach from the side.'

The rest of the squadron understood. This tactic would give the eight Hurricanes a better chance of damaging the German bombers with prolonged bursts of machine gun fire strafed along their fuselages.

Suddenly, the curtain of night was torn apart by tracers, then by the brilliant flash of a German Dornier DO215 bomber that had taken a direct hit in a fuel tank. It exploded spectacularly. The sight deterred the other bomber pilots, for they peeled off to the southwest towards the south of Ireland, jettisoning their bombs into the sea. Within seconds, however, the Hurricanes were caught up in a frantic dog-fight with a dozen or so accompanying Messerschmitts.

Edward dived and turned round again in a tight circle. He reported that he was intending to follow the fleeing bombers and inflict as much damage to them as possible. This he did alone for some fifteen minutes, hitting several Dorniers, but unable to discern whether he had 'killed' any.

But then the cooling tank in his Hurricane exploded as he took a hit from return fire, and with a frightening judder, his cockpit began to fill with smoke and fumes.

Edward cursed. He yelled into his radio to his colleagues, but there was no response, only static. His first thought was to bail out. Mentally, he rehearsed the procedure. He could hardly see for the oily smoke filling the inside of the cockpit, but he decided to stay aboard his aeroplane and try to bring it down safely. Yet there was nothing below him except for the ice-cold sea, and the prospect of spending even a minute bobbing up and down in its swell did not appeal. It did not appeal at all. Better to try and nurse the aircraft back. So he turned around, leaving the remaining Dorniers in peace. First, though, he had to find out where he was.

It was then that he realised his compass had also been damaged, and was permanently stuck, indicating southwest. His only option was to lose height and speed and try to open the cockpit to clear it of smoke and so aid visibility. His breathing was not so much of a concern, since he was wearing an oxygen mask. He descended to two and a half thousand feet, keeping a steady eye on the altimeter, and was limping along at something significantly less than a hundred miles an hour to try and save fuel. By now, the fumes were making his eyes water despite the goggles. He managed to open the cockpit canopy and the savage, deafening rush of air sucked the fumes out. After another minute he could see clearly again.

But where the dickens was he? He decided his precise location was becoming increasingly irrelevant; his priority was simply to land, just so long as it was on British soil. He determined the North Star through the open cockpit and believed that if he took his bearings from that he would be able to guide himself to south Wales. There, he would try and find somewhere suitable to land . . . but by starlight it would be difficult, more especially landing on unfamiliar ground – always provided the engine of his Hurricane would hold up, or that he would not run out of fuel . . .

He nosed the Hurricane down and descended to fifteen hundred feet, keeping his eyes on the altimeter. He could discern the sea below him, now all he needed was to put the Hurricane down. But its Merlin engine was seriously overheating and spluttering alarmingly. It seemed impossible to eke sufficient power out of it and he feared he would have to ditch the aircraft into the sea after all. He wished then that he had paid more attention to inflating the Mae West he carried, in which he would have to drift until he was eventually picked up.

Then, thankfully, below him he could see the dim outline of the coast as waves lashed ghostly white in the moonlight against looming cliffs. Relief swept over him. Wales at last.

But it was no time to be complacent. He banked to the right, in search of a stretch of flat ground where he could put the fighter down; a field, a clearing of some sort, or even a stretch of road.

He saw the lights of what had to be a farmhouse, and by the moonlight he could just about discern fields. *It's a blessing that not everybody is observing the blackout tonight,* he thought. He let down his undercarriage. The Hurricane spluttered and back-fired as he descended. Another cottage whizzed by beneath him also defying the blackout . . . hedgerows flashed by . . . stone walls. He picked his spot and straightened his path. The wheels touched the ground and the aircraft trundled on over rough ground, slowing down. *I've made it,* he told himself. Seconds later there was an instant, sickening impact as the undercarriage struck something solid and immovable. The force of the collision propelled him with sickening force into his harness, the straps of which seemed to hack relentlessly into his body, and his head jerked forward with uncontrollable ferocity. Unceremoniously the Hurricane embedded its nose into the unforgiving ground, and there it remained, tail up, suddenly silent.

- - -

| 16 |

Charles Burgayne sat back in his armchair having dictated his last letter for typing. He stretched and then leaned forward, and Libby knew from experience that he was intent on engaging her in a conversation.

'Tell me, Libby,' he said as he lowered his spectacles and peered over the top of them with soulful eyes, 'have you received a letter from Edward in the last few days?'

At once Libby felt sick. A few days had passed since Edward's last letter to her, and he had seemed cheerful enough. But already she had begun to worry. Normally she received a letter every day, but the last few days nothing. She had been reluctant to enquire whether his family had received any mail from Edward over the last day or two, aware that the family would begin to worry merely by dint of her enquiry. Now it was obvious they had received nothing.

'I haven't had a letter for three days,' she replied trying to remain in control of her emotions. 'Some days I know he doesn't even get time to write. Why? Are you very worried, Mr Burgayne?'

'Frankly, yes. It was his mother's birthday yesterday, as you know, but she didn't hear a word from him, neither a birthday card nor a telephone call . . . Unusual. He's normally so particular. Nothing in this morning's post either. Needless to say, she's fretting like billy-o, as we all are.'

'I know, it's such a worry, isn't it?' she agreed, trying to keep the angst out of her voice and desperately trying to push back tears. 'I do hope he's all right. He said to me once – if this is any comfort, Mr Burgayne – that because telegrams travel pretty quick, no news is good news.'

He smiled with gratitude at this simple logic. 'He was quite right of course. But I know he's been heavily involved in protecting the Naval bases in the southwest. And it's a fact that we and the Polish squadrons have already lost a few pilots in the prosecution of it.'

'Yes, I know,' she said softly.

He sighed deeply, which induced a coughing spasm. 'Ah, well, Libby. Back to business. Can you read back what I've said in that last letter please? I've lost my train of thought completely.'

Libby looked down at her notepad and read.

- - -

Within a mere hour of that fretful conversation, while Libby was typing the letters in her office at Buttonbridge Hall, she was aware of a commotion downstairs. She had heard the front doorbell ring, and thought nothing of it at the time, assuming that Jenkins would have answered it. Jenkins had, and now she was yelling hysterically for Mr Burgayne. Libby left her desk in high agitation, and from the gallery looked down to witness the maid in a state of panic. Her heart went to her mouth as she descended the broad, winding staircase.

'It's a telegram just come, sir,' Jenkins warbled uneasily, waving it at Charles as he approached. He looked sick with anxiety as she handed over the missive, as if it were on fire and didn't want to be burned by it.

'My God,' Charles breathed as Dorothy and Bunty also arrived in the hall simultaneously. He looked up and saw Libby descending the stairs, and she in turn saw how pale he had suddenly become.

'Do open it, Charles,' Dorothy snapped with unwitting impatience.

Charles fumbled with it, his hands shaking. 'I can't, Dorothy.'

Unable to complete the task, he handed it to Libby who had reached them.

'Read it to us, please, Libby.'

Also trembling with apprehension she tore open the telegram and took a deep breath. 'It's from the Air Ministry.'

She glanced at Charles; his face was already an icon of anguish.

'This damned war,' he groaned. 'Go on, Libby. Tell us the worst.'

Libby's eyes skimmed the message before she read it out. At once tears blurred her vision, so she wiped them away with the back of her hand and gave a great shuddering sigh, revealing to the others exactly the content of the message before she uttered a word. At last she found her voice.

'It says, "*Regret to inform you that your son Flying Officer Edward Robert Burgayne is reported missing following air combat operations on Jan 14th 1941*".'

As Charles, utterly dispirited, led Dorothy, keening and wiping tears with her handkerchief, out of the main hall with his arm around her, Libby slumped into a chair and wept piteously. She would not normally reveal her feelings for Edward in the family's presence, since their commitment to each other had not yet been officially declared, but this news was too distressing and she could not help it. Her head was suddenly swimming, her thoughts a whirl of confusion, torment, doubt . . . and little hope. To hold out any hope whatsoever seemed in vain, but many other thoughts ran through her head simultaneously. Was this the reward that fate doled out for being in love with an airman during time of war, never knowing from one minute to the next whether he was alive or dead? If so, fate was not fair. Fate was not fair at all. She had found her perfect mate in Edward, he in her; they were deeply, intensely in love, but already, too soon – much too soon – she had lost him. They'd had no chance of any life together, a life that had promised to be brim full of joy, blessed with children, and ultimately grandchildren. But evidently it was not to be. That promise of contentment in a settled existence had been cut down in its prime, savaged, mutilated, like Edward had most likely been savaged and mutilated, also in his prime, fighting bravely for his country and his country's principles.

An arm went around her. It was Bunty, sitting beside her on the arm of the chair.

'All is not lost yet, Libby,' she said kindly, quietly. 'It only says he's missing. He may well show up yet.'

'Oh, Bunty, I do hope so. But what if he's hurt, like Adrian was?' Libby blubbered, 'and nobody finds him? Oh, I can't bear to think of it.'

'Nor can I,' Bunty replied. 'Not again.'

Work was suspended for the rest of that day, and Libby was urged to return home and take the rest of the day off, and the next day if she did not feel up to work. That night she slept little and wept a great deal, but was up and about in plenty of time next morning to get to work. Her mother, with her great fund of sympathy, consoled her as much as she was able, which succeeded in inducing even more tears. Unable to face breakfast, she was back in her office at the steelworks early, defying the war and doing her utmost to overcome the inexpressible distress that it inflicted. Libby realised that work was the best place to be; it would help keep her mind off her grief. Work would be the antidote to grief, she believed, and she intended to immerse herself in it.

- - -

Hanging by his harness in the cockpit of the Hurricane, Edward Burgayne slowly became conscious of its straps biting into his shoulders as he looked through his cockpit and saw he was facing the ground. There was a persistent tap-tapping in his head, the pain was becoming unbearable, and his neck was aching like nothing had ever ached before. As he opened his eyes he was distracted from his extreme discomfort by what he thought was a flashlight shining in his peripheral vision. Painfully, he raised his head and realised the tapping sound he thought was part of the pain was actually somebody knocking on the perspex cockpit of the Hurricane with a broom handle.

Through the open cockpit he could also hear voices, and he slowly began to realise that more than one person was outside in the darkness. Evidently, he and his upturned aeroplane were the focus of some local curiosity.

'Can you hear me?' somebody called and tapped again on the canopy.

'Yes, I can hear you,' Edward croaked.

'He's still alive,' he heard another voice say. 'He just spoke.'

The flashlight was now trained on him and Edward was forced to close his eyes from the glare.

The first voice called again. 'We gonna get you out of your aeroplane.'

'Thank you,' Edward replied inadequately. 'It's much appreciated. But make it quick, will you? I'm in agony here.'

'Would it be easier to get you out if we right your aeroplane? We can yank the tail end down I t'ink, if enough of us pull on it.'

'That sounds like a great idea,' Edward called back.

'Den we'll need to fetch a rope to loop over the tail, so we can pull it down to the ground. Dermot, will ye go and fetch a rope?'

Edward waited, harkening to the voices of the people who had evidently been disturbed by his unsolicited and rather noisy arrival. Amazed by the phenomenon, a number of folk had come to investigate, despite the darkness. In his disorientation he could not make out the accents he could hear. But they did not sound particularly Welsh.

Eventually, the person who seemed to be in charge of the operation informed him that Dermot had now fetched a rope and they were looping it over the tail of the Hurricane. Within a few minutes he felt the jarring inside the cockpit that confirmed the fact, then he felt the angle of his dangling gradually change, until the tail suddenly hit the ground and he was sitting as normal. The pressure eased on his shoulders, but the flow of fresh blood momentarily made him wince.

Edward took of his gloves and released the catches on his harness. He tried to stretch, in an effort to alleviate the severe aching, realising that his sheepskin flying jacket had cushioned much of the impact. As he stood up and clambered onto the wing the small crowd of villagers applauded him and cheered. More flashlights illuminated the area around him, enough to see where he was jumping, and he landed on the soft earth.

'Are you all right, young man?' a middle-aged man enquired, and took his arm.

'I think so, and my thanks to you and your friends for getting me out of there.'

'You'd best come into the house. I got a nice tot o' Jameson's for yeh, to warm yeh up.'

'Jameson's?' Edward queried. 'That's Irish whisky, is it not?'

'To be sure. What else would we be drinking here?'

'You mean, I'm in Ireland?' he queried again, registering surprise and doubt.

'To be sure you're in Ireland. In County Cork. Where did you t'ink you was?'

'Wales,' he answered simply.

'Begorrah, then you missed your turning.' The man turned to one of his compatriots who was walking behind him. 'Dermot, will yeh fetch Fearghal O'Leary and bring him to my house.'

'Dat I will, Brendan,' Dermot replied.

'Is this Fearghal O'Leary a priest?' Edward asked. 'I don't think I need a priest.'

'Priest?' Brendan laughed. 'No he's the local garda. We'll feed yeh up and make yeh welcome, but as you're an English flyer we must hand yeh over to the police. That's the law.'

- - -

Hospitably fed and watered, Edward then met Fearghal O'Leary, who was quick to deny any responsibility for an English Hurricane pilot, and claimed the man must be handed over to the Irish Military Police.

'Can't you just let me go so I get back to the north,' Edward suggested. 'To Belfast. Once there they'll be able to get me back to my squadron.'

'I'm not sartain o' that, sir,' O'Leary replied, sipping a tot of Jameson's. 'As you're a British serviceman and we are a neutral country the Military Police must decide. I'll telephone them and ask them to come here for yeh. Then you can ask them. Can you put this gentleman up till the morning, Brendan?'

Brendan said, to be sure he would be happy to find the poor lost airman a bed, and give him a hearty breakfast next morning while they awaited the arrival of the Military Police.

As a guest in the old farmhouse belonging to Brendan and his wife, Edward was installed in a tiny bedroom in which the furnishings were scant. There was a single iron-framed bed with a brass bedhead, and a washbowl and stand with a mirror behind it, and a wicker chair. Edward undressed and shivered in the damp cold. He peered into the mirror, and even by the oil lamp he'd been provided with, he could see that his chest and shoulders were badly bruised where the straps of his harness had dug in on the impact of his landing.

He slept fitfully, acknowledging in those hours in which he remained awake, that as he had failed to return to his base he would be posted missing. They would send a telegram to his next of kin. At once he thought of Libby and the agony it would put her through. There had to be a way he could get a message to her, to them all, to let them know he was alive and well.

Next morning, as expected, two military policemen arrived at Brendan's farmhouse in a military van, which resembled a typical black maria that British police used to transport felons and prisoners. They greeted Edward cursorily, unsmiling as he gave his name and rank.

'Shall I be able to get to Belfast,' Edward asked.

The MPs looked at each other, and one of them answered. 'That's not for us to decide, Flying Officer Burgayne, but it's important you understand that Ireland is a neutral country in your war. We favour neither the British nor the Germans for fear of offending either nation. Therefore, as a British service-man you must be handed over to the appropriate authority here in Ireland, in exactly the same way we must hand over any German servicemen who stray into Irish territory.'

Their demeanour, although respectful, was far from friendly and Edward seriously considered making a run for it. But he could hardly fail to notice their weapons, and didn't fancy being shot at as he fled. So he yielded to them and bid goodbye to Brendan and his wife, thanking them for their kind hospitality as he was led away.

One of them opened the rear door of the military vehicle and said, "'Tis a long journey we have ahead of us, Flying Offi-cer. Make yourself comfortable.'

The door closed with a thud and Edward was alone again with his thoughts in relative darkness as he perched himself on the hard bench in the back of the van. He was being treated like a prisoner, and wondered just what was to become of him. The engine roared into life and the vehicle began to move forward over the farm's bumpy dirt track towards the nearest road.

A seemingly long two and a quarter hours passed, and at last the van pulled up. The engine died, and the front doors opened and shut with a metallic bang. He heard raised voices. The rear doors opened, and Edward frowned at the light streaming in. Several men, had gathered round, watching him, all in the military uniform of Ireland. Two of them grabbed him by the arms and marched him through a high wooden gate towards a hut with another gate on either side of it.

To Edward's eyes it resembled a prisoner of war camp, girded as it was by a fence about fifteen or sixteen feet high, topped with barbed wire. There was also an inner barbed wire fence, within the confines of which were several huts raised on concrete blocks. It seemed that the complex was split into two compounds by virtue of the two gates. Through one he could see Luftwaffe officers in a small group, who peered back at him. The Irish soldiers marched him through the other gate, where he was at once surrounded by RAF officers and men, somewhat to his relief.

One of them stepped forward and offered his hand. 'Flight Lieutenant Paul Martin.' They shook. 'Welcome to K-Lines.'

- - -

It was mid-morning, and the telephone on Libby's desk rang, diverting her from her thoughts. She answered it with her usual pleasantness.

'Libby, it's Bunty.'

Libby sighed with trepidation. It was good to hear Bunty's gentle, cultured voice, but was she about to reveal confirmation of Edward's death? Bunty, however, understood perfectly what agony her friend was going through and would only ever offer sympathy and support.

'Hello, Bunty.'

'Are you feeling absolutely dreadful?'

'Oh, Bunty, you, above all people, know what it's like. I'm so miserable, I want to die.'

'Well don't pop off just yet. We've just had some simply brilliant news.'

Libby's puffy eyes widened at this unexpected lifeline. 'Oh, Bunty, you mean he's okay? Please, please tell me he's okay,' she implored.

'Seems like it.'

'Oh, thank God!'

'We received a telegram two minutes ago from The Irish military. I rang you at once to put you out of your misery. He's safe and well – in Eire—'

'In Eire?' Libby closed her eyes and more tears squeezed out; but these were tears of blessed relief. 'What on earth is he doing in Eire?'

'God only knows. Anyway, Libby, you can rest easy now, knowing he's all right.'

'How soon before they let him come home?'

'We don't know that yet.'

'Gosh, Bunty, I'm so relieved. He's alive and well after all.'

'And I daresay they'll allow him to write to his nearest and dearest soon. So keep an eye out for the postman, Libby.'

'Lord, I can't believe it.' She was smiling happily through her tears. 'I'm so relieved. So relieved. I don't know if my nerves can stand all this. I'm worrying myself stupid most of the time, then I'm in the depths of despair because I think he might have been shot down. Now, I'm up in the air again knowing he's all right.' She uttered a little laugh of joy.

'Will you let Daddy know, and Hugh?'

'Course I will. Straight away. Then I'm going to treat myself to a cup of tea. Oh, dear God, I need one, I can tell you.'

'Then I'll leave you to it for now.'

'Bye, Bunty. And thank you so much for letting me know.'

'Libby, you know I couldn't bear to think of you suffering any longer than necessary. If we hear anything else I'll let you know straight away of course.'

'Thank you, thank you.' Libby put the handset in its cradle and left her office with a happy smile. At the door of Charles Burgayne's office, she knocked and eagerly awaited the response to enter. Still she would not dream of entering his office without being bidden.

At once Charles saw the change in her demeanour; the lovely smile had returned, her eyes were unexpectedly alive and bright, and his heart leapt.

'What is it, Libby?' he asked expectantly. 'You look somewhat happier.'

'It's Edward, Mr Burgayne,' she gushed breathlessly as she put her hands to her face, in a gesture that indicated the mixed emotions of relief and incredulity. Tears were trembling on her long lashes. 'He's shown up, alive and well. He's in Eire. Can you believe it? I'm so relieved. Bunty just rang me with the news.'

Charles stood up and grinned. 'Thank God . . . Oh, thank God,' he cried. 'What wonderful news.'

'I know, I know. I'm so thrilled.' Her eyes filled with tears, and Charles noted her reaction.

'Sit down a moment, Libby . . .'

She duly sat down on the chair in front of his huge desk, and wiped her tears. But she was smiling.

'It's so obvious by your tears how deeply you feel for my son.'

'Oh, I can't deny it, Mr Burgayne.' She looked into her lap, avoiding his eyes.

'And presumably he feels as deeply about you.'

She nodded, looked up at him again, her moist eyes wide and candid. 'Yes, he does, Mr Burgayne. I know he does. Every bit as deeply.'

'And of course you miss him.'

'More than anybody will ever know.'

'Tell me, honestly, Libby,' he urged gently. 'How long have you both felt that way?'

She felt herself blushing at what might be regarded as an intrusion into her personal affairs, but she continued smiling and looking into the eyes of her employer, who was, after all, the father of her sweetheart. 'About eighteen months.'

'You've both been very secretive about it,' Charles suggested. 'But you don't hide your feelings easily, do you, Libby? And neither does Edward for that matter. His mother and I both suspected romance was blossoming.'

'But you don't mind, do you?'

'Mind? Good God, no, Libby. Frankly, I'm delighted – for you both. If you are patient enough to tolerate what will seem like an endless wait in this war, I wish you every happiness.'

Libby grinned contentedly; this was another monumental step forward. 'Thank you so much, Mr Burgayne. You have no idea how much that means to me – to both of us. You see, Edward didn't want it to be known we were in love in case you all disapproved.'

He looked at her with infinite compassion. 'Why on earth would we disapprove, Libby?'

She shrugged. 'Because I'm a nobody? Because I'm from an ordinary working-class family? Because I'm just an employee of the Blowers Green Steelworks?'

'But there's nothing wrong with any of those things. Gone are the days . . .'

'I'm so glad to hear you say it, Mr Burgayne. But some people might think differently.'

'Then to hell with them, that's what I say. We have no such petty prejudices. We're not in the nineteenth century now. Times have changed. You are a necessary, admired and welcome member of the Burgayne household, and always will be. Just remember that.'

'I'll never forget it, sir.'

'Oh, and *miss*,' he said returning the address with mock formality, 'less of the conventionality. In future, please call me Charles – unless we're in front of employees of course.' He smiled affably and she thanked him again.

- - -

Shortly afterwards, another telegram arrived from the Air Ministry confirming that Edward Burgayne had been found and was being held in an Irish internment camp. Libby began to worry again when she received no immediate letter from him. Perhaps they didn't allow prisoners to write to their families, she thought, and her concerns then were that he was possibly being mistreated. The wait seemed endless but, just a few days later on her return home from work, her mother smiled as she waved a letter teasingly.

'Postmarked Eire,' Gladys announced, as proudly as if she herself had been Edward's mother.

Libby grinned, doffed her overcoat, and took it eagerly. 'Thank God,' she breathed.

She ran upstairs to her bedroom with the cherished letter and, as she threw herself onto her bed, she tore open the envelope, opened up the sheets of paper folded inside, and began to read.

> *Libby, my darling,*
>
> *I can only stress how sorry I am that I have not been able to get a letter posted to you earlier. Since they tell me here that my family has been notified of my incarceration, you might have learned by now that I am in Southern Ireland in an Irish internment camp. I won't bore you with details of the circumstances of how I lost my way – that can wait until another day – but I simply had to let you know that I am all right, and actually being treated rather well.*
>
> *I crashed my Hurricane in a field while landing in the dark, and the impact knocked me unconscious. Miraculously, the only injuries I received were a bruised chest and shoulders. I actually thought I was landing in Pembrokeshire, but I was miles out because my compass had stuck. It has since re-*

minded me of the first time I took you up in the Moth and you said afterwards how amazed you were at how I could find my way while flying. Well, it was easy then, but a different kettle of fish in the dark over the blacked-out sea when you have no markers and no compass to guide you – only the Pole Star and the light from a full moon.

Anyway, it was not until I came to and heard a gabble of voices, asking if I was all right and offering to get me out. A group of people were inspecting me with flash lamps as I hung by the straps in the open cockpit of my upended plane. Then, when they knew I was still alive and by this time awake they decided to act. The farmer, whose land I had crashed on, and his wife, were wonderfully hospitable. He took me into his house and fed me royally before he sent for the police, who then decided I was a military concern and handed me over to the Military Police. When they arrived next morning I was taken unceremoniously away.

I am now in permanent residence at an internment camp called K-Lines at the Curragh of Kildare, conveniently close to a racecourse and a golf course. There are quite a few RAF pilots and crews here who have mistakenly or unavoidably landed on Irish soil. There are some German airmen and sailors too, who have been here almost since the start of the war.

I was informed during my interview with the camp commandant, Colonel McNally, that we are allowed certain privileges not countenanced in a POW camp. Namely, we are allowed out at certain times of the day on parole, and may actually play golf! Astonishing, but true. Restrictions have been lifted here recently and we are even allowed to go to any of the three cinemas and pubs locally as long as we wear civilian clothing. The purpose of civvies, they say, is so as not to stand out among the locals, some of whom still dislike the British and are sympathetic to the aims of the IRA, or even favour the Germans. Some, on the other hand, hate the Germans and support the British. Of course, we are kept under surveillance, but they tell us it is for our own protection. We have to buy the civilian clothing – they don't provide it – but apparently my salary will be paid as usual, and I should be able to get hold of something very soon. Unfortunately we cannot just walk away when out on parole, we are honour bound to return.

I know and understand how relieved you will be that while I am interned here I am unable to fly. On the other hand, I feel such a fool for getting myself into this mess and am longing to get back into a Hurricane and do my bit.

The weather here has been dreadful, by the way, with deep snow and drifting. Just before I arrived there was an escape attempt, but I think the weather impeded the chances of the escapees getting too far, and they were all rounded up af-

ter a day or so. Still, you are obliged to try once you are shut inside the camp. It's expected, seen as a duty.

I have no doubt that my letters will be censored before they are allowed to leave here, so maybe we shouldn't bore the poor chap who has to read our missives with endless (although delightful) admissions of love and devotion. They go without saying. Suffice to say, my darling, that I love and need you awfully, and I ache to be with you again. But how long that will be really depends on how long this war is going to last. I see no end in sight yet, but if Germany invades England I urge you to try and leave the country for your own safety and go to Canada.

Meanwhile, be patient, my darling, as I too must be.

My love always,

Edward.

- - -

The Royal Hospital in Wolverhampton was the location for Bunty's training to become a nurse, but when at Buttonbridge Hall she would help out with the convalescents, as would Libby during her less busy times. It was there that a young army lieutenant named Harry Wilding, drew Bunty's attention. Harry had served in France, as Adrian had done, and had also been wounded as he'd tried to flee Dunkirk. One day she asked him whether he happened to know Adrian, but he shook his head. Sorry, he said, he did not, but the likelihood was remote with so many thousands of men involved. He was, however, ready and willing to talk about his experiences, in turn listening intently while Bunty told him about Adrian.

Harry seemed a decent and likeable chap, cheerful and good-looking, and Bunty was drawn to him. He hailed from Bury St Edmunds in Suffolk, the only son of a reasonably well-to-do family. And he was unattached.

She began to spend more time with him, watching him recover from his wounds, as confident as he was that he would be able to lead a normal life in future. This was exactly what Bunty needed. Having another man to think about was helping her overcome the pain of losing Adrian.

But, inevitably, the time came when Harry was considered well enough to leave Buttonbridge Hall, and the day prior to his departure Bunty walked with him in the grounds, hand-in-hand. It was a bright March day, typically blustery, and the daffodils, in full bloom, were abundant, uplifting the grounds of Buttonbridge Hall from the dullness of their winter sleep.

'One question I've avoided asking you, Harry,' Bunty said as she lead him towards the fishpond where she knew it would be quiet and they would not be overlooked.

'What's that, pet?' He looked at her admiringly.

'Will you have to rejoin your unit?'

He shrugged. 'I expect so. I reckon I'll have to be assessed first, though. If they think I'm fit enough, then yes, it's my guess that I shall have to go back and do a bit more.'

She sighed, looking despondent, and he imagined what was troubling her.

'Look,' he said kindly, 'I'll do my best to keep out of the way of any German bullets, but the trouble is, they travel pretty quick, so you don't generally see 'em coming.'

Bunty sighed with anxiety. 'I told myself, Harry, that I would never get too attached to a soldier or a sailor or an air-man again. Yet here I am, head over heels once more. If you do have to go back please don't get yourself killed. I don't think I could stand it.'

'Chances are, if I am recalled,' he said, 'they'll be kind and give me a sit-down job in some stores or something. I might not even have to go abroad again. How would that suit you?'

'That would suit me perfectly,' she replied happily. 'Especially if we could be together from time to time.'

'Then give us a kiss and let's set a seal on it. In the mean-time, you won't forget to write to me, will you?'

'Of course not, silly.'

They stopped walking so as to hold each other and con-centrate on a decent kiss. It was good to feel a man's lips lin-gering on hers again, and he kissed so toe-curlingly well. The promise of greater closeness was tantalizing, for Bunty missed the tenderness of intimacy as well as the passion.

'And don't you get falling for some other service chap who comes here convalescing,' he said as they broke off their em-brace. 'You kiss so damned nicely, I couldn't stand the thought of somebody else having the pleasure.' He grinned appealingly. 'D'you hear?'

She smiled back, a light of mischief shining from her blue eyes, as in the old Bunty. 'Chance would be a fine thing, Harry, but if I do, you'll be the first to know.'

'Ah, you mean the last to know, of course. That's the way it normally works.'

'If I'd already found somebody else by the time you knew, it wouldn't matter one way or the other,' she teased. 'But I promise I won't,' she added, 'if you'll promise me the same.'

'That I do.'

- - -

| 17 |

'Can I ask a huge favour, Charles?'

'No harm in asking, Libby. What is it?'

Libby had just entered Charles's office at the works and was standing holding the edge of the door, her head tilted towards it appealingly. Her dark hair was swept up and pinned in a roll, a style that enhanced the youthful set of her neck.

'I'd like a few days holiday if you can spare me . . . I had in mind the week after Easter . . .'

'Oh? Well, I daresay we can arrange for somebody else to fill in for you. But why now? The weather's likely to be inclement for a month or two yet.'

She shut the door behind her and approached his desk, smiling in anticipation of having his permission. 'I have a rather special reason, Charles.'

'Which is?

'I want to go to Ireland. I want to see Edward.'

'Ireland? But will you be allowed to see him?'

'I don't see why not. He says the rules in his internment camp seem rather relaxed.'

'To say the least.'

'If you were to try your contact in Dublin?' she suggested. 'I'm sure he would be able to help . . .'

He smiled at her enterprise, full of admiration at her natural grasp of how useful it was to have contacts, however acquired. Since Edward's internment, the British Representative in Dublin had written to Charles, telling him of his visit to the K-Lines camp to meet Edward, and to reassure him that his son was indeed in good health and being well looked-after. They had subsequently kept up a correspondence, letters which Libby had typed.

'You mean Sir John Maffey. Yes, I suppose I could ask him to try and ensure you a safe and easy passage, and to ensure that you would be able to see Edward.'

'Would you, Charles? Please?'

'Of course I will.'

'You see, Edward is allowed out of camp whenever he wants.'

'So I understand.'

'So I'm sure he'd be able to meet me. Apparently, they even encourage the internees to take Irish girlfriends to keep them happy and not homesick.'

Charles smiled. 'Some internment! But where would you stay?'

'I've no idea. An inn or hotel, I expect. There must be some.'

'So when do you want to leave for Ireland?'

'Easter Tuesday.'

'Get your pencil and pad then, my girl. Let's get a letter off to Sir John Maffey and ask if he can pull a few strings.'

Libby grinned contentedly. 'Thank you so much, Charles.'

- - -

On Tuesday 15th April, armed with a travel permit and a copy of a letter from the British Representative in Dublin, Libby stood on the deck of a ferry bound for Belfast, braving the wind and the rain as it lashed her face. She was thrilled, and not a little nervous, at the prospect of actually being with Edward soon, of being able to touch him, able to hear his voice, feel his lips on hers again.

Gulls wheeled above, their persistent shrieks a perfect contrast to the roar of the restless, surging sea. Other passengers eyed her curiously; a young woman travelling alone across the Irish sea – for this journey was not without its dangers, not least from the mines that were regularly dropped by the Luftwaffe around the approaches to Belfast. Nor did she look Irish; she looked English to the core. But she was prepared to risk all, and willingly, for the chance of being with the man she loved, however brief their tryst might turn out to be.

As she leaned against the wooden rail, relishing the buffeting of the wind, the rain, and the salty smell of the sea, they came within clear sight of land. Soon the ship was ploughing a wide stretch of water known as Belfast Lough, lined with docks, shipping, towering cranes and gantries, some of which had clearly suffered damage from recent bombings. In the distance stood church towers and steeples, and forests of tall chimneys driving smoke into the steel-grey sky. She strained her eyes for a better glimpse, and saw the hills of Ulster beyond, rendered grey by the mist of rain.

The ferry docked and Libby joined the throng of folk stepping onto the quay. She enquired of somebody if they knew how far it was to the railway station, and was duly given directions. On the way the clouds parted and the low, reddening sun burst through clear and vivid, leaving everything tinged with grey-orange. At length she arrived at the station and bought a return ticket for Dublin. The next train was not due to leave till half past ten that night owing to wartime rescheduling, so she decided to buy a newspaper, *The Belfast Telegraph,* to occupy her while she waited. Trains hissed and clanked as they pulled in and out of the station, dropping and collecting passengers. Feeling hungry, she made herself comfortable in the station cafeteria where she bought a ham sandwich and tea. She looked at the clock again; it was ten minutes to eight.

It was going to be a long wait, and she read the newspaper from cover to cover.

- - -

At length, a locomotive of the Great Northern Railway Ireland pulled in hauling its line of carriages. No sooner had Libby stepped inside one and placed her suitcase in the luggage rack of one of the compartments than she heard the sound of air raid sirens. She'd read in *The Belfast Telegraph* the criticisms and invective of how the city had been totally unprepared for the bombing raid around the docks and the shipbuilding yards just a week earlier. This information made her realise how much her journey was fraught with danger, especially now that the Luftwaffe was evidently back for another strike. How fortunate that she'd already left the docks and was on this train that was due to leave Belfast any minute.

The train, which was full, pulled out of the station slowly, its blue liveried locomotive huffing and rasping. Libby stepped out into the corridor, busy with other passengers seeking a seat, all of whom looked apprehensive. Just as apprehensively, she lowered the window in the door nearest to where she stood and looked up. After the earlier rain, the sky had cleared but for some scattered cumulous clouds which tarried. The cold glow of a three-quarter moon highlighted them and cast an eyrie glimmer over the undulating landscape despite the blackout. It was then that she heard the unmistakable drone of aircraft – a great many aircraft – audible even above the sound of the gasping locomotive and its clattering wheels.

'Did you hear the sirens this morning?' somebody asked standing close to her.

She turned to see if the person was talking to her. Evidently he was; a middle-aged man wearing a trilby hat and mackintosh.

'This morning? No,' she replied. 'I didn't arrive in Belfast till this evening.'

'English, hah?'

She nodded and turned back to the window.

'Then you should be used to the sound of sirens. But in Ulster we're not. Leastwise, we weren't. We thought the Germans had forgotten about us, but we should've known better. After all, we've got the Harland and Wolff shipbuilders and

Short's aircraft factory here. The Krauts were never going to leave *them* alone, hah?'

'No such luck,' she said sympathetically, but didn't know what else to say. Nor did she feel like encouraging further conversation.

'Well let's hope and pray that a stray bomb doesn't hit this train!'

As the train gathered speed, away from the confines of the city, the wind was buffeting her, so Libby closed the window in deference to other passengers and to keep warm. But she continued to gaze out. The insistent drone of aircraft in swarms overhead was still perceptible, and the man's comment about a stray bomb hitting the train frightened her. Belfast was in for it tonight, and no mistake. Lucky for her she had left the city, but oh, those poor people who couldn't . . .

Then, behind them the sky lit up, and Libby watched in absolute horror. The first wave of German aircraft were dropping flares which came tumbling out of the sky to bathe the whole city in a blindingly brilliant white glare, creating artificial daylight that slowly turned to orange before dying.

Using that invasive light, droves of other aircraft followed, raining incendiaries, high explosive bombs and lethal parachute mines onto Belfast. Even from the train, thankfully travelling away from the city, she could hear the incessant barrage of explosions and anti-aircraft gunfire in one long, rumbling, terrifying cacophony of sound. Even the ground beneath them seemed to transmit the resulting tremors through the floor of the moving railway carriage. Alarm, horror and even panic was visibly and audibly spreading among travellers through-out the railway carriage. Some of those passengers would have left friends, sweethearts and family behind, to suffer the con-sequences of that sickening air raid. There would be hundreds, if not thousands, of casualties that night.

Mass destruction was happening there and then, which emphasised to Libby how absolutely necessary it was for those brave young pilots like Edward, to fly out and intercept the in-cessant droves of enemy aircraft that were capable of inflicting so much material damage and loss of life. She felt a surge of pride at their unstinting courage and willingness to put their own lives at risk in the course of protecting the rest of us. She had no doubt also, that but for the dedication to duty of these men, there would have been more Luftwaffe aircraft in the skies above Belfast that night, for many would already have been downed on the way.

As the train snaked on, meandering southeast beyond Por-tadown, Libby could still see the incandescent sky to the northeast aglow with the fires and explosions that were rip-ping through Belfast. It was a sight that she would never for-get. But at least the bombs had not found the moving train.

It was well after midnight when the train arrived at Dublin's Amiens Street Station. Still horrified and preoccupied with the harrowing scenes she had witnessed, albeit from the relative safety of the train, Libby left the station, uncertain what to do next. It was late and imperative she find some-where to stay the night. It then dawned on her how bright the streets were – of course, there was no blackout here. Across the street she saw an hotel and headed for it. The sign above said, 'North Star Hotel'. At least she might be able to get a good night's sleep there before continuing her journey to Newbridge in County Kildare.

Next morning, refreshed, but still disturbed by the ghastly mental images of Belfast aflame, she returned to the station and caught the next train to Newbridge. She was getting closer to Edward and could soon be in his arms, and these pleasant thoughts began slowly to nudge away the nightmarish recollections of last night.

Once in Newbridge, she took a taxi to the Curragh, and was astounded by the number of well-tended large country houses she saw on the way. Clearly, there was wealth around here. Her heart began pounding when the taxi stopped at the gates of a compound that was enclosed by high barbed-wire fencing.

The Curragh Camp was originally built as a barracks for British troops stationed in Ireland during the occupation. Its rows of huts were now housed soldiers of the Irish Army. K-Lines, which formed a rectangle on the east side of the camp and was separate from it, was remarkably similar in outward appearance to most prisoner of war camps. It was modelled on the No.1 Internment camp which the British built on the west side to house IRA prisoners. It consisted of a rectangular perimeter barbed wire fence, which incorporated large double gates at the outer entrance. A grass corridor, patrolled by the camp guards occupied the space between the outer and inner barbed wire fences. On each of the four corners of the perimeter stood a tower, all serving as observation and gun posts. The area within the rectangular perimeter fences was divided into two compounds by a fence constructed of corrugated iron and topped with barbed wire. Both compounds adjoined a hut, which straddled the dividing fence and had a door and window allowing entrance to, and exit from, each compound. The coming and going of the internees from both compounds was controlled from this hut and known as the parole hut. 'G' compound was occupied by the German forces, and 'B' compound by the allied forces.

Libby realised that this had to be the K-Lines internment camp.

And Edward was here.

She paid the driver and thanked him, picked up her small suitcase, then braced herself for this extraordinary visit, not knowing what sort of reception she was likely to get from the guards in the building facing her, which looked the best place to start.

'I'm a visitor from England to see Flying Officer Edward Burgayne.'

'Yeh've cum ter see Burgayne?' the guard replied with a friendly grin. 'Well, I'm sartain sure he'll be glad to see yourself, miss. Yeh see dat hut over dere . . .' He pointed. 'Ask for him in dere. Boi der way, dat's a luvly hat you be wearing.'

Libby smiled graciously. 'Thank you.'

Carrying her suitcase she made her way to the next hut, which was the parole hut, and repeated her request.

'What's your name, miss?'

'Libby Shakespeare.'

'Libby Shakespeare,' he repeated, as if savouring the words on his tongue. 'So you're the possessor of dat name. For the sweet love o' Mary, 'tis a pretty name, so 'tis. I tort so when I saw it writ down. And named after the Bard.'

'You've seen my name written down?'

'To be sure. We've been told in a memorandum to expect yeh, miss, and give yeh every assistance.'

Sir John Maffey had been helpful then, according to that snippet of information.

The guard looked up at her and smiled politely. 'I'll have Burgayne sent out to yeh, once we find him. He might be in der gymnasium or in der swimming pool, you see.'

The guard left his post, she put down her case and she waited, shivering with anticipation. She was about to see Edward, at long, long last.

It seemed like an age, having come this far, but it was actually no more than three minutes before she spotted Edward through the intimidating barbed wire fences, escorted by a guard and another officer. He was smiling and, as far as she could tell from where she stood, he looked well, and was wearing civilian clothes. Her heart was pounding like mad. Slowly – it seemed an age – he approached. When he saw her standing waiting he grinned, waved excitedly, and quickened his pace. Eventually he reached her, and they embraced, while the two Irish servicemen tactfully retired to their hut.

'Look at you,' Edward said, almost breathlessly. 'You look wonderful.' He held her at arm's length and simply admired her.

'Oh, Edward.' She gave him another hug. 'I can't believe I'm actually here. I can't believe we're actually together. It must be a dream.' She felt self-conscious under his gaze, but tears of joy were making her eyes tingle, and she gave them a wipe with the back of her gloved hand. 'Gosh, just look at me. I'm such a sentimental fool, aren't I?' she added self-effacingly.

'It's absolutely wonderful to see you. You can't imagine how grateful I am you actually made the trip.'

'I just had to. Ever since you wrote and told me you were allowed out I've been hatching my plan. It seemed such a waste not to.'

'I was petrified for you when I heard about the bombing in Belfast last night.'

'You heard about it?' she asked incredulous.

'Yes. They allow us a wireless here so we can keep up to date with news of the war.'

'It was horrid – simply awful – scores of aircraft screaming overhead dropping flares, bombs and all manner of stuff. Thankfully, we just missed it. As the train pulled out of the station you could hear the planes coming over. We saw it all unfold from the train. It really was terrifying. The poor people of Belfast . . .'

'We heard about it first thing. It must've been dreadful. Thou-sands of houses have been flattened, apparently, hun-dreds dead. Of course, they don't know the full extent yet. But it's one reason I want to get back into a Hurricane – to pay the bastards back.'

'And I'm so proud of you, Edward, but so scared for you. Anyway,' she said her expression lighting up with a smile, wiping the watery remnants of tears, 'I haven't come here to discuss the war. You look well and they're treating you well, you say.'

'It's true. We're treated more like guests than prisoners.'

'So it's not so bad?'

'Well, it's a certain fact we wouldn't be treated like this in a German POW camp, nor would we get any privileges like we do here. If I have one complaint, it's that it's boring. But not now you're here,' he said warmly. 'How long can you stay?'

'Only till Saturday. Then I'll have to leave. Goodness knows what problems there'll be when I get back to Belfast.'

'Well, let's worry about that nearer the time. For now let me show you the Curragh. Have you been able to find somewhere to stay?'

'No, I've only just got here.'

'Then we'd better get you fixed up. We'll go out and find somewhere.'

'We're leaving the camp?'

'Of course.'

'What a funny old prison,' she remarked.

He laughed. 'Well, all I do is sign a parole slip, and Bob's your uncle. That chap who came to get me when you arrived is the duty parole officer.' He turned around and called to him. 'Captain Fitzpatrick! May I have a parole slip, please?'

As Edward walked towards him, the parole officer grinned and took a slip from a drawer in the desk before him. 'To return by what time?' he asked, looking Libby up and down. 'Shall we say 23.00 hours?' he suggested with a knowing look.

'Oh, Eamon, can't you make it midnight?' Edward asked with a wink.

'Pooh!' he complained. 'Oi'll likely get into big trouble, but seeing as how your luvly wife has come all the way from England to see yer, I'll mark it down as twenty-three hours fifty-nine.'

'Thank you, Eamon. I'll see if I can find a bottle of Bushmills for you,' Edward declared. 'Actually, Eamon, my wife needs somewhere to stay for a few nights. Do you recommend anywhere?'

'You know, Flying Officer Burgayne, I didn't even know you was married,' the parole officer said, looking at him with a sideways smirk. 'According to your record you're unmarried. Your next of kin is your father. And how come your luvly wife is called *Miss* Shakespeare?'

Edward winked at him in response while Libby wished that the ground would open up and swallow her. 'Well, keep it to yourself for now, eh. Eamon?'

Captain Fitzpatrick grinned with self-satisfaction that he had let Flying Officer Burgayne know that he hadn't fooled anybody with his wife baloney. 'Try Lawlor's Hotel in Naas.'

'Lawlor's . . . Of course. Thank you, Eamon.'

'Now, if you'll just sign your parole slip . . .'

Edward duly signed it. 'We'll need a taxi.'

'For the love o' Mary,' Captain Fitzpatrick exclaimed satirically, 'd'yer t'ink dis is a holiday camp?' He smiled, willingly picked up the telephone and dialled a number.

Within five minutes a taxi appeared at the main gate.

When they had departed, Captain Fitzpatrick picked up the telephone again and spoke to the receptionist at Lawlor's Hotel to let them know that an intern from K-Lines, Flying Officer Edward Burgayne, was on his way with his young wife, and would they ensure she was given a good room.

On the way to Lawlor's Libby said quietly, 'Given all this freedom, why don't you just walk away from that camp, catch a train and escape? You could be in Belfast before they even missed you. It's not as if you are wearing your RAF uniform. It would be the simplest thing.'

Edward sighed. 'But it's really not that simple, Darling.' He took her hand as they sat close to each other in the rear of the taxi. 'You saw me sign that parole slip. Well, it's a conditional release from the camp, a privilege granted by the Irish authorities, and upheld by the British government. As officers of the RAF we are obliged to honour its terms and return by the time noted on that slip. Failing to do so brings dishonour not only to ourselves, but to the RAF and our country.'

'But there's a war on, Edward,' Libby protested logically. 'And the RAF needs you – not to mention me.'

'And, believe it or not, if I scarpered while on parole, the authorities in Northern Ireland and England would only send me back here. Furthermore, I could be court martialled.'

'Why are they so strict about it? It doesn't make sense.'

'Basically, it's because our government doesn't want to offend the Irish in any way. As I understand it, the Irish, being neutral, do not allow either British or German warships to enjoy the facilities of Irish ports. If we upset them and they granted such facilities to the Germans it would be catastrophic to our Atlantic shipping, and possibly alter the outcome of the war.'

'I see . . . Well, I think I see . . . So your word is your bond.'

'Spot on, Sweetheart. However . . .' He smiled and she saw again that disarming twinkle in his eyes that she loved so much. 'On the other hand, we are obliged by the RAF to do all we can to escape and return to our squadrons, but only while we are interned and not on parole. In fact, when we're not on parole the Irish expect us to try and escape. Hence all the barbed wire and armed guards.'

'Crikey, what a cock-eyed world this war has created,' she sighed. 'So you couldn't even return home with me. And I thought I would easily persuade you.'

'I only wish I could, my love. It would be my dream. But it just ain't possible.'

As they drove through Newbridge Edward asked the taxi driver to stop, and he got out of the car.

'I won't be a minute,' he said.

Five minutes later he returned, a broad, self-satisfied grin on his face.

'You look pleased with yourself,' Libby remarked.

'Oh, I am,' he answered smugly. 'You'll see why presently.'

Presently they arrived at Lawlor's Hotel, a large country house symmetrical in its Georgian style. Libby paid the taxi driver and watched him drive off.

'Here, take your gloves off,' Edward said with the familiar gleam in his eye as he put her suitcase on the ground.

Libby looked at him puzzled.

'Now give me your hand . . . No, your left hand.'

She did as he asked, he slipped a ring on her finger, and she looked at him with all her love in her eyes.

'It's nothing special,' he said apologetically. 'I suspect it's made of brass. It's what I stopped to get in Newbridge. But so long as they see what looks like a wedding ring they'll be happy. It's an odds-on certainty that the folk who own this place are Catholics, and they could be awkward about unmarried couples . . .' He winked an eye at her, and she nodded as she realised his ploy.

The young man on the desk glanced at Libby with approval and at Edward with envy, but smiled and bade them welcome as he handed Edward the key to a room upstairs. Once there, Edward again put down Libby's suitcase, parted the curtains and looked out onto the gently rolling countryside of Eire.

'Come here,' he said softly.

She stood before him looking alluringly coy, and he took off her hat, then her coat which he tossed onto a chair in a swish of material. They fell into a passionate embrace, lips hungry for each other. It was so wonderful to feel her in his arms again after so long, to be alone with her and nobody else in the world to trouble them. They were together again at last, and it barely seemed possible. It would not have been possible, but for Libby's vision and her unwavering determination to make it happen. She could have been killed in the attempt, too, had her train's departure been delayed.

'Let's get undressed,' he whispered.

They did so quickly, and dived naked between the sheets.

'Gosh, it's chilly,' she remarked. 'Maybe we should've asked for a hot water bottle.'

He grinned contentedly. 'Absolutely no need, Sweetheart. I'll warm you up very quickly. It's a promise.'

As the cold of the sheets enveloped her she shivered and snuggled up to him, and he luxuriated in the warmth and the silky smoothness of her skin against him. He held her tight, their lips met again, and they kissed passionately, instantly entwined in earnest mutual desire. There was scarcely time for foreplay, scarcely any need. He rolled onto her, pressing himself urgently against her as he sought entry. She clutched his buttocks and, with a little gasp of pleasure, felt him slide gloriously inside her with such blissful sweetness.

'Oh, Edward,' she sighed, relishing the luscious sensations that were flowing through her. 'I've wanted you so much . . . so much . . . If only you knew . . .'

So this is how it is for a husband just come home from the wars after long years, Edward thought as he wallowed in the love she eagerly bestowed on him. The feel of her slender but accommodating body beneath him, her instinctive physical response as he moved inside her was delightfully familiar, yet because it had been so long since last they'd made love, somehow it all seemed so new, so fresh and unexplored. It was a sheer, invigorating joy.

Afterwards they lay silent in each other's arms for some time, perspiring contentedly. Outside the sun was shining and they could hear the voices of the locals as they greeted each other outside, while she lay with her eyes closed, a look of serenity on her beautiful face.

Thank God he had Libby. As well as her enthusiasm as a lover, Edward pondered her courage, her resourcefulness and willingness to risk all to share a few hours with him in Ireland. It was a measure of the strength of her love – strength she would need when he announced his intentions, which were noble enough, to his family.

'Libby, are you awake?' he whispered.

'Yes, I'm awake,' she answered softly. 'I was just thinking how lovely it would be to wake up next to you every morning.'

'On that very topic, I want to ask you something.'

'Ask away,' she sighed, and turned to face him.

'Will you marry me when all this is over?'

'Will I marry you?' She raised her head resting it in her hand propped-up on her elbow, her hair comically dishevelled as a result of their passion. 'A thousand times, yes, Edward. Of course I'll marry you.'

'We'd be happy, wouldn't we, you and me?'

'Happier together than we are apart, that's for certain.' She fingered the patch of sparse hairs that were sprouting on his chest.

'I just worry about how my folks will take the news.'

'Edward, you don't have to worry about that anymore.' She leaned forward and kissed him on the lips, her breasts brushing his chest tantalisingly. 'We have your father's blessing.'

'We do? How come?'

'Because I told him how it is between us. He was delighted. He wished us well.'

'You never said in any of your letters.'

'I would've. But now I've told you to your face. A much better way. Don't you think?'

'I know what I do think, Libby, my gorgeous little poppet . . . I want to make love to you again.'

- - -

| **18** |

On the night before she left for home, the Friday, there was a dance at Lawlor's Ballroom. Lawlor's Ballroom was not part of the hotel building, but was located in a converted carpet factory on the eastern side of Naas. It became obvious to Libby that many of Edward's RAF colleagues present had already made friends with local girls, some of them well-heeled socialites and members of the Kildare Hunt, because they danced and laughed with obvious familiarity. However, some girls were accompanied by their mothers, who were there to keep an ever-watchful eye.

Through the haze of cigarette smoke and wafts of scintillating perfume, Edward introduced Libby to a few other internees, Douglas Newport and Herbert Ricketts, crew members of a Blenheim Bomber, who had been forced to bale out over County Donegal: Aubrey Davidson, tall and good-looking with an equally handsome moustache; and Paul Martin from Norfolk, a Hurricane pilot who had got lost over Ireland in circumstances not dissimilar to Edward's.

'How long have you been at K-Lines, Paul,' Libby enquired, making conversation.

'Since early October last year,' he replied. 'Though I did make one unsuccessful attempt to escape in January – just before Edward arrived. But the weather was foul – against us more than any other factor. I've not at all given up the idea, though, I can assure you . . .' He took a quick drink from his glass. 'I have a rather lovely fiancée back home whom I'm dying to see.'

'I can understand why you're keen to get back home,' Libby replied with a smile. 'And you, Aubrey?' she asked. 'You're still here.'

'But not for want of trying to get out,' he answered. 'Actually, I try to escape on a regular basis. You might have heard, one's only obliged to try and escape when not on parole, but I must say, it is rather comfortable here. I'd just as soon be in the officers' bar as risk being shot at by Irish guards.'

'You have a bar, as well as all this freedom?' she asked incredulously.

'Well-stocked at that,' Aubrey replied. 'I must confess, I've developed a taste for Guinness since I've been here.'

They were standing near the ballroom's bar which was tended by a tall blonde girl whom they called Teagan.

'How do you get along with the German internees?' Libby asked Douglas Newport, over the sound of a quickstep the band were playing – a familiar tune.

'We don't have much to do with them,' Newport answered, hugging his beer glass to his chest. 'For obvious reasons. They come in here sometimes, sometimes visit the same pubs as we do, but they tend not to mix with us. I suppose language is as much a barrier as the war itself. In any case, it wouldn't do to get too chummy.'

The group chatted about this and that for some time, then Edward, itching to get close to Libby, leaned in her ear and said, 'They're playing a waltz, sweetheart. Dance with me.'

She put down her glass on the bar and held her hand out to him with a smile, and they stepped onto the specially sprung maple dancefloor.

'So what do you think of my fellow airmen?' he asked as they set off in a whirl.

'They all seem awfully nice,' she answered, hearing herself and at once aware that she was beginning to speak like them. 'But I do feel sorry for them. They're all itching to get away from here.'

'Not least, me,' he admitted. 'There's talk of escape all the time. They're always discussing ruses – where to dig tunnels and all that. But Paul – the Hurricane pilot from Norfolk – he's the leader of our escape committee, if you can call it that – he's got contacts.'

'He seems very posh,' she commented. 'Even posher than you.'

He saw the humour in her eyes, and said, 'He is posher than me. His father's a knight of the realm.'

'Crikey! Anyway, shall you try and escape, Edward?'

'They'll have a job to hold me back.'

'But please be careful, darling. I'd rather you were here and still in one piece than at home in several bits.'

He laughed.

'Actually, I've got something to tell you, Libby,' he said, pressing himself against her and with a dreamy look in his eyes.

'What?'

'I've managed to get special parole.'

'You mean you don't have to be back at the camp until to-morrow?'

'Oh, if only . . . I'd love nothing more than being able to sleep with you tonight – all night. But they wouldn't allow that for a minute. It would set a precedent, you see.'

'That's a shame. Shall we slip off early then,' she suggested, flicking her eyebrows provocatively. 'You mustn't be late get-ting back to camp.'

He laughed happily at her saucy suggestion, delighted at her utter lack of prudishness, her lack of inhibition. She was one in a million. 'I wanted to suggest it myself, but I'm awfully pleased that you have.'

'So could you come with me as far as Dublin tomorrow?' she asked.

'That's my avowed intention. That's what the special parole allows.'

'Oh, Edward.' She hugged him tight. 'I love you so much.'

So they slipped out of the dance unnoticed and returned to Lawlor's Hotel and her room, leaving plenty of time for Ed-ward to return to K-Lines without violating his parole.

- - -

What remained of that night was made all the more delectable, all the more passionate, because it was wrested from the peculiarity of their circumstances. Edward, the RAF pilot who was interned in a benevolent sort of prison where, incongruously, he was free to come and go as he pleased, but not allowed to return home while aching to do exactly that; Libby, the resourceful, romantic girl who needed to know that her man was thriving, and who was unshrinking in her intention to make the absolute best of their limited time together. It had been a magical few days, an unforgettable experience and she regretted nothing, save the horrors she had seen perpetrated on Belfast and its people. Yet, inevitably, the time came when she and Edward had to part.

Libby left Lawlor's Hotel early, collecting Edward from the camp on the way, so that she could catch the early train from Newbridge, then the ten o' clock from Dublin to Belfast. They said their goodbyes on the platform at Amiens Street Station, and even more goodbyes while he hurried alongside the train, keeping up with Libby at one of the open windows as it gathered speed, until he ran out of platform. Then she craned her neck to see him waving, until eventually he disappeared from view behind a hoarding. It was a timely cue for tears to fall again.

When she deliberately tried to take her mind off Edward and think about her journey, Libby was apprehensive about how things would be in Belfast. When she arrived she was presented with the evidence of the air raid, but work was already underway clearing up. Folk were smiling, and she admired their unconquerable spirit. All that remained now was to hope that the ferry to Liverpool was still operating. To her relief, it was.

- - -

Libby's return home was uneventful. Much of it she could not recall because she was absorbed in thoughts of Edward, K-Lines, and how benevolent it was to all those poor servicemen who had been unfortunate enough to have been incarcerated there. Benevolent, it certainly was, but the policy of the Irish government was not sufficiently benevolent to allow them home.

Gladys and Joe Shakespeare were relieved to see her back safely, and surprised at the extraordinary privileges the interns were able to enjoy when Libby related her experiences. Joe informed her that the Blowers Green Steelworks had been bombed while she was away, but the damage had been limited to only one area.

When she returned to work next day, Charles Burgayne was eager to see her. He called her to his office as soon as she arrived, spruce and perky, that Monday morning.

'How is he, Libby?' He sounded anxious.

'He's extremely well, Charles,' she said brightly, to immediately allay any fears.

'It's very gratifying to hear it. Very gratifying.' He coughed. 'And you enjoyed yourselves?'

'We had a lovely time. I wouldn't have missed it for the world. It was lovely to see Edward again. He sends his love, of course, to all of you.'

'His mother will be delighted as well as relieved.'

She told Charles at length about the very favourable conditions of Edward's internment, and the extent of his liberty – except of course for his extended parole and their subsequent interludes of tenderness and passion at Lawlor's Hotel – and explained, too, the concept of the parole system that allowed it.

'But I wouldn't be at all surprised if some of them try and make another break for it,' she remarked. 'They're all desperate to get back to their squadrons and fight. I just hope they don't get shot in the process.'

'You have to admire their valour,' Charles said with a solemn frown, 'but I have the feeling it would be better for Edward if he were to remain there.'

'I think so too,' Libby agreed. 'He's out of harm's way there.'

'We were also genuinely concerned for you, Libby, when we heard about the bombing raids over Belfast.'

'I was lucky, Charles. I was already on a train out when it began, but you could see it all happening in the distance.'

'We took a direct hit ourselves at the works,' he informed her. 'It's lucky nobody was killed. One or two hurt, which is a dreadful shame, but none seriously. Number Two Melting Shop is out of action meanwhile.' He shrugged resignedly and coughed again. 'We're lucky we haven't been hit before. Let's face it, as a steelworks we're a legitimate target.'

- - -

Spring turned slowly and surely into summer and, along the way, the Germans pushed the British out of Greece. London suffered the worst air raids of the war so far when 550 aircraft indiscriminately rained bombs and incendiaries on the capital, killing 1,400 civilians. The robust spirit of Londoners seemed to flag under the ferocity of the attack. In May the German battleship *Bismarck*, the terror of Atlantic shipping and reckoned to be unsinkable, was finally destroyed after a three-day chase across the ocean from Greenland. On another assault, German troops, wearing New Zealand army uniforms, invaded Crete, but were repulsed largely by New Zealand troops, as well as British and Greek forces.

In late June, the Nazis decided to invaded Russia.

On Monday, 30th June, Libby was at her desk at the steelworks when she received a message from the telephonist that a telegram had just arrived for her. She hurried to collect it, her heart in her mouth, then sat on a chair in the reception hall and opened it gingerly, while her mind was suddenly swimming with possibilities that it contained bad news about Edward.

But logic rapidly took over. It could not be. The authorities would have sent any bad news to Charles, his father, his next of kin. This must be good news, and from Edward himself. Heartened, she unfolded it and read it . . .

AM IN BELFAST AND PROSPERING STOP MORE
LATER STOP MEANWHILE DON'T WRITE STOP
PLEASE TELL FAMILY STOP EDWARD STOP

Excitedly, she ran to Charles's office and knocked, but burst in unceremoniously without waiting for a reply, waving the telegram.

'It's from Edward,' she gasped breathlessly. 'He's in Belfast. It can only mean one thing – he's escaped.'

Charles stood up, astounded. 'Are you sure?'

'Why else would he be in Belfast? He's across the border. It stands to reason he's escaped.'

'May I see?' he held his hand out for the telegram as if it might contain a further clue that she had overlooked, and she passed it to him. As he read it a smile spread over his face. 'I believe you're right, Libby. So what do we do now, I wonder?'

'We wait,' she suggested. 'He says not to write, and more later. Maybe he'll ring.'

'Maybe I should telephone the Air Ministry to see if they know anything.'

'I wouldn't,' she said assertively.

'You wouldn't? Why not?'

'Because it could draw attention to it. If they don't know about it they won't start investigating. If they do begin to pry, it could alert the wrong people perhaps, and jeopardise his chances.'

Charles looked at her with admiration as he rubbed his chin pensively. 'You're a canny girl, Libby, and I think you have a valid point. But waiting . . .' He coughed. 'This not knowing . . .'

'I know.'

'Still, we should make no ripples, just in case.'

She nodded. 'No ripples. Just in case.'

- - -

The waiting seemed interminable. Days passed with no word and no clue as to what had happened to Edward. Libby was beginning to imagine all sorts of horrendous possibilities; that he'd been recaptured and sent back to K-Lines, that he'd violated his parole and the RAF had sent him back, that he'd been shot, that he'd been run over by a bus, that it had all been some sort of cruel joke.

Then, on the following Sunday evening, after nearly a week of anxious fretting, she answered a knock on the veranda door and, magically, through the glass she saw him standing there, a perfect grin on his manly face. She rushed to open it, and flung her arms around his neck.

'Oh, Edward . . . Edward . . .' Tears of joy tingled in her eyes. 'So you did escape, after all.'

'Nine of us. Six of us made it.'

'How? How did you do it.'

'Later. Kiss me.'

They kissed, ardently and long.

'God, I've missed you,' he breathed.

Unseen, the Shakespeare's next-door neighbour, Mrs Bennett saw them as she returned from the privy at the top of the shared yard, and smiled with understanding as she tactfully averted her gaze; how agonizing it must be, she thought, to be young and in love with a serviceman in wartime.

'Come in and see mom and dad,' Libby said as they reluctantly broke off their embrace. She took his hand and turned, leading him inside.

'Look who just happened to be in the neighbourhood,' she said joyously to Gladys and Joe who, because they were sitting listening to the wireless had not heard the knock on the door.

'Well, I'll be hanged!' Joe exclaimed, getting up from his chair and offering his hand. 'It's young Edward. Thank God you'm all right, lad – our Libby's been fretting herself daft over thee . . . Turn the wireless off, Glad.'

Glad turned the wireless off.

'It's good to see you again, Mr Shakespeare. It's great to be back.' He turned to Gladys. 'Mrs Shakespeare . . . Lovely to see you again.' He bent down and kissed her filially on the cheek.

'So you escaped from that concentration camp,' Gladys exclaimed. 'Good for you. I never did trust them Irish. You only have to look at that swine de Valera.'

Edward grinned happily. 'Well, it was hardly a concentration camp,' he said. 'More like a holiday camp, to tell you the truth. But it was not home, and I'm glad to be out of it. I'm glad to be back in England.'

'I'll put the kettle on, eh? I bet you could do with a cup of tea. I know I could.' But she hesitated, standing by the door to hear more of Edward's exploit.

'When did you get back?' Libby asked.

'About three this afternoon. Dad collected me from the station.'

'So where've you been since I got your telegram? It's been ages.'

'Well, we were picked up and taken to London for a couple of days for debriefing, before we were allowed home.'

'Sit yourself down, son,' Joe invited, 'and tell us how it all happened.'

'It was all too easy really,' Edward responded as he pulled a chair from under the table and sat on it. 'We'd planned it all carefully, of course. The top and bottom of it was that we'd been to the races, and some of us had had a jolly good day—'

'The races?' Joe queried, incredulous.

'Yes, Dad,' Libby butted in. 'I forgot to tell you there's a racecourse next to the camp, and they're allowed to go.'

'Well, on our return, we all pretended to be the worse for drink, a condition not at all unusual among us, I have to confess. Later, while we played cards, we pretended to drink more, and collected lots of empty bottles around us to enhance the effect. So when the guards came to check on us later they were fooled into thinking we were all frightfully blotto. At bedtime some of our lads asked to go to the parole hut with the excuse that they wanted to send a telegram, and of course the guard on duty complied. While they were taking their time composing it, two other chaps – with perfect timing – returned from parole, signed back in, and together we overcame the guards. We didn't hurt them, of course, they were thoroughly decent chaps. All that remained was to get through the outer perimeter fence. Well, Paul Martin – you remember you talked with him, Libby – had managed to get hold of a pair of wire cutters from somewhere – I told you he had connections. Anyway, we didn't ask where they came from. The guards in the look-out towers fired some shots, but we discovered later that they only ever use blanks! In seconds we were through, and out onto the golf course.'

'Golf course?' Joe said.

'Yes, Dad, I forgot to tell you – they were allowed to play golf.'

'Glory be! I wouldn't mind being shut up in that camp meself.'

'Well, that's it, basically,' Edward concluded. 'Once outside we split up, of course, and most of us managed to get to Belfast by one means or another. I've seen Paul since in London, and he hid up in a tree for about twenty hours, he reckoned, before he crossed the border.'

'Who else made it?' Libby asked.

'Ricketts, Newport . . . You met those chaps too at the dance. The others you didn't.'

'So who didn't make it?'

'Poor old Davidson, for one. You know, the tall, good-looking chap with the moustache. The others I'm not sure about. We only planned for six to go, but nine went in all. Opportunists, the other three who saw their chance to get out, and they tried their luck. You can hardly blame them.'

'Well, what a story,' Gladys said. She was still hovering by the door ready to scurry to the brew house to fill the kettle. 'I'll make that tea . . .'

'No, wait, Mrs Shakespeare. There's something else I have to tell you, that you'll be interested to hear.' He looked at Libby and she saw that deliciously warm look in his eyes again. 'When Libby came to Ireland I asked her if she would marry me.' He reached out to where she was standing, close to him, and pulled her onto his lap giving her a hug around the waist. 'I have no idea whether she's mentioned it to you, but anyway, she said yes.'

'Our Libby!' Gladys exclaimed, emotionally. 'You never said. How come you never said?'

Libby shrugged. 'There didn't seem any need, mom. Edward was interned and he might have been there for years. There seemed no point in everybody raising their hopes when it looked like being a long wait.'

'Anyway,' Edward pressed. 'With your blessing I hope, I intend to apply for a special licence while I'm home, and I hope that within a very few days we shall be man and wife.'

'This week?' shrieked Libby excitedly. 'Gosh, Edward, you really do know how to spring a surprise. Will it be a church wedding?'

'That's my plan.'

'Gosh, I'll have to see if I can buy a decent wedding dress. Do your mother and father know, and Bunty, and Hugh?'

'Oh, yes, I've announced my intention.'

'And?'

'They're delighted, of course they are. We shall hold the wedding supper at Buttonbridge Hall. All that remains is to fix the day and book the vicar.'

- - -

| 19 |

The priority for Libby was, of course finding a wedding dress for her big day, and it was a somewhat intense business. With the help and advice of Bunty, however, she eventually chose one off the peg that fitted perfectly once a couple of darts had been introduced at the waist. Then there was the acquisition of a headdress and veil, her going away outfit, for there would joyously be time for a brief honeymoon before he was recalled to his squadron. Gladys reminded her to order a bridal bouquet, so Libby arranged to obtain a suitable one after visiting a florist in Dudley. It was fortunate that Charles had agreed to afford her two days off to get herself organised.

The Burgaynes drew up a list of those friends and family they wished to invite, and invitations had to be urgently printed and despatched, a task that fell to Bunty in Libby's absence from Buttonbridge Hall. Libby's birth certificate was required, which Gladys found after a frantic search. Then Edward obtained the marriage license, and booked the vicar and the church.

All that successfully achieved, it was his bounden duty to buy a gold ring for his bride, which they chose together two days before the wedding. Since the wedding party was to be held at Buttonbridge Hall the food had to be decided upon, obtained and prepared, and servants briefed. Everybody felt that they were at the epicentre of a whirlwind, but the whirlwind had the effect of rapidly blowing the big day in.

On the arm of her father, who was as proud as any man had a right to be, Libby walked into the cool dimness of the lovely sandstone church of St Mary the Virgin in Enville, to meet Edward. Following her was Bunty, content to be the solitary bridesmaid, her reward for the hours she spent helping to organise this wedding and the bride. Edward stood waiting for Libby, looking entirely pleased with himself, and undeniably handsome in his steel-blue RAF uniform. When she reached his side he turned to greet her and gave her a broad, happy smile, and she felt her heart pounding hard. Despite the invited guests, and well-wishers who had come to the church curious to see the event, it seemed for a few fleeting moments that they were all alone together, that there was no one else in the world but the two of them, meeting there to pledge the vows that were to bind them together as man and wife. Libby smiled back at Edward, and tears of pure sentimentality misted her beautiful eyes, but she managed to hold them back.

Ever since the day they first met, when she was invited to make up a four to play tennis, she had been attracted to Edward, and he to her. But love had not been instant, although mutual admiration had been. Love had grown, unsurely at first due to their prolonged absences from each other, yet it flourished steadily because of those same absences. Finally love blossomed and had its head, and another series of forced absences rendered this marriage desirable when the opportunity unexpectedly arose.

Yet how quickly the ceremony seemed to pass, as if it was all a dream. One minute Libby was making her vows, the gold ring was firmly on her finger, she was lifting her veil and tilting her face to receive Edward's smiling kiss. Then, before she knew it, she was in the vestry, signing the register – signing her name, Libby Shakespeare, for the last time. She was surrounded by people, being kissed, caressed, hugged, having her hand shaken, aware of a perpetual smile on her face.

Then she caught unfathomable looks on the face of Edward's best man, his brother Hugh, and abruptly felt uneasy when she recalled how he had once taken her to the secluded fishpond, bared his soul and asked her to be his. It was an unfathomable look that he bore at that moment, possibly even a look of envy, because he had failed to win her, perhaps even a look of ardent longing. Maybe it was more than either of those things she saw in his eyes, something darker; resentment perhaps, perhaps even jealousy. In that instant Libby felt inordinately sorry for Hugh. He was an enigma, indecipherable. If he was a troubled soul was it because of her? She had never really liked him, although she'd never bothered to try and understand him. Now that she was his sister-in-law perhaps she should try.

Back down the aisle again, but this time on Edward's arm. She had dismissed thoughts of Hugh and was smiling radiantly as the organ triumphantly thundered out the Wedding March. People on both sides of the aisle, smiling their admiration and best wishes, were watching her intently as she walked slowly passed them with her handsome new husband. Then they were out in the porch, greeted by warm, summer sunshine. A press photographer was facing them, who's editor had heard of Edward's recent escapades and considered that his escape from internment, just to return home and marry his sweetheart, was the very essence of romance and thoroughly newsworthy. He duly got his photographs.

The other photographer, whose services Bunty had managed to secure, took more photos. Libby's mother and father – happy, smiling figures – stood contentedly in the group along with Charles and Dorothy Burgayne as the photographer did his stuff. Then showers of confetti, tossing her bouquet to Bunty, getting into a chauffeur-driven car and being taken back to Buttonbridge Hall.

'You look stunningly beautiful,' Edward said warmly as they sat close together in the rear seat. 'Considering what little time you've had to prepare for this, I'm astonished.'

She smiled her thanks for his compliment. 'And look at you – so handsome in your uniform. Anyway,' she went on, 'I'm glad you think I look nice. I feel nice.'

Indeed, Libby seemed to have garnered even more beauty when she put on the white satin gown, the misty tulle veil, the chaplet of orange blossoms, none of which had been easily come by, and which had cost a small fortune.

'So kiss me,' he said.

She kissed him.

'I do hope my mom and dad don't show themselves up, Edward,' she remarked, out of the blue. 'They're not used to the way of life you Burgaynes are used to.'

'Is it bothering you?'

'A bit.'

'They'll be simply fine,' he said reassuringly. 'It's not as if they're bumpkins, or that my family are snobs. Anyway, I think your mother looks lovely in her new outfit.'

'Oh, she does, and I'm glad you think so, but it was a real panic finding something that she liked that isn't too old fashioned.'

'And your father,' he said. 'He looks very smart in his new suit.'

'It's not new, Edward.' She giggled at this. 'It's not even his. The trouble is, he's likely to broadcast it!'

Before long they were being driven up the long, sweeping drive of Buttonbridge Hall. At the front door they alighted from the car, watched and applauded by Jenkins, the cook, extra servants hired just for the day, the convalescent servicemen who were sufficiently mobile – some of whom Libby was acquainted with – and their nurses. Libby and Edward stood, waiting to receive their guests, which amounted to immediate members of both families, and Harry Wilding, Bunty's by now established beau, who was fully recovered from his wounds and conveniently on leave. They all returned, including the Beauchamps, long-standing friends of the Burgaynes. Libby knew of them – a little at any rate – but had never met them, so it was with some surprise that she learned they had offered to lend them their cottage retreat in Ludlow as a honeymoon hideaway.

'Edward is a lucky chap, my dear,' Harry commented to Bunty when they arrived.

'No luckier than you are, Harry,' she riposted, tongue-in-cheek.

There were one or two moments when Libby couldn't help worrying about her mother and father. Out of all the people there, they were her only family in attendance, and she felt they were uncomfortably out of their depth and on tenterhooks because of it. Irrationally, she thought about her old flame, Ron Downing, and her half-hearted attitude towards him; she'd always known that he would never be the one she would marry. What would he think of her now, if he could see her?

In the long, chandeliered dining-room the table was laid for a feast, and Libby wondered what strings the Burgaynes had pulled to get food, much of which was officially rationed. There were gold-foiled bottles of champagne and an enormous crystal bowl of iced punch. On another table under the window stood wedding gifts – a mystery collection to be explored later.

Everybody was gracious, conversation was bright, the atmosphere was jovial. Charles Burgayne was unstinting in his efforts to make Gladys and Joe feel welcome and at home, and Libby, heartened with this kind attention to her mother, was full of admiration for her new father-in-law. Her mother-in-law, too, Dorothy, was conversing with Joe as if they'd known each other years. It was all so gratifying.

The meal was served, a feast considering the constraints of rationing. Charles replenished Gladys's glass with wine, then Joe's, and the two men became mutually engrossed in reminiscences of the steelworks in the old days, and past employees. There were speeches, but only a short one from Joe, who toasted the bride and groom, to which Edward responded in true tradition. Hugh, his eyes barely leaving Libby, gave his, rather more revealing speech as best man.

'I have to congratulate Edward on his choice of bride,' he began predictably. 'The very first time I cast eyes on Libby was the day she became an employee of Blowers Green Steelworks. I have to tell you that many pretty girls have graced those corridors, and it was always a rule of mine that as a member of the family owning and running the company, I would never ingratiate myself with any of them. But when Libby appeared that day, I asked myself whether, after all, it had been a rather silly and short-sighted imperative . . .' Polite laughter . . . 'Soon after that, Libby visited Buttonbridge Hall with Bunty to make up a four for tennis, I believe – a game she plays as if she might easily qualify for Wimbledon – and, to my absolute horror, I discovered that Edward had taken her for a flight in his Gypsy Moth, for in those days Edward was not the great pilot he has since turned out to be. Well, as you can see, they made a happy landing.' Another ripple of laughter and some applause. 'So now, on behalf of the very lovely bridesmaid, my adorable sister Bunty, I give you a toast . . .'

And so it went on.

The time came for Libby to change out of her wedding dress, and Edward to swap his uniform for civvies. Libby, her arm linked in Bunty's, ascended the stairs to the enormous bedroom which had been hastily prepared for her and Edward. It was to be their room, the bedroom where they would sleep when he was on leave, where she would sleep every night after her honeymoon, because it had been decreed that even when Edward returned to his squadron, she should continue to live there as a member of the Burgayne family.

Oh, yes, she was a Burgayne now . . .

Libby kicked off her shoes. 'Would you unfasten me please?'

Bunty willingly obliged, releasing the hook and eye at the back of Libby's wedding dress, then the row of tiny buttons below it.

'Thank you,' Libby said as she slipped it off her shoulders and over her hips. 'You know, Bunty . . .' she picked up the dress from the floor. 'I'm amazed.'

'Amazed? At what?'

'Because I never expected to marry a man like Edward and live in a grand house like this.' She put the dress on a hanger and hung it from the picture rail.

'Your inferiority complex is rearing its ugly head again, Libby. For goodness' sake, stop it.'

'Oh, I expected to marry somebody, but I always pictured somebody more like that chap Ron Downing I used to see – you know – decent enough, but ordinary.' She slipped off her underskirts and stepped out of them. She was standing in her knickers and brassiere, and her flesh-coloured stockings. 'I rather saw myself in a little terraced house like ours – at best one of those semi-detached ones, if he'd been lucky enough to have a good job – and then babies perhaps. That sort of thing. But you know, Bunty, I didn't fall in love with Edward at once, although I liked him from the first. He sort of grew on me.'

'I think that's the best way,' Bunty remarked. 'That's how it was with Harry and me.'

'And I'm so happy for you, Bunty.' She began to put on her going away outfit, a light-hearted dress of printed silk, with a wide swinging skirt. 'Especially after the tragedy of Adrian's death. I thought you were never going to get over it, and there was nothing any of us could do to help you.'

Bunty put her hand on Libby's arm in a gesture of appreciation for her concern. 'I know, Libby, that if you could have done anything you would've. You're the best friend I ever had, and you understand me well. Anyway, let's not dwell on that. You were saying how you didn't fall in love with Edward straight away.'

'Oh . . . well, all I was going to say was, when we first met I could tell Edward fancied me, but I never really expected he'd fall for me the way he did, an ordinary working girl.'

'I told you, Libby, put your working girl complex away.'

'Oh, I have, believe me. I'm a Burgayne now.' She tossed her head and smiled happily. 'All the same, marrying Edward is the most wonderful, the most astonishing thing that could ever have happened to me.'

'Well,' Bunty said, her pretty head tilted cannily, 'wonderful it may be, but hardly astonishing. Not only are you preposterously beautiful, but you're so outrageously modest with it – and so terribly nice. Why shouldn't Edward fall in love with you?'

'I'm just so happy that he did.' She turned and looked at herself in the cheval mirror near the window. 'I'm ready now—how do I look?'

Bunty rolled her eyes with envy. 'You positively glow, and I'm so envious . . . Why can't I glow like you?'

Libby laughed happily. 'Oh, but you do, Bunty. You just don't see it yourself.' Which was perfectly true. 'It's why Harry has fallen in love with you. And you'll glow all the more when you two get married.'

'Well, thanks for tossing me your bouquet anyway.'

'I'm so relieved you caught it!'

- - -

The destination of the newly-weds was an old Georgian house, cleverly modernized, in Ludlow. Here, they would have absolute peace and security from intrusion, yet all the convenience that a small market town offered. There was no maid, no gardener and no cook to serve them, but that was hardly likely to faze Libby, who had lived her entire life without such help.

They arrived at the house in the evening. The low sun was already flaring behind a ridge of cloud, as if somebody had opened a furnace door and the glow was shielded behind unburnt coals. Edward drew up his MG before the brightly-painted front door and they clambered out. He took the key and opened it, then decided to carry Libby through, to her amusing shrieks of protest.

'Never mind carrying me over the threshold,' she laughed.

'And miss an age-old tradition?'

'What about all the stuff we've brought, and the suitcases?'

'Such mundane things can wait.'

Inside, he put her down and she rewarded him with a kiss.

The oak floors were strewn with rugs, and it was furnished with comfortable, cretonne-covered chairs and sofas. Flowers had been placed everywhere, in corners, on window-sills and tables.

'How kind of the Beauchamps to come and make it so pretty before we arrived,' Libby commented. 'They must have been here only yesterday.'

Edward lugged the suitcases upstairs to the large double bedroom, from which opened a dressing-room and a perfectly appointed bathroom. Together they put away the few clothes they had brought with them. While he went downstairs to heat some water, she walked over to the windows, adorned with white muslin curtains, and looked out over the undulating green hills around Ludlow. The sky was beginning to darken towards the east. Libby stood there for some time, silently reliving the day, deliciously happy, for without question this had been the loveliest and most important day of her life. After a while, she decided to change into clothes more practical, and began undressing.

Edward returned to the room as she was sitting at the dressing-table in only her knickers, brushing her abundant dark hair. It fell youthfully to her shoulders, shining, burnished, and her eyes looked so big and soft and inviting in the fading light. In the mirror she saw him coming to her and she turned to greet him. She smiled, all her love in her eyes, and he returned her smile, the warmth of desire bright in his eyes. He kicked off his shoes, doffed his jacket, his tie, his shirt, his trousers, his underpants and his socks, then scooped her up in his arms and laid her across the counterpane while she giggled contentedly. She looped her arms around his neck then raised her bottom as he slid her knickers off and down her legs. He ran his hand over the silky-smooth skin of her belly and lingered at the soft, dark delta to the south, teasing her, kissing her ardently. Then, he rolled gently onto her, and they made love leisurely, extravagantly, for the first time as man and wife.

- - -

| 20 |

The following Thursday a telegram arrived at Buttonbridge Hall. It was addressed to Edward, so Bunty decided that she should be the one to deliver it to the honeymooning couple at Ludlow, and set off at once in the Riley. She handed the telegram to Edward who read it and in turn passed it to Libby. Her heart sank; the Air Ministry was requesting him to rejoin his squadron at Exeter immediately.

'Damn!' she said. 'Why can't they leave us alone?'

The honeymoon was over, and with cruel abruptness.

'Has Harry gone back?' Edward asked conversationally.

'He left yesterday,' Bunty replied. 'Otherwise he would've come with me today. Look, while I'm here I'll help you tidy up before you leave.'

'Thanks, Bunty,' Libby said, deflated after the contentedness that this brief few days of living with Edward had brought. 'I'll go upstairs and strip the bed.'

'And I'll pack our bags,' Edward said sombrely.

Upstairs, back in the bedroom, Edward caught Libby and pulled her to him, put his hands to her waist as he looked dejectedly into her eyes. 'I'm so awfully sorry I have to go, Sweetheart,' he breathed.

She sighed with resignation. 'Duty calls, my love. We knew this couldn't last forever. We both know it can't be helped, but it's such a pity they can't just pension you off as being out of practice and a danger to everybody, since you've been interned in some foreign land.'

'After the time and money invested in training me? No such luck.'

'Shall you go back today?'

'Not a chance.' He smiled ruefully. 'I'm spending the night with you at Buttonbridge Hall. But I'll have to go back tomorrow.'

She hugged him. 'Then more waiting and waiting for you to come home on leave . . . more worrying and worrying and worrying whether you're all right . . . or not . . .'

'I know, sweetheart.' He gave her another reassuring squeeze. 'It's the same for me. But I have a job to do, and I suppose the sooner I get back and do my bit, the sooner this damned war will be over. And when it is, we can resume our lives. We'll be able to put all this madness behind us.'

'I can't wait,' she sighed, and clung to him fearfully, as if this would be the last time ever.

- - -

Breakfast next morning was a quiet, sombre affair. It was to be their last breakfast together for some time and there was so much still to be said, so many more promises to be made. But both felt inhibited to say much more than how delighted they were with the cottage in Ludlow, because of the presence of the others. Libby glanced at Edward meaningfully, and he would smile back at her with reassurance in his soft blue eyes. It was obvious that he too felt the same frustration.

Charles was to drive Edward to the station, accompanied by Libby of course. When breakfast was over Edward carried his suitcase and put it down next to his father's Bentley, which had been readied outside on the sweeping driveway alongside Hugh's Jaguar. Libby, meanwhile, was adding the final touches to her make-up upstairs. As Edward opened the boot of the car ready to stow his suitcase, Hugh appeared carrying a brown envelope.

'I just wanted to say goodbye, Edward, old man, and give you these . . .' He handed him the envelope.

Edward looked at his brother enquiringly. 'What is it?'

'Just some photos I took of Libby one spring day. I thought you might like to have them . . .'

'Thanks, Hugh,' Edward replied with a grateful smile, his curiosity at once aroused.

'So, goodbye, old chap.' Hugh patted him fraternally on the shoulder, offered his hand and they shook. 'Keep out of trouble this time, eh? And we'll see you on your next leave. In the meantime, I'll keep an eye on Libby for you.'

As Hugh slumped into his car and drove off, Edward opened the envelope and pulled out the bundle of photographs, half-plate size, of Libby in various poses taken outdoors. He looked at the first. She was laughing contentedly, her pose relaxed, but her skirt was alluringly above her knees.

He looked at the next. She was standing, legs apart, framed by the arch of some ancient, ruined building and taken from a low angle. Her skirt was blowing up around her thighs showing much more than would normally have been considered decent. Irked by what he saw and the thought of Libby, his own wife posing so flauntingly, so coquettishly, for his brother, he slid it behind the others and looked at the next with increasing indignation. On the next, Libby was seated, her face tilted to the sun, her eyes closed, basking in the warmth of the sunshine. Her back was erect, her breasts pushed hard against the light material of her dress, and again the hem of her skirt was rippling audaciously high, revealing long tracts of her thighs.

Edward sighed with frustration, and turned his head to see where she was. He did not know how to handle this situation, how to approach Libby about it, for it could not possibly go unmentioned. Libby had never told him previously that these photos had been taken.

She appeared at the front door with Charles, and they hurried towards the car. It was time to go.

'I'll sit in the front with Father,' Edward stated offishly, intent on making a point.

'You should sit in the back with Libby,' Charles suggested. 'You're not going to see her for God knows how long.'

'No, it's all right, Father. I'll sit in the front.'

Libby was hurt by this, especially when they had been married only days, and were about to be parted. On the way to the station she found herself looking silently at the back of his head as he spoke not a word to her, and only to his father when spoken to. It seemed something was amiss. But what?

They arrived at the station, and the three alighted from the Bentley. Libby glanced apprehensively at Edward, but his eyes avoided hers.

'I'll wait in the car for you, Libby,' Charles said as Edward retrieved his suitcase from the boot. 'You don't want me in the way while you say your goodbyes.' He gave her a wink.

'Thank you, Charles,' she replied, forcing a smile.

Edward put down his suitcase, shook hands with his father and gave him a hug, then picked it up again and headed for the entrance to the station, paying no heed to Libby. Libby skipped behind him mystified and irked.

'Edward! Wait for me!'

He ignored her, striding out determinedly.

'Edward, wait,' she pleaded. 'For goodness' sake . . .'

She caught up with him as he reached the booth and waited uneasily while he showed his travel warrant, which he returned to a pocket of his jacket.

'What on earth is wrong, Edward?' she asked again, and saw that now at least she had won his attention.

He regarded her with a look of disdain. 'I'll tell you what's wrong, Libby . . .' He reached inside his jacket and pulled out the brown envelope. 'Here . . .'

She took it and opened it gingerly.

'Hugh gave me those photographs just as we left. He said he thought I might like to have them.' There was sarcasm in his tone.

Folk were milling around them, travellers arriving and departing, and Libby felt not only decidedly self-conscious but helpless too. They could hardly have a row – their first ever – in full view of the travelling public, and at the very moment they were to part.

She flicked through the photos one after the other while he scrutinised her reaction. Why had she never mentioned them? Her blushes were proof of her embarrassment.

'Well?'

She looked into his eyes with an appeal for his understanding, not knowing how best to respond, but at least she understood why he was angry. 'They're just some photos Hugh took . . . oh, a long time ago,' she replied trying to make light of them. 'Before you and I were together.'

'Are you always so willing to flaunt yourself in front of others?' he asked acidly. 'Especially my own brother?'

'Oh, Edward . . .' She sighed with frustration, praying silently that she could extricate herself from this silly and unnecessary situation without too much harm to their relationship. 'Anyway, you didn't seem to mind the first time Hugh took some photos of me, did you?'

'I had no claim on you then.'

'Nor did you have any claim on me when these were taken,' she asserted in defence of their past.

'Who else have you posed for like this?' he asked with disdain.

'Nobody, Edward. Of course I haven't.'

His expression was one of suspicion. 'Really? I wonder about you, Libby. Stuff like this makes me wonder what sort of a girl I've married.'

He looked away from her, remembering that her old flame had called her a tart when he'd caught her with him after he'd driven her home one Boxing Day evening. The poor chap had been justified, too; she had been disloyal to him. Was all this – this susceptibility to be disloyal, this apparent fondness to show herself off – a flaw in her character?

She saw the hurt look in his eyes. Tears welled up and trembled on her eyelids at his implication, at the realisation that he was distressed and regarded it as her fault. 'Are you try-ing to make out I'm a tart, Edward?' she asked defiantly.

'According to these pictures you are.' His eyes pierced hers with hot resentment. 'So why didn't you tell me about them? Because you thought I might disapprove? Because you saw them as something to be ashamed of?'

'Ashamed?' she queried, her own anger rising. I'm ashamed of nothing. I have done nothing to be ashamed of. I'm em-barrassed, I admit, but only because it never occurred to me to tell you about them, because they were of no consequence. And anyway, I've never seen them before. Hugh never showed them to me. I'd forgotten all about them.'

'So . . . I repeat – why didn't you tell me?'

'I just told you, Edward. I'd forgotten all about them. And I think it was jolly mischievous of Hugh to give them to you just as we were leaving. Like I said, I've never seen the photos before. I remember him taking them – course I do. He wanted them for his camera club's annual exhibition, I suppose. It was long before you and I were together I saw no harm in it. There *was* no harm in it.'

'Is there anything else you haven't told me?' he scoffed.

'Such as?'

'Well . . . Are there any more skeletons in your cupboard?'

'Of course not . . . Oh, Edward . . .' She reached out to him, put her arms around him and laid her head on his chest submissively. 'What's got into you?' she appealed. 'Don't you know I love you with all my heart and soul? Don't you know I wouldn't do anything you disapproved of for the world? If these photos have offended you, I am so sorry, but they were taken innocently enough, believe me. Hugh asked me to pose for him. There was no ulterior motive on my part. It was just me – a single young girl having fun, enjoying being admired. If you can't understand that, Edward, then there's no hope for us.' She gave a shrug.

'The subject matter doesn't offend me, Libby,' he conceded, sounding more reasonable now. 'A beautiful girl looking extremely appealing. I'm not that much of a prude, nor a hypocrite, that I can't appreciate the aesthetics. But I doubt your judgement in allowing Hugh to even photograph you. Are you sure they were taken before we started courting?'

He was softening, thank God, and he needed her reassurance. This was hurting him as much as it was hurting her.

'Of course I'm sure,' she said earnestly. 'Look at my hairstyle. It was much shorter . . . a bob.' She pointed to it in one of the photos. 'It hasn't been like that for ages.'

He sighed profoundly then, admitting her claim, and gave her a hug. 'Very well . . . Look, I'm sorry, Libby. We can hardly part on an argument, can we?' His smile was a true apology, pleading for forgiveness. 'God knows when we'll see each other again. Promise me you won't sit for Hugh again – or anybody else for that matter.'

'Oh, Edward . . . Of course I won't,' she solemnly promised. 'I love you, I'm your wife now and I'm devoted to you. And I'll stay devoted to you while you're away. You know I will.'

'Then I apologise. I have no wish to upset you, my darling. I love you too much for that. I absolutely idolise you . . .'

'Then I forgive you.'

'So kiss me, to prove you do, and I'll forgive you for your silly outburst.'

They kissed, regardless of the people milling busily around them.

They eventually broke off, and he peered resentfully at the station clock.

'My train leaves in five minutes,' he reminded her, with a wistful smile. 'Bugger . . . Will you walk to the platform with me?'

She smiled back at him, more brightly, evidence of her tears still on her cheeks. 'Course I will. Just try and stop me.'

With arms around each other, they headed towards the train that was already standing by.

- - -

One evening some weeks later, Hugh Burgayne, having been under stress at the steelworks over some government contract, decided to seek the peace and tranquillity that the grounds of Buttonbridge Hall offered. He could not find the peace he needed inside, for talk at the dinner table seemed to be concentrated on the changes Libby wished to make to the large bedroom she was occupying, ready for when Edward was on leave. Naturally, she was aided and abetted by Bunty. This was all girls' talk to Hugh, and trivial after the trials he'd had to endure at the steelworks.

It was a balmy evening and Hugh found himself passing through the hole in the wall towards the fishpond. He sat on the pool's edge and peered into the water's lily-festooned depths, beyond their outspread floating leaves. Some of the pool's slippery occupants swam into view, silent slivers of silver and gold, that produced neat, expanding rings on the surface as they sucked up the pond skaters that dared to venture close. He had been made aware that a heron had been seen lurking near the pool, and he considered it about time the gardener regularly produced an accurate inventory of the fish stock to ascertain if they were losing any to the predator.

Hugh was shouldering greater responsibility lately at the works, but not entirely satisfactorily. His father's health was in decline and because of it he was remaining at home more, becoming less active in the day-to-day running of the substantial business. It was, of course, his chest; Charles had always suffered with his chest. As a small boy, Hugh saw his father often being laid up in winter due to bronchitis, and the weeks it sometimes took to fully recover. His problem was getting worse as the years rolled on.

Consequently, Libby too found she had less work to do as a secretary, work she had decided to continue doing, despite the fact that she was married now and a member of the Burgayne family. Hugh often wondered how she felt about the things the other girls of the typing pool were doubtless saying now she was a lady of the manor, and set apart from them. It could not be easy for her. She was bound to suffer some resentment, yet she seemed to carry it off with great aplomb.

Hugh's thoughts meandered on. He recalled the time he'd confessed his feelings for Libby. He had chosen his moment badly, for he realised now – typically much too late – that she had been annoyed with him. He'd been spouting about registering as a conscientious objector when Edward was clearly keen to do his bit in the RAF. The comparison, he understood, must have seemed odious. Even his father had not admired him that evening. But assessing on-the-fly the reactions and opinions of other folk had never been Hugh's strong point. Seeing Libby every day, dining alongside her with his mother and father every evening nowadays, and some lunchtimes and breakfast times, had not diminished his desire for her. She might be the adoring wife of his younger brother, but that did not stop him casting covert, lustful glances her way, admiring her lovely face, her beautifully proportioned body. She was oh, so delectable, so desirable.

There was a particular chair she liked to sit in in the drawing-room, and he was at pains to position himself in a chair opposite when he could, so that when she sat down or crossed her legs he might get a peep up her skirt. He had enjoyed some rewarding moments as a result.

Yet why should he languish over this one woman who never could be his, and never would be, when there were plenty of other women, any number of them, available right now? They might not all be single, but while their husbands, misguided in their patriotism, were away fighting in this ridiculous war, many married girls were happy to make themselves available to any presentable man who showed an interest, and keen enough to sample what was on offer. Not that Hugh had ever tried his luck in that respect, but he'd heard it said time and time again. Live for today was the prevalent cry, for tomorrow we might be bombed out of existence. Well, it was perfectly understandable. There was even Laura Birch to fall back on, at a push; she remained unattached and amenable. She even telephoned him at work from time to time. The truth was, Hugh was unsure of himself where women were concerned. He did not know how to talk to them, how to pass a compliment sincerely. He had no small talk; he did not know how to make girls laugh and so draw their interest. He was not especially good-looking either.

The things he did have, though, were money, education, his assured future in the steelworks, and his share of his father's inheritance which, when it finally fell into his lap, would be ample.

Deciding to leave his thoughts at the fishpond, he stood up and ambled back through the hole in the wall. He looked at his watch. It was nearly half-past eight. Coming from the house for a turn in the grounds he saw Libby, smart in a crisp summer dress that emphasised her trim waist and pert breasts. She was with Bunty, who was wearing her trainee nurses' uniform. Accompanying them was a young RAF officer on crutches; one of the current crop of convalescents. The girls walked slowly, at the airman's reduced pace, one on each side of him. They were laughing at some remark he had made. It irked Hugh that the man was able to concoct some quip that made the girls laugh. Considering his unwelcome disability, Hugh thought it odd that the man was even able to laugh, let alone make the girls laugh.

He watched their retreating figures, especially Libby's; the sway of her hips that caused her skirt to swing so appealingly, her well-turned ankles, how her calves looked so shapely. Then Bunty stopped, said something, and ran back to the house, while Libby carried on walking with this recovering RAF officer, still attentive and laughing, clearly enjoying his company, evidently hanging on his every word.

Why would she want to do that when she had Edward for her husband? Was she so easily diverted? Could she be so easily diverted? He pondered the possibility for some time. There was something about women he did not understand.

- - -

That same night, Hugh made a startling discovery.

After Libby had gone to bed his mind was still active, and he knew from experience that sleep would elude him. So he went to the attic with a flash lamp in search of a different lens for his photographic enlarger and a masking frame, so that he could make bigger and more impressive enlargements of some of his more treasured photographs. He did not use these things often, and there was not enough room to store them in his darkroom. But before he began to look he noticed a splinter of light coming up through the uneven floorboards. Over many years the joists had warped and shrunk, leaving the floor irregular and distorted. He went down on hands and knees to see, realising that this area of the attic was roughly above the seldom-used old bedroom recently taken over by Libby and Edward, and yet to be refurbished properly.

To his astonishment, he saw that he was looking directly down on Libby. She was sitting on her bed wearing only pretty French knickers, and his heart started pounding at this fortuitous discovery. She was applying face cream. He scanned the attic with the flash lamp and spotted a coat-hanger with a wire hook. He tip-toed to where it hung and straightened the hook, then returned to the gap in the floorboards. He wanted to wiggle the wire around so as to increase the size of the fissure and improve his angle of view. But it was a risky business, and he did not want to make any sound, or allow any bits to fall from above and give the game away, so he dared not push his luck too far. He could return tomorrow and effect the improvement when she was not there.

However, he remained watching for some minutes, congratulating himself on his extreme good fortune. Eventually she put the lid on the pot of face cream and stood up. She walked over to the dressing table and placed the pot on it, and he felt a familiar stirring within his trousers at the sight of her near nakedness. Then she sat in front of the mirror and brushed her hair for a while, her back towards him. After a while she got up from the dressing table and disappeared from view, reappearing after a second or two in a flimsy white nightgown. She slipped her knickers down her legs and tossed them aside, pulled the bedclothes back and slid into bed.

Then the light went out.

- - -

Dorothy Burgayne, although used to her husband's suffering, was more alarmed than usual at his recent spate of chestiness, and duly sent for the doctor.

Dr Vernon MacKenzie, a huge, robust man, arrived in due course and Dorothy greeted him cordially.

'I am so sorry to have to send for you like this, Vernon,' she said familiarly. 'I know you must be dreadfully busy.'

'Not at all, not at all,' he answered reassuringly. 'How are your convalescents faring?'

'I believe those with us at present are prospering, thank you. Leastwise, I don't think we've killed any off just yet.'

The doctor laughed, his low rumbling laugh. 'It's your husband this time, I understand.'

'I'm afraid so.'

'The old trouble?'

'Yes, the old trouble,' she sighed.

'Then let me take a look at him.'

'I made him stay in bed, Vernon.'

'Well, that's always a safe bet.'

Dr MacKenzie followed her up the sweeping staircase and to their bedroom. Charles looked swamped in the old four-poster bed, and very pale. He was propped up on a pillow reading a copy of Picture Post.

'Ah, good morning, Vernon.'

'Good morning, Charles. The old trouble, I understand.'

'The old trouble and a bit more besides, I suspect,' Charles croaked. 'I'm not normally this incapacitated at this time of year.'

'I told you, years ago, you should move to sunnier climes. You could afford it.'

Charles coughed, a long, ratchety cough, and winced at the pain. 'That might be eminently sensible, Vernon,' he wheezed, 'but entirely impracticable. I have a business to run.'

'Others are also capable of running it I understand. It'll kill you if you don't leave it be.' He put down his bag. 'So let me examine you, eh?'

The doctor opened the bag and withdrew his stethoscope. He undid the top buttons of Charles's pyjamas, pressed the pad against his chest, and listened. 'Breathe deeply.'

It induced another searing spasm of coughing.

'Try again, slowly . . . Breathe in . . . Breathe out.' The doctor put away his stethoscope. 'The coughing is painful, Charles?'

'Rather.'

'And you're short of breath when you do anything physical?'

'I haven't done anything physical for years.'

'What about climbing the stairs?'

'Yes, that makes me short of breath.'

'Has it been worse lately?'

'Markedly.'

Dr MacKenzie sighed. 'You've suffered with bronchial problems for a number of years, Charles, that much we both know.'

'Ever since I had measles as a child.'

'And you aren't getting any younger.'

'Thank you for reminding me.'

'You have also spent much of your life in the foul confines of a steelworks, among all manner of obnoxious fumes.'

'An occupational hazard, I'm afraid, Vernon.'

'But one that has aggravated your condition over the years, eh?'

'Indeed so. So what is your diagnosis this time? What is your treatment to be? The same as before?'

'Avoid the steelworks at all costs, my friend.' He patted Charles's arm matily. 'Your condition has deteriorated to emphysema. Tell me – just out of interest – have you ever played a wind instrument?'

'Indeed I have. As a young boy I used to play the trumpet.' He stopped, wheezing for breath. 'Did it for years . . . till I discovered more interesting challenges.'

'The trumpet, eh?' the doctor mused. 'Mmm . . . That figures. Emphysema is sometimes prevalent among people who've played wind instruments for some time. Straining the lungs stretches the air cells, you see, and in some cases may even tear them. Each attack of bronchitis aggravates the condition and makes it worse. There is no cure for emphysema, Charles,' Dr MacKenzie declared. 'Only treatment to alleviate the symptoms. Your room temperature must be maintained at sixty-five degrees Fahrenheit, and I am going to prescribe the usual regular steam inhalations of Friars Balsam, as well as a turpentine liniment chest rub.'

'The chest rub at least sounds exciting, Vernon,' Charles quipped. 'Perhaps we can find some pretty nurse from the convalescent ward to administer it.'

'Which would only cause you more acute breathlessness,' the doctor riposted with a smile. 'And that won't do. Sorry, old chap.'

Back downstairs in the hall Dr MacKenzie said, 'I'm rather concerned, Dorothy, about Charles's health. His condition has deteriorated without question, and I'm obliged to keep my eye on him. He is very prone to other more serious ailments, so he must be kept quiet and at rest. Don't allow him near dust or smoke, or outside in fog. Tell me, does he worry about things?'

'He worries a great deal about Edward, our younger son.'

'The RAF pilot? And well he might.' Vernon MacKenzie assumed a suitably grave expression. 'Being an aircraft pilot in wartime must be a particularly hazardous occupation.'

'Oh, please don't remind me. Edward married very recently, you know. A delightful girl. It's such a pity they can't be together to enjoy their marriage. But while this war rages . . .'

'Of course, of course . . . But life must go on, Dorothy. Now, while I'm here I'll take a look at your convalescents.'

'I'll take you through.'

'Anytime you need me, just ring.'

'Thank you, Vernon.'

- - -

'You know, Libby, I really don't think you should flirt with Pilot Officer Farnell when you accompany him in those walks he takes for therapy,' Bunty warned one evening. 'He takes it too seriously.'

'But what harm can it do?' Libby queried. 'He needs cheering up after all those awful operations to save his leg.'

'Oh, you cheer him up – there's no question about that. I've seen the way he looks at you . . .'

'Yes, I know.'

'Just so long as you don't look at him in the same way.'

'Gosh, Bunty. What *are* you suggesting?'

'It's just that when his time comes to leave he's going to be all despondent again, which could set him back somewhat. Don't forget his wife ran off with another chap. Then he was gravely injured when his plane was shot down, and they thought his leg would have to be amputated. It would be cruel if he fell in love with you to compensate.'

'Which hat are you wearing right now, Bunty? Your nurse's or an agony aunt's.'

'It doesn't matter which. The advice is the same.'

They were sitting together in the breakfast room sharing a pot of tea. It was evening and Bunty had just returned from the hospital, still wearing her uniform. The others had had dinner.

'Anyway, as far as Keith Farnell is concerned, he knows very well that I'm married, and I certainly *haven't* led him on. I wouldn't do that. I'm not interested in him that way, but he's a nice enough chap, and I see no harm in trying to cheer him up. Besides, him being RAF, he sort of makes me feel closer to Edward. I can't help having some rapport with him. I'm sure he and Edward would get on really well. Actually, I feel rather sorry for him. Why don't we give him another turn around the garden after dinner? He does need to exercise that leg.'

'Then you do it,' Bunty suggested.

'Just me?' Libby queried. 'After what you just said?'

'Yes, just you. And put him straight about a few things. He's leaving soon, I understand. And while you proceed to break the poor chap's heart I'll go up and see father. He won't mind a bit of company. How is he today?'

'About the same, I think.'

There was a pause in the conversation as they both drained their tea mugs.

'You know, Bunty,' Libby said with a sigh as she put her mug down, 'I feel at such a loose end at the moment. If Edward were home I know it would be different. But he's not. Nor is he likely to be for the foreseeable future.'

'So what's your point?'

'My point is, that I am still employed as your father's secretary, and because he is so ill and not allowed to work, I have nothing to do either, except to walk Pilot Officer Farnell and one or two others. Oh, I try and make myself busy with the convalescents, but there's not a lot I'm qualified to do, or even allowed to do except talk to them, help them with therapeutic exercises, and fetch and carry for the nurses. I think I should talk to Hugh. I'm sure there's work a-plenty I could do if I went back to the office. They still pay my wages, but I feel I'm having the money under false pretences.'

'Rest assured, the Blowers Green Steelworks can afford you, Libby. But, yes, maybe Hugh would appreciate an assistant. I imagine he's a great deal busier in father's absence and, after all, you do know the ropes. If not, there's always the convalescents. You could train to become a nurse, like me.'

Libby shook her head. 'I'm definitely not cut out to be a nurse, Bunty. I know my limitations.'

'Then why not learn to drive? There are lots of errands you could run. Why don't you learn to drive?'

'Yes, I ought to learn to drive, oughtn't I?' Libby replied, suddenly enthusiastic at the novel idea. 'I've never given it a thought, but if I could drive I could be useful in lots of ways. Can we spare the petrol for me to learn?'

'I don't think petrol is an issue at the steelworks, Libby.'

- - -

Keith Farnell was reading a newspaper in a small room attached to the ward, which had been kitted out as a sitting room for those convalescents able to get about. He spotted Libby and hailed her.

'Pilot Officer Farnell,' she greeted, formally but amiably. 'How are you today?'

'All the better for seeing you,' he answered with a broad grin of pleasure at the sight of her. 'Have you come to take me for my evening constitutional?'

'I can, if your crutches are up to it,' she answered dryly.

'For you I'd hop on my good leg to China and back. It looks like a beautiful evening out there.'

'Oh, it is.'

'No Nurse Bunty this evening?' he asked.

'She's with her father. He's not well at the moment. Maybe she'll join us in a little while.'

'Ah. So I get you all to myself for once.'

He took hold of his crutches which he'd placed handily against the wall, and eased himself off the chair. He made his way to the door and she opened it for him, to let him out into the warm summer air.

'How is your leg today?' Libby enquired as they began walking over grass, towards a clutch of elms.

'Oh, the healing continues. So much so, that I'm being let out of here.'

'So I understand. We shall miss you.'

'I'd like to think that *you* will, Libby,' he said.

'Course I shall,' she said affably. 'I shall remember you with great fondness.'

'Great fondness?' he repeated with some disdain. 'How patronising that sounds.'

'I'm sorry,' she said. 'It wasn't meant to be.'

'You see, Libby, *fondness* is hardly a word that expresses what I have come to feel for you.'

'If that's the case,' she answered, her colour rising, 'I hope I haven't given you reason to think it might be reciprocated. I'm a married woman, Keith, as you know, and I'm very much in love with my husband.'

'Yes, I understand all that despite how much it grieves me. But you must allow me to say what's in my heart. I've enjoyed your company a few times while I've been convalescing here, and you are an inspiration to me, you know. I wouldn't have improved at the rate I have if it weren't for you, for the prospect of hearing your voice, of seeing that heavenly face, of being with you on these therapeutic walks I'm obliged to take, but which you have made so enjoyable.' He smiled appealingly. 'And the joy of seeing the light in your beautiful eyes.'

'Crikey, I'm well and truly flattered,' she said, unable to think of anything else to say.

'Anyway, your husband is an RAF man, isn't he?'

'You know he is.'

'I'd like to meet him sometime.'

'Perhaps you will . . . Sometime. Who knows . . .?'

'It's just that . . . Well, Libby, if anything untoward were to befall him . . . I'd like to stake my claim . . .'

Libby shuddered. 'I really don't know what to say to that, Keith, except that I think it's a rather tactless thing to say to somebody who's married to an RAF pilot. I certainly hope and pray nothing untoward befalls him, as you put it.'

'Then I apologise for being tactless, but you must understand that life in the RAF is mighty precarious. You only have to look at me.'

'Oh, I understand it only too well, believe me.'

'So we're both realists.'

'It pays to be,' she admitted.

'But I'm also a romantic. Incurably so.'

She sighed as she looked up at him, hobbling along with the help of his crutches. 'Frankly, Keith, it's not wise to be romantic where I'm concerned. I can offer you nothing in return. I've been perfectly happy to be your friend, but that's all I could ever be – a friend. I can be nothing more. You do understand, don't you?'

'Can I write to you?'

'Would you want me to show your letters to my husband?'

He shook his head and smiled. 'Perhaps not.'

'So that means you would involve me in a conspiracy against him? You would ask me to be disloyal?'

'Absolutely.'

'Why can't you just accept my situation and be done with it?'

They stopped walking and Keith turned to face her.

'Because I am in love with you, Libby. Can't you see?'

She touched his arm, allowing her hand to rest on it as she looked up into his eyes, sympathetic to his emotions. 'You're a smashing chap, Keith,' she said. 'I like you – as a friend – but it can never be more than that. You have to understand.'

'Then you can show my letters to your husband on his return, and have a jolly good laugh about this other silly besotted airman who suffers from the unrequited love of his beautiful wife.'

'It's just a passing fancy, I'm sure,' she answered dismissively. 'You must have known lots of girls.'

'A few, yes, of course. But I knew from the moment I set eyes on you that there could never be anybody else for me. This is not some juvenile infatuation.'

'It's infatuation all the same,' she declared, touching his arm again and smiling sympathetically. 'Anyway, I think we should be going back now,' she said firmly, determined to put a stop to this in as kindly a way as she knew how.

'Now I've offended you.'

'No, of course you haven't offended me, Keith. But there's no point in harping on about it.'

Both were unaware that this earnestly emotive scene, being enacted within sight of the house, had been seen but not overheard by Hugh Burgayne, who was carrying a small Leica 35mm camera.

- - -

| 21 |

Next morning Libby was up early. She had a clear double-edged plan. The first part was to go with Hugh to the office and immerse herself in work. That in turn would ensure she was not around when Pilot Officer Keith Farnell left the house for his return home and ultimately to his squadron.

As Hugh and Libby journeyed to Dudley in his Jaguar SS, conversation was at first sparse, except for a comment from him about the relentless German advance through Russia, and how it might have lessened the possibility of Britain being invaded. Then he asked if she had heard from Edward.

'Not today yet,' she replied. 'The post hadn't arrived when we left. But I heard from him yesterday.'

'And he's well?'

'He seems in good spirits, yes. He wrote to your father, too. I think he was glad to get a letter.'

'Oh, he would be. He worries about Edward.'

'I was thinking, Hugh . . . Something Bunty suggested . . . I'd like to learn to drive a car. I'm sure I could be more useful to everybody if I could drive. I could go and visit my mom and dad a bit more regularly as well. I just need somebody with the time to teach me.'

'I could teach you,' he said, seizing the opportunity.

'But you're too busy. You're far too busy.'

'I think I'm the best judge of that,' he replied. 'I'm busy during the day, there's no question, but most evenings I could find time. Besides, I understand your friend Pilot Officer Farnell is leaving shortly, so that should give you more freedom in the evenings as well.' He looked at her askance.

'Crikey, Hugh, you make it sound as if we've been having an affair,' she answered.

'I trust you haven't been.'

She laughed, scoffing at such a preposterous notion. 'Don't be daft. I'm a happily married woman, as you well know.'

'But some women, Libby, while content enough while their husbands are around, are perfectly happy to stray when they are not.'

'Well, that doesn't apply to me, Hugh, I can assure you,' she protested. 'I'm perfectly content to wait for Edward.'

'The fact is, Libby, my dear, I've seen you and Mr Farnell together on a number of occasions walking in the grounds. You always look very chummy together.'

Libby felt she was on trial for something she had not done. 'Are you accusing me of being unfaithful to Edward?' she asked bluntly. 'Because if so, you're way off the mark. I don't dislike the man, Hugh, he's a decent chap. I actually feel sorry for him, having been severely injured in the war serving his country, and having lost his wife – who *was* unfaithful, apparently. But that's all you could ever have seen – the two of us walking the grounds. That's hardly tantamount to having an affair.'

'All the same, I'm sure Edward would be very displeased if he found out you'd even been walking the grounds of an evening with another man.'

'I think Edward would understand perfectly, and would even condone my helping a fellow RAF pilot with therapeutic exercise.'

'All the same, I'm sure you wouldn't want me to tell him.'

'I can't imagine why you'd want to anyway – especially as it's of no consequence. But if you think I've got a guilty conscience, you're wrong. I've got nothing to hide.'

'I'm glad to hear it. But it was obvious by the way he looked at you that he was smitten.'

'If he is, then that's his problem, and there's precious little I can do about it. I certainly haven't egged him on.'

'All the same, he'll doubtless be sorry to leave you behind.'

'He might be, and I daresay he'll write, because he said he would, but that doesn't mean I have to answer – though it would be discourteous not to reply.'

'Of course you wouldn't have to reply, Libby. Why encourage the idiot?'

'I've no wish to. To be fair, though, he did suggest I show any letters he might write me to Edward.'

That night, Hugh set himself up in the attic room and watched Libby undress once more. These clandestine observations were happening nightly and becoming an obsession, but he realised they were getting him nowhere – only increasing his frustration, for he was regarding himself more as merely a voyeur, cowardly, stalking; attributes hardly admirable in the eyes of the woman he wanted, if she discovered his little secret. He realised he was also jealous of the admiration she drew from other men. He was insanely jealous of Pilot Officer Farnell who had managed to gain her attention. There had to be a resolution to this torment.

If only he could somehow prise Edward and Libby apart.

Next day he left his office for a while in order to drive to Dudley town centre. There, he bought a miniature camera to take photos of Libby through the hole he'd enlarged in her ceiling.

- - -

Hugh was left alone at the dinner table the following evening. Dorothy was upstairs with Charles, who showed no improvement, and Bunty was at the hospital on her shift. In Dorothy's absence Libby had been called to the kitchen to give an opinion on some culinary matter.

He picked up the bottle of wine they'd shared at dinner and began pouring into his glass, just as Libby returned.

'Ah, Libby, would you like some more wine?' he asked.

'No thanks. I've already had a glass. It'll only make me tired. Especially if you're going to teach me to drive. I wouldn't want to fall asleep at the wheel.'

'Shall we go now, before it gets dark?'

'If it's convenient for you.'

He quickly downed what was in his glass and got up. 'It'll have to be the Jaguar, I'm afraid, since Bunty has the Riley.'

It was another balmy evening. The sun was low, glittering through the whispering foliage of the trees.

'I don't think we should go onto the roads at this stage,' Hugh said as they approached the car, 'but at least I can show you the rudiments and have you pulling away and stopping.'

He opened the driver's door and gestured for her to sit inside, and she brushed past him as she did so. 'Make yourself comfortable . . . You can adjust the seat here . . . Excuse me a moment.' He stooped down and his hand dived between her shins, brushing the skin of her calves. He lifted the hem of her skirt a little for access to the adjusting lever, and she was reminded of the time he took those photos of her and did something similar as he posed her. A coincidence?

'Now pull yourself forward . . . Comfortable?'

She nodded.

He sat on his haunches. 'Now . . . these pedals at your feet, Libby . . . Part your legs a little so you can see them . . .'

He looked up at her with unmistakable innuendo brimming from his narrowed eyes.

'That's it. Now . . . The pedal on the right is the throttle. When you press it you increase the speed of the engine and that makes you go faster. The one on the left is the clutch, and you use that when you want to change gear and stop. The one in the middle is the brake.'

'So I have three pedals, but only two feet,' she remarked.

He laughed at her girlish appraisal. 'You use your right foot to operate the throttle and the brake, the logic being that if you are using the one you won't be using the other. Before we start the car, make sure that you are in neutral . . .' He stood up again, leaned over her, making sure he rubbed his upper arm against her bosom as he reached inside the car for the gear stick to demonstrate.

He turned his head and smiled reassuringly at her, taking in her slender figure, the flawless, lightly tanned skin of her bare arms; how her light summer skirt outlined the contours of her thighs so tantalisingly as she sat. She looked so clean and fresh; he yearned to sniff her hair, her creamy skin, to experience her sweet gentle breath on his face. He'd been looking forward so much to being alone with her like this, dreaming of what he might engineer out of it.

'Perhaps it'd be better if you were showing me all this from the passenger seat,' she suggested, aware of his intentions.

'Right-ho,' he agreed perceiving that she must have rumbled him. So he walked around the car and got in beside her. 'Left foot on the clutch,' he instructed. 'Now feel your way through the gears.' He put his hand on hers and guided her through the gears; forwards, backwards, across and forwards. 'Reverse is a bit trickier . . . D'you see?'

'Yes, I've got it.' She pulled her hand from under his. 'I always was quick to pick things up,' she remarked pointedly.

'Now let's start the engine. It's been standing a while now, so we might have to use the choke. This is the choke . . . Now, make sure you're in neutral . . .' She duly checked. 'Now turn the key and press the starter . . . There . . . and don't forget to release it when the engine fires.'

Libby felt the vibration of the engine instantly as it roared into life.

'Foot on clutch . . . Now engage first gear. Handbrake off . . .' She struggled with the handbrake, and he did it for her. 'Now let the clutch out slowly, and gently put pressure on the throttle pedal.'

Of course, the engine stalled.

'Never mind,' he said patiently. 'Let's try again.'

It stalled again with an alarming judder.

She tried it several times, until she eventually felt the car move forwards. Flushed with success, she stayed in first gear, getting used to the notion that she was in control of the car, getting used to the feel of the steering, the effect of the throttle.

'Now press down on the clutch and change into second gear . . . That's good. That's rather good, Libby.'

She smiled, delighted at her minor achievement, and drove on, twisting and turning along the drive until they almost reached the huge wrought iron gates at the end. She felt for the brake, applied it too enthusiastically, and forgot about the clutch. They came to an abrupt halt and the engine stalled.

'Not bad, Libby. But don't forget to depress the clutch pedal as well as the brake pedal to stop. Now let's try a three-point turn.'

He explained the routine and she set about doing it. It was a great deal more difficult to keep the car from stalling when reversing, but after numerous attempts she began to get the feel for it. While she reversed the car, he turned to look behind through the rear window, and his arm went about the back of her seat.

'Now first gear,' he instructed.

Another stall, but at the next attempt they moved forward. But Hugh's arm remained behind her.

'Very good,' he said again. 'Now, just pull up here . . .'

They were a fair distance from the house, which was hidden from view behind the many trees that stood in the grounds. She stopped, put the car into neutral gear and applied the handbrake.

Hugh looked at her as he tickled the back of her neck experimentally. The feel of his fingers sent a shudder down her spine and she leaned forward in protest.

'Please stop it, Hugh,' she said, irritated.

'Can I ask something of you, Libby?'

'What?' she replied apprehensively.

'May I kiss you?'

She laughed, but with disdain. 'What for?'

'Simply because I'm dying to.'

'Well, you're not going to, Hugh.'

He eased himself towards her and pulled her to him, and tried to force his lips on hers. She turned her face away in indignation.

'Hugh, what on earth d'you think you're doing?'

'I told you, I want to kiss you.'

'Well, I don't want to kiss you, if you don't mind.'

'All right . . . Then will you go to bed with me?'

She laughed again at his absurdity. 'No, I will not. If I won't kiss you, I'm hardly likely to go to bed with you.'

'Oh, but the two things aren't necessarily connected, Libby,' he suggested, not about to abandon his cause. 'You could still go to bed with me, and we wouldn't have to kiss if you didn't want to. I do understand that kissing is rather more personal – more intimate, perhaps – than the actual sex act.'

'Whether or not,' she replied with increasing indignation and diminishing patience. 'I have no desire to go to bed with you. I'm married to your brother, for goodness' sake. Doesn't that mean anything to you?'

'But nobody need know. Least of all Edward. Think of the fun we'd have. They say stolen fruits are the sweetest.'

Libby saw a squirrel run down the trunk of the tree and sit for a few moments on the grass, its tail erect, before it darted up another, indifferent to the problem she was facing with Hugh. But her mind was not on the squirrel; it was concentrated on Hugh and his outlandish proposal.

'And what if I told Edward that his own brother had designs on me?'

'Why would you want to do that? You couldn't possibly.'

'I will, Hugh, if you don't stop this nonsense right away.'

'But I can't stop it. Don't you see? I fell in love with you the moment I saw you. I fell desperately in love. I've been in love with you ever since. I live and breathe you.. You're never off my mind.'

'Oh, *Hugh!*' she exclaimed, annoyed, shocked and utterly disappointed that he still felt that way. Didn't he realise how uncomfortable it made her feel? Didn't he understand what a ridiculously difficult situation his ardour was putting her in? 'You should have more grace than to say such things,' she said in admonishment. At once she wanted to escape, curl up into a ball and put her hands over her ears so she could hear no more such words. She was a married woman after all – married to his brother.

'But you must have known it all along, Libby. I didn't try to hide it. I didn't even try to hide it from Laura.'

'I would have thought my obvious love and respect for Edward, not to mention my marrying him, might have cured you of all that.'

'But it hasn't. We only have to be in the same room, and I have this terrible urge to take you in my arms and make passionate love to you. When you're close to me, within touching distance, like now, it's absolute murder. Doubtless, you are blissfully unaware of the torment it brings, Libby. Please don't be so hard on me as to refuse me.'

'I have to refuse you, Hugh, Of course I do—'

In a last-ditch effort to seduce her he ran his hand up her skirt, let it rest on her thigh just above the knee and relished the fleeting moment of contact with her delightfully smooth flesh.

She did not consider it such a clever move on his part, but neither did it shock her, for she was beyond being surprised at his antics, and for a split second she did not react. 'What do you think you are doing, Hugh?'

'Feeling your leg, of course.'

'How dare you!' she protested, and slapped his face as hard as she could for his presumptuous arrogance. She opened the car door and jumped out, then hurried back towards the house, darting between the trees, avoiding the edge of the drive. Tears trembled on her long lashes as she ran. *How dare he ... Who does he think he is?*

- - -

That night Hugh was on sentry duty again in the attic room, accompanied by a new miniature camera, ready and waiting to secretly spy on and photograph Libby as she undressed and prepared herself for bed. It had been a hot day, and its warmth and sultriness lingered. He watched her remove her light summer dress, her underskirt then, to his unqualified joy, her knickers and her brassiere. She was standing there stark naked except for her gold wedding ring that glinted on her finger, and this lack of any clothing whatsoever was for the sake of keeping cool. Hugh's mouth went very dry, and he stared transfixed, goggle-eyed and sweating, his heart pounding like a drum in concert with the disturbance that was demanding more space inside his trousers. Her breasts were ripe and beautiful like fresh fruit, more ripe and more beautiful than Laura Birch's. Her triangle of dark hair, too, was a magnet for his eyes as he watched her spread herself on top of the counterpane with ultimate femininity and grace, before she reached over to turn out the light.

He lay there for a long time afterwards, mental images of her nakedness filling his thoughts. Eventually – perhaps it was even half an hour later – he got up from the floor, his frustration absolute. She had already turned him down that evening, had had the gall to stop him. Perhaps his approach was too clumsy, too unsophisticated for her tastes. It was not his fault that he did not know how to win over women. It was not his fault that he was not the glib-talking ladies' man his brother was, or even Pilot Officer Keith Farrell. She should understand and make allowances.

That slap she gave him was hardly deserved.

Indeed, she might end up being deeply sorry for that.

He took off his shoes and quietly, stealthily, crept down the back stairs and made his way to the landing and Libby's room. Breathing hard, a lump in his dry throat, he stood outside the door in the darkness. The rest of the household was already in bed and asleep. His mother and father were in the other wing, as was Bunty, and the servants. Why hadn't he thought of this before? It was a desperate measure, but he was desperate; desperate to have her, but also desperate to make her see she had chosen the wrong man, that he could still make her the most pampered of women if she were amenable. His only decision now was whether to wait a little longer to be sure she was asleep, or simply go in there at once.

He couldn't wait. Patience had never been one of his virtues.

Gently, he tried the doorknob and it turned. The catch released with a metallic click, and he pushed the door open. He could smell her sweetness, could hear the faint sound of her steady breathing. At once he was affected. How was it possible that one girl could have such a massive impact on a man? She was asleep already. His eyes were accustomed to the darkness, and he could just discern the pale, slender curves of her body as she lay sprawled tantalisingly naked on top of her bed. Her dark hair was loose, and flowing over her pillow like rivers of ink.

He decided to undress; it would be pointless to waste this golden opportunity and not feel her blissfully smooth skin pressing against his own. His eyes never leaving her, he took off his clothes and they fell to the floor. He approached the bed, lay down on the side where Edward would sleep, and remained still for a moment, just looking at the soft curve of her throat and the delectable mounds of her breasts. How delightful it would be to nuzzle his face in their spongy smoothness.

Well, very, very soon . . .

His heart was pounding like a drum, the blood was coursing through his veins, and his mouth was bone dry. After this, she would either love him irreversibly, or hate him. But at least . . .

Gently, he reached out to her and let his hand skim lightly over her belly. The unbelievable smoothness of her skin made him want to weep, it was so unutterably beautiful. He could feel the enticing warmth of her body radiating towards him. His hand ventured carefully to her bare thighs and luxuriated in their silkiness, less moist than earlier when he had snatched that quick, defiant grope up her skirt. Encouraged, he roamed smoothly upwards and reached her mound of soft hair . . . Oh, bliss . . . She stirred, parted her thighs and sighed, and his heart pounded with anticipation as he caressed her gently in that soft, moist place.

'Oh, Edward,' she breathed softly.

In the darkness her response was immediate. Her arm came around him, her mouth was on his, and she snuggled her body to him, sighing contentedly. He cupped one firm round buttock in his hand as she pressed herself against him, then ran it gently over her thigh. His luck was in at last. This woman was far too desirable to be the property of one man. Gently, he rolled onto her, enjoying these stolen, but incredibly delicious kisses she had denied him earlier.

But for Libby, rousing from a dreamy sleep, there was something different about those kisses. They did not feel like Edward's kisses, did not taste like Edward's kisses. Funny the tricks dreams play on you. It quickly dawned on her – Edward was not at home. Or had he returned on leave unexpectedly in the night and slipped into bed with her?

'Edward?' She sighed contentedly, smiling to herself in the darkness. 'You're home . . .'

This was no dream after all. Edward was on top of her, her legs were apart, and she was ready and eager to receive him as he pressed urgently for entry. But she could feel that he was not properly lined up– a lack of practice, maybe.

In a flash, in an earthquake, in a striking revelation she was alert, and understood perfectly that Edward was not expected. If he were coming home she would have known beforehand.

This man naked lying on top of her was not Edward. She would not put it past Hugh to try his luck.

Deftly, forcibly, she shoved him off. He clawed back at her and she rolled over, out of his reach. She switched on her bed-side lamp.

'Hugh! For God's sake!' she shrieked in horror. 'What on earth d'you think you're playing at?'

For once he looked decidedly sheepish, blinking at the brightness of the light as he slid off the bed. Libby instinctively wrapped the counterpane around herself for both modesty and protection.

'Are you mad?' she cried, thoroughly outraged.

'Only for you,' he answered pathetically, almost apologeti-cally. 'I couldn't help myself, Libby. But you know how I feel.'

'I didn't know anybody could be so underhand. You should be locked up. You are mad.'

She could find no words strong enough to express the aversion she felt. She was beginning to feel that she could con-sider neither herself, nor her virtue, safe in this house while Edward was away. There was a lock on the door, but never had she thought for a moment that she ought to use it in the family home of her husband. From now on, though, she must keep the door locked; to prevent another invasion of her pri-vacy by her lust-crazed, demented brother-in-law.

'I'm not ashamed. Libby,' Hugh said regaining his defiance, recovering his composure. He suddenly remembered the slap and was feeling justified in his behaviour. 'I want you, and I gave you fair warning.'

'That you did, but never would I have thought you could stoop so low as to try and take me in my sleep. If you ever come near me again I swear I shall tell your father.'

'I wouldn't, if I were you,' he said ominously. 'It would be all too easy for me to tell Edward how you invited me to your room while he was away.'

'You wouldn't dare tell such lies.'

'Wouldn't I?' He smirked as he strutted across the bedroom, unabashed, and picked up his clothes. 'Consider this a truce we have for now, Mrs Burgayne – but for you at any rate it'll be an uneasy one. I suggest you consider your position very carefully. It might be so much simpler, and so much more to your advantage to submit. Think on it.'

'I'll do no such thing. Now will you please bugger off,' she said vehemently, the vocabulary of the working girl unintentionally surfacing, 'and never trouble me again.'

- - -

Next morning, Hugh arose early with the intention of leaving for the office without Libby. Before he went, though, he sought Jenkins, and found her in the breakfast room laying the table for the others.

'Margaret.'

'Yes, Mr Hugh?' she answered sweetly, aware that he often looked at her with interest and admiration, and in her naivety was flattered by it.

'Whatever post we receive from now on, I want you to put it away unseen by anybody, and hand it to me on my return home. I don't want my father troubled unduly.'

'All right.'

'Do you understand what I'm asking?'

'Yes,' Jenkins shrugged. 'You want me to hand you all the post and not give it anybody else.'

'That's correct.'

'But what if somebody else gets to the post first?'

'You know what time the post arrives, Margaret. Be sure you are there, ready and waiting for the postman.'

'What about if it's a letter from Mr Edward for the new Mrs Burgayne?'

'You know what Mr Edward's letters look like? You recognise his hand-writing?'

'Oh, yes, Mr Hugh.'

'Then let *the new Mrs Burgayne* have them. But only letters from Edward. All others you will hold onto for me. I repeat – keep all other post and hand it to me – nobody else.'

'I'll see to it, Mr Hugh.'

- - -

| 22 |

Libby realized that when learning to drive her virtue was more likely to be left intact if Bunty would teach her and allow her to practise in the Riley. This she did throughout August, and gradually became a proficient and confident driver. On the last Sunday in August, accompanied by Bunty, she took Edward's MG and, with the canvas hood lowered and the wind blowing through their hair in the summer sunshine, they left Buttonbridge Hall to spend the day with Gladys and Joe Shakespeare.

Libby's absence that day presented Hugh with a perfect opportunity to do what he had been contemplating ever since she had so unfeelingly spurned his love and rebuffed his advances, for Hugh was nothing if not vindictive. Withholding her favours, for which he was so ravenously hungry, was nothing short of a crime in his eyes. She needed to understand that neither he nor his feelings were to be trifled with. In the end he would have her. He just needed to clear the path.

So he sat in Libby's office in Buttonbridge Hall and fed two sheets of paper between the rollers of her typewriter, and separated them with a sheet of carbon paper. He squared them up neatly, and began to type; a letter he had more or less mentally composed already.

31ˢᵗ August 1941
Buttonbridge Hall

Dear Edward,

First and foremost I must give you the latest news on Father. Dr MacKenzie has been calling regularly, administering potions and poultices, but the old man as yet shows no detectable signs of improvement. If anything, he is worse. It seems his bronchial problems emanate from when he was a young man and will never improve entirely. His spirits are also low, because he is unable to usefully occupy himself, having been made to give up working, at least until such time as there might be some upturn in his condition. That, however, is very unlikely in my opinion. He has also lost his appetite, and is barely eating anything, and has lost much weight in consequence.

Rest assured that he is enjoying the best care possible, so I would not want you to worry about him unduly, or even consider applying for compassionate leave to visit at this stage.

However, there is another particular turn of events, about which I feel it is my duty as your brother, and acting head of the family, to inform you. It grieves me greatly to have to write on the subject, but after due consideration of the seri-

ousness of the problem and how it directly affects you, I feel I have no choice.

You may or may not know that a young airman was convalescing here at Buttonbridge Hall by the name of Pilot Officer Keith Farnell. It seems that he and Libby, your beloved wife, struck up quite some friendship after you had returned to active duty following your internment in Ireland and your subsequent marriage. As evidence of this I enclose some photographs that I managed to take of them together in the grounds, and I'm sure you will easily discern, merely by their poses, the obvious familiarity that exists between them. It transpires that letters have passed between them since his return home, and I have been fortunate, inasmuch as I have been able to acquire a couple that Libby received from him. They are enclosed for your edification and enlightenment. You will agree, I am certain, that there can be no doubt from the strong emotions and desires expressed in these letters that PO Farnell and your wife are, or have been, conducting an illicit and ardent love affair, albeit at a distance and by post for the time being. Unfortunately, I have not been able to get hold of her replies, for obvious reasons, but I have no reason to suppose they are any less fervent. And all this while she is no doubt also writing love letters to you. One cannot begin to comprehend the fickleness of women.

It pains me even more to relate that I myself have been propositioned by your wife on more than one occasion, even invited to her bedroom. Needless to say, I was appalled, not to mention affronted that she would even consider that I could betray my loyalty to my own brother, but some people, regrettably, do not share our moral values. I would not normally have mentioned these occurrences, but in the context of the foregoing I am confident you will agree that it is entirely relevant and reveals a pattern to her behaviour and her lax morals.

I have no reason to suppose there have not been others. Indeed, I saw Libby once meet that other person she was friendly with when she first commenced her employment at Blowers Green Steelworks. It was outside the works and it was when you two had begun your then undeclared courtship. His name eludes me.

I perceived from the outset that your liaison with Libby was both foolhardy and doomed. You may recall that I tried in my own way to warn you of this, and to register my disapproval. The old saying "There are none so blind as those who will not see" certainly holds true in this case. One must put it down to the impetuosity of youth. I even tried to discourage her, but my words fell on deaf ears. After all, to a common working girl, you were quite some catch, and she was hardly likely to let go easily.

So I trust the foregoing will open your eyes to the diabolical flaw in the character of Libby Shakespeare and the things of which she is capable.

I deeply regret having to inform you of these appalling events for I know the revelation will upset you greatly, but I would be failing in my duty as a brother if I were to ignore them and allow them to remain concealed. Edward, you are young enough and strong enough to put all this behind you and start anew. A better life, with a woman more suitable and more responsible, on your return from active service, is what I earnestly wish for you.

Affectionately yours,

Hugh.

Hugh pulled the letter from the typewriter, read it through, and satisfied that it adroitly made the points he wished to convey, he signed it. He slid it into the envelope, along with the incriminating letters from Keith Farnell that he had intercepted, and the tell-tale photographs. When he had sealed it, pocketed the carbon copy and destroyed the carbon paper, he drove to the nearest pillar box to post his malicious communication, somewhat pleased with his efforts.

On his return from his trip to the pillar box to post his venom, Hugh rang for Jenkins. She emerged from the kitchen, smiled when she saw him and stood facing him with her hands clasped in front of her girlishly.

'Yes, Mr Hugh?'

'Margaret, will you take a pot of tea and a bottle of whisky to my room, please?'

'Very good, Mr Hugh,' she replied and bobbed a neat curtsey.

'Do you know where my mother is?'

'I believe she's helping out with the convalescents, Mr Hugh.'

'Thank you.'

He climbed the staircase. On his way to his room he tapped on the door of his father's bedroom, opened it and peeped inside. Charles was evidently asleep and alone. He left and in his own bedroom he took off his shoes and sat on his bed, propping himself up with two plump pillows. Presently, Jenkins tapped on the door and he called her to come in. She appeared, carrying a tray bearing the teapot, a cup and saucer, a bottle of whisky and a glass.

'Thank you, Margaret,' he said with a grin. 'If there's anybody in this household who I know I can count on, it's you.'

Margaret blushed becomingly. 'Thank you, Mr Hugh.'

'How old are you, Margaret, if you'll pardon my asking?'

'Twenty-four,' Mr Hugh.

'So how long have you been with us at Buttonbridge Hall? A few years now?'

'Ever since I was fifteen, Mr Hugh.'

'That's a long time.'

'Would you like me to give the pot a stir, Mr Hugh, or would you like me to pour you a glass of whisky?'

'Yes, pour me a glass of whisky, please. We'll let the tea brew a few minutes.'

She poured the whisky and handed it to him. He took the glass with his right hand, but with his left hand he reached out and took her hand, detaining her.

'Sit beside me, Margaret,' he said smoothly. 'I've been dying to have a chat with you.'

'Oh, really?' She sat compliantly beside him on the bed, and looked at him expectantly, while he still held her hand.

He sipped the whisky, and looked into her eyes, while she returned his look with a great deal of uncertainty and coyness.

'You're a very pretty girl,' he said softly.

'D'you really think so, Mr Hugh?'

'I wouldn't say so if I didn't think it, and I expect you have a great many admirers.'

She shrugged. 'Working here I don't get the chance to go out looking for admirers,' she answered.

'So you don't have a sweetheart?'

'I ain't had a sweetheart since I was seventeen,' she answered.

'That's a shame. Here . . . would you like a sip of my whisky?'

'D'you think I should? What if Mrs Burgayne found out?'

'Well I shan't tell her, Margaret. Go on . . .' he handed her the glass, and she took a sip.

'Mmm, whisky's nice. ain't it? Thank you, Mr Hugh.'

'There's plenty more where that came from. Have more.'

She smiled, her blue eyes creasing into a look of conspiracy over the rim of the glass as she took another sip.

'I have a confession to make, Margaret,' he breathed, as she handed the glass back to him.

'Oh? What sort of confession?'

'I'm drawn to you . . . very much so.'

'Crumbs, Mr Hugh. I don't know what to say.'

'Well, it's true,' he affirmed. 'Very much so.'

'But I'm just a maid.'

'And I'm just a man,' he answered, surprised at the ingenuity of his response and encouraged by it, as well as by Margaret's apparent delight at the revelation – or was it surprise? 'So I was wondering, Margaret, if you might consider being *my* sweetheart. I ended my engagement to Miss Birch some time ago.'

'I know you did, Mr Hugh. D'you really mean it though?' she asked. 'It's a bit sudden. It's something I wasn't expecting.'

'Well, do you need time to think about it?'

'No, no,' she declared without hesitation. 'I'd be that proud to be your girl, Mr Hugh—'

He squeezed her hand. 'Just call me "Hugh" – when we are alone at any rate. But don't mention our little arrangement to anybody else. It must be our secret for the time being.'

'So when shall we have time to be together?' she asked.

'Leave that to me. I'll take you out, wine and dine you on your evening off. We'll certainly fix something. In the meantime, we do live in the same house . . .'

'But I'm in the attic . . . Hugh – with other servants.'

'If you are careful, you don't need to be in the attic all the time. Not every night at any rate. If you get my meaning.'

'You mean I should come to your room . . . in the middle o' the night?'

'What a clever girl. It sounds like a perfect arrangement. Would you be prepared to?'

'Oh, I couldn't,' she said with maidenly reserve, even though her face was an icon of both pleasure and bewilderment.

'Of course you could, and I want you to. Say you will, Margaret.'

'I don't know . . . Mr Hugh . . . So soon, I mean.'

'Don't be so diffident, Margaret. Why wait? You like me enough, don't you?'

'I've always liked you . . .'

'Well then . . . Come to my room tonight.'

She nodded uncertainly, her eyes avoiding his.

'Promise?'

'Yes, I suppose so,' she yielded. 'If you're really sure. If you really want me to.'

'I do. So let's set a seal on it, shall we, Margaret? Kiss me.'

She offered her lips hesitantly at first, still unable to believe this was happening to her. Yes, she had always liked Mr Hugh, even as a young girl of fifteen and he was about nineteen. Their lips met, and he could taste the sweetness of the whisky she had just sipped. Her response remained tentative for a few seconds, but as their lips lingered, pressed together in that first kiss, she became less inhibited, obviously taking pleasure from it.

'That was nice,' she whispered when they broke off.

'I'm glad you like it,' he said. 'So let's try it again.'

As they kissed once more he eased her backwards, so she was lying beside him on his bed. His hand felt beneath the ribbons of her apron and unfastened the buttons of her blouse. When he broke off their kiss, she looked into his eyes, and smiled confirming her complicity. His heart was racing, his breathing heavy. Had he finally made a conquest of an attractive, beddable girl, albeit their maid of many years, who was prepared to share his bed in a few stolen moments?

'Your tea will be cold,' she remarked in a vain attempt to reclaim some modesty.

'Never mind the tea, Margaret. You're much tastier than the tea.' He kissed her again, pulled up the hem of her skirt and ran his hand up the inside of her thigh. She offered no resistance as his hand reached her bare skin above the tops of her stockings, and proceeded on its course inside the leg of her knickers.

- - -

The pink hue of an early September dawn was turning to turquoise over the English Channel as two southbound Hurricanes scanned the skies, patrolling for German aircraft. Over the last few days and nights the Biggin Hill RAF base had been attacked again and reduced to a shambles by one-thousand-pound bombs dropped by a small formation of a dozen bombers approaching at low level and undetected by radar.

Workshops, barracks, stores, hangars and W.A.A.F quarters were destroyed, and 39 personnel lost their lives. The following day, in a high-level attack, the Operations Block took a direct hit. There was no reason to suppose other airfields would not be likewise attacked, hence the aerial patrols of the Hurricanes.

Pilot Officer Royston Hughes was flying one of them, the other was piloted by Flying Officer Edward Burgayne, cruising at 16,000 feet. Edward's eyes, through the tears which misted them, instinctively searched every section of the sky around him, above and below. A long way off, a speck in the sky, an unidentifiable aeroplane was limping for the French coast with a plume of smoke trailing; somebody else's victim, and they made no pursuit.

Then the voice of Royston Hughes rasped through the headphones. Six fighters, he said, possibly Messerschmitt 109Fs, were approaching at a height of about 12,000 feet. Edward gave the order to descend and engage them. The danger was that if an enemy plane could get behind you and beneath you, you were at his mercy. Conversely, if you could get behind and below the enemy planes you would enjoy a clear advantage.

But Edward Burgayne had lost all enthusiasm for any chase. Bigger, more important things were preoccupying him – personal things. Only the day before he had received an extremely disturbing letter from his brother Hugh. Hugh rarely wrote, and the very rarity of correspondence from Hugh served to underline its gravity; and the information it contained was grave indeed. Edward was scarcely able to believe that Libby, to whom he had given his all and whom he believed he could trust implicitly, could betray him after all. His doubts about her and her integrity had been first raised when Hugh had presented him with that batch of photos as he was leaving Buttonbridge Hall to rejoin his squadron. Now Hugh had produced even more evidence, unmistakeable in the form of love letters from a man of whom he had no prior knowledge, and clear black and white photographs, which showed her holding affectionately onto the arm of another airman as she stood smiling coquettishly at him with her big expressive eyes. That look, he had always believed, was reserved only for him.

It was heart-breaking to have one's illusions shattered, to be told that the woman you adored was not worth a light. In the torment of sleepless nights he had pondered over and over their moments together, searching for some clue that would give the lie to Hugh's devastating claims. Yet all he could ever recall was Libby's eager response to him, her unstinting demonstrations of love. But to turn all that on its head, was that same eager response, those same unstinting demonstrations of love, merely the subterfuge of a woman out to sell herself to a man she considered worth having, or – even worse – the baser instincts of sexual gratification? He understood there were such women; they were often discussed bawdily in the mess rooms, referred to as nymphomaniacs, and everybody wanted to meet at least one in his life, or so they said. Maybe Libby one such nymphomaniac, if Hugh's further assertion that she had even propositioned him was anything to go by.

He had been blinded by love, by desire, and ought to have seen it coming. He pondered the first time they made love, when her eagerness, her lack of modesty belied her claims to virginity; virginity which she had effected convincingly enough at the time. Had she not undressed in front of him without turning a hair, flaunting her nakedness before him in the ferns of Enville Common? Hardly the behaviour of the demure young thing she purported to be. In hindsight, how easy her seduction had been; her forwardness had astonished yet delighted him. In truth it had been tantamount to her seducing him.

Having received Hugh's letter, Edward had decided not to write again to Libby until he had considered the matter further. It would be difficult to know what to say to her ever again after receiving this intelligence. How could he write and accuse her of having affairs and blame her for the impending break-up of their marriage without revealing that it was Hugh who had fed him the information? But if he failed to write, what then? She had to know how things stood between them and the reason why. It was an impossible situation, and his mind was in a whirlwind of confusion because of it. He was hardly mentally fit to be flying his Hurricane– deprived of sleep, of the love of his wife, having to make split-second decisions that could jeopardise the life of his fellow pilot Royston Hughes.

He flew on, obsessed with these thoughts, with Royston flying alongside just a few feet to his left. The Messerschmitts had evidently spotted the pair of Hurricanes and were preparing to attack, peeling off from their formation to come on broadside.

Then began a terrific dogfight. Royston Hughes manoeuvred himself cleverly and opened fire, disabling two of the Messerschmitts. He screamed with triumph through Edward's headphones as he saw them lose altitude, riddled with bullet holes, spewing black smoke behind them.

Edward watched all this passively, almost as if he were a spectator and aloof from the action. Partly through sheer mental fatigue, partly through the acute heartache he was suffering, what he was doing now seemed triflingly unimportant in comparison. Once he had been happy, oh so happy, but would he ever be happy again? He had loved that girl Libby Shakespeare with all his heart and soul, but could he ever love any woman again? Would he ever be able to trust any woman in future? What he now knew put a different perspective on every aspect of his existence. So was there any point in living? And here was the perfect opportunity to escape this life and all its ineffable tribulations . . . with honour.

He saw the line of tracers from one of the Messerschmitts that were intended for him and had time to either dive or climb to avoid them. But he did neither. Even he was unsure whether he maintained his course through fatigue, apathy, indecision, or whether it was entirely deliberate.

The first bullet ripped into the Hurricane's nose, ripping away the fuel lines to the engine, which spluttered and died in a stream of flames that lapped around fuselage and over the cockpit. The next two strafed the length of the fuselage and the tail, blasting part of the rudder away.

Edward was still conscious, but unmoved, still impassive, still aloof, utterly fatalistic as his Hurricane nose-dived uncontrollably towards the sea below, failing to respond to his fellow pilot's shouts in his headphones.

- - -

After some anxious days devoid of a letter from Edward, and enquiries to Jenkins about the reliability of the post, Libby sought the advice of Hugh. They had hardly spoken since that awful night when he had invaded her bed, and the mutual hostility was palpable.

'Jenkins tells me you've given instructions that all post is handed only to you,' she said coolly on his return from the steelworks one evening. 'Are there any letters from Edward you might have been hiding from me?' She flashed a look of sheer scorn that was unmistakeable in its message.

'Indeed not, Libby,' he replied, his haughtiness matching her disdain. 'Jenkins has instructions to hand you any correspondence addressed to you personally. It's only business mail I'm concerned about, merely to protect my father from the worry of dealing with it while he is so ill.'

'I see,' she said politely. 'But you might as well know how worried I am that I've received nothing from Edward for a few days now. I think it fair you should know. Unless, of course, he has written to his father or mother, in which case I would appreciate being made aware of it for my own peace of mind.'

'There have been no letters at all from Edward.'

'Are you sure?' Tears welled in her eyes.

'Of course I'm sure,' he declared, resentful of her implication.

'Then perhaps you should be worried too.'

- - -

A telegram from the air ministry arrived that same evening, addressed to Mrs Edward Burgayne. She took it from the telegram boy, trembling with trepidation, having been down this path before. That time it had turned out well, but the heart-rending anxiety, the devastation, the feeling again that life suddenly seemed pointless, was unbearable. Whatever it said in this telegram, she was going to suffer those same traumatic emotions once more, whether or not it would turn out well this time. But there was no escaping it. So she opened the telegram and read it, watched apprehensively by Dorothy and Bunty.

THE AIR MINISTRY REGRETS TO INFORM YOU THAT YOUR HUSBAND FLYING OFFICER EDWARD BURGAYNE HAS BEEN REPORTED MISSING IN ACTION BELIEVED KILLED FOLLOWING OPERATIONS OVER THE ENGLISH CHANNEL ON THE MORNING OF 3/9/41 STOP LETTER TO FOLLOW STOP

Libby fell into the arms of Bunty and wept hysterically. Dorothy gently prised the telegram from Libby's fingers and crept away to break the dreadful news to Charles, leaving Libby to grieve in Bunty's tender care.

Charles was sitting in a wicker armchair in the bedroom, wearing his dressing gown. His hair was awry, and he had not shaved that day, so that grey whiskers sprouted from his cheeks and chin, exaggerating his pallidness. He looked up when Dorothy entered, at once alarmed by the grave expression on her face.

'What is it, my dear?' he wheezed. 'You look as if you've lost a pound and found sixpence.'

'Here, Charles. This just arrived.' She offered him the telegram. 'It's bad news, I'm afraid.'

'Edward?'

She nodded. 'You'd better read it.'

'I can't. Read it to me.'

She duly read it.

A cold shudder ran down his spine. 'My God,' he whispered, as tears started rimming his eyes. 'It's as I always feared—' A spasm of painful coughing seized him, interrupting him. Eventually it subsided and he continued. 'I rue the day I gave him that damned Gypsy Moth. Why ever did I encourage him to fly?'

'You weren't to know there would be a war, Charles,' Dorothy consoled, struggling to maintain her composure. 'Or that he would be so intimately involved in it. And even if you hadn't given it him, who's to say he wouldn't have become an RAF pilot anyway? He was always mad on planes.'

Charles shook his head and wept. 'I feel responsible,' he croaked. 'I contrived to kill my own son. I have helped to engineer his death.'

'We don't know he's dead, Charles.' Dorothy knelt beside him and took his hand. 'He's reported missing. He might still show up.'

'Over the English Channel? If he crashed or was shot down over the English Channel . . . he would have drowned anyway.'

'But there is hope, Charles. We must be patient, and pray that he is still alive.'

'Some hope,' he answered despondently. 'How is Libby taking it?'

'She's utterly distraught.'

'That was a silly question. I'd have expected her to be nothing less.'

- - -

The promised letter arrived two harrowing days later. Jenkins, realising what it was and its importance, sought Libby as soon as the post arrived and handed it to her. She was sitting with Bunty in the breakfast room, pushing an uneaten strip of bacon, her ration for the week, around her plate. When Jenkins appeared, she looked up forlornly.

'I think your letter has arrived, ma'am,' she remarked softly.

'Oh, Margaret, thank you.' Libby got up to receive the letter, and opened it as she sat down again. As she read its contents tears formed once more in her eyes that were already red from continued weeping. There seemed to be no end to this anguish.

'What does it say, Libby?' Bunty asked gently.

Libby handed it over and Bunty digested its contents.

RAF Exeter.

6 September 1941

Dear Mrs Burgayne,

By the time you receive this letter, you will already have received a telegram informing you that your husband, Flying Officer Edward Burgayne has been reported missing as a result of Air Operations. It is with sincere regret that I write to you conveying as I do the feelings of my entire Squadron. On the morning of 3 September at approximately seven o' clock Edward and a colleague, Pilot Officer Royston Hughes, took off from this aerodrome to patrol the skies over the English Channel for signs of approaching enemy aircraft. The enemy has been conducting low level and high-level attacks on our aerodromes with a view to crippling our air superiority. Unfortunately, your husband failed to return, and his aircraft was seen losing height and in a severely damaged condition by PO Hughes.

Your husband always displayed keenness and considerable ability, and had many friends. We lost one of our finest and bravest men when his aircraft failed to return, and one for which a great future had already been mapped out with this Squadron. His presence is greatly missed and his loss is regretted by all.

Your husband's personal affects have been gathered together and will be retained here for a short period in the hope that better news will be received. You may be aware that in quite a large percentage of cases aircrew reported missing are eventually reported prisoner-of-war, and I hope that this may give you some comfort in your anxiety. If that is the case it is likely that THE RED CROSS will inform you before I get to hear.

It behoves me to explain that the telegram notifying you of the casualty of your husband, was sent with the object of avoiding his chance of escape being prejudiced by undue publicity, in case he is still alive and at large. This is a precaution in the case of all missing personal.

Once again please accept the deep sympathy of us all, and let us hope that we may soon have some good news of the safety of your husband.

> *Yours Sincerely*
> *B. Rossiter*
> *Wing Commander*

- - -

| 23 |

Libby hurried up the stairs to show the letter to Charles, and tapped gently on the door of his bedroom. He was grievously affected by the loss of his younger son, which had had an adverse effect on his overall condition. When she entered he was alone, slumped in his wicker chair in the window that looked out onto the grounds of Buttonbridge Hall. But his eyes were shut to the world.

'Charles?' she said gently, in case he was asleep.

He roused, slowly turning his head to face her. He looked like death, and Libby was alarmed at his apparent worsening. He was so vastly changed from the proud, confident captain of industry she had worked with and admired.

'Libby,' he croaked, and managed a smile. 'Come and sit by me.'

She did as she was bid, pulling the stool from the dressing table close to him.

'This letter just arrived, Charles. It's from Edward's Wing Commander. Full of regrets, of course, but offering some hope. Would you like to read it?'

'My eyes are not so good, Libby. Please read it to me.'

She read it out, slowly and precisely.

'It's not like the last time when he turned up in Ireland, is it?' she commented with a profound sigh. 'This is altogether different.'

'Altogether more serious,' he gasped, finding breathing more difficult. 'It really doesn't offer much in the way of hope.'

'But he might turn up,' she said, in an effort to cheer him a little. 'Even if he's alive and been captured, at least he'll be freed when the war ends.'

'Whenever that might be,' Charles replied dolefully.

'Are you comfortable, Charles? Is there something I can get you while I'm here?'

'You're a good girl, Libby,' he said with a sad smile. 'I hope and pray that Edward turns up for you. I've never seen him so happy as when he's with you.'

'It's the same for me too, you know. I'm like a ship without a sail.'

'I know, my dear.' He reached for her hand, and she met him halfway, clasping his affectionately. 'It must be so painful for you.'

'Painful for us all . . . But, Charles, I do have some good news that might cheer you. At least I hope it does.'

He looked at her enquiringly, the light in his eyes, dimmed for so long, brightening a little. 'Do tell me.'

'I'm having Edward's baby . . .'

It took a second or two to sink in, coming, as it did, as a complete surprise. 'But that's simply wonderful news, Libby.

You're going to give us a grandchild. Oh, I couldn't be more pleased. Congratulations, my dear.'

'Thank you. I knew that would please you. I do hope it's a boy and that he's the image of his daddy.'

Charles's smile was one of delight. 'Oh, wait till the rest of the family know.'

'No, Charles, I don't want anybody else to know yet.' Certainly, she did not want Hugh to know. 'This is between us two for the time being. It's not absolutely certain yet, although I am fairly sure.'

'Well, it's just the tonic everybody needs.'

'Please, Charles. Please don't say anything yet. Let me tell everybody in my own time.'

He squeezed her hand. 'Very well . . . I just hope I don't talk in my sleep and blurt it out in front of Dorothy.'

She smiled affectionately. 'Thank you . . . Also . . . you've always been exceptionally good to me, Charles, always truly kind. I want to thank you for that as well.'

'Because I've always thought the world of you, Libby. And I'm proud and delighted that you are my daughter-in-law. I just hope the future bodes well for you.'

'Mmm,' she agreed. 'So do I.'

'Well, speaking frankly – and realistically in the event of the worst scenario – If dear Edward does not show up – and we all pray he will – you should know that the Burgaynes will always look after you and your baby when it arrives. Your child will be a Burgayne, Libby. He, or she, will be treated as such. Always remember that.'

Libby was touched, and tears trembled on her long lashes. 'Thank you, Charles. Naturally, I've suspected for a week or two that I've been carrying a child, and it has been a concern as to what would happen if Edward were ever lost – even before he was lost. It's pretty hazardous being an RAF pilot.'

'Too hazardous for my taste,' Charles concurred. He sighed, deeply, gasping for breath.

'Are you all right?' Libby asked, alarmed at this unexpected change in his breathing.

'I feel quite hot and faint all of a sudden. Could you please help me into bed?'

'Of course.'

She stood up, and helped him to his feet, steadying him as she took the few awkward steps to his bed. He slumped down and, as he rested back on his pillows, she lifted his legs and tucked his feet into bed, then helped him lean forward so she could plump up his pillows. He was sweating profusely, and his breathing was coming in sharp rasps.

'Thank you,' he said, polite as ever, even in his extreme discomfort.

'I'll call a nurse from the convalescents' room.'

'No, stay, Libby' he implored. 'Dorothy will be here very shortly. Tell me what names you have thought of for your baby.'

'I haven't given it much thought yet,' she admitted. 'But if it's a boy, then I shall call him Edward. Certainly Edward.'

'A good choice, and hardly surprising. And if it's a girl?'

'Mmm . . . I need more notice.'

He smiled through his suffering, and closed his eyes, his breathing still laboured. Within a couple of minutes it was clear he was asleep, and Libby planted a kiss on his cheek before she tip-toed out of the room.

She immediately sought Dorothy, and Dorothy hurried to his room, then hurried back downstairs to the telephone to call Dr MacKenzie.

'Charles is running a temperature, Vernon, and I am rather concerned,' she explained.

'I see. I'll be there shortly.'

Dr MacKenzie arrived within half an hour, and at once examined his ailing patient.

'So what's up with me now?' Charles asked resignedly.

'Pneumonia, I'm afraid, old chap.'

'Pneumonia? Hell . . . As if my family haven't got enough to concern them right now.'

'I know, Charles. And it's exactly the condition I was hoping we would avoid,' the doctor added.

'Will you tell the family, Vernon, or shall I?'

'I'll break it to them, old chap. You're going to need some special attention.'

- - -

Charles Burgayne passed away on Sunday 21st September 1941. Libby sat with him much of the time during his suffering, watching this once great man, a true gentleman, fade away. In the early stages, Dr MacKenzie said it was possible he might recover, but Libby could see that even he didn't really believe recovery was likely. Besides his illness, Charles had taken the additional punishment of the loss of his son, and felt partly responsible for that loss. The trauma of grief had taken its toll and had expedited his death, for he had lost the will to fight for his life.

Buttonbridge Hall was engulfed in sorrow. The loss of Edward was hard enough to bear, for there was still no news, but the death of Charles doubled the grief.

The funeral was held on Friday 27th at St Mary's in Enville which, from its lofty elevation, overlooked the huddle of the village, its public house, its barns and fine houses. As the clock struck twelve, every pew inside the ancient sandstone church was filled. The Burgayne family were huddled in the front pew, behind them relatives, friends and business associates, as well as a numerous contingent from the steelworks, including Joe Shakespeare, Libby's father. Only a few short weeks ago Libby had been married here.

Then everybody filed outside to the churchyard in a sombre procession and stood in random groups around the precisely cut rectangular hole in the ground. The day was grey, misty and autumnal, and spots of rain rustled and pattered in the tops of the trees.

Libby looked out across the valley behind the village and recalled the first time she had watched Edward, Adrian and Bunty riding across with others, hooves thundering and hounds baying during the first Boxing Day Hunt she'd been invited to. Little did she realise then that she would be looking across the same valley, uncannily silent on this day, mourning

Edward's loss in war just a few short years later, and the death of his father also.

Dorothy Burgayne sniffed and wiped her tears, and Hugh, with a great show of filial love, put a comforting arm around her. Bunty shifted silently to Libby's side, and she felt her friend's arm around her waist. Libby realised that Bunty too needed comforting, so they gloomily held onto each other like the devoted sisters they had become.

For the entire family, but for Libby especially, this was a double funeral. The only thing missing today was Edward's body, but only God knew where he lay. The tears came, irrepressible, insistent. A million tears she had cried already, but clearly it was not over yet. Helplessness and grief still sickened her, as did the sense of futility of loving somebody, when that person's life could be snuffed out so easily and so unjustly. She resented the hopeless waste that made a mockery of his bravery and his sensitivity, for he had been a sensitive man. His loss, and the loss of others like him everywhere, was the consequence of the ambitions and politics of remote and aloof people in positions of extreme power, and had been wrought by their agencies. It was a further manifestation of man's inhumanity to man, and the suffering that such inhumanity caused to ordinary people was beyond endurance.

She begrudged too the premature demise through more natural causes of Charles, a man she had always admired and had grown to love as a daughter loves a father. These sudden, unexpected deaths disdained all the striving for betterment, negated the value of wealth and position, for neither money nor influence, however abundant, could have made Charles a well man. Nor could they bring Edward back.

Yet inside her was growing the next Burgayne; Edward's child. However much of a mockery death made of her hopes and her dreams, she must protect this life, for it was all she would ever have of Edward now.

- - -

To take her mind off things, and to try and make herself useful, Libby did her best to immerse herself in work, and drove herself every day to the steelworks. She occupied the same office she had occupied before and found that she missed Charles greatly. She half expected him to call her to his office, or venture into hers and ask her to do this or that for him, but because it didn't happen her sense of his loss was accentuated.

The other girls whom she had befriended and had got to know well, seemed to shed their resentment of her heightened status, and were genuinely sorry that after such a tragically short time married, she was now, suddenly, a widow. She was one of them again, unconditionally accepted, for they all sensed her sadness and shared in it. After all, they were equally likely to suffer similarly, since the husbands and sweethearts of most were fighting this dreadful war in the army, the air force or the navy. But for all that spiritual closeness, there were still material differences between Libby and the others, although most closed their eyes to those differences. When she went home she did not go back to a small, damp terraced house where baths were relatively infrequent and taken in a tin tub in the scullery, with a cold and draughty privy in the back yard, but to a mansion in acres of beautiful, wooded grounds, with bathrooms and servants. She even had the use of a motorcar with which to drive herself to and from work. Yet they seemed to forgive her for that too.

Hugh was evidently still smarting over her rejecting his ardent advances, for he rarely spoke to Libby, which is the reason she drove herself to work in Edward's MG. When he did deign to speak it was curtly.

Yet Hugh still harboured this dark, secret lust for Libby, fuelled by his still regular, secret spying on her through the crack in the floor of the attic, and despite his covert affair with Margaret Jenkins. By now he had built up quite a collection of photographs, some showing Libby naked and some scantily clad in her underwear, which he kept in a file marked 'LS' in a draw of a cabinet in his cellar darkroom. It was a sin that she was going to waste, unloved and unserviced in that big bed in that vast, all but empty house. He strove to think of the best way of getting her to be his friend again, and ultimately his lover. After all, his father was no longer alive so could not be an obstacle, Edward was out of the way, Bunty was spending more and more time in nurses' accommodation at the Royal Hospital in Wolverhampton, and his mother would be oblivious to anything anyway because of her grief.

Besides, he controlled everything now. He had ultimate power, over the works, over his employees, over his father's entire estate, and even over his mother. He could do just as he pleased, and nobody would dare gainsay him.

He was God.

To demonstrate the fact, he would do away with his father's Bentley which he had inherited. He had never liked the car anyway; it was far too stodgy for a go-ahead chap in his late twenties. The trouble was, you weren't allowed to buy a new car under wartime restrictions. If only he could get hold of one of those American jobs – a Cord, or a Cadillac would be much preferable – much better suited to the image of himself as the wealthy, dashing young man about town he was keen to promote. It could only do his standing with women a power of good.

Then he had a brilliant idea. He thought he could see a way to gain Libby's friendship, her admiration, and a route into her underwear. He rang her office.

'Libby, it's Hugh. Would you like to step into my office a moment?'

She put down the receiver, got up, and made her way to Hugh's office with a notepad and pencil, wondering why on earth he wasn't using his own secretary. She tapped on his door, and waited for him to acknowledge her.

'Sit down, Libby,' he said pleasantly.

'What can I do for you, Hugh?'

'You can listen to me.' He smiled, an amiable smile, which had the opposite effect to that which he was trying to achieve and immediately put Libby on her guard. 'I wish to offer the hand of friendship, Libby. We live in the same house, you and me, and I see no sense in us living in enmity. Don't you think it would be much more comfortable, much more agreeable if we could forget our differences and get on with our lives as friends?'

'It sounds logical,' she replied, growing even more sceptical of his intentions.

'I understand how you have suffered, your grief over Edward. I know too how fond you were of my father. I would like to make some recompense.'

'So what are you proposing?' she asked, wary of him.

'First of all, I propose to give you my Jaguar car. You've done very well learning to drive so quickly. It's yours, to use as you please. It's small recompense.'

'That's very generous, Hugh . . . Forgive me if I sound cynical, though, but what do you want in return?'

He held his hands up in a gesture of candidness. 'Nothing. There are no strings attached. I merely want us to live in peace and accord.'

'If you believe your generosity will grant you access to my bedroom, you are very much mistaken.'

'That is being cynical, Libby,' he answered calmly. 'Anyway, you lock your bedroom door,' he added, and she wondered how he knew that if he hadn't tried to get in.

'It's very kind, and I thank you, Hugh, but I don't know if I should accept your offer. You see, Edward's MG is now mine. It falls to me as his widow, so I don't need another car. I can only drive one car at a time.'

'So you are spurning my offer?'

'I wish you wouldn't look at it like that. It's simply that I see no practical reason to own another car when the one I have is perfectly adequate. But I do appreciate your offer of a truce between us. As you say, it will make life much more agreeable at Buttonbridge Hall, instead of us trying to avoid each other.'

'So we have a truce at least?'

'You're my brother-in-law, so for goodness' sake let's have a truce,' she agreed. 'I welcome a truce.'

Hugh had broken the ice, and laid the foundations for his plan, but his idea of a truce was somewhat different to Libby's. To him it meant a resumption of former endeavours, with Libby remaining friendly and even becoming compliant. To Libby it meant a truce, pure and simple.

- - -

A week passed and Dorothy, having developed a cold, was sent packing to bed by Hugh with a bottle of aspirin. He had become overbearing and impatient with his mother, had come to regard her as a burden since his father had died. Bunty was in Wolverhampton. So he was alone with Libby who was sitting on one of the settees in the drawing-room reading the latest issue of *Picture Post* and its update on the war. Hugh sat himself beside her.

'Don't you get lonely nowadays, Libby?' he asked clumsily.

'How could I possibly be lonely with you at my side?' she answered.

The sarcasm went straight over Hugh's head and he said, 'Do you mean that, Libby? If I thought you meant it I'd kiss you.'

For a man who was capable of running a steelworks, which he did with ample aplomb, he could be decidedly dim, she thought.

'There's no need to get excited, I can assure you,' she replied. 'I was being sarcastic.' She resumed reading *Picture Post*, feigning a casualness she did not feel, for he was up to his old tricks again.

His arm came around her shoulder and gave her a hug. 'I'd like to think that I could be more than just a friend, you know, more than just your brother-in-law,' he said smoothly. 'I've always admired you tremendously, Libby, you know that. And with Edward not around anymore.'

Libby shifted smartly along the settee away from him. 'That's just about the most insensitive thing anybody could say to me, Hugh,' she protested, pushing back tears. 'Do you think that just because Edward has been posted missing—?'

'And is most certainly dead,' he interjected.

She sighed. 'Do you think that just because Edward has been posted missing,' she repeated patiently, 'I don't love him anymore? He's on my mind constantly. I never stop thinking about him, hoping that I'll receive some news that he's alive and well, and in some prisoner of war camp in Germany. Don't you know that that's all I live for now? Yet you seem incapable of comprehending it. You seem incapable of understanding anybody's feelings but your own.'

'You're right on that count, I understand my own well enough. I understand that I want you and that I've wanted you from the outset, yet you are always so standoffish . . . and it hurts. Are you such a cold fish?'

'Not with the right person.'

'You mean somebody like Pilot Officer Farnell?'

'No, I don't mean somebody like Pilot Officer Farnell,' she answered indignantly.

'Have you heard from him since he left?'

'No, I haven't. Why should I?'

'You and he seemed very fond. So he had his fun and scarpered, eh, disappearing into the land of Babylon?'

'I really don't know what you mean, Hugh, but it sounds offensive. I thought we had a truce. I thought we agreed not to rub each other up the wrong way.'

'That's true, and I'm sorry. I just get so frustrated with you so near and yet so far away.'

'There's nothing I can do to help you there.'

'But there is, Libby, don't you see? Just give yourself up to me. I'll care for you, I'll look after you. I'll make you the happiest woman in the world. You can have whatever you want. Your wish is my command. I'm a wealthy man since my father died. I control his entire estate. You could have access to it all, through me. All you have to do is sleep with me.'

'Is that all?'

'Well, you know what people do when they sleep together?'

'I have a vague notion,' she replied, trying to hide her disdain.

'I hope it might help sway you . . . This too . . .'

He leaned over and kissed her on the lips, and his hand went straight to her breast, slightly plumper now.

'Hugh!' she protested, pulling away.

'Oh, come on, Libby,' he said impatiently. 'Grow up.'

In that instant, he pushed her down so that she was lying on the settee. He spread himself on top of her, still trying to kiss her, his free hand clawing at her skirt. She turned her face from him, protesting vehemently, trying to push his hand away from her thighs, which he was now groping having pulled her skirt up. But he was bigger and stronger than she was. He forced his knees between her legs, hurting her as she resisted, and she yelled in complaint. His hand went around a cheek of her bottom and she could feel the elastic of her knickers tighten as he yanked on them.

'*Hugh!*' she shrieked again. She began thumping his back with clenched fists, but it made no difference. He was tugging her knickers relentlessly down her legs, and she felt them rip under the strain as she fought. Pressing his whole weight upon her, pinning her down, he unfastened his fly and she felt him unleash himself. Unless she could do something drastic in the next few seconds . . . She was about to be raped. The thought made her feel nauseous and she screamed. She had idly wondered occasionally how she would feel if she were to be raped, not thinking for a minute that it would ever happen. Yet here she was now, held fast and hard beneath a strong maniac intent on having his way.

'You must understand, Libby,' he rasped through clenched teeth as he put all his strength into tearing away her knickers, 'that I am the master in this house, and so long as you live under this roof you will do as I want you to. The sooner you accept this, the happier you will be.'

The last resisting threads of torn cotton and elastic gave way, and he pulled her knickers away from her and tossed them aside. Libby made one last gasping attempt to free herself, to shove him away. She managed to get one arm free, and she brought her hand up to his face, and tore down it, feeling the resistance of his temple and the flesh of his cheek as she dug her fingernails in deep.

He yelled with pain, loosed her, but slapped her hard across the face in retaliation.

'You minx!' he roared. 'You'll not get away with that.'

'*Hugh!*' a voice called conveying absolute disapproval. 'I have never witnessed such scandalous behaviour in all my life.' It was Dorothy. She was standing watching in outraged astonishment, hands on hips. Libby had no idea how long she had been there, but her intervention at any rate was timely. 'You should be utterly ashamed of yourself . . .' She approached Libby, who was struggling to regain her composure, feeling suddenly embarrassed and undressed minus her one significant item of underwear. 'Libby, my dear . . . Are you all right?'

Libby, flushed from her struggle, ran her fingers through her hair which was all over her face in an unruly mop. She picked up her torn knickers from the floor and threw them scornfully at Hugh as a souvenir. Shamefacedly, he restored his drooping member to its rightful place.

'Thank you, Dorothy,' she gasped breathlessly. 'I hope you could tell I wasn't a willing party to all that.'

'That much was obvious,' Dorothy replied with new-found contempt for Hugh in her icy look and her voice.

'I think I'm all right, Dorothy, but thanks only to you. You couldn't have cut it any finer, though.'

'My dear, I can't think what has come over him.'

'Well one thing's for certain,' Libby said, smoothing the creases out of her skirt self-consciously. 'I can't stay in this house a moment longer.'

'You're leaving?'

'I must. Tonight. Would you stay a moment longer with *him* on the loose?'

'I confess, in your position I would not, after witnessing what I have just witnessed. But it's not my wish that you leave, Libby.'

'Until now it's been my wish to stay, Dorothy. But I can't any longer. So I shall pack my things and go. I've never been so humiliated in all my life.' She glared at Hugh. 'This isn't the first time he's tried this, Dorothy, and I really have no intention of putting up with it any longer.'

'I really had no idea, Libby.'

Just then, Jenkins appeared, alerted by Libby's screams and curious to know what the fuss was about in case she could be of help. Dorothy saw her and shepherded her quickly away.

'There's no need for you to be concerned, Jenkins,' Dorothy said calmly. 'Libby just had a little fright, but it's all over now.'

'I thought somebody was being murdered,' Jenkins re-marked, sceptical of the inadequate explanation as she looked at Hugh and his scratched face with suspicion.

'Oh, somebody might be very soon, if he's not careful.'

Libby rushed upstairs to her room, packed as many of her things as she could cram into a suitcase, and left in the MG.

- - -

When Dorothy had gone to bed, and Hugh had evidently re-tired to his room, Margaret Jenkins stole upstairs and tapped gently on his door. He opened it.

'Come in, Margaret,' he whispered, still in a state of agita-tion.

'What was all that fuss about earlier with young Mrs Bur-gayne?'

Hugh sighed heavily, sat on his bed and ran his fingers through his hair. 'We had an argument . . . She's a very silly, self-willed young woman, and I hate her.'

'What was the argument about?'

'Oh, nothing to concern you.'

'But you were holding a pair of torn knickers, Hugh. Hers, I suppose?'

'Oh, yes, they were hers all right. She took them off in front of me. She wanted to seduce me, the trollop. Tried to force herself on to me. When I shoved her away, she began scream-ing, as if I were trying to rape her.'

'But you weren't?' she asked dubiously.

'Of course I wasn't. Why would I want her anyway when I've got you?'

'So why did she scratch your face?'

'Anger? Vindictiveness? Because I wouldn't go along with her antics, I suppose.'

Margaret sighed and smiled with relief, content for now to believe his every word. 'Well, she's gone. She drove off in Mr Edward's sports car.'

'I couldn't be more pleased. Gone for good, I hope . . . Come here, my sweetheart.'

Compliantly, she joined him on the bed, but she was only half-convinced of his version of the story.

'Has everybody gone to bed now?' he enquired.

'Yes. I told the others to go up as well. I said there were a few jobs I still had to do.'

'You're a shrewd girl, Margaret. So let's get undressed, and make the most of it. I want you . . . badly . . .'

- - -

| 24 |

Bunty returned home next day to enjoy some free time away from the hospital. Exams were approaching and she needed somewhere quiet to study, and Buttonbridge Hall was the ideal place. Besides, she would have some mail to catch up on. There were sure to be letters from Harry Wilding, and she looked forward to reading them and answering them; a bit of sentimentality was a welcome change from the grimness and sadness of the hospital wards.

Just before seven o' clock she pulled up in front of the house, and it struck her how quickly the nights were drawing in. She was glad to be home before dark, for driving in the blackout was hazardous and wearing. The evening was cool and dark clouds loitered above the treetops in the western sky as she made her way across the tarmacadamed drive to the front door.

Inside, she looked for the unclaimed mail, on the vast and ancient chest of drawers on which it normally stood, but there was none.

Odd.

'I'm home,' she called.

The house felt strange, cold, lacking in atmosphere, and she put it down to the difference the death of her father had made.

Jenkins appeared. Her ready smile and her usual cheerfulness had disappeared.

'Hello, Margaret. Where is everybody?'

'Oh, Mr Hugh's in the cellar, miss Bunty, working in his darkroom, and Mrs Burgayne is in the drawing-room.'

'Thank you, Margaret.' She pointed to the old chest of drawers. 'Is there no post for me?'

'Er . . . Mr Hugh still insists he takes all the post, miss Bunty.'

'Oh, really? Then I'll see what post he has of mine when I've said hello to my mother, and chastise him for being so presumptuous.'

Bunty took off her jacket and handed it to Jenkins, then headed for the drawing-room. She greeted Dorothy with a kiss and sat on the settee beside her, eased off her sensible shoes and crossed her legs.

'How have you been, Mother?'

'Me? *I've* been quite all right considering,' Dorothy replied ominously, and looked up from the knitting of socks that was occupying her for the war effort.

'You make it sound as if nobody else is.'

'There *has* been a problem, Bunty.' She frowned. '*Quite* a problem, in fact.'

'Concerning who?'

'Concerning Libby.'

'Libby? Where is Libby?'

'Unfortunately, she's left.'

'Left? You mean she's gone? Left Buttonbridge Hall?'

'That's exactly what I mean.'

'Gone to her mother and father, do you think?'

'I presume so.'

'How come, Mother? What's happened?'

'I'm afraid her presence had become too much for Hugh.'

'In what way? I'm not entirely sure what you mean.'

'In the worst possible way that a man can be affected by a thoroughly pretty girl.'

'Oh . . .' Bunty nodded her understanding. 'I always knew he fancied her. So you've sent her away? Mother, I can't believe you've sent her away because of that.'

'I haven't sent her away.' Dorothy resumed knitting. 'I didn't want her to go. She left of her own free will, and frankly, I would've done the same in her position. Hugh has made life here impossible for her. He tried to rape her, you know.'

'He *what?*'

'Just as I say, dear – he tried to rape her. In this very room. On this very sofa. I had gone to bed early with a cold, but shortly afterwards I heard these frightful screams. I intervened at what appeared to be a critical moment—'

'Oh, spare me the details, Mother.'

'Well, Hugh hasn't forgiven me for the interruption, and I haven't forgiven him either, for being such a callous bounder. So we co-exist in a world of silent brooding.'

'The blithering idiot.'

'His father would have gone mad.'

'Father would've *killed* him.'

Dorothy sighed profoundly and put down her knitting. 'Anyway, I'm so happy to see you, Bunty. Now I'll have somebody to talk to.'

'But poor Libby,' Bunty sighed, appalled. 'I must go and see her. She'll have gone back to her parents for certain. Has she been in touch with you since, Mother?'

'No, she hasn't been in touch.'

'What a complete and utter cretin Hugh is. He's grabbed hold of my post as well, so Jenkins tells me. Where does he keep it? Do you know?'

'In his room, I imagine. He decided to have the post so his father wouldn't have the worry of dealing with business communications while he was ill.'

'But all business stuff goes to the works,' Bunty argued logically. She shrugged. 'He certainly gets some strange notions. I take it there's no news of Edward?'

'None, dear, sadly.'

Bunty watched tears well up in her mother's eyes at mention of Edward's name, and decided she should change the subject.

'How are the convalescents?'

'Thriving, as far as I am aware. We've taken in three new chaps in the past week.'

'Maybe I should go and inspect them. There might be a likely candidate among them,' she said flippantly.

'Oh, don't joke about such things, Bunty. Hugh insists that Libby's been having an affair with one RAF chap.'

Bunty gasped with indignation. 'Whatever Hugh might think, Mother, I can assure you that Libby most certainly has not. I know her, and she's not that sort of girl. She idolised Edward.'

'That's what I always like to think, but Hugh was adamant.'

'Well he's bloody-well wrong,' she protested vehemently. 'He's way off the mark. So when did he tell you this pack of lies? Before or after his skirmish with Libby?'

'After . . . during a fit of remorse. No doubt trying to justify his beastly attack on her.'

'The poor girl. I'm going to give him a piece of my mind.'

'Please, say nothing, Bunty. All's quiet now. Let sleeping dogs lie.'

'Jenkins says he's in the cellar. Buggering about in his darkroom, I expect. I'm going to see him.'

'Don't say anything, Bunty.'

'I'm making no such promise, Mother.'

So Bunty grabbed a flash lamp and made her way to the cellar, prepared for a fight. The door to the area he used as his darkroom was shut, and when she tried it she found it was locked.

'Hugh?' she called. 'It's Bunty. Can I come in?'

'Wait,' he called back tersely. 'I'm in the middle of something.'

'Well hurry, it's damned chilly down here.' She wrapped her arms around herself in an effort to ward off the cold, and waited.

Eventually she heard him unlock the door, and open it. The only light was from his orange safety lights by which he did his photographic printing. She caught a whiff of hypo.

'What d'you want?' He was distinctly abrupt.

'Oh good evening, Hugh, how lovely to see you,' she said with exaggerated sarcasm. 'Gosh, I haven't seen you for ages and all you can say is "What d'you want?". Well, first of all I want my mail. What right have you to stash it away?'

'You can have your mail when I go upstairs.'

'What right have you to stash away anybody's mail, come to that?' she queried, stressing the point.

'Is there anything else?' he asked, avoiding giving an answer.

'Yes, as a matter of fact there is. I just heard about your disgraceful conduct with Libby. You really ought to be ashamed of yourself, Hugh. Have you no sense? Have you no regard for the way the poor girl feels about Edward, grieving over him as she is? A decent, innocent girl like that.'

'Innocent?' he muttered scornfully. 'She's hardly innocent.'

'Oh, I know what you think,' Bunty hissed with equal disdain. 'You're stupid enough to think she was having an affair with Pilot Officer Farnell.'

'As a matter of fact, I do. I have some photographs of the two of them together that prove it.'

'Do you now? Do show me.'

He switched on the main light, went to the filing cabinet, and opened the top draw guardedly, his back turned towards her in an effort to block her view. This made her all the more curious, so while he flipped through various files she tried to peer around him for a glimpse of the contents of the filing cabinet. After some seconds he handed her two prints, which certainly depicted Libby and Keith Farnell together. She was looking into his eyes and laughing, and her arm was on his in a gesture of familiarity.

'You bloody fool,' Bunty scoffed. 'These don't prove anything. Libby is just a friendly sort of girl. She always thinks the best of everybody, and she's sharing a joke with Keith. She always touches people she gets on with. She's the sort of person who does it without thinking. It's her nature. It means nothing.'

'Think what you like,' he said pompously. 'I know what I saw.'

'Whatever you saw – or think you saw – it gives you no right to try and *rape* her. Who on earth do you think you are? God? – Sitting in judgement? The poor, poor girl. I presume that because she can't stand the sight of you anymore she's given up her job, too?'

'There was a letter of resignation from her at the works, yes.'

'So now she has no means of supporting herself. That's *awfully* good, Hugh. That really is *terribly* clever, and so considerate of you. Do you realise what a true and abiding scoundrel you are?'

- - -

Gladys and Joe Shakespeare were entirely happy to receive Libby back into their home, and she occupied her old bedroom looking out onto Hill Street.

'When the bab comes, our Libby, we'll clear out the box-room so's we can put a cot in there, eh?' Gladys was happy to suggest one day. 'It'll be lovely having a bab in the house. It'll keep us young.'

Libby smiled indulgently, pleased that they were pleased. Their attitude made life so much more bearable, and she soon settled into the unpretentious roll of their dependent young daughter once again, as if it had never been any different, as if it had never been interrupted by the brief months living at Buttonbridge Hall as the young bride of Edward Burgayne.

She had been back in Hill Street no more than a week when a letter arrived from Irene Attwood, one of her old school friends. When last they had seen each other, at the dance held at the Grammar School, they had all expressed a wish to hold a reunion four years later. Irene had tracked down most of their friends and had hired a room at the Dudley Arms Hotel for Saturday 8th November at 7.30 p.m. Was Libby engaged or even married yet? It would be lovely to see her and catch up on each other's lives since leaving school. And would she RSVP as soon as possible?

So Libby replied. Yes, she would love to see the others, to find out how they were getting on in this awful war.

On the same day that the letter arrived, so did Bunty. The two girls greeted each other tearfully, with sisterly hugs, and

Libby suggested Bunty should sit and have a cup of tea with Gladys while she changed and made herself presentable, for they would go out. So Libby went upstairs to her room, changed and made herself more presentable to the outside world.

'I'm ready,' she announced as she opened the stairs door. 'See you later, mom.'

The air had a definite autumnal nip as she and Bunty walked down the entry to the Riley and clambered into it.

'So where are we going?' Bunty enquired.

'Anywhere,' Libby replied. 'Just drive off and stop somewhere quiet. I didn't want to talk in front of my mom and dad.'

'I imagine they don't know everything, then?' Bunty said, starting the engine. 'I heard from my mother about your awful spat with Hugh. What a complete arsehole he is. I really gave him a piece of my mind. I can only apologise for his outlandish behaviour.' She put the car into gear and drove off.

'It's over and done with, Bunty, and I never want to see him again. But you're right – my mom and dad know nothing of what happened. It would only upset them . . . Then there's something you don't know, Bunty . . . I'm having Edward's baby.'

Bunty stopped the car at once, in the middle of Hill Street where it levelled out at the top.

'That's absolutely the best news I've heard in years. Brilliant! You're delighted, of course?'

'Of course.' She grinned, pleased at Bunty's reaction.

A Post Office van, coming over the brow of the hill behind them honked his horn in protest at the position of the Riley occupying the road, and the driver glared as he drove past.

Bunty bobbed her tongue out to him. 'I really ought to move. I'll just pull over here . . . Crikey, that's a hell of view from here.'

'Hardly pretty, though. That's West Bromwich and Tipton and Smethwick.'

'So when is the baby due?'

'Sometime towards the end of April, I imagine.'

'Gosh! Let's see . . . You must've conceived on your honey-moon.'

'Of course. When else?' She laughed self-consciously. 'In Ludlow. Or maybe even at Buttonbridge Hall when we returned – the night before Edward rejoined his squadron. I like to think it was that night . . . We hardly slept . . .'

'I should hope you didn't,' Bunty remarked. 'Of course, there's no news of poor Edward. Have you given up hope?'

Libby sighed. 'I try to be optimistic, Bunty,' she replied, composed. 'But if he were still alive, somebody somewhere would have found him by now, and he'd either be held in a prisoner of war camp or sent back to his squadron, depending on who found him. But because there's no word either way, I'm inclined to think he's lying at the bottom of the sea, probably still in his shattered Hurricane.'

'Crikey, Libby, you paint a horrifying picture. But we have much in common, you and me. I lost Adrian and was convinced my world had ended. Now you've lost Edward, and no doubt you think your world has ended too. But it hasn't, believe me. You'll get over the heartache. It'll take time, but you *will* get over it, I promise.'

'At least I've got his baby to look forward to, Bunty,' she sighed. 'At least I shall have something of Edward to remind me of him. He'd be so proud . . .'

'So he would,' Bunty concurred softly. 'So am I. Bloody hell, I'm going to be an aunty, for Christ's sake. I want to be the child's godmother, too. Will you let me?'

Libby laughed. 'Course. I would've asked you anyway . . . So what's the latest on Harry Wilding?'

'He's got a desk job with the Royal Army Ordinance Corps. No more front-line fighting. You have to agree it's much safer.'

'Oh, Bunty, that's good to hear. But I don't mean his army career. I mean the romance.'

'Oh . . .' Bunty beamed. 'Well, the fool's asked me to marry him . . . and I think I will, actually . . .'

'Oh, Bunty, that's brilliant.' Libby took her friend's hand and squeezed it. 'I'm so pleased for you. So when is it to be?'

'Not decided yet. We can wait till this damned war's over and then do it, or do it when he's next on leave.' She shrugged. 'What would you do?'

'Are you in love with him?'

'Yes, I'm in love with him. Madly.'

'Then why wait?'

'Mmm . . . There is a certain logic to that, Libby.'

- - -

When she attended the school reunion at the Dudley Arms Hotel, Libby was surprised at how many of her old school friends smoked. Smoke hung in a dense blue cloud in the assembly room, and it made her eyes water. Her clothes and hair would reek of it.

But she overlooked it for now, delighted to see her old friends again. In the four years that had passed, several had married, most to servicemen who were away fighting in the war. Libby, along with Irene Attwood and Doreen Gilbert, her closest school pals, drifted off into their own private clique where they supped as they brought each other up to date with their lives. Libby told her story to sincere expressions of sympathy at the recent loss of her husband, rendered all the more poignant since she admitted she was already pregnant with his child.

'So what shall you do?' Doreen asked.

'Well, I'll try and find another job till I get too big and can't work anymore,' Libby answered. 'I can't expect my dad to keep me, and the baby will be another burden for him when it arrives. The trouble is, firms don't want to employ somebody who's going to have to leave soon to have a child.'

'What about when it's born? Will you still work?'

'I won't be able to,' Libby said. 'I could hardly expect my mother to look after my child while I went out to work. Anyway, I shall want to look after the baby myself.'

'I think his family ought to help you out,' Irene remarked, trying to be helpful. 'I mean to say, it's not as if they're short of money if they own that big steelworks down Peartree Lane. And it will be their grandchild.'

'If Edward's father were still alive they would, Irene,' Libby said. 'But I don't get on with the new head of the family, Edward's older brother. He's the reason I gave up my job there and moved out of their home.'

'You fell out with him entirely?'

'You could put it that way. So I don't expect to get a penny, because of him. But neither would I want anything off *him*.'

'So what happened to that chap Ron who you used to go out with?' Doreen enquired. 'He was a nice chap. A steady sort. Wouldn't you fancy seeing him again?'

Libby shrugged and smiled. 'Once I'd met Edward, I wasn't interested in Ron anymore,' she replied. 'Anyway, I presume he's in the army or air force now, like most other chaps, if the Germans haven't got him yet.'

'He's in the army,' Irene declared.

'How d'you know that?' Libby asked.

'One of the girls I work with lives near him, and she knows him. We were talking about you and it cropped up how you used to go out with him. That's how it came to light.'

'Whether or not,' Libby remarked. 'Why talk about him? Let's talk about you two. Tell me what you've been up to.'

- - -

| 25 |

Weeks and months passed, and the gruesome war spread and grew ever more gruesome. Hong Kong fell to the Japanese and the Allies failed to stem their relentless advance through Malaya. In February of 1942 the Japanese had taken Singapore. The Germans were getting the better of the British 8th Army in the Western Desert too. At the end of March the RAF began a terror bombing campaign, dropping thousands of incendiary bombs on German cities. The Nazis responded in April by bombing those grand British cities that were listed in their Baedeker guidebook, with the result that Exeter, Bath, Norwich and York were all hit. But the Germans were meeting fiercer resistance than they bargained for from the Red Army in Russia, which was making heavy demands on manpower and machinery. It seemed the Germans might have bitten off more than they could chew.

Libby was slowly coming to terms with the loss of Edward. Some days were better than others. Some days she tended to dwell on thoughts of him for longer than she should, and made herself miserable in the process, for thinking of him was painful. The lack of any news told her he had never been found, otherwise she would have heard; Bunty would be quick enough to inform her of any letter or telegram that arrived.

On 30th April, Libby was full of reflections, and feeling particularly downcast. Her child was due but still she had no pains, no signs that the birth was imminent. She could feel it kicking healthily inside her, so she was not worried about going over her time a little. All the same, she wished she could have it over and done with so she could sleep more comfortably and move around more easily. In the afternoon, she decided to take a walk, despite her big belly, and told her mother she reckoned she would be about an hour. She wanted to be alone, to walk in the soft April rains under the canopy of trees that was Oakham Road, and remember Edward. With normal walking you could walk as far as the golf links in less than fifteen minutes. At Libby's slower pace, twenty.

As she walked, her mind became full of him, and the precious moments they had shared. Memories flooded back ceaselessly. She recalled the very first time she met him when she had been invited to Buttonbridge Hall to make up a four at tennis, and Bunty was doing her best to entice Adrian into a love affair. Little did Libby think then that she would eventually become Edward's wife, much less his widow. It was the widowhood that was so brutal a circumstance, a circumstance that really tore at her emotions. She had enjoyed so little time as his wife, had so little time to enjoy marriage before he was so cruelly snatched away. No longer could she talk to him, no longer could she touch him, take his hand, feel his sweet lips on hers, be caressed by his warmth . . . It also hurt that her child would never know its father.

She recalled the exhilaration of that flight with him in his beloved Gypsy Moth and how privileged she had been to have shared the experienced with him; because of it she could appreciate his love of flying. It was something she would never forget. Then there was the garden party and that disturbing photographic session with that frightful idiot Hugh when, she now unmistakeably realised, he had deliberately tried to take advantage, and had the brassbound audacity to feel her leg. She remembered the first evenings out in foursomes with Bunty and Adrian, dancing so close to Edward at the Stewponey, talking with him, laughing, eating fish and chips from Wall Heath late at night; that first cold Boxing Day when she was invited to see the Enville Hunt. She had been so lucky to have done all that, an ordinary working girl. She recalled Edward's precious serious kiss just before he returned to Cambridge, when Ron so curtly interrupted them by tapping on the window of the car. Was that an omen for the future which she had not recognised? She asked herself why they had held back their love, she and Edward. Why didn't they make the most of what time they had while they had the chance, by committing to each other before he finished his university studies? They could have met during those times; she could have travelled to Cambridge for weekends, or they could have met halfway. What languid, loving nights they would have had.

But, instead, they waited. Then, there was that first night they made love in the open air at Enville Common, hidden amongst the ferns. She'd been on top of the world. Never had she felt so happy, so close to anybody. She recalled how she was as nervous as he was, but how she'd tried not to show it, and actually led that fateful expedition into virgin territory. Then the long, long wait before they could be together again, and the weird but vigorously romantic time in Ireland. She recalled the joy and pride she felt when Edward escaped and announced that they should be married, and the panic to get everything organised in a week. Now he was gone, and the promise of happiness was gone with him.

How futile it had all been, but for the fact that she was about to have his child. The child might restrict her, but she would not mind; she loved the child already, and spending nearly all her time with it would be a joy. She had no thoughts, no notions of meeting another man when the passage of time had finally healed her broken heart. She could love no other man like she loved Edward. Her child would be her saviour.

The rain came heavier, drumming on the burgeoning spring foliage of the trees around her, but she walked on defiantly. If only she'd thought to bring a brolly. She turned up her collar and nestled deeper inside her coat. The rain and the wind could not hurt her. She would weather it, like she'd weathered the heartache. The relentless rain, however, began to seep into her coat; her hair, hatless, was becoming limp and bedraggled and the drops trickled down her face like an overabundance of tears. What would Edward think of her if he could see her now, with her nine-month belly and soaked to her very skin, looking decidedly unglamorous? She hardly looked like the pristine and personal private secretary she had once been at the height of her efficiency. But she would weather it. She would re-emerge from this all the wiser, all the more worldly, and all the more compassionately.

And then she felt it; the first pang that told her that her baby was on its way.

- - -

Elizabeth Bunty Burgayne was born 1st May 1942, a healthy baby weighing seven pounds five ounces, with blue eyes like her father and dark hair like her mother. As the days and weeks passed it became clearer that little Elizabeth was destined to inherit her mother's looks and daintiness.

Motherhood came naturally to Libby. She idolised her child and watched her bloom into a healthy, contented baby. Elizabeth helped take her mind off Edward, as she knew she would, although she would have given anything to see Edward with his child; he would have been so appreciative, so admiring, so proud. Gladys and Joe both doted on the baby and it seemed to Libby that all she had to do was feed the fragile and precious bundle.

Libby's figure soon returned to its former slenderness and her belly, she was pleased to see, was flat and free of stretch marks. What excess weight she had put on during her pregnancy she soon lost, although it was challenging to get fat on the reduced diet enforced by food rationing.

Then, one day in the heat of August, Libby and Gladys were taking a break from the day's chores, enjoying a cup of tea. Libby took advantage of the break to feed Elizabeth and the baby was at her breast, when they heard a knock on the door of the veranda. Gladys, corsets creaking and with a sigh at the interruption, got up to answer it. 'Oh, my God!' she exclaimed. 'Look who it is.'

Libby, alerted by her mother's surprised utterance, stood up to get a look, her heart suddenly pounding. Could it be Edward?

'Jesus Christ!' she said to herself.

Wearing his uniform, standing there, waiting to be let in, was Ron Downing,

Libby's immediate hopes just as quickly collapsed, but Gladys greeted him with a broad smile as if he was a long-lost son. 'Come in, my lad. How nice to see you. You home on leave?'

'Yes, I got a few days leave, Mrs Shakespeare,' Ron replied, a little unsure of himself and what welcome, if any, he might receive. 'I thought I'd come and say hello to you and Libby. I heard she's had a bit of bad luck.'

'It's nice of you to think of her,' Gladys said. 'She's in the house feeding the baby. Come and say hello. She'll be that surprised to see you.'

Ron was a little embarrassed to witness Libby with a child at her breast, but she knew better than to rob the baby of her feed and induce squawks and tears of protestation. So she carried on unruffled. He tried not to look, but she smiled her greeting at him from her chair with fewer inhibitions. Childbirth had taught her that where babies were concerned, bashfulness and self-consciousness were entirely out of place.

'You won't mind if I don't get up, Ron.'

'Don't worry, chick, I can see you've got your hands full.' He smiled amiably. 'How are you anyway?'

'Well, thank you.' She looked him up and down appraisingly. 'You too. You look very smart in your uniform.'

'Think so?'

'I do. Don't you think so, Mom?'

'He looks very smart,' Gladys agreed.

Ron smiled appreciatively. 'So who's this little person?'

'This is Elizabeth,' Libby informed him. 'And isn't she beautiful?' She eased the child away from her nipple and turned her towards Ron, so he could see her. 'Don't you think so?'

'She's gorgeous,' he agreed. Little Elizabeth, robbed of her dinner, opened her eyes momentarily in protest and he saw how vividly blue and clear they were. He also saw how exceptionally smooth and appealing Libby's pale, exposed breast was, but Libby did not appear to mind. She returned to feeding the child who continued suckling keenly.

'I heard you'd got married, Libby,' he said, trying to tread carefully. 'I bumped into somebody who knows Irene who you were at school with. She said your husband was posted missing.'

'Yes,' Libby replied economically.

'I'm ever so sorry. It must have been horrible for you, especially as you was having a baby as well.'

'Well, you can imagine, can't you?'

'And there's nothing more been heard of him?'

Libby shook her head and glanced at the baby. 'And you, Ron?' she said, turning the emphasis away from herself. 'Are you courting, or engaged, or anything?'

'Me? No.' He wanted to say that there could never be anybody but Libby Shakespeare for him, but he thought better than to let it be known there and then, even though she was the only reason he was there.

'I'm surprised,' she commented. 'A nice-looking chap like you. I'd have thought the girls would've been falling over themselves. Are you sure there's nobody?'

'Well, nobody serious . . . It seems as if all those couples who are serious get wed quick. This war has led to more and more folk getting married earlier – rush jobs.'

Libby raised her eyebrows. 'Me included, I suppose. But Edward and me would've got married anyway, war or no war. So how long are you on leave?'

'Three days. Not long. But while I'm on leave, Libby.' He paused. 'If you fancy going out one night . . .'

'Oh, that would be nice, our Libby,' Gladys intervened, hardly masking her enthusiasm. 'Why don't you? Once the baby's been fed and put to bed, I can look after her.'

Ron looked at Libby imploringly, awaiting her response.

'I think my mother's keen to get me paired off with somebody again,' Libby joked.

'Oh, don't be daft, our Libby. But it wouldn't hurt to go out with Ron. You used to go out with him often enough . . .'

'For old times' sake, eh, Libby?' Ron said brightly. 'You can tell me all about your husband. I'd like to hear.'

Libby smiled. The baby had finished feeding, and while Ron's eyes were averted momentarily, she discreetly wiped her breast and covered herself up, then put the baby to her shoulder to coax up any wind.

'Okay, if you like,' she agreed. 'But I can't promise I'll be the best company you've ever had.'

'It'll be nice just to catch up on each other's lives after so long,' Ron said. 'We'll have plenty to tell each other, I reckon.'

Ron stayed about half an hour over a cup of tea. Secretly he wondered how he would feel if the little child before him had been his. Under different circumstances she might have been. She really was a lovely little thing.

'Can I hold the baby a minute?' he asked.

'Are you sure?' Libby looked at him doubtfully.

'Yes,' he reassured her. 'I'd like to.'

Libby passed Elizabeth to him carefully. He held her tentatively at first, then with greater confidence when she did not struggle to escape his arms like some vigorous young puppy. He rocked the baby gently for a minute or two, looking down at her with tenderness.

'She's like you, Libby,' he said, handing her back.

'Everybody says so, but I can see her daddy in her more and more.'

- - -

Ron called for Libby the following evening. It was warm and sultry, as August generally is in England, and the sun was low in the sky casting an orange tinge over the landscape. They walked together up Oakham Road, where Libby had walked alone the day before Elizabeth was born.

'I was really sorry to hear about your husband,' he said sincerely. 'I think it's a terrible thing for somebody your age to be a widow. So many good lads have perished fighting in this war, and there's so many girls like you . . . in the same boat, I mean.'

'Oh, I know,' she replied. 'I know I'm not the only one. But it really doesn't help much.'

'No, I don't suppose it does.'

'So what about you, Ron? What have you been up to? It's been years since we last saw each other.'

'It has,' he agreed. 'I joined up soon after the outbreak of war. I was sent to France and got out okay in the mad scramble of Dunkirk. I've just got back from the Western Desert. Rommel's been giving us a bit of a bashing out there, but now Montgomery's taken over you'll see a change.'

'How are your folks?'

'Mom and Dad are okay.'

'Give them my best wishes.'

'Course I will. They send theirs, by the way.'

They walked on in silence for what seemed like an age. Conversation did not seem to flow naturally like it used to, and Libby put it down to mutual nervousness. After all, she had rejected him in favour of Edward; it must be playing on his mind, she thought. It was certainly playing on hers.

'I've never been interested in anybody else but you, you know, Libby,' he suddenly remarked, breaking the silence.

'There's plenty other fish in the sea, though, Ron.'

'Oh, you say that, but having lost the love of your life, does it feel that way to you?'

'No,' she admitted, and smiled sadly. 'I take your point.'

'Well there you are then ... Anyway, who knows ... When this war's over, you and me could do worse than get back together again.'

She laughed at that, not dismissively but self-consciously. 'You're a glutton for punishment. I'd have thought you'd have had enough of me after the merry dance I led you before.'

'Never. If I thought there was a chance of it, I'd wait for you.'

'You mean you'd be prepared to take on another man's child as well? Your old rival's child?'

'Course. Little Elizabeth would be all part of the bargain, eh?'

'Well, I can make no promises, Ron,' she said gently. 'You have to understand that Edward was the whole world to me. It's going to take me a long time to get over him. Elizabeth helps, of course – I love her to bits – but as yet I can't see that far into the future.'

'I understand, chick,' he said kindly. 'But there'll come a time when this war's over, and folk will start to lead normal lives again. You'll need a man to look after you, to help you bring up your baby. You can't depend on your father to keep you. You'll need a bit of security in your life, and so will Elizabeth. I'm prepared to provide it if I'm spared this war. I'd just like you to bear it in mind.'

'You're a good and kind soul, Ron,' she answered, touched by his compassion, but which made so much sense. She took his arm as they walked. 'You're decent and reliable, the sort of man many a girl would give her all for, and I appreciate your offer. But it's too much of a sacrifice for you to make. It's too soon for me yet in any case. I'd be no good for you. I'm still raw from losing Edward. Ask me in another two years if this damned war is still on then – if you still feel the same.'

- - -

| 26 |

Two years passed and the war ground on. During that time Bunty married her Harry Wilding, but while he remained in the army she remained nominally at Buttonbridge Hall, although she spent most of her time at the Royal Hospital in Wolverhampton. She found it impossible to live in the same house as Hugh. He had contrived to commandeer his father's entire estate, and allowed his mother a pittance only for clothing and the little luxuries of life when, throughout her married life, she had been used to having the best of everything, and in abundance. To satisfy the law he made her a director of Blowers Green Steelworks, but unpaid, and made all decisions himself; he controlled the company entirely. Dorothy was allowed no independence, and became almost a prisoner in what used to be her husband's house. Since Charles's death Hugh held the deeds and effectively owned the property. He suffered the convalescents only because he didn't relish a confrontation with the Red Cross, and any resulting adverse publicity, for it would not do his image any favours if he cast them out or made life awkward for them.

Nor had Bunty seen any of her father's inheritance that she felt sure was due to her. Consequently she had to live on nurses' pay. No doubt there was recourse through the courts to what was rightfully hers, but the potential costs of litigation precluded her from doing anything. So she decided to wait until the war was over and she had settled down to a normal life with Harry, before she embarked on something which was undesirable anyway, and would tear apart what remained of the Burgayne family.

Elizabeth had her second birthday, and Libby her twenty-fifth, and Gladys made a cake with which to celebrate, despite the constraints of sugar rationing. Bunty, by this time a fully-fledged nurse, was invited to the little party, and they all made a pleasant evening of it. Aunty Bunty helped put Elizabeth to bed and read her a story; she had been allowed to stay up later than usual since it was her birthday. Gladys and Joe retired to bed at half-past ten, with the excuse that Joe must be fresh for work next morning, but diplomatically leaving Bunty and Libby to talk, which they did over a bottle of beer.

Bunty brought Libby up to date with Hugh's latest tyrannies.

'I'm certain there's something going on between Hugh and that maid Jenkins. You remember Jenkins?'

'Course I do. She was always courteous to me.'

'Well, you were always courteous to her, Libby.'

'So what makes you think there's something going on?'

'Their body language when they're in the same room together – the looks and expressions that pass between them.

I've got no concrete proof of it, of course, and mother's said nothing, but I'm suspicious.'

'Poor Jenkins if she's got herself mixed up with him.'

'I've a good mind to ask her outright next time I visit mother.'

'Well do keep me informed,' Libby requested. 'Meanwhile, what news of Harry's pen-pushing in the Royal Army Ordinance Corps in France.

'It will be grand to have him on leave again, but I don't expect to see him now before the end of the war,' Bunty said resignedly. 'How about Ron? What's happening with him?'

'Oh, we still write,' Libby replied. 'He's asked me to marry him and, I must say, the older I get, the more it appeals. After all, I can't allow myself and Elizabeth to be a burden on my mom and dad forever.'

'Is that the only thing that would induce you into marriage again? Being a burden on your mother and father?'

'It's a valid consideration.'

'So you might marry Ron, but not because you are in love with him?' Bunty queried.

'He knows how I feel, Bunty,' Libby answered defensively.

'But you're still a young woman, Libby, and in your prime. If you're anything like me you still have a healthy sexual appetite too, although it can't be satisfied very often – more's the pity. Would Ron do for you in that department, if you don't actually love him?'

'If I were Ron's wife, of course he would have to do for me. I suppose those kind of bedroom activities would have to be part of the arrangement, whether or no. Lots of girls marry, Bunty, but not always for love. Life isn't like that. Some women marry for security, for a roof over their heads. Anyway, Ron is not actually repulsive. In fact, he's quite handsome – he's certainly improved with age. It's just that I never used to fancy him that way. And as you get older, I imagine the physical side of things becomes less important.'

'Not to me it doesn't, and nor will it to you, I suspect. Not for a long time yet. You and Edward were like rabbits – at it at every opportunity. You said so yourself.'

Libby grinned impishly. 'We were. We couldn't get enough of each other. It was an addiction. Nothing will ever come close to that again. Nothing.'

'So when Ron is about his nightly exercise upon you, you will be lying back and thinking of Edward—'

'Wishing it could be Edward.'

'So it won't be the same, Libby, because it's not Edward. You will resent it. It will become a chore.'

Libby sighed. 'I think I know this, Bunty.'

'Yet you are prepared to put up with it for the sake of being a burden on your parents?'

She shrugged resignedly. 'I think I must.'

'And is this forthcoming marriage – of which I don't really approve – imminent?'

Libby shrugged again, typically. 'That I don't know. It depends on whether he gets some leave soon.'

'Well, I ask you to think about it very seriously.'

'I have thought about it seriously, Bunty,' Libby replied, avoiding Bunty's eyes in her admonishment. 'Very seriously . . .' Then she looked up at her more challengingly. 'Do I take it then, that you wouldn't consider being my maid-of-honour?'

Bunty sighed. 'You are my best friend, Libby, and I think the world of you, so I will do whatever you want. It's simply that I don't – I can't – condone your marrying Ron. Nor will it be fair on him, don't you see? There must be hundreds of chaps more worthy of you. Chaps you'd really fancy. Chaps who would adore you . . . and Elizabeth.'

'Ron would be good with Elizabeth.'

'So would any number of men. I just think you're making the ghastly mistake of going along with the first man who offers himself. Don't do it, Libby. After Edward, you're vulnerable. I think you're still on the rebound, even after all this time.'

- - -

Despite Bunty's protestations, Libby agreed to marry Ron Downing. She had thought it through very carefully and the benefits seemed to outweigh the impediments. Ron was a good man, he loved her, he would cherish her, and he would be a sound father to Elizabeth. He understood what Libby had gone through and was prepared to make allowances if her responses to him were not as heartfelt as they had been with Edward. All this they had discussed very frankly in a series of letters. In time, she would grow to love him dearly, he had predicted, and she was inclined to agree that she might – if nothing else, he was deserving of her love. The days, the dreams of living her life as Edward Burgayne's devoted wife, in the secure embrace of a wealthy and influential family, had long disappeared. What a fabulous dream it had been, but she had to face reality.

The war by this time was all but won, and Ron was due home on leave for Christmas before being posted to the Ardennes where the Germans were making a last-ditch attempt to recapture Antwerp in Belgium so as to cut off supplies to the advancing Allied armies. Libby had made all necessary arrangements for the registry office wedding. All that remained was for Ron to appear – he was due home on 20th December 1944 – and to obtain the special licence that would enable them to become man and wife on Friday 22nd, just in time for a very merry Christmas.

On the 19th, the day before Ron was due, Libby took Elizabeth in her pushchair to the Post Office in St John's Road on Kates Hill to collect her allowance. There was a telephone kiosk on the corner there, and she had arranged to ring Bunty who would be home at Buttonbridge Hall that day. It was cold and damp, but people were wearing smiles on their faces at the welcome prospect of Christmas, victory and an end to the war.

'It's all set, Bunty,' Libby said into the handset. 'I'm just waiting for him to get home on leave. We shall be married on Friday . . .'

Silence.

'Say something, Bunty . . . Oh, please wish me well.'

'Oh, Libby, of course I wish you well,' came the reply at last. 'I shall be there, don't worry.'

'Well I know you don't think it's for the best, but I have to make my own mind up about these things, don't I? And it would make all the difference knowing I have your support. If Edward were still alive I wouldn't be doing this anyway. But Ron's a good man. We'll be all right with him.'

'Ignore me, Libby. I'm a silly romantic at heart, and I just don't see much romance in what you're doing, that's all. With Edward, it *was* romantic.'

Libby decided to ignore the remark. Her forthcoming marriage was not romantic; but it was practical. 'So will you come to the house first on Friday?'

'Yes, I'll come to your house.'

'Good – then we shall depend on you for a lift, so come early, because there'll be lots to do.'

'You actually sound quite excited, Libby.'

'Do I?

'Yes, you do.'

'I suppose I am, really.'

'How's my niece, by the way?'

'Oh, she's fine, except that she got covered in writing ink this morning, the little monkey. Mom left a bottle within her reach. Of course, she managed to get hold of it and opened it. It went everywhere. I just hope we can wash it off her by Friday.'

Bunty chuckled. 'Kids! What I wouldn't give for a houseful.'

'Your chance will come, Bunty.'

'Yours too, what?'

Libby heaved a sigh. 'Who knows . . . Anyway, I'd better go – the pennies will be running out. See you Friday.'

They said their goodbyes, Libby put down the receiver and carried Elizabeth back to her pushchair. Yes, she was really quite excited now at the prospect of marrying Ron.

- - -

Bunty made her way back to the drawing-room where her mother was sewing a button on a blouse she'd had for years. Jenkins arrived there at the same time carrying a tray on which stood a pot of tea and two cups and saucers. She set them down on an occasional table and set them out neatly.

'Well, it's all set,' Bunty announced resignedly. 'Libby's marrying her old sweetheart when he arrives back on leave for Christmas. I don't hold with it – I think she's doing it for the wrong reasons – but she has her own ideas. She has her own life to live.'

Dorothy cut the cotton thread and put her needle back into a pincushion. 'I think I can understand how she feels,' she commented. 'A young woman with a child must be anxious that they are both cared for. It's her duty as a mother to see that her child gets the best on offer.'

Jenkins was listening, and hesitated to go.

'I can understand that, Mommy, but she doesn't love this chap, although she does like him. More as an old friend, though, than a paramour.'

'But that's nice,' Dorothy said. 'If that's the case, maybe he won't make too many demands on her.'

'I think the boot's on the other foot, Mommy. She won't make many demands on him, but I think it'll be a different kettle of fish with him. He's hungry for her, and has been for years. He'll not be able to keep his hands off her.'

'Oh, Bunty, you can be quite coarse sometimes. It's so unbecoming. I'm sure it must be mixing with common nurses that does it.'

'I've always called a spade a spade, Mother.'

'Young Mrs Burgayne's getting married again?' Jenkins interjected, still hovering.

'On Friday, Margaret. Didn't you know?'

'I had no idea, Mrs Wilding. But I wouldn't have thought it the proper thing to do under the circumstances.'

'What circumstances? As a widow, she is free to marry if she so desires. I just don't think she's chosen the right man. Or, put another way, I don't think the right man has chosen her, for that's what it amounts to.'

'Does Mr Hugh know that young Mrs Burgayne is to remarry, miss?'

'One presumes he knows. He must have heard us talking about it unless his ears are bunged up with wax. Why? Does his opinion matter? Libby is not bound by his unorthodox rules like my mother and the rest of the staff are.'

'No, I just wondered, miss,' Jenkins said, and made a rapid exit.

- - -

Friday morning arrived, the big day, and after breakfast Bunty rang for Jenkins to come to her room to help her get ready.

She was sitting wearing only her underwear, rolling up her stockings and looking pensive when Jenkins arrived.

'I think I shall need a vest on today if I'm going to have to stand out in the cold, Margaret. What do you think?'

'Yes, I think so, Mrs Wilding. I would if I were you at any rate. It's seems a bit chilly out.'

'There's one in my drawer over there.'

Jenkins went to the chest of drawers. She withdrew a vest and placed it on Bunty's bed.

'I think young Mrs Burgayne's very wrong to get wed again, miss,' Jenkins declared out of the blue.

'So you agree with me, then, Margaret?'

'Well, I mean, ma'am, what about if Mr Edward's still alive in a prisoner of war camp, and he comes home after the war and finds his wife has got married to somebody else?'

'That would be tragic, I agree. Not to mention the fact that it would render her second marriage illegal. But we all know there's little chance of it happening in this case.'

'Pardon me for saying so, ma'am, but I reckon Mr Edward is still alive.'

Bunty looked at her with a frown of curiosity. 'What on earth makes you think that?'

Jenkins shrugged. 'There have been letters . . .'

'Letters? What kind of letters?'

'Letters, ma'am.' She shrugged again guiltily and her colour rose.

Bunty's heart started pounding hard. 'Letters from whom, Margaret? You *must* tell me.'

'I dunno who from, ma'am . . . Mr Hugh always had them.'

'Letters from Edward?' Bunty asked with incredulity.

'Letters . . . And cards.'

Bunty felt herself go hot. 'So where are these letters now?'

'I dunno, ma'am. Like I say, Mr Hugh always had them.'

'Yes, he did, didn't he?' Bunty said, instantly prepared to give the notion more credibility than heretofore.

Letters . . .

If there had been letters about Edward, why hadn't Hugh handed them over? What would he do with such letters anyway? He was a stickler for order and organisation. Maybe they were still around somewhere . . .

'If he knows I've said anything, ma'am, he'll kill me,' Jenkins bleated.

'No, he won't,' Bunty said impatiently. 'Because I shan't implicate you. Look, you can go now. I can manage from here on.'

'If you're sure, ma'am.'

'I'm sure. Go and make my mother a cup of tea or something. And be sure not to say a word to Hugh about this conversation.'

'Very good, ma'am.' Jenkins left the room, closing the door behind her.

What letters? Surely Hugh would never hide letters that revealed information about Edward, even if such letters existed. Yet he had given orders that all letters be vetted by him when their father was ill. He had even taken hold of her own letters until she had fought him over it. What other letters had he withheld? Had he never rescinded that order he gave? Was Jenkins still faithfully handing him the mail every day – even now? To what purpose? But what if the person for whom the letters were intended was not here to receive them? What if that person was Libby? Bunty's thoughts raced on, gathering momentum by the second. Hugh had tried to rape Libby. He had become totally obnoxious when he had not been allowed to have his way and was made to look a villain. His true colours had come to the fore. His regard for Libby had subsequently turned somersaults and, since she had uncovered the monumental flaws in his character, that high regard had since disintegrated to absolute contempt. Would he, could he have kept all letters addressed to her out of pure spite? He was certainly capable of it. You only had to witness how he treated his mother to realise how ruthless he could be.

Then Bunty remembered the incident when she had to ask him for her own mail – letters from Harry. She'd had to go to him in his darkroom and suffer the ignominy of awaiting his convenience to retrieve them. Once inside he showed her photographs of Libby and Keith Farnell, which he kept in a file in *that filing cabinet . . .*

Bunty quickly finished dressing herself. She put on her coat and hurried to the cellar. The entrance was outside in the cold, down some stone steps on the north side of the house. The door was locked. The key had to be somewhere. Back in the house, she rushed upstairs to Hugh's room. This door was not locked. Jenkins had been in, neatly made his bed, tidied up and dusted. There was a dressing table, a tallboy, a chest of drawers. The key to the cellar should be somewhere. She rifled through them. In the fifth drawer she found a bunch of keys. One was large and old, made of iron, big and bulky but smoothed through years of use. Maybe this was it.

She took it and raced outside again and down the stone steps to the cellar. She inserted the key and it turned in the lock. She opened the door, and hurried across to the partitioned area which was the darkroom. That door was locked too. Bunty fumbled through the assortment of keys looking for a likely contender. She tried a couple, then one fitted the lock and it turned without resistance. That door opened too. She flipped the switch that turned on the light, and headed directly for the filing cabinet. Hugh had opened the top drawer to find the photos when she had been there before. She tugged on it, but that, too, was locked. Of course, it would be. Once more she sorted through the keys and found one that looked about right. She inserted it into the keyhole and it slid in unhindered. It turned . . . She pulled the drawer again, and it glided open . . .

Bunty was breathing hard by this time, trembling. What on earth was she likely to find in here? What evidence of Hugh's vindictiveness was she likely to uncover? She shuddered at the prospect. God, if he were to come in here right now he would kill her. She flipped through the files, lined up precisely and squarely in the deep drawer. They were all neatly labelled; Bank, Cameras, Cars, Chemicals, Legal, Developers, Fixers, Insurance, LS, Miscellaneous, Receipts, Records Various, Sheet Music, . . . One stood out in that alphabetical list. No name, just initials.

LS . . .

Libby Shakespeare . . .

Bunty withdrew the file, laid it on the dry bench and opened it. She gasped when she saw how many photographs there were of Libby in various stages of undress, many taken when she was stark naked. They all had one thing in common; each was taken from a position above her, looking almost directly down on her. Possibly shot through a spy hole if the fuzzy outline at the edges of most was anything to go by. How could he? How could he possibly be so insensitive as to invade her sacred privacy? The wife of his own brother.

Bunty continued to flip through the photos and papers. The photos he'd already shown her of Libby with Keith Farnell were there, and still they proved nothing. Then she came across a carbon copy of a typewritten letter . . . How typical of Hugh to keep a carbon copy – 'for the sake of good order' – that was always one of his sayings. She pulled it out. It was addressed to Edward, and dated 31st August 1941 – just a few short days before he was reported missing. She read the letter with increasing horror. It told Edward of Libby's 'affair' with Keith Farnell, how she had even tried to entice Hugh into her bedroom. It painted the poor innocent girl a whore, and was written in a very convincing style.

Bunty was incensed. This very letter might have been the cause of Edward's death. Saddened to the point of despondency he could have made sure he got himself killed in action,

tantamount to committing suicide, rather than suffer the pain
and anguish of what his loving, caring brother had so elo-
quently yet so wickedly described. But surely, Edward would
never believe such nonsense? Surely he would have seen
straight through it. Events, however, suggested not.

She put the letter down, scarcely able to believe that Hugh
could be so vicious as to write so maliciously to his own
brother, a letter that could so easily have shaped Edward's destiny; indeed, the destiny of each of them. Then she came across
another, still in its envelope. It bore the emblem of the Red
Cross. She opened it with trembling hands . . .

Friday 28th November 1941

Dear Mrs Burgayne,

*It is with some trepidation that I write this letter. Part of
our remit is to trace missing relatives via our international
network and our work is invaluable in bringing comfort and
succour to missing servicemen and their relatives from all
countries.*

*It has come to our attention that your husband was posted
missing believed killed on September 3rd 1941 as a result of
air combat. However, reports from our network suggest that
an RAF pilot was picked up in the English Channel at about
08.00 hours of that morning by a German motor torpedo boat.
We are hopeful that this airman was indeed your husband.
With the help and co-operation of the Air Ministry we are
actively seeking confirmation from the German Authorities*

that Flying Officer Edward Burgayne is alive and well and is interned in a German Prisoner of War camp.

As soon as we have more information we shall of course be in touch.

Yours faithfully,

Richard H Charlton

pp The British Red Cross

Surely this was what Jenkins meant when she said there had been letters. She would have seen the red cross on the envelope and put two and two together. Yet either her loyalty to Hugh, or her absolute fear of him, had prevented her from saying anything to anybody about it until Libby's second marriage was imminent.

And look how imminent that was! She looked at her watch anxiously.

There was another letter. Also in a Red Cross envelope. She tore it open angrily, read it avidly.

14th January 1942

Dear Mrs Burgayne,

It is with very great pleasure that subsequent to my previous letter, I can inform to you that due to the invaluable help from the Air Ministry, information has been secured regarding the fate of your husband Flying Officer Edward Bur-

gayne. He is reported to be interned currently in Dulag Luft Dulag 12, a transit camp for receiving and debriefing captured RAF personnel prior to transit to a Prisoner of War camp. Dulag 12 is situated at Grosstychow in former Polish territory. How long your husband might remain there is not known.

It is important for you to know that the Red Cross operates a postal message scheme which you would be advised to use to contact your husband. Most Citizens' Advice Bureaux act as Red Cross Postal Message Bureaux, but those that do not will be able to give the address of your nearest despatching centre.

Personal messages of not more than 20 words, exclusive of names and addresses are allowed. Christian and surnames, as well as full addresses of sender and addressee must be given, and a statement of the relationship. The whole should be written in block capitals. An unstamped envelope bearing senders name and address should be handed in with the message for postage of reply. Cost, including reply, one shilling. You are advised to use this method of correspondence to establish contact, and until more direct methods might be possible ...

Bunty found evidence that Hugh had used the Red Cross as a means of contacting Edward, because there was a letter card from Edward bearing official German rubber stamp marks and sent via the Red Cross. She was relieved to see that t was written in his own hand.

> *Hugh,*
>
> *Devastated to hear of father's death. Dearly want to be home. What news of Libby? Moving to POW camp soon.*

Bunty's eyes filled with tears when she read it. Edward was still alive when everybody believed he was dead and had rearranged their lives accordingly. Suddenly she was aware of his raw emotions as he went through all this unnecessary suffering, not knowing what was happening, the absolute and total frustration at being unable to influence matters, particularly where Libby was concerned. *'What news of Libby?'* he had said. Oh, the poor, poor man. Bunty wept long and hard for him. The poor chap would have been heartbroken to have received all the venomous lies about his wife. It must surely have affected him monstrously.

She eventually wiped her tears and came across another letter card:

> *Hugh,*
>
> *Now at Stalag Luft 6 near a town called Heydekrug. Polish Lithuanian border. What news of Libby? Please let me have news.*

Hugh obviously risked sending a full letter for the next document was another carbon copy of a typewritten letter.

4ᵗʰ May 1943

Flying Officer Hugh Burgayne,

Stalag Luft 6

Heydekrug

Germany

Dear Edward,

It is indeed good to know that you are finally settled in Stalag Luft 6 with other Allied airmen I imagine, for what must prove to be very stimulating company.

As for Libby, she left Buttonbridge Hall shortly after Father passed away. She also resigned her job as secretary. Clearly, she was seeking pastures new. I understand that only a month ago she gave birth to a child, a daughter, who clearly could not have been yours some year and a half after your absence. I undertook some undercover investigation, and it appears that her former sweetheart might be the child's father. This merely bears out what I told you before ...

Bunty was flabbergasted and horrified when she read this. Hugh had actually confirmed that Libby had had a child, but claimed its birth to be a year later than the actual birth so that Edward could hardly begin to imagine himself as the father. Such vile wickedness. And he cited Ron Downing as the father.

She had seen enough. What she had seen sickened her. But she needed this proof. So she picked up the letters and letter-cards, and one photograph of the naked Libby, and put them to one side. The rest, she replaced in the file, which she in turn returned carefully to the drawer in the filing cabinet. She locked it up, took the documents she'd put to one side, turned off the light, left the darkroom and locked that too, then emerged from the cellar into the dull chill of that enlightening December day.

She looked at her watch. She had to stop this wedding. It was nearly twelve. She should have been at Libby's house by now. The wedding was arranged for one o' clock. Just enough time. She hurried back to her room and grabbed the keys to the Riley, said goodbye to her mother, and left.

- - -

| 27 |

Libby looked every inch a war bride in her best coat and a new hat, a pair of new nylon stockings that gave her legs a sleek and shapely look, and high-heeled shoes – all very proper for a wedding. Fastened to the lapel of her coat was a pink silk rose. Anticipating Bunty's arrival, she was standing at the bottom of the entry, and on tenterhooks, pondering this highly significant day that was to change her life yet again. Her friend was late, exceedingly late, however, and the Shakespeare family were depending on Bunty to convey them to the Registry Office for her marriage to Ron. He would be there already, anxious at her non-arrival.

Maybe Bunty had changed her mind about attending this wedding, since she did not wholeheartedly condone it. Yet Libby knew Bunty well enough to realise that she would have got a message somehow if she had not intended to show. Therefore something unforeseen must be delaying her.

After a wait that seemed eternal, Bunty drew up outside number 20 and jumped out of the car. Her expression suggested she was wound-up about something. Also, she was carrying documents, which she held up for Libby to see, as if there was some significance to them. Mysterious . . .

'Crikey, you're late, Bunty,' Libby admonished mildly. 'Ron will think I've changed my mind.'

'Then Ron will have to get used to the idea, Libby,' Bunty said as she hurried round the car to the pavement.

'What on earth can you mean?'

'It so happens you've got to change your mind, my girl. You can't marry Ron. Not while you're still married.'

Libby looked at Bunty almost with disparagement. She would never have believed that Bunty might employ such insensitive tactics to prevent this marriage.

'What on earth do you mean, Bunty?'

Bunty was at her side now, waving the papers in Libby's face. 'Edward is alive and well. I discovered it only this morning. In the nick of time, don't you know.'

'If this is some kind of sick joke . . .'

'If this is any kind of joke, it's not a bit funny, I agree,' Bunty remarked. 'But it is true and a reason to be joyful. Look at these papers, Libby. Edward's own dear brother Hugh – may God damn him till eternity – has hidden from all of us the fact that Edward is alive and well, and in some POW camp in Germany. He's known it for two years, and the proof is here.'

'Edward is alive?' Libby reeled at the news, and Bunty steadied her. 'Oh, God . . . Really? Is he really alive, Bunty?'

'Absolutely.'

'But how can you be so sure?' Tears welled up instantly and lingered on Libby's long lashes for a second before trickling down her face. Then her expression changed, to one of resentment. 'If this is a ploy, Bunty Burgayne, it's the cruellest ever and I'll never forgive you . . .'

'It's no ploy, Libby, nor is it a dream,' Bunty said gently, putting her arms around her. 'I would never subject you to that and you know it. So pinch yourself . . . Edward is alive and well. Get it? . . . I promise you he is.'

'Oh, Bunty . . . Is this really true?'

'I keep telling you.' Bunty gasped with frustration, unable to comprehend Libby's reticence to accept what she was being told what she'd been longing to hear. 'Why won't you believe me when it's all you've wanted to hear for years?'

'I want to believe it – course I do.'

'Then read these letters, Libby. They tell us that Edward is a prisoner of war at some camp called Stalag Luft 6 . . . It's an absolute fact.' She handed her the documents.

So Libby read the letters from the Red Cross and was convinced that Edward was alive after all. She looked at Bunty, and a smile lightened her face that only a minute ago had been clouded with confusion and doubt.

'Oh, Bunty, this is such brilliant news, but it's so hard to take in after all this time . . . It's as if a dreadful mist has suddenly been lifted from my eyes, and I can see where I'm going again. D'you think I'll be able to go and see him, like I did when I went to Ireland?'

'Don't be daft. We're at war with Germany. We weren't at war with Ireland.'

'But why would Hugh want to hide it from us all? I don't understand.'

'I'll tell you why. It's because he's an idiot. He was jealous of Edward, jealous of the fact that you were in love with Edward and Edward was in love with you.'

'Well I knew that, but never did I dream that he could stoop so low as to hide his actual existence and his whereabouts from me – or from you his family for that matter. He's evil, Bunty. I think he's mad.'

'He needs certifying,' Bunty remarked. 'I'm afraid, though, that what I have to tell you next will take the gloss off this wonderful news.'

'Oh, no! What?'

'Hugh has evidently tried to turn Edward against you . . . by inventing ridiculous lies. Here . . . You'd better read the lot.'

'Let's go in the house then. I'm frozen.'

'No, Libby. Better read them here before your mother and father realise what's happening. Then we'll decide how best to tackle what we have to do next.'

'About Ron, you mean?'

'About Ron first, then about Edward.'

So Libby read. When she reached the awful, incredible lies that Hugh had formulated so calculatingly, her mouth dropped open and her moist eyes widened with horror.

'I can't believe he would do this,' she said softly, looking at Bunty. 'I can't believe anybody would want to do this.'

'Neither can I,' Bunty replied. 'I would never have thought him capable of such evil, for that's what it is. It's Hugh's way of getting back at you for refusing him.'

'But this is scandalous, Bunty.'

'Actually, it's libellous.'

'He should be put away,' Libby claimed. 'He must be sick. He should be put in a mental home . . . And what if Edward believed all this rubbish?'

'Being realistic, it must have had some effect. It's my view that when he read that awful first letter from Hugh, he was heartbroken. He would have received it the same day or the day before he was shot down.'

'You mean he might have deliberately got in the way of some German plane, so he'd get shot down?' Libby suggested.

'I think it's possible. Look at the date. He was definitely shot down the same day, or the day after he received the letter.'

'My God . . . Oh, Edward, Edward . . .' She clenched her fists in frustration and anger, and more tears came. There was nothing she could do to rectify the situation.

'There's more, Libby,' Bunty warned. 'Hugh's also been spying on you. Take a look at this . . .' She handed Libby the photograph. 'It's just one of many. There must have been a crack or a hole in your bedroom ceiling. Anyway, I shall investigate that when I get back home.'

Libby looked at the photo. 'The perverted swine!' she exclaimed with mounting disdain. 'I never liked Hugh, you know Bunty. Something I could never quite put my finger on, but there was always something about him I couldn't stand. Something dark, something creepy. I was right all along.'

'I know,' Bunty agreed, and gave her a sisterly hug.

'Ah well . . .' Libby gave a juddering sigh, then forced a smile through her tears, which to Bunty, who knew her well, seemed like a smile of relief. 'So the wedding's off. I'd better let him know.'

'Well, at least you don't have to sacrifice yourself after all.'

'I don't, do I?'

Bunty perceived an element of acquiescence in those few words, acknowledging that she would indeed have been sacrificing herself to Ron.

'Come on inside now, Bunty. We'd better let mom and dad know.'

Gladys and Joe were dumbfounded but delighted, and vastly relieved to learn that Edward was alive and presumably well, but Gladys felt pangs of sorrow for Ron, who for years had idolised and waited for Libby.

'As one heart's mended, another's broken,' she declared with a sigh. 'But that's life . . .' She gave Libby a hug. 'I'm so happy for you, my flower. At least, when this war's over, you'll be back together.'

Libby nodded and finally began to sob. 'I know,' she cried, mopping up tears in her dainty handkerchief. 'But you know one of the best things that's come out of this? Elizabeth will get to know and love her real live daddy after all.'

Bunty drove Libby directly to the Registry Office in Dudley. It was well after one o' clock when they arrived, and Ron, resplendent in army uniform, was standing outside on the pavement waiting agitatedly for the arrival of his bride. Already he was thinking that she was not going to show, so when he saw the car draw up and Libby open the door he smiled and went to greet her, prepared to forgive her for keeping him waiting so long. But when he saw that she had so obviously been crying, he was instantly full of foreboding.

'Take this,' Bunty said, handing her the letter from the Red Cross confirming Edward's internment. 'You might need it as proof.'

Libby stepped out of the car as calmly as she could.

'I thought you were never coming,' Ron said, and took her hand.

'But I had to come, Ron,' she replied as placidly as she knew how.

'What's up, Libby?' He had read her well.

Bunty watched from the car, but could not hear how Libby explained the situation. She saw her take Ron to one side and look earnestly into his eyes as she revealed that her dear beloved Edward was still alive after all. He stood, patiently listening, rolled his eyes disbelievingly, looked away, asked her something and looked at her again with utter dejection, keeping perfectly still while she gave her reply. Then he nodded in Bunty's direction and they both turned to glance at her. Bunty gave them a little wave of her fingers and smiled. Libby unfolded the letter from the Red Cross and handed it to Ron; the ultimate proof that she was not simply trying to wriggle out of their arrangement. Poor Ron read it, and assumed the look of a man who had just been handed a death sentence. He had been so close to attaining his dream, but it was being snatched away from him at the very last minute. Bunty felt inordinately sorry for him as she continued watching, for she acknowledged that he was a decent man.

There was no need for Bunty to hear the conversation, she could see it being played out, and it was ineffably poignant; the strong, brave soldier wiping his eyes as he began to weep for the love of a woman he could not have, the sympathy that was manifest on the exquisite face of this woman he loved as she denied him what he wanted most in the world. He nodded, finally convinced of the situation, wiped an eye again with the back of his hand, then took Libby's hand and kissed her tenderly on the cheek. He turned away; she turned away and headed back to the car.

Libby opened the door and slumped into the seat.

'How do you feel now?' Bunty enquired.

'Drained. Completely drained.'

'Hardly surprising.'

'Talk about cutting it fine,' Libby said. 'He's just gone in to tell the registrar the wedding's off.'

'It's been a funny old day. Can we go yet?'

'Yes, let's go, Bunty . . . You know, that's the most awful thing I think I've ever had to do in my life.'

'You do tend to get yourself into some scrapes with men,' Bunty replied, tongue-in-cheek as she started the engine.

'But I don't mean to . . . Ever.' She settled herself more comfortably in the car, glad that the ordeal of facing Ron was done with. Another chapter of her life was over, and it was time to move on. 'How long d'you think it will be before the war's over, Bunty?'

'Hard to say exactly, but not long, I think.' She put the car into gear and they moved off. 'The Home Guard has been stood down and the Germans are being defeated on every front. Months, if not weeks, I'd say.'

'And then Edward will be released, and he'll be home again. Gosh, I can hardly wait.'

Bunty turned her head and smiled. 'I still can't believe I found out just in time. It was only because of what Margaret Jenkins said this morning – that Hugh had taken letters confirming Edward's POW status. It must've been a guilty conscience on her part having known about it and not letting us know earlier, and fateful for you. You see, it wouldn't have been right to marry Ron. You'd have been a bigamist.'

'Crikey! I hadn't thought of that. Anyway, what's going to happen about Hugh? We surely can't let him get away with what he's done.'

'Frankly, Libby, I don't know what we should do. He'll have to be confronted, of course, and he'll have to write to Edward again, apologising for his stupid lies and for keeping from you the fact that he's in a POW camp. Beyond that, I don't know.'

Bunty said goodbye to Libby and her folks later that afternoon. She must, she said, tell her mother the awful truth about Hugh and the brilliant news about Edward before Hugh returned home from his office. And together they must decide what should be done.

- - -

'My God, I never realised I had spawned a monster when I had Hugh,' Dorothy Burgayne remarked after she had listened with open-mouthed astonishment to what Bunty had to say. 'What could have made him turn out the way he has? He's always had the best of everything – the best education, the best opportunities. How many other men of thirty inherit a company as large and as successful as the Blowers Green Steelworks?'

'Maybe that's the trouble,' Bunty suggested. 'He's had too much far too easily, and therefore expected everything else to fall in his lap. Even Libby. The problem remains, Mommy, what to do about him.'

'Well, first we must tell him we know everything, and let him know exactly how we feel.'

'That'll really be some punishment,' Bunty said sarcastically. 'Can't we stretch him on a rack, or tar and feather him and then set fire to him? Preferably all three? It's no less than he deserves.'

'Our disdain will be sufficient,' Dorothy said. 'His own sense of shame will be punishment enough.'

'Is he capable of feeling shame?'

'If not, Bunty, he is lost.'

'Well I believe he is already lost. So when shall we tell him?'

'After dinner.'

Hugh duly returned from work. Jenkins magically appeared in the hall simultaneously and fluttered around him. He went upstairs, washed and changed, flipped through the day's newspaper, and finally went down to dinner.

It was a morbidly silent affair, with nobody able or willing to make normal conversation. Bunty's scornful glances at Hugh were like daggers. Jenkins could sense the atmosphere as she hovered, and was on tenterhooks. It was obvious to her that something radical was afoot, especially in view of her revelations to Bunty earlier.

Then, halfway through the fish course, Dorothy crashed down her knife and fork, dabbed her mouth with her napkin and got up, unable to control her resentment.

'I'm sorry,' she said to Bunty, 'but I cannot sit at the same table with my own son, and it breaks my heart.' Tears flooded her eyes, and she rushed out of the room.

'What's that all about?' Hugh remarked with measured scorn.

'About you, actually,' Bunty replied with even greater contempt.

'Me? What am I supposed to have done?'

Bunty turned to Jenkins. 'Margaret, please leave us now, would you? There are certain private things I need to discuss with my brother.'

Jenkins gave Bunty a cutting look, glanced at Hugh apprehensively, then scurried from the room, certain she was about to be implicated.

'I have been to see Libby today, Hugh,' Bunty began. 'It was her wedding day.'

'Oh? Did it go off well?'

'Much better than any of us could have imagined, actually. She's incredibly happy. Very happily married.'

'Did she marry that ne'er-do-well she used to see before?'

'D'you mean the father of her child?'

He looked at her puzzled. 'Is he the father of her child?'

'Yes, she's married to the father of her child. Shouldn't she be?'

'Hang on, you've lost me here,' he said. 'Are you saying the chap she's married today is the father of her child?'

Bunty smiled; she was confounding him. 'I'm saying the chap she is married to is the father of her child,' she confirmed, but twisting the words.

'You're talking in riddles, Bunty.'

'No, I'm not. It's perfectly straightforward. Edward is the father of her child and that's who she is married to.'

'But Edward was posted missing. Libby was going to marry this other chap. This ne'er-do-well.'

'She was . . . But since she discovered that Edward is still alive and well in a prisoner of war camp called Stalag 6, somewhere in Germany, she could hardly marry the ne'er-do-well, as you insist on calling him, could she?'

Hugh felt himself go hot. 'I suppose not. But where did she get this news, Bunty. How on earth did she discover Edward is still alive?'

'By letters from the Red Cross initially.'

'Oh?' He looked at her apprehensively.

'Yes. First there was one that said an airman had been picked up from the sea by a German torpedo boat, then another some little time after confirmed it was Edward, stating he'd been traced to a reception centre for captured Allied airmen.'

'Really? That's wonderful news.' He hunched his shoulders in the manner that he did when he had a conflict on his hands, and Bunty saw that he was flustered.

'Yes, it's wonderful news. Then she read a copy of a letter written by Edward's loving brother, claiming she'd been having a torrid affair with another airman called Keith Farnell in this very house . . . It was quite awful, and utterly malicious and, if she's got any sense, she will sue for libel. Also, the effect it had on poor Edward was to make him go out in his aeroplane with the intention of getting himself shot down.'

'You can't prove that—'

'Ah . . .' Bunty smiled triumphantly. It was tantamount to an admission of guilt, however inadvertently given. But her smile quickly turned to an icy glare. 'You should be utterly ashamed of yourself, Hugh. How could you be so evil? Do you realise the heartache you have caused the people you are supposed to love? Do you understand what unhappiness and chaos you have created within your own kith and kin with your damned pointless lies and your insane meddling? What were you thinking of? And those horrible photographs you sneaked of Libby in her bedroom. It's the behaviour of an unspeakable creep. Father would be appalled.'

'You've been in my darkroom, going through my files.'

'And a good thing, too,' she rasped, 'else we should never have discovered your insanity. Did you really think you could get away with it? We should have you committed. And what sort of reception will you get from Edward once he is back home? The war is nearly over now, and he'll be released soon. If I were him I'd happily strangle you.'

'I hadn't considered that possibility. I merely thought he would thank me for exposing Libby for what she is.'

'Well, whatever you want Edward to think she is, was not enough to stop you wanting her for yourself. Is that what this is all about? Jealousy? Spite? I always thought you too big a man to be troubled by such trivialities. I was patently wrong.'

Hugh Burgayne left Buttonbridge Hall the next morning, Saturday, and did not return. When it was discovered that Margaret Jenkins was also missing it confirmed what everybody suspected. Christmas came and went, and still they did not return. Subsequent enquiries, instigated with the help of the police after the Christmas break, revealed that Hugh had obviously visited his office at some time and that the petty cash was missing. When it was time to go to the bank to fetch the money required to pay wages, it was discovered that company cheque books were also missing. The bank had insisted that when Dorothy was made a director following Charles's death, her signature should appear on cheques as well as Hugh's. Hugh, however, had been in the habit of bringing company chequebooks home so she could sign blank cheques which would be used to pay pending obligations. Thus he had been able to withdraw substantial amounts of cash, leaving the company almost bereft of working capital.

In her capacity as a director of Blowers Green Steelworks, Dorothy, assisted by Bunty, was obliged to visit the bank and urgently negotiate facilities to overdraw so that wages and suppliers could be paid in order for the company to remain in business.

Hugh Burgayne had disappeared off the face of the earth accompanied by Jenkins, taking his own and much of the company's wealth with him.

- - -

At the first opportunity after Christmas in 1944, Libby visited the Citizens' Advice Bureau so that she could send a note to Edward using the Red Cross Postal Message Scheme. It had occurred to her how strange it was that she had seen nothing in the correspondence that Bunty had retrieved from Hugh's file, that Edward had tried to contact her directly. This set alarm bells ringing. Had he been convinced by Hugh's meddling letter and decided to shun her in future? If so, it was possible she might have nothing to look forward to but the divorce courts on his return.

Her note to Edward, consisting of the limiting 20 words only, was hardly sufficient to tell him all and let him know how she felt. But she did her best, and it read:

JUST DISCOVERED HUGH'S LIES. HUGH HID FACT YOU ARE NO LONGER MISSING. LOVE YOU ALWAYS. YOU HAVE A DAUGHTER. WRITE.

She waited anxiously for a reply, but no reply came. Weeks passed, and the weeks turned into months. By May 4th, when Field Marshall Montgomery received the Germans' surrender in his tent pitched on Lünebeurg Heath south of Hamburg, she still had not received word. How wonderful it would be to hear from him on her birthday. Surely, he would not forget her birthday.

But still no word came, and Libby was back to weeping, beside herself with worry and frustration, because there was literally nothing more she could do.

- - -

| 28 |

Edward Burgayne never received the message that Libby sent via the Red Cross. In mid-July 1944 – months earlier than she actually sent it, and unbeknownst to Libby – he and three thousand other prisoners of war were shifted out of Stalag Luft 6 at Heydekrug near the Polish-Lithuanian border, in order to avoid the advancing Russians. After a gruelling journey, crammed into horse trucks, they arrived at another camp in Torun in Poland where they remained for only three weeks before being moved again. This time they were sent by train, via Bromberg & Stettin in northern Germany, to Falling-bostel, lying twenty miles north of Hanover.

The prisoner of war camp at Fallingbostel was already dangerously overcrowded and conditions were atrocious. The place was guarded not by the Luftwaffe, but by German Army personnel, hardened soldiers rewarded with some respite after a punishing campaign on the Eastern Front, and unwilling to accept that they were losing the war.

The Allied bombing campaign had annihilated Germany's infrastructure, with the consequence that fresh supplies of

food, clothing and other essentials were virtually non-exis-
tent. Nevertheless, Edward was heartened to see American
airmen in action during this time. Waves of aircraft – Liber-
ators and Forts, escorted by long-range fighters – flew over
the camp day after day to targets further south. His optimism
turned to anguish, though, as scores of German fighters, including unbelievably fast new jet fighters, tore into the tight
formations firing cannons and rockets. But this was war; this
was what air forces did. Every now and then one of the big
bombers would fall out of the formation in flames. The rest
of the wing would then close up the gap and fly on, inevitably
into a barrage of anti-aircraft fire as it approached the target.
If only he could be up there with them, defending them in his
Hurricane . . .

At Christmas in 1944 food began to arrive from the Red
Cross and a parcel of cigarettes arrived in January 1945. By
March the supply of everything had dried up, and the Ger-
mans' rations, too, had dwindled to nothing. Come April, the
Germans hurriedly left the camp, chased by Russians hell-bent
on revenge.

On the 16th the Americans turned up. They delivered food
and drink to the starving prisoners that same night, and over
the next two days worked on a plan to transport everyone
home. Those interned longest were allowed to leave first, and
Edward was of the opinion that the whole operation was mag-
nificently organised.

He duly left Fallingbostel on April 20th. Along with hundreds of other British prisoners of war he was taken first to

Belgium. From there he was flown to Aylesbury in Bucking-hamshire, where he arrived on April 22nd. Tea, food and cig-arettes were laid on, since the RAF stations in England were already gearing up to receive returning prisoners of war. He was one of the early arrivals. Next day he was taken to RAF Cosford near Wolverhampton, where he was medically exam-ined, debriefed, and kitted out . . .

Only when he was so close to home did he try to examine his feelings and emotions objectively. For so long he had been incarcerated, cut off from the civilised world. He had been un-able to influence things that were going on at home, and there had been such a debilitating lack of information. He'd received no word at all from Libby during his entire internment, when he knew well enough that the Red Cross had let her know where he was by dint of the notes from Hugh. That same dearth of correspondence served only to reinforce the com-ments Hugh had made about Libby in that awful letter he'd re-ceived.

That soul-destroying information had unbalanced him, prompted him to offer himself as an easy target to be shot down, for he foresaw no further joy in living. Having survived it so miraculously, he was forced to consider, in retrospect, how reckless he had been. He began to wonder whether Fate had played a hand, and he, a fatalist, imagined there had to be a reason. He began to believe there could be life after Libby nev-ertheless, and that Fate must have chosen him to participate.

Then the doubts would return, and he would tell himself again and again that it could not be true, that there must be some hideous misunderstanding somewhere, that Libby must still love him. Yet how could she when he had heard nothing at all from her in all his years pent up in German prisoner-of-war camps? He had received not a word. He debated it with himself endlessly. She had obviously given up the wait, had been tempted elsewhere as Hugh had told him. This train of thought had been fortified by tales his fellow POWs related, about their own beloveds deserting them in favour of a new lover who was conveniently at hand. For the sake of his sanity, which had been tested to the limit, for the sake of finality, for the sake of a solution, Edward had to mentally let go of Libby. He had to let go of his hopes, his dreams, and his love for her.

Yet still he dreamed of her. Still he dreamed of their easy relationship, the tenderness, the glorious intimacy they had shared, and when he awoke he would suffer again the heartache and anger that relentlessly resurged because of it.

He could not live with doubts; it was not possible. He had to believe one thing or the other, and it was easier to let go, to try and forget her, for she was evidently unworthy of his love or even remembrance. He'd had to shut Libby from his thoughts as far as possible and accept that, like so many other wives and fiancées he'd heard about from fellow prisoners, she was fickle, possibly promiscuous and in her nature to stray. Besides, he could do nothing about it either way from within the distant, ghastly confines of Stalag Luft 6.

That other letter from Hugh, that other sickening missive, which he received prior to the exodus from Stalag Luft 6, claiming there was an illegitimate child, merely served to confirm her easy virtue. It had unsettled him again, but so much more than anything else. The very idea that Libby might have had a child by some other chap – and out of wedlock – was utterly abhorrent. Yet he had no option but to accept it. Other men's wives were unfaithful, why not his?

It was natural to give credence to Hugh's letters, sent out of a duty inspired by brotherly love. There was no reason to disbelieve what he read in them. Yet it was an absolute living nightmare; it was pure hell, insufferable. He endured it, but prayed every day that a letter from Libby, telling him that she loved him deeply and looked forward to his release at the earliest moment, would liberate him from that hell.

Yet no such letter came. Nor would it.

- - -

There was a telephone booth in the main reception centre at RAF Cosford. After a few days there Edward believed he ought to contact his family, which he had hitherto delayed doing. He really ought to let them know he was back in England, and find out once and for all when Libby had left Buttonbridge Hall. It was one rather large loose end that needed to be tidied up at the earliest possible moment, so that he could re-embark on some sort of settled life. But first he had to muster up the courage. He did not have the strength to endure the savage confirmation of the truth. Whilst he never lacked the courage to fly his Hurricane into a potentially fatal dog fight, he lacked the mettle to face up to what had plagued him for years, and which was now inevitable; the awful proof that Libby had betrayed him and had had a child by another man.

He stood looking at the telephone for some time, preoccupied, willing himself to use it. After some minutes of indecision, he slipped two pennies into the slot, lifted the receiver and made his call.

His mother answered, he pressed Button A, and the coins dropped with a clatter.

'Mother, it's me, Edward . . .' There were some seconds of uncertainty while Dorothy, suddenly bewildered at the thoroughly unexpected sound of Edward's voice, collected herself . . . 'Mother?' he said again.

'Edward? Is that really you?' Her response told of her absolute incredulity at hearing his voice.

'Yes, it's really me, Mother. Don't you recognise my voice? How have you been keeping?'

'Oh, Edward, Edward, where are you?'

'I'm at RAF Cosford, believe it or not.'

'Cosford? Gosh! You're so near? Well, thank God you're back so soon. Our world has fallen apart here since you were reported missing and your poor dear father passed away. I can't begin to tell you . . . But how are you, dear?'

'Reasonably well, all things considered. Lost a fair bit of weight, though, since last time you saw me. Not enough to eat, especially lately . . . What about Libby, Mother? What happened there?'

'Libby? Libby hasn't lived here for more than three years. But that's a story on its own.'

'So it's true . . .' he breathed, and sighed heavily as his world finally caved in.

'When are you coming home, dear?'

'I can't say, Mother,' he answered despondently. 'Very soon I hope, but it depends on when the RAF will release me.'

'Bunty's here. Would you like a word with her?'

'I would.'

'Hang on then while I go and get her.'

There was a long delay while Dorothy located Bunty and brought her to the telephone. Meanwhile, he was concerned that his money would run out if she didn't hurry.

'Edward?' It was Bunty's voice at last. 'You're at Cosford I hear.'

'Bunty,' he greeted economically. 'Yes, I'm at Cosford. Listen, I think my money's due to run out of this infernal telephone very soon, and I have no more change.'

'Thank God you're back in England. When shall we see you?'

'Just as soon as I can.'

'Can you receive visitors?'

'I imagine so.'

'Excellent. I'm going to visit you tomorrow morning. There's so much to tell you. I'm married now too, you know.'

'Really?' He accepted the information with genuine pleasure. It was the best news he'd heard in years. 'Good for you, Bunty. Congratulations. I do hope it works out well. Now tell me—'

The line went dead; the money had run out. He slammed the receiver back in its cradle and glared at it resentfully for a few seconds. Tears welled up in his eyes and he wept. Bunty was the one person who was most likely to have news about Libby, but still nothing was resolved. He was no nearer an explanation. And she could not ring him back because she didn't know the number.

After some time he sensed a presence beside him. He wiped his eyes and returned his handkerchief to his pocket.

'Let me guess . . . It's a woman . . .'

Edward turned to see a fellow RAF officer, of higher rank, standing next to him; a complete stranger. He nodded morbidly. 'Something like that, sir.'

'Nothing new there. Fickle creatures, women. Prepared to bugger off with the milkman if he takes their fancy, some of 'em.'

'Thank you, sir,' Edward replied curtly. 'But that's not the sort of information I need.'

'Expect nothing, and you won't be disappointed,' the officer said, undeterred. 'That's the worst that can happen, and when it does you know you've hit rock bottom. From then on things can only get better. Are you prepared to accept the worst on that basis?'

'I thought I would be able to, sir. I'd sort of conditioned myself to accept it. I'm not so sure now, though.'

'I know. You've been to hell and back. You've seen it all – the horrors, the depths of human depravity and the suffering. You've witnessed cruelty, wickedness, filth, squalor. I could go on – things that would horrify you in peacetime and in normal daily life, yet you took it all in your stride. What you're facing now is no different. You'll take it all in your stride as well. You've no option, when all's said and done.'

Edward forced a smile. 'I believe you might be right, sir.'

'I know I'm right. I'm speaking from experience.'

'Sorry to hear that, sir.'

'I was married once, you know, to a beautiful girl whom I absolutely idolised,' the stranger went on, evidently intent on saying more. 'We promised each other the world, that whatever happened in this war we would wait, and remain faithful. But you know what? While I was away fighting in the RAF for king and country, she was distracted. Some glib-talking young buck, no doubt extremely handsome and I daresay sporting a huge dick, talked himself into her underwear and she ran off with him. That's the trouble with beautiful girls – you daren't rest while your back's turned, because some cad will be trying his luck. And women are susceptible – so susceptible. Anyway, I was devastated. I was also angry and wanted to get my own back, and I believed the most vengeful way was to steal somebody else's wife. It seemed fair – somebody had stolen mine after all. And the world owed me that one solitary favour to redress the balance.

'And, do you know, I met one such girl who was an absolutely ideal candidate. A terrific girl – a peach of a girl. I'd been on bombers – a Pilot Officer in those days – and we got shot down. I was wounded in the leg and it was touch and go whether I'd actually keep the bally thing. The first thought of the surgeons was to lop it off, but they decided to try and mend it instead with some pretty heroic surgical techniques they were trying. I had countless operations, but they saved my leg, and I was sent to convalesce at a place not far from here called Buttonbridge Hall. It was there I met a delightful young woman who was married to the son of the owner of the house, by the name of Burgayne – also an RAF chap it transpired. Well, I fell head over heels for this girl . . . Libby, her name was . . . and naturally, I plied my charm with a vengeance. She was wonderful to me. She helped me recover, accompanied me around the grounds on therapeutic walks that were supposed to exercise my leg. She listened patiently to my tales of woe. Never have I met a woman more sympathetic or easier to talk to. She was a real gem. She had a sister-in-law too, I remember, called Bunty – also a tasty dish.'

'But this girl Libby,' Edward prompted, intrigued by the tale so far. 'Did you get anywhere with her?'

The other officer shook his head. 'She was definitely not available for those sort of shenanigans. She was recently wed, was very much in love with her husband, and was not about to stray. In fairness to her, she told me exactly that from the outset. From the very first suggestion I made that I was interested in her, she told me she could never be unfaithful, that it was not in her nature. Undaunted, however, I subsequently wrote to her, words of undying love that might have swayed a lesser mortal. But they didn't sway Libby Burgayne. Not one solitary inch.' He laughed, shaking his head as he relived his own foolishness. 'I never heard a word from her, from that day to this. But what a woman. What a girl to be married to. Such loyalty, such steadfastness. So you see, it just goes to prove that not all girls are tarred with the same brush.'

Edward held out his hand to his superior officer with a smile. 'Flying Officer Edward Burgayne, sir. Thank you for that information. You've quite given me something to think about.'

'Burgayne? Of Buttonbridge Hall? Well, I'm blowed.' He took Edward's hand and they shook. 'Flight Lieutenant Keith Farnell.'

'Yes, I gathered that, sir . . .'

'Well, congratulations on your choice of bride.'

'Thank you, sir.'

All the worrying, the doubts, the fears, the frustration, the desolation, the anger, the futility and heartache – especially the heartache – that had been pent up for years and growing like a canker, all seemed to drain away from him in those few seconds. There had never been any hope, and now, suddenly, there was. According to this man, Libby was a gem – loyal, steadfast and true, and that mattered more than anything. Might she still be waiting for him after all?

Yet the question of the child still remained. What she had told Keith Farnell might have been true at the time, but years had slipped by. She might, after all, have grown tired of waiting, as so many did, and sought solace and romance in somebody else's arms. And all that Keith Farnell said conflicted directly with what Hugh had written. He put a handkerchief to his face to wipe tears away and stepped outside the building into the darkness of the evening.

The sky was clear, the moon and the stars were bright. A perfect night for flying, he thought. But his flying days were over. He no longer saw himself as the greatest flyer ever to take to the skies. He would resign his commission.

And tomorrow, he would see Bunty, and find out for sure what had gone on. He had a thousand questions.

- - -

When Bunty rapped on the veranda door at 20 Hill Street next morning Libby answered it. She could tell by the expression on Bunty's face that something significant had happened.

'Bunty,' she greeted uneasily. 'Come in.'

'Come on, girl, spruce yourself up, I'm taking you and Elizabeth out.'

'But—'

'No buts. I want you looking your absolute beautiful best – both of you. I'm taking you out, I said.'

'Where are you taking us?' Libby laughed, safe in her assessment that it was not going to be awful with Bunty in blustering mood.

'Somewhere special. But it's for me to know and you not to find out until we get there.'

'I won't go with you if you won't tell me,' Libby teased.

'Suit yourself,' Bunty replied, feigning nonchalance, 'but it's somewhere extra special, and you're the one who'll be missing out, believe me. Persuade her, please, Gladys.'

'Fancy a cup of tea while you wait for her to get ready, Bunty?' Gladys enquired.

'That would be really rather spiffing, Mrs Shakespeare, thank you.'

So Bunty sat and talked to Gladys and supped a cup of tea while Libby and Elizabeth got ready upstairs. She dodged Gladys's questions about Edward, giving no clue as to where she was about to take them.

When the stairs door opened, Libby stepped down the last step in a simple cotton dress with a tasteful floral print, nylon stockings and high heels. Her hair was perfect and her make-up exquisite.

'I didn't mean that you had to outshine me so vividly, Libby Burgayne,' Bunty said in mock protest. 'My God, you look divine. Doesn't she, Gladys?'

'I wish I knew who she gets her looks from,' Gladys replied. 'It certainly ain't me – nor her dad neither.'

Then Elizabeth appeared treading gingerly down the stairs behind Libby, clinging to the handrail as she'd been taught. She was clean and spruce in a pale-yellow cotton dress, white ankle socks and dainty shoes, her hair tied in two bunches with matching ribbons.

'And you, young lady . . . I can see you're going to take after your mommy. You look nice enough to eat, Elizabeth.'

'Fank you, Aunty Bunty,' Elizabeth replied with becoming coyness. 'Where are you taking us? Mommy says she wants to know.'

'Mommy will know soon enough, darling. Somewhere rather special as I've already said – special for both of you.'

They bid Gladys goodbye, filed through the entry to the street and got into Bunty's car.

'Heard from Ron?' Bunty enquired casually.

'No,' was the matter-of-fact reply.

'Did you expect to?'

'Not really.'

From then on Bunty steered the conversation in the direction of generalities; about Harry, about the war, about anything and everything, avoiding any reference to Edward. They drove through Sedgley, then through the centre of Wolverhampton, and were out in the pleasant suburb of Tettenhall, where the road was overhung with a grotto of trees, before Libby commented that this was quite a long journey for them to take by car. Bunty drove on, confident she was travelling in the right direction, into open countryside, and then through the sleepy, attractive village of Albrighton. She could hear the incessant drone of aeroplanes flying low overhead, some taking off and others landing one after the other, which betokened the close proximity of an aerodrome. Bunty slowed down.

'Is this an RAF station?' Libby asked.

'I certainly hope so.'

'Is this where you're taking us?'

'When I can find the way in,' Bunty replied dismissively.

At once Libby became excited and apprehensive. 'Why here?'

'You'll see.'

Anxiety stirred within her. It must have something to do with Edward. But what? Perhaps it was the Commanding Officer from his squadron who was here and wished to see her. But why? To tell her he was dead after all and hand over all his personal effects, which so far she had not seen? No, he would have sent a letter, his things in a parcel. Besides, Bunty's demeanour would be different. All manner of possibilities ran through her mind, except the correct one.

Bunty turned into the base and stopped at a barrier. She got out of the car, closed the door behind her and talked with the guard. Libby saw how he smiled, and she knew then it was nothing too grave. The guard pointed towards one of the buildings, Bunty thanked him, returned to the car and, once the barrier was raised, drove on.

'We're in,' she said economically, and pulled up outside a brick building. She turned to Libby. 'Wait here you two,' and then disappeared inside offering no further explanation.

Inside the building, she approached the RAF man sitting at a desk.

'I'm a visitor for Flying Officer Edward Burgayne, a recently returned prisoner-of-war,' she announced.

The man smiled. 'I'll see if I can get him found and sent here.' He saw the wedding ring on her finger. 'Are you his wife?'

'I'm his sister.'

'Ah.'

The man picked up the telephone and started making enquiries. He smiled at Bunty, and said, 'Got him. He's on his way.'

'Is there somewhere private I can talk to him?'

'Yes, there's a room over there.' He pointed to a closed door and Bunty thanked him.

'I'll wait here for him. Which way will he come?'

'Through the door behind me, I imagine. He'll be coming from that direction.'

'He won't come in the way I did?'

'Doubtful.'

Bunty nodded, satisfied that Edward would not see Libby until she had prepared him.

After a wait that seemed interminable, Edward arrived, and Bunty was staggered at how thin and gaunt he was. But they rushed towards each other and hugged.

'Oh, Edward,' she sighed, 'it's wonderful to see you back.' She let go of him and looked him up and down. 'But you're so painfully thin. Are you quite well?'

'The doctors tell me I'll almost certainly survive,' he said flippantly, as if it would be a great disappointment if he did. 'The last few months we were half starved. Our calorie intake fell to about eight hundred a day, I'm told, then to nothing – due to food shortages. But I'll soon put weight on when I'm home. Anyway, look at you, you look wonderful.'

'Well, I'm a married woman now,' she confirmed proudly. 'Mrs Harry Wilding, no less. He's an army chap. Met him at

Buttonbridge Hall when he was a convalescent. He's in Belgium now with Eisenhower's lot, clearing up.'

'I met another convalescent from Buttonbridge Hall last night,' Edward declared.

'Oh? Who was that?'

'A chap called Keith Farnell. A Flight Lieutenant stationed here. Did you know him?'

'Bloody hell!' Bunty exclaimed. 'I remember Keith Farnell very well. Fancy him being stationed here. He was terribly sweet on Libby.'

'So he said – before he knew who I was. He said some awfully nice things about her.'

'So he should,' Bunty said. 'Libby was always very patient with him. Actually, I need to talk to you about Keith Farnell . . . And Libby.'

'So did they have an affair?'

'No, absolutely not, Edward . . . But I know Hugh wrote to you and told you they did. I found copies of the despicable letters he sent you, because he kept carbon copies. There was not a word of truth in either of them, except for the part where he said she'd left Buttonbridge Hall. She did, but only because he made her life hell. She went back to live with her mother and father. There was never ever any question of wanton infidelity, Edward.'

'Oh, Bunty, I desperately want to believe that.'

'You'd do well to believe it, Edward.' Bunty was reminded of Libby's intention to marry Ron Downing. Somehow she had to prepare Edward for that too, but she did not relish the prospect. 'Well, you must be aware, Edward, that she believed you were dead. We all did. What you're not aware of, but what you must understand and take into account, is that Hugh intercepted the correspondence the Red Cross sent to Libby telling her first that you had been found, and later that you were alive and well in a prisoner-of-war camp. He never passed it on to her – deliberately. She had absolutely no idea you were still alive. Nor did the rest of us.'

He looked at Bunty apprehensively. 'I see . . . But why would he do that?'

'Spite. Jealousy. Because he's a complete arsehole. But more of that later.'

He was still uneasy. 'So have there been other men? Is that what you're about to tell me?'

'Libby has been through hell, Edward, as we all have – the same as you have. So you must bear in mind that she believed you were dead. She has her own story to tell, and I wouldn't dream of trying to tell it for her. That's all I want to say on her behalf . . . But there is one more thing . . . Hugh . . . After proving himself to be such an out-and-out bastard he's disappeared, and hasn't been seen or heard of for months. Driven by shame at what he's done to this family, I have no doubt. Strangely though, Margaret Jenkins, our maid of long-standing, disappeared at the same time. We think it's more than coincidental. It seems certain that she's pregnant, according to some snippets of information that cook gave us, and it can only be with Hugh's child. Hugh has also robbed the company, leaving it bereft of working capital, and we're having to borrow heavily from the bank. Our insurers are investigating of course. We shall expect you to take the helm at Blowers Green Steelworks as soon as you're fit enough, and see if together we can't get through the crisis.'

'There's my career sorted out then,' he said. 'But fancy Hugh . . .' He frowned with concern. 'It's unbelievable.'

'You'll learn more later. There's much more. Anyway—'

'Anyway . . . Back to Libby . . . Is it true she has a child?'

'Yes, Edward. She has a child . . .'

He groaned. He had been so obsessed with the notion, so plagued by it for so long, that he failed to recognise Bunty's smile as indicative of something to be happy about. To him, it was a nightmare come true. As he inwardly grimaced at the profound disappointment, he hardly paid any attention when Bunty said, 'Now, just wait here. I have a surprise for you . . .'

- - -

| 29 |

Bunty hurried outside. In the Riley Elizabeth was sitting in Libby's lap, and they were playing a game. Libby looked up inquiringly when Bunty opened the driver's door and sat back in the car.

'Are we leaving?'

'No . . .' Bunty turned to face Libby. 'Libby, I brought you here to see Edward—'

Libby gasped, putting her hand to her mouth in shock. 'Edward?' she queried, incredulous. 'You mean he's here? At Cosford? Not in Germany?'

'Yes, he's here at Cosford. We learned only yesterday. Actually, to be more precise, he's inside that building . . .' She nodded in the general direction.

'Have you seen him?'

'Yes, I've just seen him.'

At once, Libby opened the car door. 'Then I must go to him straight away.'

Bunty held her arm firmly. 'Wait, Libby. Listen to me first.'

Libby sat back in the chair reluctantly, apprehensive about what Bunty was going to say. 'Well?'

'He's been through hell, Libby, and it shows. He's painfully thin, having been half-starved these last few months, but he told me the doctors say he'll be okay. Those letters Hugh sent have obviously had an effect, and he's certainly not convinced that you've been faithful. I would be careful how you tell him you were due to be married to Ron. In fact, if I were you I wouldn't mention it at all yet. Not until he's settled and confident again of your love. He might think the worst. Elizabeth is also a worry, because he never knew you were pregnant, and Hugh misled him about who her father is. You can thank him for that, too.'

'You didn't tell him he has a daughter, then?'

'I believe you must have that pleasure. You have to convince him of your love and your loyalty. Only you can prove to Edward that he is Elizabeth's father. So I think you should go and see him first without her.'

'But she's the ace up my sleeve.'

'Not yet, she isn't, Libby. You have to convince him first.'

'Do you think he still wants me?' she asked, the awful possibility that he didn't entered her thoughts for the first time like a bolt of lightning.

'I'm certain he does, but just remember he's had doubts about you. You'll need all your patience and understanding to help him overcome those doubts.'

Libby sighed. 'Should I go in and see him now?' she asked.

'Yes, do. Go . . .'

She stepped out of the car, and felt herself trembling. What could she expect? Was Edward so weak, physically and mentally, that Bunty had seen fit to brief her first, to forewarn her? It was one aspect of his condition she had not considered.

She entered the building and the door swung shut behind her. At the far end of the room in which she found herself, a man in RAF uniform was sitting at a desk. He looked up when he saw her, and she followed his eyes as he nodded towards a door to that private little interview room in which Edward sat, waiting. To make sure, she pointed towards the door and raised her eyebrows questioningly, and the man nodded again with a benevolent smile, as if he knew.

Tentatively, quietly, she pushed it open. He was sitting at a table, his head in his hands, and he neither saw nor heard her enter. He looked desperately thin, as Bunty had warned her, and his hair had lost its youthful sheen. His fingers were bony, his nails cracked and in poor condition, and his skin sallow and flaky.

God . . . She sighed heavily as her heart went out to him.

'Edward,' she whispered.

Warily, he looked up. His eyes were sunken and dark-rimmed but, as he saw her, they instantly brightened.

'Libby!' At once he stood up. 'My God . . .'

'Edward . . . Oh, my Edward . . .' She held her arms out to him and at once they grasped each other tightly. Her eyes were shut tight in the ecstasy of simply holding him again, but tears leaked out from her closed lids and rolled down her cheek. He felt so thin; her poor Edward was so frail compared to how he had been the last time she'd seen him.

'Oh, Edward.' She was unable to say more yet, for pent-up emotion seemed to constrict her vocal chords, and prevent her mouth from forming words. Eventually, she managed, in a snuffle, to utter, 'Oh, my darling . . . What on earth have they done to you?'

'Libby, it's so good to see you. You're looking as lovely as ever.' He gave her another squeeze. 'You're certainly a sight for sore eyes.'

'If anybody had told me when I got out of bed this morning that I would be holding you in my arms by eleven o' clock, I would never have believed them,' she said, looking up into his eyes, which were as wet with tears as her own.

At sight of his tears she began to shake with weeping, and held him as tightly as she could. He lifted her chin and looked into her wet eyes, clear and round and earnest.

'I can't believe it's you,' he said in a croak, and a great sob of a sigh juddered through his gaunt body. 'My God, I've yearned for this moment, but despaired of it ever coming to pass. Oh, Libby . . . Libby . . . Libby . . .'

He screwed his eyes up and hugged her so tightly, and it was as if he could not get enough of the sound of her name, or the joy of saying it.

'Are you still mine?' he asked softly into her ear, tears rolling down his sallow cheeks. 'It's been so long, Libby . . . Tell me you're still mine.'

'Of course I'm still yours,' she said tenderly, and planted a kiss on his cracked, dry lips. 'If you still want me.' She looked at him imploringly.

'More than anything. More than anything in the world.'

'I've missed you so much, Edward. I've needed you so much, I can't begin to tell you . . . Life without you has been awful . . . so lonely . . .'

'We had so little time together before all this,' he breathed, his voice breaking up with emotion.

'I know, I know,' she replied. 'If it hadn't been for our—' She stopped herself saying it and gazed fervently into his eyes. 'I have the most beautiful surprise for you, Edward.'

'A surprise? D'you think I need more surprises?'

'This one is special – extra-special.'

'Then surprise me.'

'You have a daughter.'

There. It was out. She felt him tauten at the mention of a child, understood why, understood why Bunty had taken the trouble to prime her, and realised she had to proceed very carefully, as Bunty had predicted.

'She'll be three on Tuesday,' Libby went on, prudently giving him a straight fact to consider, 'and she's called Elizabeth Bunty. Elizabeth after Princess Elizabeth, not me – Bunty after – well, guess who. She's just dying to meet her daddy. I've told her so much about you.'

He let go of her, and she stood before him as if silently accused of some heinous crime. Suddenly she felt vulnerable, because she was aware that in his mind, poisoned by Hugh, her integrity, her honesty, was on trial.

'Edward . . .' she said his name assertively. Never had she shrunk from being forthright and now was not the time to begin. 'I'm aware of your doubts about being Elizabeth's father, but I can assure you, you are. She was born on the first of May, nineteen forty-two, just nine months after we were married. Do you remember our honeymoon in Ludlow, Edward? Do you remember the hours we spent, before you were recalled to your squadron, making love till we were sore? It's hardly any surprise that I conceived then, is it? It would have been more surprising if I hadn't . . . I can show you her birth certificate.'

He was at once convinced and his frown changed to a broad, open smile, made possible by the sensations of relief and happiness that now flowed through him at last, supplanting the anxiety and doubts that had made his life a living hell.

'Oh, Libby,' he sighed. 'How could I ever have doubted you?' He took her in his arms again, and held her tight.

'I suppose it's natural to have doubts when you're away from somebody for so long,' she said matter-of-factly. 'And I know it wasn't helped any by Hugh's stupidity either—'

'If ever I lay my hands on him . . .' Edward said, finding it unnecessary to finish his sentence.

'It's over and done with, my darling. Forget him. Everything is going to come right for us at last. We have each other again. We've always had each other. Even when I thought you were dead, I was still yours. Always.'

'You were never tempted?'

'I was seldom short of offers,' she admitted, smiling. 'But I've never been interested in anybody else that way.'

'Hugh said in one of his letters that you were seeing that chap Ron again, who you used to see years ago. Was that true?'

She had not reckoned on explaining those circumstances yet, and Bunty had advised her to avoid the issue for the time being. But it had been introduced, and she decided it was as well to get it into the open and be done with it, once and for all. So she told Edward the story of how she honestly believed she was a war widow and that she had agreed to marry Ron.

'And did you love him, by this time?'

'I was never in love with him, Edward. Oh, I liked him. He was a nice, decent chap. He was supportive, and he would've been a good stepfather to Elizabeth. But I was never in love with him.'

'Did you ever sleep with him?'

'Never,' she answered simply. 'The chance never cropped up anyway. He was always away doing his army service.'

'Would you have done?'

'Only if I'd married him, but not until. But if I'd married him, it would have been bigamy anyway, and the marriage would not have been legal.'

'That's true. But he was prepared to take on my daughter?'

'Yes. Oh, yes.'

Edward sighed. 'I'm glad you've told me all this, my darling. Maybe we expect too much of people, maybe I expected too much of you. But we are only flesh and blood, after all, afflicted by all the weaknesses, the inclinations and instincts of mere flesh and blood. I could hardly have blamed you if you had married Ron, illegally or not. The fact that you didn't has saved us a lot of bother and him a lot of heartache. I imagine he didn't take kindly to being let down, though?'

'He was disappointed to say the least . . . but in view of the circumstances he was very understanding.'

'Have you heard from him since?'

'No.' She laughed self-consciously. 'Bunty asked me that, too.'

'Oh, Libby . . .'

'What, my love?' She regarded him anxiously.

'Shall we sit down? I feel rather tired and I'm aching rather, standing up. I really have to get fit again.'

'Of course, and I'll help you to get fit.' She should have realised he was not as strong as he used to be after his ordeals; he needed building up.

So they sat opposite each other at the table in that bare, chilly, unromantic room.

'Do you remember Pilot Officer Keith Farnell?' he asked.

'Yes . . .' She felt her heart rate quicken.

'He's here . . . at Cosford. I bumped into him last night, quite coincidentally. We got talking . . .'

'You did?'

'He told me he'd been a convalescent at Buttonbridge Hall. He said some awfully nice things about you, quite unprompted. He implied the exact opposite of what Hugh had written.'

'I should hope so,' she responded. 'How did he seem? His leg was severely injured.'

'Well, he was limping a bit. But other than that he seemed fine. Would you like to see him while you're here?'

'Not particularly,' she said. 'I'm here to see you, not him.'

He took her hands in his and looked into her eyes.

'Let me just gaze at you for a few moments,' he said, and smiled warmly. 'You're as beautiful as ever . . . I really don't deserve you, doubting you the way I have. And look at me . . . I'm just a scrawny, screwed up ex-prisoner-of-war whose mind has been so poisoned that everything has got twisted out of all proportion. Anyway, I imagine you'll be pleased to learn that I've already decided to resign my commission. I'll do my damnedest to be a good husband for you, Libby, but I fear you might have to be patient with me sometimes.'

'Oh, Edward, I'm just so happy you're home,' she replied sincerely. 'I can't wait to get you back to Buttonbridge Hall and make it our home again. And I'll look after you properly to build you up. I'll make you well again. I promise.'

'It seems I'm going to be busy running the steelworks, according to Bunty.'

'When you're fit and well. And I'll help you all I can,' she replied enthusiastically. 'I know a bit about what goes on at the steelworks. I didn't work with your father all that time and not pick up a few tips, you know.'

He laughed. 'I think we'll be all right after all, you and me, Libby,' he said, feeling infinitely happier and brighter.

'Of course we shall. Would you like to meet your daughter now?'

'Is she here?'

'She's outside with her Aunty Bunty.'

'Oh, my God.' He gulped with renewed nervousness. 'I do hope she's going to like me.'

'She's going to love you. Come on. Do you feel up to walking?'

'Just try and stop me!'

As they stepped outside into the warm spring sunshine together, hand in hand, they saw Bunty playing with Elizabeth on a patch of mown grass.

'Is that her?' Edward enquired, his eyes alive now with the sincere, gentle look about them that Libby had always loved.

'That's her, the little tinker.'

It was a monumental moment for him. A lump came to his throat and his eyes welled up with tears again. 'She's absolutely beautiful, Libby,' he sighed inadequately. 'Look at her lovely thick dark hair. She's the image of you.'

'But she has your eyes, Edward, and no mistake.'

Libby called her, and when Elizabeth looked up from her game with Bunty, she beckoned her. Bunty urged her forward and the little girl came running over, while Edward sat on his haunches to be at her level, waiting, a broad expectant grin on his face. She ran directly to him and he caught her in his arms, picked her up and hugged her. He was indescribably moved that this child, his child, who had never seen him before and only knew him by what her mother and others had told her, could be so instantaneously generous with her affection. He fell in love with her at once, and made a private vow that he would be the best father any child could have. He would do his utmost to make up for the years lost.

'Are you weally my daddy?' she asked, with the sort of wide-eyed innocence that would have utterly demolished the hardest of hearts.

'Oh, yes, I'm your daddy all right,' Edward replied. 'And it's your birthday soon, isn't it?'

The child nodded earnestly, looking directly into his eyes. 'I'll be fwee on the first of May,' she declared.

'On May Day,' Daddy said, as if it were a great surprise. 'We'll see if we can rig up a Maypole especially for you, and we can all dance around it. Would you like that?'

Elizabeth nodded with adorable juvenile eagerness.

Libby looked on moist-eyed but content – oh, utterly content.

'And you've been looking after Mommy for me while I've been away?'

The child nodded again, and grinned.

'Good girl. Now daddy's back to look after both of you, and I shan't be going away again.' Edward turned to Libby. 'It's a travesty I've been shut away for so long. I'm absolutely devastated that I've missed three years of her life – three years of her growing up. And she really is beautiful, Libby – the image of you.'

'She's a little madam,' Libby asserted with infinite tenderness in her eyes. 'I can see she'll be able to twist you round her little finger.'

'Oh, there's no doubt about it,' he happily admitted. 'But I want her to. With all my heart I want her to.'

'Anyway, she'll benefit from her father's presence.'

'Which she'll get – in abundance.' He gave the child another hug, reached out and took Libby's hand, and the three of them held each other, savouring these moments that in the years to come would remain vivid, poignant, but extraordinarily happy memories.

- - -

Edward Burgayne resigned his commission on 13th May, the day that Winston Churchill announced in a broadcast to the nation, that the war with Germany was officially over. In the meantime, he was allowed home to celebrate Elizabeth's third birthday and Libby's twenty-sixth a week later. She moved back to Buttonbridge Hall and was happy to regard it as her home once again. It would also be Elizabeth's home, and Libby was well aware that their child would benefit from both the cultural and physical environment. And with a child in the house, the atmosphere was at once restored.

But, even more than that, a new and challenging adventure, another chapter in their lives, and in the future of the Blowers Green Steelworks, had begun . . .

The End

Author's Note

The K-Lines internment camp at the Curragh near Kildare in Eire actually existed, and is well-documented. It was built in 1939 to house and detain servicemen from both Axis and Allied Forces captured on Irish soil during World War II. It was situated on the east side of the Curragh Camp which was originally built to house troops during the British occupation of Ireland. Handed over after occupation, it has been used by the Irish Army ever since.

Whilst Edward Burgayne is a fictional character engaged in fictional exploits, I have used, for the sake of authenticity, the actual names of those members of the Irish Local Defence Forces who guarded them. All dialogue attributable to them is the product of my imagination, however. Other characters, with the exception of actual historic personages and real places, are also entirely fictional.

It is a historical fact that internees of K-Lines were allowed out on parole, and honour bound to return by the time appointed. They were indeed also free to use the local hostelries, visit the cinemas, play golf, enjoy the local racecourse on race days, and fraternise with local girls. At the end of the war, of those internees who remained in the camp, many decided to stay and make the area their home.

It is also a fact that they were duty-bound to attempt escape once within the confines of the camp and not bound by the terms of their parole. Many did escape, some successfully, some unsuccessfully.

Nancy Carson

2021

About the Author

Nancy Carson was born and bred in the Black Country, that part of the English West Midlands that lies between the eastern fringes of Wolverhampton and the western edges of Birmingham. Dudley was her home town, and though she has travelled widely she still lives no more than 6 miles from her birthplace.

Nancy has always been a 'people-watcher' and believes this has given her a clear insight into human interactions – male and female – especially when it comes to relationships. So, her stories spring from the broad canvas of human nature. The characters that populate them have often been inspired from life, as have the situations she sometimes places them in. Many have been embellished, some not.

Nancy Carson is the author of several published novels.

Other Novels by Nancy Carson

Trilogy:

The Dressmaker's Daughter

The Factory Girl

Rags to Riches

Stand Alone Novels:

A Family Affair

Daisy's Betrayal

Poppy's Dilemma

The Railway Girl

Honour Thy Father

Duology:

A Country Girl

A Fallen Woman

Short Story:

The Girl from the Opera House